WIN... ...H
–1886–

# WINCHESTER
## –1886–

## WILLIAM W. JOHNSTONE
*with J. A. Johnstone*

**PINNACLE BOOKS**
Kensington Publishing Corp.
www.kensingtonbooks.com

PINNACLE BOOKS are published by

Kensington Publishing Corp.
119 West 40th Street
New York, NY 10018

PUBLISHER'S NOTE
Following the death of William W. Johnstone, the Johnstone family is working with a carefully selected writer to organize and complete Mr. Johnstone's outlines and many unfinished manuscripts to create additional novels in all of his series like The Last Gunfighter, Mountain Man, and Eagles, among others. This novel was inspired by Mr. Johnstone's superb storytelling.

All Kensington titles, imprints, and distributed lines are available at special quantity discounts for bulk purchases for sales promotions, premiums, fund-raising, educational, or institutional use. Special book excerpts or customized printings can also be created to fit specific needs. For details, write or phone the office of the Kensington special sales manager: Kensington Publishing Corp., 119 West 40th Street, New York, NY 10018, attn: Special Sales Department; phone 1-800-221-2647.

ISBN-13: 978-0-7860-3646-2
ISBN-10: 0-7860-3646-X

First printing: February 2015

10 9 8 7 6 5 4 3 2 1

Printed in the United States of America

First electronic edition: February 2015

ISBN-13: 978-0-7860-3647-9
ISBN-10: 0-7860-3647-8

# PROLOGUE

**Fort Smith, Arkansas**
**Spring 1899**

When he was older, though still a young man, serving as a deputy marshal for the United States District Court for the Western District of Arkansas, James Mann would ignore irritating questions.

"Why do you carry that cannon of a rifle?"

"You got some prejudice against short guns?"

"Reckon you'll run into any elephants down in the Winding Stair Mountains?"

He seldom carried a revolver on his hip, and when he did, Mann hardly ever pulled that Colt from its holster. Yet always—*always*—he had that Winchester 1886 rifle. It chambered the .50-100-450 round and .50 calibers favored by a few old buffalo hunters in single-shot rifles, but rarely found in lever-action repeaters.

Mann's Winchester '86 looked older than it actually was, the stock and forestock battered and badly scratched, the barrel losing some of its bluing. Yet it was always clean.

Always loaded.

And quite often cocked.

A drummer who had traveled all the way from North Haven, Connecticut, once offered Mann a Marlin '89 . . . free, with a year's supply of ammunition. Mann turned him down cold.

When Mann won a turkey shoot, Buffalo Bill Cody said he would pay $1,500 for that rifle and give Mann a brand-spanking new one in return. Mann thanked Colonel Cody for the offer, but said he liked his rifle just fine. He was used to it. It was like family.

Truth was, that rifle *was* family. Blood kin.

He did, however, answer one question. After testifying in one of Judge Rogers's trials—Rogers having replaced Isaac Parker a few years back—Mann had retired to the Texas Corner Saloon on Garrison Avenue. Alone. The rifle lay on the table next to a pitcher of beer.

The owner of that watering hole, Katie Crockett, dropped into the seat across from Mann. "Rough day at the courthouse?"

"No more than usual."

By that time, practically everybody from western Arkansas to the Chickasaw Nation had heard about the trial, how the defense attorney had accused Mann of abusing his power, using a .50-caliber weapon on a seventeen-year-old kid, forcing the doctor to saw off the boy's right leg, which had been shattered by two shots from Mann's Winchester.

Never mind that that boy had killed five people in cold blood and had been trying to make Mann number six.

Katie drew a long finger down the Winchester's barrel. "You and this gun . . ."

He poured her some of the beer.

She shook her head. "I don't see how it's all worth it."

"What?"

"The abuse you get for carrying it."

He lifted his stein in salute. "It's worth it."

"Why?" Katie asked.

He drank some beer, and she figured he would just shrug off her question the way he always did when anyone asked him what made that beat-up rifle so special.

But he put the stein on the table, wiped his mouth, and locked his eyes on Katie's for a moment, before falling onto that well-used, often-criticized Winchester. "My uncle," Deputy Marshal James Mann said softly, "went a long way to get this rifle. For me."

# CHAPTER ONE

*Randall County, Texas*
*Late summer 1894*

"Kris," James said to his sister, shaking his head. "I'm too old to play that game."

"You're yeller!" his kid brother Jacob said with a challenging sneer.

Beside him, his twelve-year-old sister dangled the Montgomery Ward & Co. catalog, showing off imported China fruit plates like she was clerking at the mercantile in McAdam, which passed for a town in the Texas Panhandle.

Eight-year-old Jacob lost his sneer. "Please," he begged.

James Mann stared at him then at Kris, before dropping his gaze to the *McGuffey's Sixth Eclectic Reader*. He was making his way through the book for the fourth time, and, honestly, how many times did his ma and pa expect him to read a scene from George Coleman's *The Poor Gentleman*? Besides, Ma was shopping in McAdam, and Pa was working on the Fort Worth-Denver City Railroad up around Amarillo. The Potter County seat wasn't much more than a speck of dust on a map, but Amarillo boasted a bigger population than McAdam.

Since James had finished his chores and had been assigned the grim duty of keeping his younger siblings out of trouble, that child's game seemed a whole lot more appealing than reading *McGuffey's*.

He slammed the book shut, hearing Jacob's squeal of delight as he slid the *Reader* across the desktop, and pushed himself to his feet. "No whining when you don't get what you want!"

Following Kris and Jacob, he pushed his way through the curtain that separated what Ma and Pa called the parlor, and into what they called the dining room. Another curtain separated the winter kitchen, and beyond that lay his parents' bedroom and finally the room he shared with his brother and sister. All were separated by rugs or blankets that Ma called curtains and Pa called walls.

The Mann home, a long rectangle built with three-inch siding and three-inch roof boards, stretched thirty-four feet one inch long and eight feet, nine inches wide, while the ceiling rose nine feet from the floor. The only heat came from the Windsor steel range in the kitchen. The only air came from the front door, which slid open, and the windows Pa had cut into the northeast corner of the parlor and the southwest corner of Ma and Pa's bedroom. At one time, the home had hauled railroad supplies from Fort Worth. The wheelbase and carriage had been removed from the boxcar, although the freight's handbrake wheel and grab irons remained on the outside . . . in case someone needed to climb up on the roof to set the brake and keep the Mann home from blowing away.

Jacob was young enough to still find living in a converted boxcar an adventure. At sixteen, James Mann had outgrown such silly thoughts, although he was about to take part in a game he hadn't played with Kris and Jacob in years.

The door had been left open to allow a breeze, for the Texas Panhandle turned into a furnace in August, and the nearest shade trees could be found in the Palo Duro country, a hard day's ride southwest.

Kris and Jacob already sat at the roughhewn table, the thick Montgomery Ward catalog in front of them. James took his seat across from them, giving his younger siblings the advantage. He would be looking at the catalog pages upside down, but, well, he didn't plan on winning anything. It wasn't like anything they allegedly won would actually show up on Christmas morning. It was simply a kid's game.

They called the game "My Page." Shortly after Ma picked up the winter catalog at the nearest mercantile wherever they were living, the Mann children would sit at the table, and see what they might ask Santa Claus to bring them. They'd open the book, slap a hand on a page, shout out, "My page!" and pick something they might want.

It had worked a lot better, or at least a little fairer,

before Jacob had been born, when either Kris or James would actually get a page. By the time Jacob became old enough to play, James figured he had grown too old to play. Besides, his reflexes had always been quick—almost as fast as his namesake uncle's—so he had left the child's game to Kris and Jacob. And let them complain and argue and eventually get into a brother-sister fight because Kris had slammed her hand on the page with the Kipling books on purpose, knowing how much Jacob loved Kipling even if Ma was already reading to him.

"You only get five gifts," Kris explained, "so you better watch what you go for."

Like anyone really wanted to find a turkey feather duster or whitewash brush under the tree on Christmas Day.

James turned in his seat, looking through the open door at the flat expanse of nothingness that was the Texas Panhandle. Out there, you could see forever, to tomorrow, to the day after tomorrow, to Canada, it felt like. He wanted desperately to light out for himself, but Ma wouldn't have any of that. She wanted her oldest son to go to college, maybe wind up teaching school. She certainly didn't want him to wind up in that fading but still wild town called Tascosa, north of Amarillo, and work cattle for thirty a month and found. Nor did she want James to follow in his Uncle Borden's boot steps, serving as an express agent, risking his life riding the rails with payrolls and letters and such. Borden, the oldest, worked for the Adams Express Company and usually found himself on Missouri-Kansas-Texas trains, but he had gotten James's father, Millard, the job on the Fort Worth and Denver before Jacob were born.

James could remember little of Wichita Falls, the town near Fort Worth, other than it had been poorly named. It usually had little water to begin with, let alone enough to make a waterfall.

Three years later, the line had stretched out to Harold, just some thirty-four miles. In '86, when Millard had been promoted to assistant foreman, the line had grown to Chillicothe. A year later, it had reached the Canadian River, and the Manns had made themselves a home out of a boxcar five miles from the town of McAdam. Eventually, the rail line had moved into New Mexico Territory and joined up with the crews laying track from Denver and Millard bossed a crew working on a new spur line.

James would not have minded working for the railroad one bit, even if he had to swing a sixteen-pound sledgehammer in the Texas heat. Yet what he really wanted was to follow his Uncle Jimmy's line of work. Riding for Judge Isaac Parker's deputy marshals in Arkansas and the Indian Nations, bringing bad men to justice, seeing some wild country. It sounded a lot more promising, a lot more adventurous, than rocking along in a locked express car as a train sped through the night. It certainly held more promise than bossing a bunch of thick-skulled Irishmen who sweated out the whiskey they had consumed the night before at some hell-on-wheels while lugging two hundred-pound crossties for the rail pullers and gandy dancers.

But there he was, practically a man, babysitting and about to play "My Page."

"I go first," Kris said.

"No," Jacob whined. "I wanna."

"Too bad."

"But . . . Ja-aaames!"

Shaking his head, wishing he had stayed in the parlor with his Reader, James refrained from muttering an oath. "Let Jacob go first."

Kris frowned. "How come?"

"He's the youngest."

"You're just saying that because he's a boy. Like you."

"I'm a man," James declared.

Jacob and Kris giggled, and Jacob pulled the book closer to him. Kris relented, and Jacob opened the catalog. He went deep, probably toward the tables and such, if James remembered correctly, let the pages flutter, and released his hold.

It fell open to two pages of baby carriages. Jacob was ready, hand about to slam down, but he stopped himself from making a critical mistake and risk winding up with a canopy top baby carriage with brushed carpet and matching steel wheels.

No one moved. James was about to slide the catalog toward his sister, when Kris's hand slammed down on the page without the advertisement in the corner.

"My page!" she yelled.

"You want a baby carriage?" Jacob turned up his nose.

"For my doll." She pulled the catalog closer, whispering, "Let's see." She studied the three rows of offerings, before pointing to one at the bottom corner.

Jacob shook his head, but James pulled the catalog toward him, turned it around, and studied it . . . like old times, when he was a boy. "Twelve dollars and fifty cents?" He smiled.

"It's silk laced," Kris said.

"For a doll?" Jacob sighed. "Girls!"

"Well . . ." James slid the catalog back to his sister.

She quickly turned it around, opened it, let some pages fall, and dropped the corner. Capes and cloaks. No one made a move. August came too hot for anyone to think about winter clothing, although they had seen just how harsh Panhandle winters could be.

It was James's turn. Purposely, he let his pages open to the index.

"Aw, c'mon!" Jacob pulled the book to him. Collars and suspenders. No interest.

Kris's turn. James saw what he was looking for and made a quick grasp, laughing when Jacob's hand landed on page 131 as James moved his hand to his hair, and scratched his head.

"My page!" Jacob shouted. He lifted his hand, realizing where his hand had dropped. "Dang it!" He glared at his brother. "That's not fair."

Kris was laughing so hard, tears formed in her

eyes. "What are you going to ask for, Jacob, the rose sprays or the straw hats?"

"But them is girls hats!"

"You'll look good in that one." She pointed to one with fancy edges and trimmings. Available in white, ecru, brown, navy blue, and cardinal.

"Fine." Jacob said. "I'll take the orange blossoms."

"You getting married?" James asked.

Kris pulled the catalog, opened the pages, let one end fall. James decided he might as well play along, so he wound up asking for a dozen packages of Rochelle salts—which made Jacob feel better.

So the game went. Jacob wound up with a Waltham watch, and it did not matter to him that Kris said it was a ladies watch. He liked the stars on the hunter's case, anyway. Kris got a roman charm shaped like a heart with a ruby, pearl, and sapphire. Jacob picked a leather-covered trunk—Sultan according to Montgomery Ward & Co.— He could use it as a fort or place to hide. Kris chose a ladies saddle, just beating Jacob to the page.

"You ain't even trying!" Jacob complained to James.

"I'm trying," James protested. "You two are just too fast for me."

"All you got is some salts."

"I like salt."

The next round, James wound up with a Cheviot suit. He opted for the round cornered sack suit in gray plaid made of wool cassimere. He let Jacob beat him to one of the pages of saddles, and exploded in laughter, as did Jacob, when Kris tried to get a piece of wallpaper, thinking it was fancy lace, but the breeze came in strong and flipped the pages to where Kris wound up with a Spanish curb bit.

"You can use it with your saddle," James told her.

"You just need a horse," Jacob added.

It was James's turn. He stood the book up on its spine and just pulled his hands away, watching the catalog pages spread, flutter, and fall. It landed open. Jacob's hand headed for one of the pages as James saw the muzzle-loading shotguns on one upper page. He spotted the Winchester repeaters on the facing page and couldn't help himself. His hand shot out, barely landing on the page just ahead of Jacob's hand, and he heard himself calling out, "My page!"

"Dang it!" Jacob pulled his hand back. "I wanted that rifle!"

"You're too young to have a rifle," Kris said.

James withdrew his hand, and stared at where his hand had fallen. He felt guilty, but only slightly. "I'll let you shoot it," he offered.

"Which one?" Kris asked, even though she had no use for guns.

James's finger tapped on the bottom of the page, and Jacob pulled the catalog toward him, leaned forward, and read, "Winchester Repeating Rifles— Model 1886."

Kris leaned over. "That's twenty-one dollars," she sang out. "And you scold me for wanting a twelve dollar baby carriage?"

"That's the factory price," James corrected. "The catalog doesn't charge that much." He pointed to the second row of numbers. "Fourteen dollars and eighteen cents." He had been studying that catalog, poring over that page, since Ma had brought the book home from McAdam Mercantile a week ago.

Reaching for the catalog, wanting to see, to dream some more, he thought of what it must be like to hold a rifle like that in his hands. All Pa owned were a Jenks carbine in .54 caliber that his father had carried during the Civil War and a Colt hammerless double-barrel shotgun in twelve gauge. Pa had let him fire the shotgun, even let him go hunting for rabbits and quail, but never the rifle. Pa didn't own a short gun, but Uncle Jimmy did, preferring the 1873 model Winchester.

"Promise I can shoot it?" Jacob demanded.

James choked off a laugh. He had as much chance of getting a large-caliber repeating rifle at Christmas as Kris had of getting a $12.50 baby carriage for her doll. Besides, she was getting too old to play dolls. And he was too old to play that silly game.

"They's lots of models." Jacob put his elbows on the table, chin atop his fingers, and studied the catalog page. Only one illustration but about a dozen typed descriptions. "Which one you want?"

James knew exactly and found himself reaching across the table and pulling the book toward him.

A voice outside startled him. "What are y'all younguns doing?"

# CHAPTER TWO

**Denison**

Both barrels of the Wm. Moore & Grey twelve-gauge belched fire and buckshot, filling Lynn's Variety Saloon with thick white smoke while the explosion and reverberations drowned out the brief cries of the man Danny Waco gunned down, shooting from his hip.

Ducking beneath the smoke, he shifted the shotgun to his left hand, his right quickly reaching across his body to pull the short-barreled Colt from a cross-draw holster. His thumb eared back the hammer, but he did not fire. He didn't have to. Even through the drifting smoke, he knew that the man he had just shot no longer posed any threat.

He could see where buckshot had punctured a calendar and splintered some siding. A table had been overturned. The dead man had fallen into a chair, the momentum sending it sliding across the floor and slamming against the wall. He had tumbled onto the floor next to the side door through which he had entered the saloon. The chair, however, remained upright, next to another table where a pitcher of beer stood undisturbed. The drummer sitting next to the pitcher looked so pale, Waco figured that the dude would soon drop dead from an apoplexy.

That struck Waco as uproariously funny. Laughing, he lowered the hammer on the Colt and used the barrel to push up the brim of his hat. "That beer ain't gonna help you none," he told the drummer, who still did not move. "You need rye." Waco turned toward the bartender, who likewise stood like a statue, and snapped a finger.

Crossing the floor to the batwing doors, empty shotgun in left hand, loaded Colt in right, Waco leaned against the doors and swung halfway onto the boardwalk.

The lady across the dusty street at Mrs. Wong's Millinery Company quickly looked away and busied herself, digging in her purse to fetch the key to her business. An old black man stood, broom in hand, in front of the mercantile, and a cowboy had reined in his strawberry roan a few rods from the saloon. Quickly, the waddie turned his horse around and trotted to the Mexican saloon at the edge of town.

Waco's gaze landed on the marshal's office. The door remained shut.

Picturing the town law hearing the shotgun blast and freezing in fear, Waco laughed again.

With a fresh shave and haircut and new blue shirt, Danny Waco figured he looked his best. If the lawman lying on the Variety's floor had been lucky, and things had turned out differently, at least Danny Waco would have made a fine corpse. Better than the lawdog, anyway, who had been hit with both loads of the double-barrel twelve gauge. The deputy still gripped a Smith & Wesson No. 2 in his right hand. Unlike two barrels of double-ought buckshot, a little .32 rimfire would not have ripped a body apart.

A slim man, Waco wore a pinstriped vest of black wool and gray pants stuck into his new boots showing off the cathedral arch stitching. A black porkpie hat set atop his neatly coiffed hair. His blue eyes missed nothing. Nor did his ears.

The chiming of spurs turned his attention back to the smoky saloon. Gil Millican had risen from the table where he and Waco had been sitting, sharing a bottle of Old Overholt with Tonkawa Tom and Mr. Percy Frick. Millican and The Tonk rode with Waco. Mr. Percy Frick had a job two stops down from Denison working for the Katy, which was what everyone called the Missouri-Kansas-Texas Railroad.

The Tonk glanced at Frick, whose mouth hung open, drawing flies, and whose face seemed frozen in shock. Shaking his head in contempt, The Tonk joined Millican by the wall, staring at the corpse. At least The Tonk had sense enough to look outside first, before closing the door and nodding at Waco.

"This boy's a deputy marshal," Millican drawled.

"I hoped so." Waco listened to the batwing doors pounding back and forth, back and forth, as he walked back to his table. "That's how he identified himself, ain't it? I mean, I'd hate to send a man to meet his maker with a lie on his lips." He slid into his seat, and grinned at Mr. Frick, who did not notice.

The Tonk whistled, then mumbled, "That's one tight pattern of buckshot."

"Yeah!" Triggering the top lever, Waco snapped open the barrels and ejected the shells, tossing them toward the spittoon but missing. Smoke wafted from the barrels. "It's the lightest shotgun I ever held." He leaned forward, kissed the barrels, still warm to his lips. "Don't weigh more 'n five pounds, I guess. Hardly even kicks. And I had double-ought in both barrels." He held the barrel closer to Mr. Frick, but Mr. Frick saw nothing.

It was a beautiful weapon, and Waco knew all about weapons. His father had been a gunsmith, lauded as one of the best in Fort Worth. His father had taught young Danny all he ever needed to know about guns, about shooting, and hunting. Sometimes, Waco regretted killing his old man.

The Damascus barrels were twenty-eight inches. Waco had considered sawing them down, which would have certainly widened the pattern, but it would have ruined the gun. His late father had preached that one didn't ruin a piece of art by taking a hacksaw to its barrels, and Waco's English-made shotgun was indeed a thing of beauty. Prettier than the watch he had taken off his poor old dad. Or even that soiled dove he had known in Caldwell.

The barrels chambered twelve gauge, but the

frame seemed to have been originally a twenty gauge, which would explain just how light the shotgun felt in Waco's hands. He brought the gun closer, admiring the engraved scrollwork, the smoothness of the deep brown barrels, the walnut stock and grip, the swivel eyes for a sling at the bottom of the barrel and stock.

*Yes, sir,* Danny Waco thought, *Wm. Moore & Grey of 43 Old Bond Street sure know how to make a shotgun.* It killed mighty fine. If he ever made his way to London, he would look the boys up and compliment them on their artwork.

The shotgun disappeared onto Waco's lap as he fished a fresh pair of two-and-a-half-inch shells from his vest pocket.

Fingering the twelve-gauge in his lap, Waco turned toward the wall. "You boys gonna just stand there gawking. We're talking business over here." He looked back toward the beer-jerker. "And you. Yeah, you. I told you to take that drummer a shot of rye. Have one yourself. It'll get your blood flowing again."

When The Tonk and Millican were seated, Waco put the shotgun on the table, reached over, and pried the shot glass from Mr. Frick's hand. "Mr. Frick," he said, casually. "Mr. Frick," he repeated in a placating tone. "Frick!" He tossed the whiskey into the man's face.

Percy Frick blinked rapidly, caught his breath and turned to face Waco. Rather hesitantly, he looked back at the dead body near the wall. "Y-y-you . . . killed . . . him."

"That's right," Waco said casually, refilling the shot glass. "He came in here, interrupting our conversation."

Waco slid the glass in front of Frick's shaking right hand.

"But . . ." Frick seemed to discover the whiskey. He lifted the tumbler, shot down the rye, and coughed.

The Tonk refilled the glass, shooting a grin that Waco ignored.

For a moment, Waco and his men thought Mr. Frick might throw up, but the railroad clerk shot down another two ounces of rye.

"Now . . ." Waco grinned. "Let's get back to business."

"You killed him," Mr. Frick repeated.

"We've covered that already, Mr. Frick. Yes. He's dead. Can't get any deader."

"But he was a lawman."

"Correct. A deputy United States marshal riding for Isaac Parker's court. Or so he said. But the key word there, Mr. Frick, is *was*. He *was* a lawman." Waco sipped his own rye, careful to not shoot it down. Good rye was hard to come by in a place like Denison. "Now he's a corpse."

Frick shuddered. "I didn't think anybody would get killed."

"Then you don't know Danny Waco," Millican said, and immediately regretted it as Waco's eyes burned into him. Millican cleared his throat, topped off Frick's glass, and decided to check the dead lawman for any papers, coin, watches, anything that might come in handy. He had already lifted the Smith & Wesson, which stuck out of the right mule-ear pocket on his checkered trousers.

While Mr. Frick tried to come to grips with what had just happened before his eyes, Waco sighed and looked at the bartender. "Did you recognize the lawman, Charles?" The man hadn't taken rye to the drummer, but the drummer still hadn't moved.

The bartender blinked. "No, Danny. I sure didn't."

"Are we friends, Charles?" Waco scratched the back of his neck. It always itched after a haircut. Those tonsorial artists used talcum powder like it was whiskey, not wasting any.

"Well . . ." The beer jerker understood. "He just rode into town yesterday evening, Mr. Waco."

"Looking for me?"

"He didn't say, Mr. Waco. When he dropped in yesterday, he said he was on his way to Bonham to pick up a prisoner."

Waco smiled. "Guess the prisoner will have to wait." He sipped the rye again. "But you didn't mention him, Charles, when Mr. Frick and the boys and me set down to discuss our business. Didn't mention that a federal lawdog was hanging around these parts."

The barkeep frowned and used the bar towel to wipe the sweat beading on his forehead. "Honest, Mr. Waco, I didn't think he was still in town. I figured he'd lit a shuck for Bonham by this time of day. That's the truth, Mr. Waco."

"Mister?" Waco laughed again. "It's Danny, Charles. We're friends, aren't we?"

"Yes, sir."

"Now take that drummer a shot of rye. Pour the beer over his head if he doesn't respond."

The barkeep's head bobbed. The towel dropped to the floor.

"Only an extradition paper, Danny," Gil Millican said, holding up some bloodstained papers, which he tossed beside the dead man's hat. "No warrants that I see."

"Charles is likely right. He probably slept in this fine hot morning. Spotted us as we come to meet Mr. Frick. Decided to make himself famous by becoming the lucky law who got Danny Waco." He held up his glass in a mocking toast to the dead man. "Sorry it didn't turn out that way."

He killed the rye, and swung around in his chair to face the railroad clerk. "Are you feeling better, Mr. Frick?"

He did not respond immediately, then said, "You killed a federal lawman."

Waco sighed, put his elbows on the table, and rubbed the bridge of his nose. This might take all day, and even in Denison, that town marshal couldn't spend much longer locked in his office. He would have to visit the privy before long, and despite the little arrangement he had with Danny Waco, a man had just been shotgunned to death in the city limits. The marshal had likely figured out, that man rode for the hanging judge up north in Arkansas. Even as far south as Texas, Isaac Parker threw a lot of weight.

"Mr. Frick." Waco rubbed his nose another few

seconds, then lowered his hand. "Would it make you feel better if I told you he wasn't the first?"

"But . . ."

Waco shook his head and that silenced the clerk. Waco's left hand moved toward his vest. From the lower left pocket, he withdrew his father's watch. He laid it on the table next to the shotgun.

It was thirty, maybe even forty years old, probably older than Danny Waco himself. Swiss made, in a fourteen-karat gold case, a key-wind with Roman numerals and gold Breguet hands. The big hand struck twelve, and the repeater began chiming.

Waco said, "My daddy always used to comment how this watch sings like a bird. It's real pretty, don't you think?"

Frick seemed to nod. Whether voluntarily or not, Waco wasn't sure.

"Time's running out, Mr. Frick. I agreed to meet you here in Denison." He hooked his thumb toward the dead man. "Risked my own life, and the lives of Tonkawa Tom and Gil there. We met you here, because you didn't want anybody to see you with the likes of us. But now we need to come to an understanding. An agreement."

"I . . . I . . . I j-just—"

"Yes." The song had ended, and the watch returned to Waco's vest. "You didn't think anyone would get killed. But someone did. And someone else could die, too."

Waco picked up the shotgun, and planted both barrels on Mr. Frick's nose.

"You came to Gil, Mr. Frick. Remember? You said you could provide us with some useful information. Train schedules. Payrolls. Things like that. Isn't that right, to the best of your recollection?"

"But I d-d-didn't . . . he's . . . d-d-dead."

With a heavy sigh, Danny Waco pulled the trigger.

# CHAPTER THREE

***Randall County***

The spurs jingled, but only then did James Mann hear the snorting and pawing of a horse—no, two horses—outside by the hitching rail. He turned swiftly, trying to shove the Montgomery Ward & Co. catalog toward Kris, and felt the chair tilting back too far. He sang out and crashed onto the floor of the boxcar.

His uncle, Jimmy Mann, stepped up into the home, laughing, extending his right arm toward him. Jimmy's left hand gripped that battered old '73 Winchester carbine.

Reluctantly, James Mann let his uncle pull him to his feet. He dusted himself off and felt his face flush with more embarrassment as his father stepped into their home.

Millard Mann had always been the no-nonsense type, big, bronzed, and broad-shouldered, with hard hands and thick fingers, usually calloused, scarred, scraped, bruised, or bleeding—sometimes all of those. He wore a burgundy shirt of thin cotton, duck trousers held up with suspenders, a straw hat, and lace-up boots. Sandy hair, and hazel eyes, with a well-chewed cigar clenched in his teeth, shredded and soggy but never lighted. He towered over his brother, but something always struck James and many others, that Jimmy Mann was the dangerous one. Jimmy Mann was the killer. Millard was just a big cuss, hard-working, but fairly gentle.

"What are y'all doing?" Millard asked.

"Playing My Page!" Jacob pointed to the catalog, still open to the page with all the rifles.

"Y'all still playing that game?" Jimmy chuckled, righting the chair with one hand. He sat down, slid the Winchester carbine onto the table, and pulled the catalog closer. "Montgomery Ward's selling Winchesters, eh?" He shook his head and winked at Jacob. "Which one did you want? One like mine?" He patted the scratched stock of his rifle.

"I wasn't fast enough," Jacob said. "It wasn't my page."

"Kris?" Jimmy pushed up the brim of his hat.

Kris shook her head. Jacob pointed at James.

"I was just . . ." James didn't know what to say. Sixteen years old, playing a game children played.

"You want some coffee, Jimmy?" Millard asked.

"Sure. That'll cut the dust."

James felt his uncle's eyes boring through him while his father headed to the stove.

"So," Jimmy said, "you want a '73 Winchester? I can always pass down mine. Get me a new one from our piles of contraband firearms." He rubbed Jacob's hair. "You'd be surprised how many guns can be bought real cheap just outside the jail at Fort Smith."

"He wants that one." Kris pointed to the illustration.

Deputy Marshal Jimmy Mann bent his head over the page. "Winchester Repeating Rifles—Model 1886," he read aloud. "All have case-hardened lockplates and mountings. Prices on longer or shorter barrels on application. Let's see. What else? Carbines can be furnished twenty-two inches, round barrels, eight pounds, in any of these calibers."

He looked back at James. "Which caliber, son?"

Shrugging, James tried to explain. "I was just trying to keep Kris and Jacob busy. Out of trouble. I mean . . ." The excuse died in his throat as his father came back with two cups of coffee and set one beside the Winchester '73's lever.

Jimmy Mann turned his attention to the coffee, sipping it, but read silently. He laughed. "You see these calibers, Millard?"

His head shook.

"Well, .40-82, .45-70, .45-90. Smallest one is a .38-56."

After a sip of coffee, Millard said, "Soldiers fire a .45-70 in their Springfields, I believe."

"Uh-huh. So did buffalo hunters. Rifle like that might come in handy, Millard, out here in the Panhandle. In case you run across any buffalo. Are there any buffalo left in these parts?"

With a grin, Millard hooked a thumb behind

him. "Not unless you count those shaggies Charlie Goodnight has taken to saving."

"Uh-huh." Jimmy turned back toward his nephew. "I would not advise shooting anything that Charlie Goodnight owns, James." Back to Millard, "How about elephants?"

He laughed.

"Rhinoceroses? Man, that's hard to say. Hippopotamuses? That's not any easier. Y'all been overrun by dragons lately?"

Kris and Jacob were giggling, and James's face turned beet red.

"You really want this rifle, James?"

All he could do was shrug.

"Boy your age should have a rifle, I guess."

"What about me?" Jacob cried out.

"Not this Winchester," Jimmy said, tapping the catalog page. "It'd be like shooting a cannon."

"I'd like a cannon, too," Jacob said.

Laughing, Deputy Marshal Jimmy Mann ran his fingers through Jacob's hair again, and looked up at his older brother.

"We had rifles when we were younger than James, Millard."

"Those were different times, Jim." Sterner now, the humor was gone from his voice.

"Not that different, Millard, and not that long ago." After swallowing down two more gulps of coffee, Jimmy pushed himself away from the table, dragging the carbine with him. "Come on, James. Let's see what you can do with my Winchester." It was a carbine with a twenty-inch barrel, held twelve shots and fired a .44-40 center-fire cartridge.

The 1873 Model Winchester brought glory and wealth to Oliver Winchester and the company he had established. The company had developed the .44-40 cartridge, which would become so popular, Colt—and other manufacturers of revolvers—would soon come out with short guns that fired the same caliber. Needing only one cartridge for either revolver or rifle would come in handy. For lawmen. And outlaws.

Oliver Winchester, of course, hoped for an Army contract, but Army purchasers were stingy sorts. Those repeating rifles shot fast. Too fast. What's more, a rifle could hold fifteen rounds and a carbine twelve. The U.S. Army felt a lot better keeping their soldiers with single-shot Springfields. It would save ammunition, and, therefore, save money.

Maybe not lives, though. George Custer and his 7th Cavalry boys proved that at the Little Big Horn when they found themselves overmatched by Indian warriors, many of whom carried Winchester repeaters.

The original '73s came in various models—Sporting Rifle, carbine, and even musket. Round or octagonal barrels were available, and specialties could be ordered from the factory—five dollars for nickel plating, extra trimmings in nickel for three dollars, silver for five dollars, or gold for ten dollars. A pair of set triggers would cost four dollars. A fancy walnut stock, or even checking butt stock and forearm was an option. Case-hardening, swivels and sling straps, fancy wood, cases, boxes, even heavier barrels could be ordered. And engraving? That could run the buyer anywhere from five dollars to one hundred dollars.

A typical Winchester ran from twenty-four to twenty-seven dollars.

"They test every sporting rifle," Jimmy explained as he set an empty airtight atop a corral post. "Barrels considered of 'extra merit' they turn into special rifles. Called them 'One of a Thousand,' and sold them for a hundred bucks. Other good-shooting barrels considered 'One of a Hundred,' had another twenty bucks tacked on to the price."

"What one did you get, Uncle Jimmy?" Jacob called out.

Jimmy's long legs carried him from the corral. "Just a run-of-the-mill carbine. Nothing fancy. But it shoots true." He started to toss the Winchester to James, thought better of it, and kept walking until he handed the weapon to his nephew, while calling out to Jacob.

"Jake. You'd do me a favor if you'd grab the reins to your pa's horse and lead him over this way."

Kris couldn't help herself. "That's right. James is likely to kill Pa's horse."

"That ain't it at all," Uncle Jimmy said.

James just stared at the weapon he had been offered. He took it, feeling his throat turn dry, and brought it close to his chest. He felt his body tremble.

"Should I fetch your horse, Uncle Jimmy?" Kris called out, pointing at that wiry, rangy, but tough brown mustang.

"No. Old Buck, he's used to shots. But Millard's sorrel, she ain't been trained proper."

Standing in the wide doorway, Millard watched, coffee cup in his hand.

Jimmy Mann was thirty-five years old, tall, lean, his face leathery, his Stetson stained and battered. A lot like that Winchester. He dressed not as a lawman, but as some thirty-a-month cowboy, with worn, scuffed boots and spurs. Leather chaps the color of adobe protected his pants and a pair of deerskin gloves stuck out of one pocket. He wore a shell belt across his waist, a large knife sheathed on his left hip, and a long-barreled Colt holstered on his right. The cuffs on his red and white-checked collarless shirt looked frayed, but not as badly as the ragged bandanna of faded blue calico hanging around his neck. The pockets of his brown vest held the makings for a smoke, a silver watch, and a pencil and small notebook. Most people would probably have dismissed him as a saddle tramp, unless they saw that six-pointed badge pinned to the lapel of his vest.

Or his eyes. A pale, cold blue.

James remembered a conversation he had overheard between his father and a railroad executive.

"Your brother's eyes," the railroad man had said and then shook his head. "They have the look of a vicious man-killer."

"That's what Jimmy is," his father had said.

"All right," Jimmy said softly. He stood to James's right. "Go ahead. Bring the carbine up."

The Winchester felt heavier than James had

expected, though not as heavy or as cumbersome as his father's shotgun and single-shot carbine.

Near the trigger, the saddle ring affixed on the metal just before the walnut stock began to flip and he almost dropped the weapon. He thought his uncle would laugh or maybe take the carbine from his hands.

But Uncle Jimmy said softly, "Don't worry about a thing, James. Keep your finger off the trigger till you're ready. You'll be fine."

He started to work the lever, but his uncle's head shook. "All you have to do is bring the hammer back. There's already a round in the chamber."

James studied his uncle. "Isn't that dangerous?"

"Can be. Can also save a lawman's life."

James slipped three fingers inside the lever, his trigger finger resting against the guard, his thumb on the hammer. The rear sight could be adjusted, and he thought about asking his uncle about that, but decided against it. The corral stood only thirty yards away, and the sight seemed to be at the lowest level.

His thumb pulled the hammer back slowly, clicking once, again. The trigger moved forward, then back. The stock settled against his shoulder. He looked down the barrel, then at his uncle. "Do I close one eye or leave both open? I've heard . . . well, I've read that . . . well . . ."

"Whatever comes natural."

That was easy. He couldn't see the front sight with both eyes open, so he closed his left one and sighted down on the old can of peaches. It was harder than he thought it would be. That can was tiny. He almost couldn't find it in the sights. And the Winchester would not keep still. Round and round it circled. The wind began blowing harder.

*How do you allow for the wind?* he wondered. *Does it matter at this distance?*

The carbine spoke, slamming him back, and smoke burned his eyes. James stepped away, lowering the Winchester, trying to find the airtight of peaches. His ears were ringing, but he could manage to hear his father's sorrel, snorting, dancing around nervously. He could also hear Jacob and Kris . . . sniggering.

Jacob sang out, "He missed!"

His father stepped out of the doorway to take the reins to the sorrel, began rubbing the horse's neck, whispering something to calm down the mare.

Sure enough, James could see the can, sitting undisturbed atop the fencepost. He sighed. His shoulder began to throb from the carbine's kick.

"You did fine, James," his uncle said. "It takes some getting used to, but you didn't miss by much. Next time, take a deep breath before you shoot, then release all that air, and squeeze the trigger. Gently. Real gently. Cock it again."

James jerked the lever forward, saw the metal atop the carbine slide backward as a brass bed appeared, skyrocketing a smoking casing that flipped up and over and landed near his feet. He saw the new cartridge, ready to be shoved into the chamber. He drew the lever back, leaning closer to the Winchester, now warm. It didn't weave so much this time. He sucked in his breath, held it, slowly exhaled, and squeezed the trigger.

"Missed!" Kris sang out.

Jacob echoed, "Again. He's lousy! Let me shoot it, Uncle Jimmy."

"Quiet." It was his father who spoke. "He hit the post."

"Just an inch or two below the can," Uncle Jimmy said. "Surprised it didn't knock the can off its perch."

"Better than you did when you shot your first rifle," Millard pointed out.

Laughing, Jimmy took the carbine from James's hands. "That's because that flintlock Pa had was probably twice as tall as you or me both." He immediately began fishing a cartridge from his belt, feeding it into the loading gate. He put a second .44-40 round into the rifle, then jacked the lever, sending the spent cartridge spinning skyward. Lowering the hammer, he pushed the metal slide up to cover the ejecting mechanism.

He shook his head and walked to his horse, which had barely even noticed the two shots that had been fired. "That old Lancaster was likely as old as George Washington's daddy."

The shooting exhibition over, all five Manns trooped back to the old boxcar. Jimmy again slid the Winchester onto the table, sat in his chair, took another sip of coffee, and pulled the catalog toward him for closer inspection.

Not knowing what else to do, James sat beside him. He couldn't help himself. He massaged his shoulder. Come morning, he figured, there'd most likely be a bruise.

"One thing you should know, James," his uncle said, "is that this rifle"—he tapped the image on the page—"is gonna kick a whole lot harder than my carbine."

James immediately lowered his hand.

"What caliber do you fancy?"

"Uncle Jimmy . . . I was—"

"I'd say the .45-70."

Millard sat down. "Jimmy, I think that's too much gun. Besides, he's—"

"Come on, Mil," Jimmy shot out, voice animated, though maybe not angry. "We were shooting when we were Jacob's age. Besides, the railroad might be pushing through, but this country isn't civilized yet. Not hardly."

"Is that why you come, Uncle Jimmy?" Kris asked from the doorway.

Behind her, Jacob clapped his hands. "You chasing varmints? To fetch them back so they can swing?"

Jimmy started to take in a deep breath, stopped, finished, and blew it out. Shaking his head, he laughed. "I came to visit my brother and his brood. Even Judge Parker and Marshal Carroll have been known to give a good deputy time off . . . on occasion." He slid the catalog toward James and put his finger on the drawing of the rifle. "Round barrel or octagon?"

"What's the difference?"

"Depends on who you ask. Some say one's more

accurate, others say it's the other. Round's harder to make, or used to be. But you saw mine. Octagon's heavier. Doesn't heat up as fast as a round bore. More metal makes it stiffer, too. So, some folks will argue that makes it shoot more accurately. But others disagree." He sipped coffee again.

"Here's what you need to know, kid. It ain't the rifle. It ain't never the rifle. It's the fella shooting it."

James let that sink in.

"A .45-70's a big slug. My carbine holds twelve rounds. This here '86 will hold nine. And that's a rifle. It'll be"—he looked back at the page—"six inches longer and heavier than my carbine. This what you want?"

"I guess so." James was hesitant, but it was absolutely the rifle he longed to hold.

Jimmy looked across the table at his brother. "I can get one of these when I get back to Arkansas. Might not be brand-spanking new, but it'll be cheaper than what Montgomery Ward sells them for. But I don't want to do nothing that'll go against your and Libbie's wishes. So is it all right for me to get James here a rifle?" He winked. "In case y'all get attacked by a herd of dragons?"

# CHAPTER FOUR

**Denison**

Often, Danny Waco made himself laugh, but this joke . . . how glorious. He put the shotgun on the table, almost doubled over, and eventually had to wipe the tears from his eyes with the ends of his bandanna. Still sniffing, he stood, rounded the table, and looked down at the body of Mr. Percy Frick.

"Y-y-you're . . . c-c-crazy," Frick whined.

"Me? Crazy?" Waco leaned his head back and laughed harder. "No, Mr. Frick. I'm a calm businessman. But I can show you crazy."

Immediately the humor vanished and Waco's eyes turned cold.

"Up, Frick. That barrel was empty, but the other one ain't, and if you don't get up and stop actin' like a snivelin' coward, you'll get what that deputy over yonder got. Only you won't be as pretty as he is. Not from this range." Waco thumbed back one hammer while bringing the stock tight against his right shoulder.

The railroad clerk screamed, and covered his face with his hands as if that could protect him from double-ought buck.

"Up, Frick!"

"D-d-don't . . . sh-sh-shoot. P-p-please."

*"Don't . . . shoot . . . please,"* Waco mocked the clerk. "Up, Frick, or I pull this trigger and you don't ever get up." His voice cracked. Blood rushed to his brain, flushing his face. "Ever!"

Folks from the Mexican border towns and all the way up to the Dakotas—those who knew him, or knew of him, or had seen him when he got riled— all agreed that Danny Waco was not the kind of person anyone wanted to anger. His fuse was short, and his temper explosive. He could be funny, witty, sometimes even charming, but underneath all of that laughter, the pranks, and the smart-aleck comments lay a raw, violent edge.

Others put it differently. "Danny Waco," they would say, "is mad as a hatter."

Of course, no one ever said that to his face.

His first name wasn't Danny, or Daniel, and his last name wasn't Waco. His father had named him Lyman. Another reason, he figured, to put four .45 slugs into his old man. His last name he never shared with anyone, but a good newspaper reporter could figure that out easy enough. Go to Fort Worth. Look at the old newspapers from about ten years back. Find the articles in all the city's papers that mentioned the discovery of the body of Fort

Worth's favorite gunsmith. Actually, some would not limit Cahal De Baróid's talents to the city limits, or even Tarrant County, or even the Lone Star State. The poor old man was found in his shop, his shirt still smoldering from the muzzle blasts from a Colt .45 held at point-blank range.

The coroner's inquest ruled that Cahal De Baróid of Fort Worth by way of Savannah, Georgia, and County Mayo, Ireland, met his death from four .45 bullets fired with murderous intent by person or persons unknown. But everyone, especially the newspaper reporters, knew the killer was De Baróid's no-account son, Lyman.

*Lyman. Stupid name,* Waco thought. *Not even Irish.* He had been saddled with his mother's maiden name, Leimann, which the Americans had corrupted into Lyman.

German immigrants, the Leimanns-Lymans had taught Cahal De Baróid everything they knew about making firearms. Danny's mother had died of diphtheria, which had almost called Danny to glory, too, but Danny was too tough to die. Too wild.

He had left Fort Worth with all the money he could find on his father's body and in the gun shop's till, and plenty of powder, pistols, and rifles. He had given himself a new name, a name to be feared. Danny Waco.

Funny thing was, Danny had never set foot in Waco.

"Last chance, Frick. We're already short on time, thanks to that dead dog lying yonder. The town law won't stay locked in his office forever, so we need to talk, and you need to light a shuck back home. If the marshal questions you as a witness to this act of violence, your name gets in the newspapers, bosses get telegrams, and your bosses with the Katy start to wonder just why you came all the way to Denison to do your drinking. *Up.* Get up now or make this hayseed town's undertaker mighty happy for the extra business Danny Waco gave him today."

Mr. Percy Frick, clerk for the Katy, scrambled to his feet, found his chair, made himself sit into it, and tried not to shake his way back onto the dirty floor.

"That's better." Waco returned to his chair and his Old Overholt. "Now, have another drink, Mr. Frick, and let's get down to particulars."

# CHAPTER FIVE

*Parsons, Kansas*
*Autumn 1894*

It was not a .45-70.

It was even bigger.

Deputy Marshal Jimmy Mann took the rifle his brother, Borden, handed him at the depot. Over the years, Jimmy had held a Sharps Big Fifty a few times, even shot one of those old buffalo guns a time or two, but never had he seen anything like this. He looked at the caliber stamped on the top of the barrel just behind the sight.

50-100
450

Jimmy couldn't help himself. Shaking his head, he laughed.

"What's so funny?" Borden asked.

Lowering the rifle, Jimmy said, "Well, I'm just thinking how much I'd love to see Millard's face when our nephew shoots this baby for the first time. Millard thinks a .45-70 is too much for James."

"Millard's right."

Jimmy looked into his brother's eyes. "You underestimate that boy. You and Millard both."

Borden Mann shrugged. He was dressed in the silly cap with the brass insignia and silly tan uniform his bosses required of their express agents, along with worn boots. A shiny gun belt with a revolver holstered, butt forward, was high on his left hip. "Is it what you want?" Jimmy Mann studied the weapon. Once again, he grinned.

His name was Moses, and he led the Winchester Repeating Arms Company out of the wilderness.

Back in 1876, to celebrate the American Centennial, Oliver Winchester and his company, still enjoying the success and profits from their 1866 and 1873 models, decided to bring out a new repeating rifle. They tried to do something no other gun maker had ever imagined—create and massproduce a repeating rifle chambered for fullpowdered center-fire cartridges. The Winchester Model 1876, commonly called the Centennial, fired the company's new 350-grain, .45-75 cartridge, basically a replicated .45-70 Government but in a shorter brass case.

Oliver Winchester had heard the complaints

about the '66 and '73 models. Not enough firepower. Didn't shoot true at long range. Hit a buffalo with that caliber, and the big shaggy would likely think he'd been bitten by a mosquito. So he and his designers and gun makers came up with the Centennial. It looked like the '73, only heavier, with a frame an inch and a half longer, and a shot cartridge that was eleven-sixteenths of an inch longer than Winchester's .44-40.

A rifle like that could help buffalo hunters slaughter those massive herds on the Western plains. A carbine, with a twenty-two-inch barrel, would chamber nine cartridges and weigh eight and a quarter pounds—before it was loaded. No repeating rifle had ever dared fire such a heavy, powerful round.

In 1876, Winchester introduced the new rifle at the Centennial Exhibition in Philadelphia. The North-West Mounted Police bought scores of such rifles for their Mounties patrolling western Canada. That Eastern politician who dearly loved the West, Theodore Roosevelt, used it on several hunts. Texas Rangers were known to ride with them and shoot with deadly accuracy. When the Apache Indian Geronimo called it quits back in '86 and surrendered at Skeleton Canyon, he was carrying a Winchester '76.

There were just a few problems. The rifle couldn't handle .45-70 loads, at least, not safely. In that regard, considering how popular .45-70 Government calibers were across the United States and its territories, the Centennial proved to be a failure.

What's more, Oliver Winchester really wanted to land a beefy contract with the U.S. War Department, and the Army didn't like the Centennial.

Drop a '76, and it might bust apart. The rear sight easily came loose, but shooting a rifle with that much power, sights needed to be secure. Besides, Winchesters just couldn't handle the .45-70 Government, and that's what the U.S. government wanted.

That was what brought the Winchester Repeating Arms Company to the doorstep of John Moses Browning.

Browning's father had left Illinois with thousands of Mormons back in 1852, settling in Ogden, Utah, where John Moses entered the world three years later. By the time he was seven, he was working in his father's gun shop. In the late 1870s, he was tinkering with new ideas, and developed a single-shot rifle that the Winchester Repeating Arms Company noticed. Winchester paid $8,000 for the design, and began producing its Low Wall and High Wall single shots that put the fear of God, or rather, the Winchester Repeating Arms Company, into the minds of executives with Springfield and Remington companies known for their single-shot rifles.

Winchester knew whom to turn to when in need of an excellent repeating rifle.

Company executives asked Browning to come up with a repeating rifle that could handle .45-70 Government rounds—and maybe even more powerful cartridges. Browning did just that, got the patent, and took a train to New Haven, Connecticut, with his brother, Matt, but stopped first to visit Schoverling, Daly & Gales in New York City. Since 1865, if a man wanted to sell guns, buy a great weapon, or get an expert opinion on any rifle, shotgun or revolver, he dropped in at the shop on Broadway to see what Charles Daly, August Schoverling, and Joseph Gales thought.

Browning handed his rifle to Daly and held his breath.

Daly adjusted his spectacles, looked over the rifle, and returned it. "John Browning, I know I don't have to tell you this, but what you are holding is the best rifle in the world."

Standing behind the counter, Schoverling added, "*Nein*. He is holding da future of da Vinchester Arms Company."

"A Big Fifty." Jimmy shook his head. "In a Winchester."

Borden pulled a cartridge from his jacket pocket. "This is what it shoots." Into his brother's hands, he dropped a chunk of lead a half-inch wide that weighed 450 grains.

Jimmy examined the rifle closely. Blasted out of a twenty-six-inch barrel by a hundred grains of powder, it had a twist rate of one turn per fifty-four inches, which was needed to fire a load that heavy. The weight of the octagon barrel was also necessary.

No pistol grip, just the standard stock. No shotgun or rubber butt-plate, either. James's shoulder would surely hurt after feeling that standard crescent butt-plate practically tear off his shoulder. No engraving. No set triggers. No tang sights. It looked like an ordinary Winchester.

*No,* Jimmy corrected. *It resembles a Howitzer on a Winchester frame.* He rubbed his finger over the serial number. 70630.

"A wolfer ordered it," Borden said. "Left the warehouse this past January."

Jimmy looked up. "That's a lot of rifle for a guy chasing wolves."

"Because Nels Who Smells hated wolves," Borden said.

Jimmy checked the action, working the lever. The rifle had been cleaned religiously. which did not make sense to him. Most wolfers he had run across were filthy, miserable men that were unfit for company unless you were a grayback.

"Why is Nels selling it?"

"He's not. Town marshal is. To pay for Nels's funeral. I told Mark—that's our local lawman—that you were interested in a Winchester Model '86. Mark told me. I wired you. Here you are."

Looking around, Jimmy made sure nobody was staring out one of the hotel's second-story windows before he sighted across the street at the façade. Great balance. Heavy, but it felt right, comfortable, the perfect rifle—even better than his '73.

Winchester had paid John Moses Browning $50,000 for the design. Ask Deputy Marshal

Jimmy Mann, however, and he'd tell you how Browning should have held out for more.

Still, Jimmy had reservations. His nephew was sixteen. Millard would hound him something fierce for sending a .50-100-450 to that kid. And the next time he visited them in Texas, Jimmy's sister-in-law would make him rue the day he had even answered Borden's telegraph and ridden up to Parsons.

He looked at his brother. "What do you think?"

"You?" Borden chuckled. "You're asking me? For my advice?"

"You are my oldest brother," Jimmy said. *Who looks ridiculous—like some pale-skinned Mexican Rurale— in that outfit the express company makes you wear.*

"You won't find a better price. Funerals are cheap here in Parsons."

The Labette County seat twenty-something miles from the Cherokee Nation, Parsons had been founded in 1870 with the arrival of the Katy. The railroad was still pretty much the only thing of any substance to the wind-blown town. Everything— food, rooms, beer, women, lives—came cheap, but Parsons wasn't as wild as Baxter Springs to the southeast had been years ago. And it didn't have a bunch of dead Daltons to brag about as Coffeyville had to the southwest.

A bad thought struck Jimmy. "How did Nels die?"

"He didn't blow his head off with his own rifle, if that's what you mean."

"It isn't," Jimmy said, though it was.

"You know wolfers," Borden explained. "He

came in, got his bounty from the county sheriff. No hotel would take him, of course. Don't want any travelers on the Katy to complain about getting infested with bugs. He paid for a stall in the livery, paid for rotgut from some whiskey runner heading into your jurisdiction. Got drunk. Passed out. Vomited in his sleep. And choked to death."

"Bad ending." Jimmy shook his head.

"Good riddance." Borden waited for Jimmy to stare at him, and then smiled.

"How does it shoot?"

The train whistle blew. Jimmy knew that he would have to make a decision soon.

"Mark—again, that's our local lawman. He cleaned it up, took it north of town, said he bagged an antelope at four hundred yards without hardly aiming. I know what you're thinking, Jimmy, but Mark's not prone to brag."

"So why doesn't Mark want to keep this rifle for himself?"

"Because tigers and lions and even bears aren't common in Parsons, Kansas, little brother."

"I haven't seen many in McAdam, Texas, either."

"Mark's gunshot tore up a lot of good meat on that antelope. It's like I said, Jimmy, that's a big gun for a kid."

"He'll be seventeen in April. I remember our pa saying the same thing when you got your '66."

Borden smiled. "And when you got your '73."

Porters began helping women and children onto the train, while the conductor seemed to be giving

Borden and Jimmy the evil eye. Steam hissed, and the locomotive grunted.

Typically, Jimmy Mann made his choices quickly. Working mostly in the Indian Nations, he had to. Yet he didn't want to disappoint the boy Millard had named after the black sheep of the Mann family. On the other hand, luck had eluded Jimmy as he searched for an '86 Winchester in Fort Smith . . . in Tahlequah . . . McAlester . . . Van Buren. Few .45-70s could be found, and when one came available, the owner had priced the rifle as though it were a "One of a Thousand."

"Five dollars, Jimmy. But I need to know right now." Borden wasn't kidding around.

The conductor yelled, "All aboard."

Borden took the Winchester from Jimmy's hands and made his way to the open door of the express car. Jimmy's boots didn't move. At least, not at first. Then he started running, catching up right after Borden climbed into the car and two black men working for the Katy were about to close the door.

"Can you get it to James?" Jimmy yelled up.

Borden held up a hand, and the men stopped the door.

"You bet. I can get it to Fort Worth. With ammunition to boot. Got a box all ready to ship it. And I can telegraph a fellow I know with the Fort Worth and Denver City to take it the rest of the way." He smiled. "Won't be long now until our nephew is proud to be a Mann."

"Yeah. And his ma and pa will be out for my hair."

"You want to ride along with me?" Borden asked.

"Can't." Jimmy's head shook. "I'm supposed to meet up with some Indian policemen in Lightning Creek in two days. They think Danny Waco's been in those parts."

Borden's head bobbed grimly, and the two black men finished closing the door. The train lurched forward, starting its journey south toward the Indian Nations. Relief swept through Jimmy as he watched the train rumble, hissing, belching, squeaking, squealing. He smiled, picturing his nephew's face.

Then he remembered something.

He ran alongside the train, catching up to the express car, pounding on that heavy door with his fist. "Borden! Hey, Borden! I owe you five dollars. Plus the freight charges." He had to stop, to keep from falling off the depot's platform.

Yet Borden's words carried over the grating of iron as the train pulled out of the station. "You don't owe me a thing, Jimmy."

# CHAPTER SIX

*Spavina Creek Crossing, Cherokee Nation*

There were different ways to rob a train.

You could derail it, but Danny Waco found that method to be quite destructive, messy, and, above all, needlessly noisy. Besides, send the engine crashing off the tracks and the boiler might explode, spraying chunks of wood and iron like grapeshot into the bodies of greedy outlaws.

You could board the train at a station, just get on like a regular passenger, and wait for a good moment and likely place and start the ball. Waco didn't care much for that way, either. You had to leave some of your gang and horses at the place you'd designated to stop the train. He didn't like splitting up his men. What would happen if some passenger recognized the bandits and started shooting? Besides, at least one person had to climb atop a car, and make his way on the rooftops to the engine, where he would force the crew to pull the brake lever. Plenty risky.

For Waco, however, the biggest drawback was that you actually had to buy a ticket to board the train.

Or you could find a remote location, pile debris atop the tracks, and make the train stop. He had tried that once. Seeing the blockade, the wily engineer opened up the throttle, and simply ran right through the ties and logs, leaving Waco red-faced and the butt of jokes for two or three weeks.

To Danny Waco, it seemed the best way was to pound on the door to the pump house. "Open the door, old man! The bridge is washed out, and the Number Four's comin' this way!" He slammed his rifle butt against the door again, stepped back, and smiled at himself.

Inside the pump house, feet shuffled across the floor, a man sniffed his nose, then blew it, cursed, and fumbled with the latch. The door opened, and a ridiculous-looking old-timer in his nightshirt and sleeping hat poked his head through the opening.

"What you talkin' 'bout? I jus' checked that bridge an hour ago."

"Washed out, I tell you."

"It ain't rained since August."

"Up country, I guess, got a gulley-washer. Mister, that Number Four is just up the tracks."

"The Four ain't due for three more hours. Must be the Flyer."

"Well, I don't want the Flyer's crew to get killed, neither," Waco said. "But thank-you, kindly." He smashed the old man's face with the Winchester's stock, and the man fell backward into the pump house with a cry and a crash.

"You ain't gonna kill him, are you, Waco?"

Waco grunted, tossed the rifle to The Tonk, and pushed open the door. "No, Ted Dunegan, I ain't. I ain't gonna kill him. I ain't gonna tell him that Ted Dunegan, who has blond hair and a big mouth, looks to be about twenty years old, and who married that squaw at Bluejacket, was with me. And I sure ain't gonna use nobody's name."

The Tonk grinned.

Muttering a curse and shaking his head, Waco went inside the pump house, taking the rope Gil Millican tossed him, and knelt by the moaning bridge watcher's body. "Strike a match, Ted Dunegan," he whispered. "I can't see a thing in here."

Mounted on his horse a few rods from the hut, Dunegan, of course, couldn't even hear Waco's command. Millican fished a Lucifer from his vest pocket, and used his thumbnail to light the match. He knelt, cupping a hand, giving Danny Waco enough light to tie the watchman's hands behind his back.

"You rest, old-timer." Waco patted the man's bald head. He grabbed the nightcap, and stuffed it inside the gent's mouth, then used the tails of the plaid nightshirt to wipe the blood off his hands. "We'll take care of the Number Four, me and Ted Dunegan and the boys."

He rose, and after Millican lighted another match, saw what he needed. Stepping to the table, Waco found a bonus. He picked up the bottle, sniffed it, shook it to make sure there was enough left, and grabbed the cork. Once the cork was back on tight, he tossed the Old Crow to Millican.

Carrying two lanterns, Waco followed Millican outside, closing the door behind him.

"The Flyer comes by first," Waco told the boys. "Ted Dunegan, you let that one go on ahead. That's not the one we want."

"How do I do that . . . ?" Dunegan lived up the tracks and had just learned not to use a gang member's name during the course of a train robbery.

Waco tossed him a lantern. "Light it, wave it. You'll be standing on the side of the tracks. Don't worry. You won't get hurt."

"What if it stops anyway?"

Waco glared. That was the trouble these days. He couldn't find smart outlaws, just kids and drunkards and punks with big mouths.

"You'll be waving the white lantern," Waco said through clenched teeth. "That means all's fine. The Flyer will zip on by. After that, we wait."

Lifting the second lantern he had taken from the pump house, Waco continued. "When we hear the second train coming, three hours or so from now, you'll stand on the tracks and raise and wave this one. It has red glass. That will signal the engineer to stop, that the bridge or tracks are damaged."

"I stand on the tracks?"

"There's plenty of time for the train to stop." Waco's head shook, and he set the red-glassed lantern on the bench beside the pump house. He had found three other men—if you could call them *men*—to help pull off this robbery. He didn't know if they were as stupid as Ted Dunegan, but at least they were quiet, and didn't ask fool questions. Or call Waco by his name.

"Now, loosen the cinches on your saddles and hobble your horses in the woods yonder. Then sit down, have a smoke, enjoy yourselves. No drinkin', though. Just water from the pump house. We'll do our celebratin' at Lightnin' Creek tomorrow. All except you, Ted Dunegan. Once you get your share, I'd advise you to light a shuck for parts unknown. I don't think that watchman will forget your name. Or mine, neither. Mine I don't rightly care about. I'm already a well-known hombre. But come tomorrow, Ted Dunegan, the law will be chasin' you down for the loud-mouthed fool you are."

The first train went through forty-five minutes later. Waco checked his watch, nodding with satisfaction, and telling Millican, "That temperance lecture I gave the boys? It don't apply to us veterans."

Grinning, Millican withdrew the bottle of Old Crow from the back pocket of his trousers, uncorked the bourbon, and took a swig before tossing the bottle to Waco. The Tonk did not imbibe—a good thing, considering how little the bridge watchman had left for his visitors.

Two hours later, Waco felt pretty good. Just enough bourbon to make him forget all about that idiot Ted Dunegan and think about spending all that money Mr. Percy Frick, clerk for the Katy down in Texas, told him would be aboard tonight's southbound No. 4.

An hour later, that feeling was gone.

Two hours after that, Waco paced the tracks back and forth, cursing, swearing that he would ride to Texas to kill that gutless wonder they'd met in Denison, Mr. Percy Frick.

"Boss," Millican said, "something happened to the train is all. Remember, the bridge watcher said the Number Four would be coming this way."

That stopped the pacing. Waco chewed on his bottom lip for a moment, then strode straight to the pump house, kicking open the door. Kneeling in the darkness, he rolled the old man onto his back, then jerked out the gag he had fashioned from the nightcap. "You said the Number Four was coming through."

Weeping, the man moved his head back and forth.

That prompted Waco to slap the frightened man twice. "I can't see. It's a new moon, you fool." He swore, turned and shouted, "One of you boys bring me the lantern. The clear one. Not the red one."

A short while later, The Tonk held the white lantern in the doorway.

"The Number Four?" Waco repeated.

"Supposed to be here around twelve-fifteen," the man said.

Waco fished his daddy's watch out of his vest pocket, let it dangle from the gold chain. "It's three-oh-seven. I think you and that Katy clerk tried to pull the wool over my eyes—and that's not something people live to brag about."

The bald head jerked toward the table. "Sch-sched-ule . . . it's . . . on . . . th-th-the t-t-table."

The Tonk stepped toward the table, lowered the lantern, and picked up a sheet. His eyes moved back and forth, up and down, and he was about to say something, but stopped.

He didn't have to speak. Waco heard the train's whistle in the night.

Sometimes, it was hard to figure out what an outlaw was thinking. Waco just didn't understand why more train robbers didn't operate the way he did. It worked fine and dandy.

He stood beside the express car, banging on the door with the stock of his Winchester.

Loose-lipped Ted Dunegan had done his job, had waved that red-glassed lantern, and brought the Baldwin engine to a stop. Locomotive, tinder, baggage car, express car, two coaches, smoking car, Pullman sleeper, and caboose all stopped behind it. The conductor had hurried from one of the coaches, wanting to know what had happened to the bridge, and Millican had drawn his revolver and pressed the barrel between the fat man's double chins.

The Tonk kept his Greener trained on the brake-man, conductor, and engineer. Waco sent loud-mouthed Ted Dunegan of Bluejacket and the three other men to relieve the passengers of any valuables. That left the express car to Waco and Millican.

"Mr. Express man . . ." Waco butted the Winchester on the ground. "Open the door, sir."

No answer.

"Loyalty is something you give your mama, your preacher, not the Adams Express Agency. Nobody gets hurt if you do as I say. I'll even write a letter of recommendation to your ramrods in New York City, citin' you for bravery."

Silence.

Waco turned to The Tonk. "Leave 'em prisoners with me. Go to one of the coaches and bring back a woman. Young, old, mother, grandmother, kid . . . I don't care." He spoke loud enough for the express agent inside the car to hear.

Millican moved toward the engineer, brakeman, and conductor, covering them with the revolver.

Waco shouted up at the express car. "Mr. Express man. Here's what's gonna happen. One of my partners—who is not Ted Dunegan of Bluejacket— is goin' to the coaches. He'll bring back a woman. Maybe a kid. Maybe a nun. Perhaps a grandmother or mother-to-be. When she gets here, I'll count to ten. If that door ain't open at nine, I shoot the petticoat down—"

The conductor's gasp was cut short by Gil Millican, who buffaloed him with the barrel of his Smith & Wesson No. 2, a big-bore center-fire .32 with a seven-inch barrel that had gotten a lot of use in the past twenty years. The portly man fell to his knees, moaning softly, holding his head. The engineer and brakeman did not move, barely even breathed.

From the coaches came a few muffled gunshots, shouts, laughter, and screams.

The boys were likely burning lead, trying to put the fear of God into the passengers, make them co-operate. Waco stared down the rails, watching the lights that shone out of the windows, casting eerie shadows on the ground. He looked at his watch again. Time became precious. They wanted to be well out of the area before daybreak.

"Why were you late?" Waco asked the engineer.

"I don't know, sir," the man answered. "Zeke and me was part of a crew change in Vinita."

Waco spit in disgust. He could hear the boys in the coaches clearly, shouting like fools who had run off with a box of candy from some hayseed mercantile.

"Look at this, Vern. Two double eagles!"

"I got me a diamond stickpin, Joey. Hey, what you hidin' in your boot there, mister?"

Waco would be mighty glad to get shun of these boys. Let the law catch them in two days—three at the most—and haul them back to Fort Smith to rot in the dungeon, then be sentenced by Judge Parker.

He felt better when he saw The Tonk, herding a woman toward him with his Greener.

The Tonk said nothing when they stopped a few feet in front of Waco, but the woman had a mouth on her.

"What is the meaning of this, you swine?"

Well, the old broad had spunk. Waco gave her that. A heavyset women with gray hair in a bun, dressed in light gray wool, Waco figured her as a grandmother. Maybe a preacher's wife.

"Ma'am." Waco tipped his hat and smiled. "We're just testin' the efficiency of the Katy and the Adams Express Company, and hope you would help us out. What's your name?"

She folded her arms, and snorted.

"Where are you bound?"

She glared.

Waco pulled the short-barreled Colt. "Seriously, ma'am, we need to know what name to put on your tombstone."

The arms fell, and she stepped back, mouth opening as Waco thumbed back the hammer.

"Last chance, Mr. Express man. I kill this old biddy. Then I send my pard back to fetch another woman."

The old lady's eyes rolled into the back of her head, her knees buckled, and she fell. The Tonk made no attempt to catch her, nor did Waco.

Their attention had turned to the express car. They watched with faces beaming and weapons trained at the door, which slowly slid open.

# CHAPTER SEVEN

Borden Mann stopped the door after it slid maybe a foot. He couldn't see much outside, just darkness and shadows.

"Keep it comin', Mr. Express man," a voice called. "I can still shoot this ol' lady."

It had to be Danny Waco. Who else had such gall? Back in Parsons, Jimmy had said that Cherokees had spotted Waco in the area. Borden wished his kid brother had taken him up on the offer and hitched a ride on the Katy. He tried to work up enough saliva in his mouth to spit, but couldn't. He swallowed and called out, "I'm tossing out my revolver."

"You do that. Real careful. Then open that door all the way. I want to see what a brave, but smart, express agent looks like."

He drew the revolver from the stiff holster and stared at it. It was one of Remington's New Model Pocket Army .44-40s, which the company had given him, brand-spanking new back in '89, shipped directly from Hartley and Graham's gun shop in New York. Remington had made only a few of these weapons, which looked more like a Colt than the old Remington 1875s. It had a five-and-a-half inch barrel, and, like most men, Borden kept only five loads in the chamber.

Most men never loaded the chamber underneath the hammer. Nobody wanted to accidentally shoot himself in the leg or blow off a big toe. Well, Jimmy always kept "six beans in the wheel." But Borden wasn't his younger brother.

"My patience is wearin' thin."

Five shots. He didn't have any extra ammunition. Then he looked at the box on the desk, the one holding the Winchester '86 and one box of twenty .50-100-450 cartridges.

He knew Danny Waco wasn't bluffing. An old woman was out there, and if shooting started, the woman would die. So would Borden Mann. He had done his best, but maybe he could see if he could bluff Danny Waco.

The Remington flew through the crack. He heard it *thunk* on the ground, then he gripped the door, slid it open, and let the light from the lantern on the wall shine on three outlaws, part of the train's crew, and a woman lying spread-eagle on the ground. His eyes locked on her, and then found Danny Waco.

"She just decided to take a little siesta, Brave Express man." Waco holstered his revolver but raised his Winchester at Borden, waving the barrel to motion Borden to raise his hands and back away from the door.

A big, burly Indian went into the baggage car with Waco, leaving another white man covering the engineer and brakeman with a long-barreled revolver. The conductor remained on his knees, holding his head with one hand, his right hand on the ground. The old woman did not move.

Using the barrel of his carbine, Waco prodded Borden Mann back against the letterboxes and cubbyholes. The Tonk kept both barrels of a sawed-off shotgun trained on Borden as well.

Waco knocked off Borden's cap, grinned, then moved to the safe, kneeling on the floor, and looking back at Borden. "You want to open it up?"

"I don't have a key."

"Ain't you the messenger?"

Borden wet his lips.

"I mean, you're the only one I seen wearing that stupid cap with a bit of brass that says Adams Express on it."

Borden said, "I have no key."

"Who else would have the key?"

Borden said nothing.

"I hate brave express agents." With a heavy sigh, Danny Waco turned to the Indian, who was busy rifling through the letters and packages. "Tom, blow this brave man's head off."

The Indian had ripped open a letter, and was smelling the pink stationery. Frowning, he wadded up the note, tossed it to the floor, and turned around, bringing the stock of the shotgun to his shoulder. Borden stared into the cavernous Damascus barrels, sawed down to just in front of the forestock. Ten gauge, by the looks of them. Yet he refused to turn away, refused to close his eyes. He just waited.

"Tom," Waco said, "let's not play games. Instead of killing him, kill the conductor. Then the old crone. Then tell Gil to shoot the brakeman. Maybe that'll get this brave man to finding us that key."

The Indian grinned, stepped over some boxes he had tossed onto the floor, and aimed the shotgun through the opening. "Step aside, Gil. You don't want to get hit by no buckshot. Hey, Conductor. Look up. You should see this." The big Indian snorted, and his face hardened.

They would do it, of course. Borden knew that plain enough. If you believed the stories, Danny Waco had already killed twenty men between Mexico and Montana. He would let the Indian kill the conductor and the woman passenger, still fainted dead away on the ground.

Borden knew something else, too. No matter what happened, Waco would kill him. That's why he and the Indian kept using names. No matter who else died, it would be Borden's last evening on earth. "Waco."

The Indian turned around, lowering the shotgun. Waco grinned. "You know me?"

"I know of you."

"Then you know I'm a man of my word."

Borden didn't respond to that. He found his chair in the corner, and sat, brought up his left leg, and tugged and tugged until that old boot came off. Next, he pulled off his sock, reached inside, and pulled out the key. He tossed it to Danny Waco.

"You're a bright man, Mr. Express man. Real smart." Waco turned to the safe, put the key in the lock.

"There's nothing in there," Borden said.

The outlaw sniggered. "Right. That's why you keep the key in your sock. No, Mr. Express man, I think I'll find forty thousand dollars worth of greenbacks in this safe, courtesy of the American Cotton Company of Denison, Texas."

Borden's face paled. He dropped his boot.

The safe door opened, and Danny Waco roared in rage. Papers and letters flew out of the safe, followed by a pouch of coins, and some banknotes. But nothing resembling a giant payroll for a north Texas cotton firm.

Waco came up, moving like a rattlesnake, striking. The Winchester's barrel sliced across Borden's head, and Borden fell from the chair. Head throbbing, he saw dots of orange and gold and red and white flash before him. He groaned. Bringing his left hand to his temple, he felt the blood.

"Where is it?" Waco roared.

"Where's . . . what?" Borden tried to at least sit up, but Waco put his right foot on his chest, pressing down . . . hard.

"The American Cotton Company payroll?"

He shook his head. "Wrong train."

The Winchester slashed again, cutting Borden's cheek, and loosening a few molars. "This is the Number Four, mister, and my informant in Texas said it was on this train."

"No," Borden said. "The Four derailed. This is the Sixteen. Why we're late."

The boot came off Borden's chest, and Waco began slamming the Winchester's stock against boxes and cubbyholes, splintering the wood, sending papers and packages onto the tabletop, the floor, and the sacks. He swore vilely, moved to the safe, kicked the door shut, and even banged his head against the wall.

Borden Mann managed to smile, until another voice said from outside, "He's lyin', Waco."

Waco whirled, stormed to the doorway, "What the hell do you know about anything, Ted Dunegan of Bluejacket way? And why ain't you up with the passengers?"

"We've plucked 'em of all they got, Waco. Joey and Mal's with 'em, makin' sure they don't try nothin' foolish. Vern went to fetch our horses. But he's lyin', Danny. This is the Number Four."

"How do you know?"

"Passenger told us."

Borden felt his stomach turn over. He had managed to pull himself up, leaning back against the sacks packed three feet high off the floor, blinking the blood out of his eyes, tasting more blood on his tongue and lips. His vision had cleared somewhat, enough that he could see Waco standing over him, could see the barrel aimed at his chest.

"You heard that, didn't you?" Waco asked.

"I heard," Borden answered.

"I don't tolerate liars. So who do I kill? You? Or do I dispatch Ted Dunegan to kill one of the Katy's passengers?"

Borden turned his head and spit out blood. "This is the Number Four, but there's no payroll."

"My man in Texas . . . he knows things."

Borden's head bobbed. Even that hurt. He cringed, tried to shake off the pain, and smiled. "He set you up, Danny. The payroll. We put it on the Flyer."

"The Flyer!" Dunegan cried out, followed by some curses, and a fist slamming against the express car's wall. "Waco . . . you told me to let that train go by."

Borden laughed—until Waco kicked him in the chest, knocking him to his side.

Waco walked back and forth, knocking over packages, kicking boxes, cursing, screaming, shouting out that he'd ride to Texas and personally kill Mr. Percy Frick.

Borden tried to catch his breath. He pulled himself back to a seated position, smiling with satisfaction at the irate, almost insane, outlaw. He saw this young kid—must have been Ted Dunegan—climb into the car, and begin opening letters, packages. To Borden's right, the big Indian Waco had called Tonk was doing the same.

Moments later, Waco had calmed down. "What are you doin'?"

"Seein' if there's anything valuable in this mail," said the young outlaw, a blond-headed, pock-marked kid with peach fuzz for a mustache. He found a check, folded it, and stuck it inside his vest pocket.

"How much did we get off the passengers and crew?" Waco asked.

Peach Fuzz, Mr. Ted Dunegan of Bluejacket, shrugged. "Not forty thousand dollars. Not by a long shot."

Waco cursed again. "Percy Frick's a dead man." He knelt to pick up the purse of coins he had tossed out of the safe. He pulled on the string, tugged it open, and cursed again. "Nickels." He glowered at Borden. "Who puts nickels in a safe?"

Borden didn't answer. He saw the Greener leaning against the handle of a McCormick's reaper in the back of the coach, and saw the legs of the big Indian. Heard him opening a box, and Borden's heart sank.

"Well, here's somethin'."

"Money?" Waco looked up.

"Better."

Borden heard the metallic sound of a rifle being cocked.

"That's a sweet action." The trigger pulled, snapping loudly.

Borden saw the Winchester '86 sailing across the room into Danny Waco's hands.

"A rifle?" Dunegan spit onto the floor. "It ain't worth forty thousand dollars, is it?"

"Shut up." Waco had left his Winchester lying on the floor. He studied the rifle that had once belonged to Nels Who Smells, but was supposed to be going to James Mann in McAdam, Texas. Cocked it again, pulled the trigger, then flipped the gun around, staring down the barrel. "I've seen caves smaller than this." He grinned.

"Yeah," the Indian said. "Here."

Waco shifted the big rifle, sticking it underneath his left armpit, and held up his hands like some ballist awaiting the throw of a baseball. Instead, he caught the box of shells the Indian had tossed, green paper with the image of a bullet in the center.

"For Winchester Repeating Rifle, Model 1886," Waco read and laughed. "Fifty caliber, hundred grains of powder, and a four-hundred-fifty grain chunk of lead for a bullet."

"That would stop a train," the Indian said.

"No." Borden tried to stand, but the Indian knocked him down. Borden pushed himself up. "You're not taking my nephew's rifle."

Again, he tried to get to his feet, but the Indian kicked him in the side. He felt his ribs break and landed hard on his back, groaning, spitting up blood again.

"Your nephew, eh?" Waco's voice, then the sound of the rifle being cocked, but only halfway.

"McAdam, Texas." It was the kid, Dunegan. He had crossed the room, and found the box Borden had put the rifle in. "James Mann, General Delivery."

"James Mann." Waco sounded interested. "I know a Mann. Deputy marshal who rides for Judge

Parker's court. Goes by the name Jimmy. I call him something else." He laughed. "He probably calls me something else, too. I didn't know that ol' lawdog had family. Don't see how he had the time, seein' how he's been on my trail for years."

"He . . . doesn't . . ." Just speaking hurt Borden.

"Doesn't what?" Waco stood over him.

"Have a . . . family."

"You know Jimmy Mann?"

"My . . . brother . . ."

Waco laughed. He finished cocking the rifle, braced the stock against his thigh, and held a bullet, one he had pulled from the box of cartridges the Indian had tossed him. He fed the long brass shell into the gate, and cocked the rifle again. "Well, now. This robbery might turn out to be a fine success after all. So Jimmy Mann's your brother, eh?"

Borden nodded as best he could. "And I promise you, Waco. You take my nephew's rifle. And we'll hunt you down . . . if it takes us . . . to the ends of the earth."

The rifle's stock came up to Waco's right shoulder. He leaned over, sighting down. Borden Mann looked into the massive barrel.

"Well, Mr. Express man, I promise you something, too, something you, your lawdog brother, and your little nephew can count on." He waited, but Borden Mann would give this road agent no satisfaction. "I promise you that they'll have to have a closed casket at your funeral."

# CHAPTER EIGHT

*Vinita*

"You don't want to see him, Marshal." The conductor's head looked abnormal, wrapped with thick white strips of linen, heavily padded on the top where someone had buffaloed him with a six-shooter. He was a fat man to begin with, out of breath, probably still in pain, but he held up his hand, and somehow managed to stop Jimmy Mann from charging into the freight room at the Vinita depot. "You want to remember Borden as he was alive."

Mann stepped back. His legs and butt felt sore from riding so hard from Lightning Creek. He needed sleep, a bath, and a shave. He wanted a whiskey. No, what he wanted was to see his brother . . . alive.

He could feel all the stares boring into him, felt as if he could hear their whispers. Indians, blacks, and whites had crowded onto the town's main street, next to the depot that served the Katy and the St. Louis and San Francisco Railway. News traveled fast in Indian Territory. He figured people had come to town all the way from Honey Creek and Coody's Bluff to see the show.

He stood, Winchester in his right hand, trying to dam the tears that wanted to break free. He wanted to push past the fat conductor, and find his brother, cradle his head in his lap. Instead, he steeled himself, sucked in a deep breath, and asked, "What happened?"

"It was Danny Waco." The conductor brought up a fat hand and gently fingered the bandage on his head.

*Waco.* Jimmy had a warrant in his saddlebags for him. Danny Waco was the reason he had ridden to Lightning Creek to meet up with three Creek officers of the United States Indian Police out of Muskogee. He had left the Indians at Lightning Creek once a deputy marshal had brought word of what had happened at Spavina Creek Crossing, but all the lawman had told him was that the Katy No. 4 had been robbed, that his brother had been killed.

"Waco," Jimmy said.

"He coldcocked the bridge watcher," the engineer said. "Had one of his men wavin' the red lantern. I didn't suspect nothin'. Figgered the bridge was out, so I stopped the train. Sorry, Marshal."

Jimmy's head shook. It wasn't the engineer's fault. What else could he have done? Ignored the warning signal and stormed on ahead, risking the lives of his crew and his passengers if the bridge indeed had been damaged?

"He knew of the payroll," the conductor said.

"What payroll?"

"The Adams Express Company was hauling forty thousand dollars to Denison, Texas," the conductor answered. "He knew we were carrying it."

"How?"

"Informant." This came from the bespectacled deputy marshal who had ridden all morning the twenty miles to Lightning Creek. He had ridden four horses to get there, then used up three more on the return trip. Even Jimmy, who had borrowed two of the Indian policemen's mounts, had had trouble keeping up with the old man's pace.

A tall, lean Cherokee with long gray hair and a scarred face, Jackson Sixpersons also served on the U.S. Indian Police, but the judge and district marshal liked deputizing some Indians as federal marshals, too. Good politics for one reason. Nobody knew the Indian Nations as well as those Indians for another. A good man, maybe sixty years old, who rode like a Cherokee forty years younger, Sixpersons reached into his jacket and pulled out a notepad, which he flipped open. "Clerk named Percy Frick. Down in Texas. Denison maybe." Sixpersons looked up above his eyeglasses, but said no more.

The conductor filled in. "I telegraphed the marshals in Texas. They'll find that man, arrest him."

"How did you know his name?" Jimmy asked.

"When he didn't find the money, Waco started

cussing him," the conductor said. "He thought he'd been double-crossed by—"

"Waco didn't find the money?" Jimmy interrupted.

"No." The conductor swallowed. "Thanks to your brother. After the train stopped, Borden kept the door to the express car locked until Waco threatened to murder a passenger, an old woman, in cold blood. While Waco and the other six bandits were kept out of the express car, Borden had opened the safe, hidden the money in a flour sack on the floor, put the key in one of his socks, and pulled his boot back on over it.

"We found the money after they rode off," the conductor said. "Ol' Borden . . . he bluffed Danny Waco good."

*Yeah. Only it had cost Borden his life.* "What did they get?" Jimmy looked at Deputy Marshal Sixpersons.

He flipped open his notebook, and began reading his notes. "Don't know what they got from the express car. Not till we hear from the express company."

"But," the conductor chimed in, "the Adams Express Company and the Katy have already posted a thousand dollar reward for the capture of Danny Waco."

That brought the price on Waco's head to $4,250.

"For the murder of your brother."

Jimmy nodded.

Sixpersons went on. "Maybe four hundred and fifty in cash, coin, jewelry, and watches. They got

some stuff out of the mail, but we don't know
what."

"Not the haul they were after, though," the conductor said.

"They got that big rifle, too," Sixpersons said.
"The one you were sending to your brother's boy."

That did it. Jimmy felt his stomach overturning,
felt as if he might faint. He moved to the bench in
front of the ticket agent's window and collapsed
onto the hard seat, bringing his Winchester to his
lap, swearing softly.

Sixpersons followed Jimmy to the bench. "I
found the box Borden had put it in. Sorry, Jimmy."

He sniffed, nodded. Maybe even said, "Yeah." He
wasn't sure.

"Jimmy . . ." The Indian marshal waited until
Jimmy looked up.

"He used the rifle on Borden."

Late in the day, it had turned warm, almost hot
for the time of year, but Jimmy Mann suddenly felt
cold down to his bones. He started to second-guess
everything he had done. *If I had listened to Borden . . .
He said that .50-caliber cannon was too much gun for
James. If I had said yes to Borden, had ridden down with
him . . .*

He saw himself as Borden, lying on the floor of
the express car, looking up into the barrel of that
.50-100-450. Or maybe he was lying on his stomach,
feeling the barrel of that cannon on the back of his
head. Either way, nobody had to explain to him any
further why the conductor didn't want Jimmy to
see Borden's body.

"The train was running late," the conductor said. "Got delayed at Russet Peak. We changed crews here, and after they stopped the train, robbed it, killed . . . well, they ordered the engineer to back up the train all the way back here. We telegraphed Muskogee, Parsons, Fort Smith, Denison . . ."

He kept on talking, but Jimmy wasn't listening. He was hearing his brother, yelling at him through the closed door of the express car, *You don't owe me a thing, Jimmy.*

"Yes, I do, Borden," Jimmy whispered.

"What's that?" the conductor asked.

Jimmy shook his head. "Get my brother out of that freight room," he said, the anger rising in his voice. He could feel his neck burning, his ears reddening. "He's not a shipment of farm implements."

"We didn't know—"

He cut off the conductor with a glare. "Get him to an undertaker. Put him in the best coffin. His wife and family live in Olathe, Kansas. That's where you send his body."

"Well . . ." the conductor began. "We figured you'd want to go with him."

"I'm going somewhere else," Jimmy snapped, and made himself stand. "Which way did they go?"

The conductor lost his voice. The engineer stared at his big boots. But the brakeman said, "We wouldn't know, sir. They had us backin' down the tracks before they'd taken off."

"But we know some names." Sixpersons looked back at his notepad. "Ted Dunegan." He looked up. "Young whippersnapper who married Adsila

Conley, ol' Gawonii's youngest daughter. Thinks the world owes him something. Bound to get into a scrape like this. Lives up at Bluejacket."

Jimmy's thumb rubbed against the hammer of the carbine he still held. "They used names?"

The brakeman answered. "Yes, sir. I think that man Waco got riled by Dunegan."

"Murt," the conductor said, "the bridge watchman said the same thing. Dunegan used Waco's name, and that set off Waco. You know how he is, Marshal. Anything might set him off. He repeatedly used Dunegan's name. Even described him, said where he lived."

"And the others?" Jimmy asked.

Sixpersons returned to his notebook. "They didn't wear masks. Young, full of spunk. Not smart. Just like Ted Dunegan. One was called Vern. Another Joey. And the other, Mal, maybe Hal."

"Probably friends of Dunegan?" Jimmy asked.

Sixpersons shrugged, and slid the notebook back into his jacket pocket. "The other two, we both know."

Jimmy's head bobbed. "Tonkawa Tom. And Gil Millican."

The Indian lawman confirmed that with a nod.

"What about Cutter Carl?"

"Reckon you didn't hear. Cutter Carl walked into three rounds of buckshot at Double Spring nine days back."

"Who got him?"

Another shrug. Sixpersons glanced at his piebald gelding, and Jimmy Mann understood. He could see the stock of Sixperson's Winchester '87, a lever-action twelve-gauge shotgun, protruding from the scabbard. The Cherokee peace officer removed his spectacles and began cleaning the lenses with the ends of his red polka-dot bandanna.

Sixpersons' eyesight might be failing, but that shotgun had proved to be an equalizer.

"Any idea where we might find those boys?" Jimmy asked.

The conductor said, "Posse rode off around noon to Spavina Creek, hoping to pick up the trail."

*Noon.* Jimmy held back the oath forming on his lips. They had burned all morning trying to round up enough men to go after the robbers, the murderers.

"Haven't heard back from any of our boys," the conductor said. "But I don't think Danny Waco would let that punk Dunegan or any of those others keep him company, not after what happened last night. My guess is they've all scattered."

The engineer added, "If they're smart."

"They aren't smart." Sixpersons put his eyeglasses back on and folded his arms.

"No," Jimmy agreed. "They aren't." He borrowed the Cherokee's notebook, wrote down some names, Borden's address in Olathe, instructions to telegraph the marshal's office at Fort Smith, to send word to Millard Mann in McAdam, Texas, and a few other details. He ripped out the pages, and handed them to the conductor.

"If you want a hotel, Marshal," the conductor said, "I'm sure we can help. I mean, you've ridden long and hard just to get here."

Jimmy shook his head. "Where's the livery?" As good as Old Buck was, he knew his horse wouldn't be fit for riding for another three or four days. Nor would the other mounts he'd almost run to death just to get to Vinita. He hoped he could find a good horse at the livery.

"Well, Marshal," the conductor said, "if you're bound for Bluejacket to see if you can capture Ted Dunegan, we can get you a train. The Number Four's still here."

*Ride the train that had carried Borden to his death?* "No thank-you. I prefer a horse." Jimmy moved quickly. He had found his purpose. He'd track down Danny Waco and avenge Borden. He'd get his nephew's rifle back. No matter the cost.

Only when he reached the edge of the platform did he stop, turn, and look across the station toward Jackson Sixpersons. "You coming?"

The Cherokee lawman grinned.

# CHAPTER NINE

*Bluejacket*

North of Vinita, deputy marshals Jimmy Mann and Jackson Sixpersons arrived in Bluejacket, a speck of dust on the Katy line that some people called a town. Named after a Shawnee Indian sky pilot who did his preaching nearby, Bluejacket catered to farmers and merchants. Those that dealt with farmers went to bed early. The town slept. Not even a dog barked as the two lawmen watered their horses in front of what some people might have consider a hotel.

They rode on, out of the limits of the recently incorporated town, turning at the fork in the road and following the trail east toward Shawnee, Wyandot, and Quapaw land. Two miles east, they moved down a trail that cut through the woods. When they reached the clearing two hundred yards from the pike, Sixpersons reined in his paint horse and slid from the saddle.

The Winchester shotgun slid easily from the scabbard without a sound. He tilted his head forward and knelt down. "Someone's smoking," he whispered.

Jimmy took a knee beside the old Cherokee, holding the Winchester carbine by the barrel. "Those eyeglasses are good," he said after he spotted the on-and-off orange glow from the open door of a barn.

"My age, they got to be."

Jimmy smiled and surveyed the Dunegan spread. No, not Ted Dunegan's. It was Adsila Conley's place, or rather old man Gawonii's. A cad like Ted Dunegan had only married a girl like Adsila for her land . . . and to get on the tribal rolls.

Adsila made brooms. Jimmy doubted if Ted Dunegan even swept the floor.

Not much cover, not that Jimmy could remember or see in the darkness, anyway. The skies were turning gray in the east, and the sun would be rising before long. A hundred yards from where he and Sixpersons knelt to the cabin. The barn lay maybe twenty yards to the east and north of the cabin. If Jimmy remembered correctly, a lean-to and a corral lay in front of the cabin, a well was off to the side, a two-seat privy and some sort of shed stood in the back near a garden. He heard chickens clucking and added a coop next to the barn to his mental list. In less than an hour, the roosters would start crowing. No horses that he could see. They would be in the barn, guarded by the man with the cigarette.

If someone was guarding the horses . . .

"How many do you think?" Jimmy asked.

"Too dark to read sign."

"I know. I'm asking you to guess."

"Not Waco, The Tonk, or Millican."

Jimmy's head bobbed. He wet his lips. Flaring yellow light came from the cabin's lone window and through the cracks in the door, and he could smell smoke from the chimney. Suddenly, the cabin door opened, bathing the porch and grassy ground with light.

Instinctively, Jimmy and Sixpersons ducked, although at that distance and the lack of light, not to mention the pecan trees and blackjack oaks, no one from the cabin or barn could see them.

"Hey, Mal!" yelled the voice from the cabin. "You want eggs?"

The orange glow disappeared, then sparks flew on the ground a few feet in front of the barn door. The guard flicked away his cigarette. "All I want," he called out, "is to get out of Indian Territory!"

The man at the cabin door chuckled. "Give us fifteen minutes. We'll eat. Then ride."

The door closed, leaving only the faint rays of light shining through the cracks. It wasn't much of a cabin.

Jimmy glanced to the east.

"Well, that settles that." Sixpersons reached for his notebook.

"Settles what?"

The Cherokee pulled a pencil he kept in the band around his battered black Stetson. With just enough light, he could see he had found a blank page. He wrote three letters, then closed the pad, and returned it to his jacket and the pencil back to his hat. "His name is Mal. Not Hal."

Jimmy let out a long breath. "The sun won't be up in fifteen minutes."

Sixpersons merely grunted.

"And your shotgun won't do us any good from up here."

Joints popping, Sixpersons rose to his feet and pulled his hat down with his free hand. "Give me ten minutes. I'll kill Mal. You wait. Till they come out. Then start the ball."

Ten minutes. Then five. Maybe. Jimmy hobbled the horses, and found a stump to sit on. He set the Winchester on his lap, turned the carbine, and pushed down on the piece of brass in the stock, opening the compartment for his cleaning rod. Or where some men kept extra cartridges. Jimmy had fetched the greasy rag from his saddlebag, which he drew into the rod, then swabbed the barrel three times. The rod returned to the compartment, which he closed. The rag he tossed at his feet. Carefully, he eased back the hammer, hearing the two clicks, hoping the sound wouldn't carry all the way down to the barn past the chickens.

He straightened, staring into the predawn grayness, leaving the Winchester cocked and on his lap.

He could make out the house and the door. The rooster crowed, although the sun had yet to appear.

His hat came off. He dropped it to his left.

It was time, he guessed and brought the Winchester up, leaning the barrel against a sturdy pecan, sighting down at the door. *Mal should be dead.*

The door opened, the cabin's light silhouetting a tall figure in the doorway. *Idiot,* Jimmy thought. He could call down a warning, announce himself as a deputy marshal. Yeah, he could. Instead, he squeezed the trigger.

His ears rang from the explosion, which drowned out the bedlam a hundred yards below of chickens, groans, and screams. He stood, jacking another round into the carbine, moving away from where he had just fired. He saw shadows in the doorway. Fired again. Once more.

Curses and shouts came from the cabin. Someone screamed, "Mal! Mal! Bring the horses!"

Mal, of course, could not answer.

Jimmy had moved away, ducking to his knees, levering the Winchester. The door closed, stopping the light. Jimmy put two more .44-40 slugs through the door.

He heard footsteps, knew he had missed someone. He could blame it on the darkness, the muzzle flashes from his own rifle blinding him, or the fact that he was bone-tired and needed sleep. He understood that one man hadn't gone inside the cabin and was running toward the barn. Jimmy swung his carbine in the general direction, but his eyes wouldn't cooperate. And he didn't want to risk the shot.

A second later, he heard the roar of a shotgun, saw the belching flame, and heard a gasp, a groan.

A sudden silence settled over the farm, but only briefly, followed by a sound that the wind carried through the trees, maybe all across the Cherokee Nation.

"Boys . . . they've . . . kilt me."

Jimmy fetched his hat, and moved away from the woods, following the trail to the Conley-Dunegan cabin. When he reached the corral, he squatted behind a post, and fingered a bullet from his shell belt. He slid it into the carbine's loading gate, repeating the process until the Winchester's tube was full. "I'm a federal officer!" he yelled. "You boys are wanted for the robbery of the Katy and the murder of an express agent!"

"Yeah," came a frightened answer. "Well . . . I got a Cherokee squaw in here. And if you and your posse don't skedaddle, she's a dead injun."

Jimmy wet his lips. "Makes no never mind to me."

"I ain't bluffin'."

"I ain't either. I hate Indians. Especially Cherokees." He grinned, wishing he could see the look on Sixpersons' face right then. "And squaws . . . Kill her."

These boys weren't of Danny Waco's caliber. They wouldn't hurt a woman. Few men in the West would. Jimmy tried to tell himself that a few times, but he did look up at the sky and whisper, "Lord, you know what I'm doing. Don't let me down."

"I don't know. . . . I don't know nothin' 'bout no robbery." The voice inside the cabin started cracking.

It hit Jimmy. *I*. The voice said, *"I."* Not *we*. He frowned. Four men should be there if they were the new recruits Waco had used for the train robbery. Mal was in the barn, likely dead. Sixpersons had killed another one running for the barn and the horses. Jimmy doubted if he could have missed that figure standing in the lighted doorway with his first shot. That left one.

"Who are you?"

No answer.

"Who are you?"

Still nothing.

Jimmy frowned. "Where's Danny Waco?"

"He . . . who?"

"You heard me."

"I don't know no Danny Waco."

"That figures. Seeing how you botched that robbery. Left forty thousand dollars in greenbacks hidden in a flour sack in the express car. Yeah, no way a smart man like Danny Waco led that robbery."

"You're lying!"

"Wait until your trial."

A barrage of profanity followed. Then silence.

Jimmy glanced at the barn. In the light of dawn, he could see it clearly, could see Sixpersons moving toward the man he'd blown apart with his lever-action shotgun. The Cherokee knelt by the dead man. A short moment later, Sixpersons looked up, shaking his head. He moved slowly, carefully, to the corner of the cabin, disappearing around the side.

The sun was coming up. Jimmy knew he wouldn't have to wait much longer. Still, he moved to another spot just a few yards away. In his line of work, he didn't want to stay put.

"Ted Dunegan!" Jimmy yelled. "You don't stand a chance. We got twenty deputies and Indian policemen out here."

"I ain't Ted Dunegan!" the voice called back. "And I got a Cherokee squaw in here."

"Where's Ted?"

"You gut-shot him, lawman! He's dyin'." A pause. "Mal! Mal! Mal, are you all right?"

"Mal's dead." Taking a guess, Jimmy added, "So is Joey."

"I'm Joey!"

Jimmy smiled. "Then Vern's dead." He let that sink in, before trying another tack. "Listen, Joey, two of your partners are dead. Another will be before long. You're wanted for robbery and murder—"

"I didn't blow that dude's head off. I didn't even know he was dead till—"

Jimmy's Winchester roared. He jacked the lever, shot again. "That dude," he screamed, "was my brother!"

He almost fired again, till his reason returned,

and he remembered that Adsila Conley remained inside that cabin. Those shutters and doors seemed too thin to stop a .44-40 bullet. He waited until his heart had stopped pounding, until he pushed back that rage and then he tried again. "Joey, all I really want is Danny Waco."

"He ain't here."

"I know that. What I want—"

"Here's what I want, lawman!"

Jimmy listened, but nothing else came, at least not for two minutes.

"I want two horses saddled out front. Right now. I'm comin' out. And I got this Cherokee gal with me. You don't do like I say, she's a dead squaw."

Muttering an oath, Jimmy again moved to another position, picking up the hat he had left, and, in a crouch, darted to the well. It would offer better cover than the corral fence, and give him a better shot, too. He dropped the hat in the dust beside the well, his left hand slid down the carbine to the front sight, and his thumb flipped up the sight. His right thumb pulled back the hammer, and he rested the gun on the side of the well's rock walls. He waited.

The sun had risen, but the usual sounds of birds chirping did not come with the dawn. The chickens had stopped their panicky squawks, and the roosters did not crow. The door flew open. Jimmy could see the boots, toes pointed toward the ceiling, and he knew that would be Ted Dunegan. A moment later, two figures blocked his view of the dying, would-be outlaw.

Joey stepped onto the porch, his right arm squeezing Adsila's stomach. His left hand was holding what looked to be a short-barreled Colt against her temple. "Where are those horses?" he yelled.

Jimmy shot a glance at Sixpersons, who had ducked away from the corner and was leaning against the log cabin, holding his shotgun. Quickly, Jimmy's right eye found the sight. He squeezed his left one shut but did not answer.

"Where are those horses?" Joey called, speaking in the general direction of the corral.

Jimmy kept quiet.

Joey's head kept jerking around, looking everywhere for that posse of twenty lawmen.

Once he let out his breath, Jimmy Mann squeezed the trigger.


"Nice shot," Adsila Conley said. *"Wado."*

"You're welcome." Jimmy leaned the carbine against the wall and knelt down, prying the Colt out of Joey's dead hand.

Sixpersons stared down at the dead killer. He didn't say anything. Didn't have to.

Jimmy could tell by the look on the old man's face that he disapproved, but Jimmy decided he was just an old Cherokee, protective of a young girl like Adsila.

They followed the Cherokee girl inside the cabin, picked up Ted Dunegan, and carried him, screaming in agony, to the bed in the corner. Unceremoniously they dropped him on the quilt.

"For mercy's sake," Dunegan moaned, "take off my boots."

Jimmy sat on the bed beside the dying fool's head. He let Sixpersons remove the boots.

"Oh, for the love of God, might I have some whiskey?"

"Whiskey'll kill you." Sixpersons dropped the last boot on the floor, the spurs chiming.

"You want some coffee?" Adsila was already heading to the stove.

"Thank you," Jimmy said. The place smelled of fried eggs and bacon. And blood, and urine, for Ted Dunegan had wet his britches. And gunpowder.

And death.

"Water," Ted Dunegan moaned. "Water. Please, I'm so thirsty."

"Ted," Jimmy said softly. "I need to know about Danny Waco."

"Adsila," the dying husband called out. "Honey, I'll take even some Choctaw beer." He blinked, sniffed, coughed. Blood seeped from his mouth, and he tried to swallow. His eyes finally focused on Jimmy. "I swear . . . I didn't know he was gonna kill that agent."

"I know that." The words were tight. Jimmy pressed his lips together. "Where did Waco go?"

"Didn't even . . ." Another savage coughing spell. By the time Dunegan was finished, blood drenched the pillow.

Adsila handed Jimmy a cup of steaming black coffee. Sixpersons stood at the foot of the bed rolling a smoke. He stuck the cigarette into his mouth and accepted the cup Adsila offered him.

"Adsila," Dunegan said softly, pleadingly. "Honey, could you . . . just bring me some whiskey. Please!"

She looked down at him, spit in his face, and walked back to the stove.

Dunegan began crying. Saying how he didn't want to die, that this shouldn't have happened to him.

"Waco," Jimmy said. "What about Danny Waco?"

The outlaw sniffed. "Cheated us . . . didn't give us all our share."

A match flared. Sixpersons lighted his cigarette.

"Just ten dollars." Dunegan coughed again. "Each." He smiled, though, and his fingers slid into his vest pocket, withdrawing a piece of paper. "But I fooled him. I got . . ." The paper slipped. "This."

Jimmy reached over, unfolded the check, saw it was made out to one Elizabeth Vestal for $17.32. He handed it to Jackson Sixpersons.

Ted Dunegan would die for $17.32.

"Where did Waco, The Tonk, and Gil Millican go?" Jimmy asked.

Nothing. Ted Dunegan seemed to be staring at something on the ceiling.

"They double-crossed you, Ted," Jimmy said softly. "Took off with most of the money and left you here to die."

"Mal said we shouldn't stop," Ted whimpered. "Said we should just keep ridin', that the law would catch us. Where's Mal?"

Sixpersons blew a smoke ring toward the ceiling. "In Hell." He sipped his coffee.

"Ted," Jimmy tried again, knowing he was about out of time. "Danny Waco. Where did he go? Did he say anything? Give you any idea?"

Dunegan laughed. "Waco? He wouldn't tell us nothin'." He cursed Waco, and shook his head. Suddenly, his right hand shot up, gripped Jimmy's vest, and pulled him down. "But"—Dunegan groaned—"I heard . . . Gil. . . . He . . . said . . . Cald . . . well. . . ." Death rattled in the outlaw's breath.

Jimmy pried the man's fingers from his vest, letting the arm drop to the dead man's chest.

# CHAPTER TEN

*Caldwell, Kansas*

Once upon a time, Caldwell had been a rip-roaring cow town. You could get drunk, find a hurdy-gurdy girl, gamble sun-up to sun-up for weeks on end, race up and down Main Street, even kill a gent you figured was cheating you. Basically, you could do anything and everything, and the law left you alone.

Of course, ten years ago, the town marshal, a hard-rock named Henry Brown, had ridden over with some pals of his to rob the bank in Medicine Lodge. They didn't come back, having gotten caught by the law, and killed by the populace.

*Those days,* Danny Waco lamented, *were but a fond memory.*

Oh, you could still get drunk in Caldwell, gamble, and maybe even find a petticoat that didn't charge too much, but the wildness had departed. So had the cowboys. Just last year, the town had served as the jumping-off point for homesteaders, boomers, and sooners, after the Cherokees sold the Outlet, and the Strip had been opened for settlement. About the only people racing down Main Street were farmers, and they didn't move fast at all. But since the Rock Island had laid tracks into Caldwell, and railroaders loved to drink and gamble, a man like Danny Waco could find something to occupy his time.

He reined in the buckskin, let two farm wagons pass, turned in front of the opera house, and crossed the street to the hitching rail in front of Dick's Saloon & Gambling Emporium.

"You sure this is a good idea, Danny?" Gil Millican stopped his bay, leaned to the right, and spit out a river of tobacco juice.

"We're out of Indian Territory, ain't we?" The leather squeaked as Waco slid from the saddle. He pulled the .50-caliber rifle from the scabbard on the left side of the saddle. The one on the right held the London-made shotgun, which he left.

"Yeah, but by, what? A mile? Two?"

"You're thirsty, ain't you?"

Near the Osage Agency in the Nations, Waco had traded his old Winchester and one of the pocket watches from the Katy robbery for three fresh horses. He looked hard at the buckskin, blind in its right eye, almost asleep. Before long, they would need more horses, but he wasn't about to spend money on horses.

He ducked underneath the hitching rail and stepped onto the boardwalk, out of the sun. Another farmer in bib-and-brace overalls and his brood rode out of town, heading south, toward the Strip and his hundred and sixty acres.

"Let's cut the dust. Find a card game. Get some real money."

In a tight town like Caldwell, it would take ten years to win the $40,000 they had thought that they would have already.

Reluctantly, Millican dismounted.

The Tonk remained on his sorrel.

"Get us a pack mule," Waco told the Indian. "And supplies that can get us to Ogallala." He bowed as a woman in a calico dress walked past him, basket in her hand.

The lady didn't even give him or Millican the time of day.

Waco stared at Millican. "Is Nebraska far enough from the law for you?"

"I reckon." Millican hooked the tobacco from his mouth and tossed it onto the dirty street.

"Careful," The Tonk said. "Constable might fine you for that."

Cursing and shaking his head, Millican pushed his way through the batwing doors and into Dick's.

Waco told The Tonk, "See if they've got some shells for this baby." With a grin, he hefted the Winchester 1886.

The Tonk frowned. "I doubt if you'll find anything larger than a pitchfork in this town these days."

Well, Waco had what was left of that one box of shells. He'd put one into the express agent's face. Five more were in the Winchester's tubular magazine. That would have to last him. Besides, if Caldwell didn't carry his caliber at any of the mercantiles, he'd probably have better luck up north in Wichita. It was bigger than Caldwell. Although Wichita was once just as wild, it was just as boring as Caldwell these days.

"Just do it," Waco snapped. He pointed north. "There used to be a wagon yard up the street, right before you get out of town. We'll meet you there tonight."

With a quick nod, The Tonk left, and Waco went inside Dick's.


Dehner McIntyre leaned back in his chair, leaving the paste cards on the green felt. He smoothed his thin mustache as he watched the thin gent who needed a new set of clothes, a bath, and a shave join that other saddle tramp at the bar. Most people would have dismissed both men as just a couple of thirty-a-month waddies riding the grub line. McIntyre, however, lowered the legs of his chair onto the wooden floor and played the black ace on the queen. "Danny Waco," he whispered to himself and gathered up the cards.

Waco wasn't all the gambler noticed. He saw the

Winchester the man-killer held in his right hand. It was something else the sodbusters that came to Caldwell would mistakenly dismiss as just another repeating rifle. McIntyre knew a thing or two about guns, and that was one of John Browning's 1886 models—the most powerful repeating rifle in the country.

On his last birthday, McIntyre had turned forty-five. He was getting a little long in the tooth to be playing cards in towns like Caldwell, but for the life of him, he couldn't figure out what else to do. Go back to Georgia? Twenty-seven years later, he would likely find some people who would still like to lynch him in Savannah.

He wore fancy black boots, the tops inlaid with the aces of spades, for which he had paid a fortune down in Spanish Fort, Texas. His trousers were striped in gold, tan, olive, and red—so people noticed him when he walked into a dining room or just down the boardwalk. A pair of fine leather suspenders kept them up. He wondered if that clerk at that store in Carthage, Missouri, had ever figured out that the suspenders were missing. His shirt was bright white cotton, with a bib front and stand-up collar, covered by a double-breasted vest with a shawl collar in crimson canvas and a gold paisley ascot with an emerald stickpin. That Chinaman over in Hunnewell was probably still waiting to be paid for the starching. The four-button frock coat was tan, trimmed along the lapels and placket with brown, and if one didn't look too carefully, he might not notice how frayed the cuffs were or the small bullet holes in the right tails. Topping his head was a fine top hat of brown with a matching bound edge and grosgrain ribbon. He had stolen it from an undertaker in Coffeyville.

McIntyre reached for the beer, which he had been nursing for the past two hours. He sipped some, then again smoothed his mustache, once darker but now light with gray hairs, and began dealing another round of solitaire.

For the past six months, he had been riding a losing streak, bad cards following bad cards, and bad luck compounding lousy luck. Suddenly, he figured things might be looking up.

"You just playin' with yourself. Or you let anybody sit in?"

McIntyre lifted his eyes. That hadn't taken long at all. Danny Waco and a slightly taller fellow with a black hat stood in front of him.

"I'm just waiting for the next train to Dodge City," McIntyre said, sounding just like the Southern gentleman his daddy had hoped he would grow up to be. He gathered the cards, motioning at the empty chairs opposite him. "But sit down. The train doesn't pull out until seven-fifteen."

They sat down, and McIntyre's Adam's apple bobbed at the sight of the bottle of rye that Waco slammed on the table. The gambler wet his lips and cleared his throat. "Do you mind?" He slid the mug of beer toward Waco.

"Liquor on beer?" Waco lifted the bottle.

McIntyre smiled warmly. "The nectar of the gods."

Waco topped the beer with two fingers of rye,

then filled his partner's glass, and withdrew a large amount of greenbacks from his vest pocket.

McIntyre opened the fancy case next to him and brought out some chips. "How much do you wish to buy in for?"

Waco grunted. "How 'bout three hundred? Or is that too rich for your belly?"

With a grin, McIntyre slid stacks of blue, red, and white chips across the table, before looking at the other man. "And you, sir?"

The man dropped five golden eagles on the table. "Just a hundred."

"Very good, sir."

*Four hundred bucks.* That was more money than Dehner McIntyre had seen in three months, and $397.42 more than he had in his pockets. Still, he took $500 in chips for himself, and began shuffling the deck.

He felt good—until Danny Waco laid the big Winchester on the table.

When Waco raked in a good-sized pot, McIntyre shook his head, pushed back his hat and smiled, "You're a man of luck, sir."

"Luck?" Waco laughed. "It's skill."

Pointing at the almost empty bottle of rye, McIntyre said, "Well, I think we need some refreshments. How about if I buy us a new bottle?"

"Suits me." Waco's partner was a man apparently named Gil.

McIntyre bowed graciously, pushed his chair

from the table, and walked to the bar. He pulled his wallet from the inside pocket of his coat. "A bottle of your best rye, Horace." Through sleight of hand, he handed over a five-dollar bill he had pocketed from the cash Waco had used to buy into the poker game.

He leaned forward, finding a match, and fished an old cigar—his last—from another pocket. As the bartender ducked to find a bottle of something that wouldn't blind a railroader, McIntyre whispered as he struck the match, cupped his hands, and lighted the cheroot. "Get the marshal. That's Danny Waco over there."

The barkeep looked up, his face draining of all color.

"Just act normal," the gambler said quietly, calmly. "How about that bottle?" he said loud enough for Waco to hear, and leaned forward, whispering again, "Find that scalawag you call a peace officer. Tell him to bring the vigilantes. Get them over here. Pronto."

Reaching down, he took the bottle the bartender had, thanked him loudly, and returned to the poker table.

Two men in black broadcloth suits entered the saloon, shot a glance at the table, and moved to the bar.

"Danny," Waco's partner said.

Waco was already studying the men, then grinned,

and focused on the cards McIntyre had dealt. "They ain't no threat." He bet a blue chip.

*Not a threat?* McIntyre's head shook. He recognized both men as members of the Border Queen City Vigilance Committee. They were part of the reason he was waiting for the northbound train to pull out of town.

Gil swore, but matched the bet with his nine of clubs showing. McIntyre looked at the ace of diamonds in front of Waco's hand, and also bet.

He let the pot build. Three watches had found their way from the road agents' pockets, along with most of the chips, a diamond pin, a mother of pearl broach, plus some silver, gold, and greenbacks.

Three other men had entered the saloon, ordering a pitcher of beer and three glasses, but neither Waco nor Gil even considered them.

McIntyre couldn't blame them. He let Waco raise, saw Gil call, then he called himself, and dealt the last cards up. King of clubs to Waco, whose face revealed just that smirk he'd been showing since his first two cards. The queen of hearts went to Gil, who frowned, lousy poker player that he was. He knew the queen didn't help him at all.

So did McIntyre, who'd dealt himself the king of spades.

"Holy . . ." Gil whistled. "He's buckin' for a royal flush, Danny."

Sure enough, McIntyre had a queen, jack, ten, and king—all spades—showing.

"Yeah." Waco was still smirking. "But I've been

playin' poker for years, and I ain't never seen no one deal a royal flush."

Waco bet a hundred. A good bet, even facing a possible straight flush, since he had two pair—aces and kings—showing.

"Man!" Gil looked at his hole card for the umpteenth time. He shot Waco a glance, then smiled at McIntyre. "I don't think you got the biggie, but a flush maybe. But . . . Awe. it's only poker!" He called Waco's bet with the last of his chips and cash. He held a nine of clubs, six of spades, six of diamonds, and queen of hearts. He was betting against a flush—a possible royal flush, at that—and two high pair that could easily be a full house.

"Well . . ." McIntyre didn't look at his hole card. "Like the man said, it is poker." He matched the bet, and casually raised $500.

Waco shook his head.

"He's bluffin'," Gil said.

"Of course he is." Waco pushed the rest of his chips onto the table. "That's all I got, and it's table stakes."

"How about that Winchester?" McIntyre asked.

Waco glanced at the big rifle. "That's too much rifle for a dude like you."

Grinning, McIntyre pulled the emerald stickpin from his ascot, dangled it, and dropped it on the pile of chips and plunder. "A side bet. My pin against your rifle. What kind of punkin slinger is that, anyhow?"

"Fifty caliber," Waco answered, looked at the pin,

then grinning, slid the Winchester into the center of the table. His right hand disappeared briefly and came up with a Colt, which he slid where the Winchester had been resting. He kept his eyes locked on the gambler.

McIntyre looked at Gil. "It's up to you, sir."

Sighing, the man polished off the rye in his shot glass, and turned over his hole card. "I want you boys to see what I'm folding." The six of hearts fell atop his cards. "Sure hope my luck's better in Nebraska. Three sixes. I hope one of you ain't bluffin'."

"I ain't much for bluffin'," Waco said, grinning as he lifted his hole card. "And I know you ain't got no royal flush, gamblin' man, because I got the ace of spades right here."

He dropped the card, revealing a full house, aces over kings.

Gil let out with an old rebel yell, shook his head in disbelief, and refilled his glass with rye. "That's a hand, ol' pal!" He turned toward the men at the bar and the table, who were concentrating on the poker game.

"It most certainly is, friends," McIntyre said, letting Waco reach for the pot with both hands before springing his trap. The fingers on the gambler's left hand turned over his hole card. Danny Waco froze, and the man called Gil swore.

# CHAPTER ELEVEN

The nine of spades.

Not a royal flush, but a straight flush beat a full house any day of the week.

Waco shot back, his right hand going for the Colt, but a Remington over-and-under derringer appeared in McIntyre's hand. Those twin .41-caliber barrels just a few feet from Waco's nose stopped him.

"Don't." The Southern charm could no longer be detected in the voice of Dehner McIntyre, native of Georgia, cheater at cards.

A half dozen cocked revolvers punctuated the gambler's order. Danny Waco and his partner became statues as the batwing doors pounded and six other men armed with shotguns entered Dick's.

"Your Indian friend is waiting at Miller's livery," said Greg Mason, the head of Caldwell's vigilantes. He gripped a Schofield .45 in his right hand.

"This sharper . . . He . . ." Waco stopped. He

wasn't about to beg, and the look on those vigilantes' faces told him they cared nary a whit whether he had been cheated or not.

"You and your boys are leaving town," Mason said.

Waco nodded. He had been run out of better burgs than this hayseed town. Besides, being asked to leave sure beat being locked up in jail to wait extradition to Judge Parker's court for trial, conviction, and hanging. He picked up the bottle of rye, and stared at Dehner McIntyre, who calmly raked in his winnings.

"I'll be seeing you, mister," Waco said icily.

The gambler slid the Winchester off the table, pressing the stock against his thigh, and worked the lever. A giant .50-100-450 popped out and bounced across the floor. His grin held no warmth or humor, either. "I look forward to the visit."

When the two outlaws stormed through the batwing doors, most members of the Border Queen City Vigilance Committee followed them, never lowering their shotguns, rifles, or revolvers, bound and determined to make sure they, indeed, left Caldwell. After they had passed the plate-glass window, McIntyre thumbed back the Winchester's hammer and laid the big rifle on the table.

Mason stood in front of him. "And you're to be on that train, gambler. Don't forget it."

"Of course." McIntyre returned the emerald stickpin to its proper place in his ascot. "Would you mind handing me that shell?"

The vigilante nodded to one of his associates, who bent, knees popping, and fingered the giant bullet, which he tossed onto the pile of money, chips, and plunder in front of McIntyre. Then, they were gone, too.

McIntyre picked up one of the watches, pressed on the button and watched the case, engraved with a large elk and foliage, open. The large Springfield Watch Company model felt heavy—probably solid silver—with roman numerals and blue spade hands. The time read 5:37. He slipped it inside his vest pocket.

The 7:15, of course, would pull out for Wichita on time, but McIntyre would not be on it. He was no fool. Waco and his gang would want that big Winchester, the money, the watches, everything McIntyre had cheated them out of. They would want him dead, too, and he had told them he was going to Dodge City.

So, most likely, they would either meet him in Wichita, when he had to change trains. Or in Wellington. They might even wait till he got to Dodge City. Life used to be cheap in Dodge, but civilization had reached that old cattle town, too.

Well, McIntyre would outsmart them. His luck was turning, he felt, and he had seen Dodge City before. Maybe Ogallala, Nebraska. Or west to Denver. He had plenty of money, a .50-caliber repeating rifle, and he figured he could buy a horse at Miller's livery—as soon as the vigilantes made sure Danny Waco had left Caldwell.

### Vinita, Cherokee Nation

After leaving the corpses with the undertaker, Deputy U.S. Marshal Jimmy Mann walked toward the depot, Jackson Sixpersons right behind him.

"I need to get to Caldwell, Kansas," Jimmy told the agent. He showed him his badge. "Fast as possible."

"Let me see what I can get for you, Marshal." The agent hurried away from the window and began flipping through books on a table.

Turning, Jimmy saw Sixpersons' frown. "I know. By the time I get to Caldwell, Waco will be gone. But I can pick up his trail there." Jimmy forced a smile. "Maybe even get some sleep on the train. You've been hounding me—" He stopped.

The Cherokee lawman kept shaking his head.

"Waco went to Caldwell," Jimmy said, sharper.

"Your jurisdiction," Sixpersons reminded him, "ends at the state line."

Jimmy tapped the badge. "This here says I am a *United States* deputy marshal."

"And your commission says for the Western District of Arkansas including the Indian Nations. Not Kansas."

The agent was back. "I can get you on the Katy to Parsons. Then to Cherryvale. Then Winfield. To Wellington. Down to Caldwell. It'll get you to Caldwell, if everything stays on schedule, which they won't, by . . ."

Jimmy didn't care. He simply nodded, his cold eyes boring straight through Sixpersons.

"I kinda hoped you'd see things my way, Jackson," Jimmy said after a long while.

The Indian's face looked sad. It was about the first time Jimmy had ever seen the Cherokee reveal any emotion.

"Badge means something to me, Jimmy," Sixpersons said. "So does my word."

With an understanding nod, Jimmy turned to gather the assortment of tickets the agent had given him. A few moments later, he stopped in front of Sixpersons, who handed him the battered Winchester '73. "He was my brother, Jackson."

The Cherokee nodded. "I know. This is something you have to do. But I can't go with you."

It was better this way, Jimmy figured. He didn't know how long it would take him to track down Danny Waco and that .50-caliber Winchester—nor did he care. And there was a good chance anyone traveling with Jimmy Mann might get killed. He could use a friend, a good man, plus that shotgun Sixpersons wielded, but he didn't want the old Cherokee lawman to get hurt. Besides, Sixpersons was right. This was something he had to do. Alone.

"You'll telegraph Fort Smith for me? Tell them . . ." *Tell them what? That I am resigning my commission, but will still use the badge to get whatever I need? That I am forgetting that oath I recited with my right hand over the judge's Bible? That I would kill Danny Waco—in cold blood if I had to?*

Sixpersons only nodded.

"And take care of Old Buck for me?" No reason in loading Buck on the train, Jimmy thought, taking him across the Indian Nations and Kansas. Maybe even farther.

Again, Sixpersons nodded.

"So long." Jimmy didn't offer to shake the Cherokee's hand, but his right held the Winchester and his left the bundle of tickets for various trains.

The Cherokee pulled a pouch from his pocket, and passed it to Jimmy, who shook his head. "That badge won't get you everything. You'll need some money. More than I do."

"All right." Jimmy slipped the rifle under his arm, took the beaded leather pouch, slipped it into his pocket. "And if the railroad pays anything for those idiots we brought in . . ."

"I'll save half for you." The Cherokee grinned, his head nodding his farewell.

Jimmy went toward the rails. Sixpersons walked to the hitching rail.

### Wellington, Kansas

"He ain't on the train, Danny."

The locomotive churned coal-black smoke, the taste heavy on Danny Waco's tongue. He stared at Gil Millican, and looked at the passengers disembarking the train from Caldwell. A drummer in a plaid suit. A nun.

Wellington didn't bustle like Kansas City or Omaha. At 9:30 P.M., the town was asleep, seeming as dull as Caldwell. That cheating sharper, Dehner McIntyre, couldn't have slipped off the train, gotten off.

Spitting into a trashcan, Waco swore. "He never got on."

Millican's eyes widened. "He said—"

"I know what he said." Waco made a beeline for the horses. That lousy gambler had his cash, had his Winchester.

"He said he was goin' to Dodge," Millican said. "Maybe we can meet him there."

Pulling the newspaper he had picked up from some tyke of a hawker at the depot, Waco shoved the *Times* under Millican's eyes. "We can't go to Dodge City," he snapped. "Law won't be so gutless in Dodge City. They'll be after that reward the Katy's posted."

"What about your rifle?"

Waco wadded the newspaper into a ball and tossed it underneath one of the train's coaches. "Maybe it'll show up in Nebraska." He saw The Tonk waiting across the street with the horses and pack mule. He knew they needed to put some distance between themselves and the Indian Nations, and Wellington, Kansas. Even Dodge City wasn't that far from the reach of the law. He hated to run, hated to give up on killing Dehner McIntyre and fetching that Winchester '86. But he didn't want to die.

### Kiowa County

Camping along the banks of the Medicine Lodge River, Dehner McIntyre had money in his pockets, coffee in the pot on the fire, a fine blue roan with some Tennessee Walker in her blood, and a twenty-five-cent cigar in his mouth.

He ran a rag over the Winchester's barrel, and began to wonder just what he needed with a .50-caliber rifle. Gamblers didn't use rifles, especially gamblers like him, who knew how to deal off the bottom of the deck, how to palm cards. Men like him used hideaway guns like that Remington derringer.

On the other hand, a derringer wouldn't bring down a deer. He probably couldn't even hit a rabbit with that little popgun, and it was a long way to Hays City. Luck was still running with McIntyre, and he had decided to try his luck in Hays, leaving Dodge City to the likes of Danny Waco and his men.

### Caldwell

He stared hard into Greg Mason's eyes until the full-time newspaper editor and part-time vigilante looked away and motioned to the bartender to bring a bottle of something that wouldn't blind a man. "Did you know he robbed a train in the Nations?" Jimmy asked again.

The bartender found a bottle of Jameson, and Mason poured two fingers in a tumbler for Jimmy Mann and four fingers for himself.

Jimmy laid his Winchester on the bar. "I asked you a question. Twice."

Mason shot down his liquor, and quickly refilled the glass. "I didn't know, Marshal." He let out a heavy sigh.

*Well,* Jimmy thought, *what did I expect?* He sipped the Irish whiskey. "But you knew he was wanted—"

Swearing bitterly, Mason turned around and gave Jimmy an equally hard stare. "What did you expect me to do? Get the citizens of this town—maybe even their kids and dogs—shot to pieces? This isn't Caldwell ten years ago, Marshal. It's a town full of good people with good children. Most of them cater to farmers. You come to Caldwell, chances are you'll see a bunch of farm families. What's Waco's reward up to these days? A thousand dollars? Five? Even if it was ten thousand dollars, I don't think that's worth risking the lives of women and children. Do you?" He didn't wait for an answer. "It seemed to me that the best thing to do was get those gunmen out of town. But I guess that's something you just don't understand."

Jimmy finished the whiskey, and surprised the vigilante. "I understand."

Each had another whiskey.

"I don't know, Marshal," Mason said wearily. "Had I known about the Katy robbery . . . had I known about your brother . . ." The whiskey went down. He corked the bottle, which made Jimmy relieved. As much as he wanted to get drunk, he knew he couldn't afford that.

"It's all right," Jimmy said. "Wasn't your fight. It's my fight. Which way did Waco go?"

"We pointed him north," the vigilante said. "Wellington? Wichita?" Suddenly, Mason paused, rubbed his nose, and cocked his head, thinking.

"Go on."

"Well, there was a gambler in town. He took Waco and one of his men for a pile of money."

Jimmy waited.

"Gambler's name was Dehner McIntyre. We were running him out of town, too. A sharper, he was. Marshal at Hunnewell had sent me a telegraph about him, which is why we'd asked him to take the next train north."

He knew where the vigilante was pointing, what he was thinking. If this Dehner McIntyre busted Danny Waco at a poker table, that wasn't something that Waco would let lie. A man like Danny Waco would go after the gambler.

"Do you know where McIntyre was going?"

"He said Dodge City."

*Dodge City. Wonderful.* It couldn't have been Coffeyville or Wichita, someplace close. Dodge lay about a nine- or ten-day ride northwest of Caldwell, but Jimmy had spotted a good-looking sorrel at the livery. He was sick of riding trains. Every face of every crewmember reminded him of Borden or Millard. Sometimes even his nephew, James. It was time to leave the rails behind and sit in a saddle. For if he caught up with Danny Waco, he'd likely need a horse when the chase really began.

"You said Waco had two men with him," Jimmy said.

Mason's head bobbed. "That we saw. Saddle tramp and an Indian. They rode out with him, of course."

"Did one of them have a big Winchester?" Jimmy asked.

# CHAPTER TWELVE

### *Along the Arkansas River*

He hated this country. Flat. Windy. Hot, even for the Moon Of Lying Side To Side. Tall grass blew, and storm clouds to the north and west blackened the afternoon skies. The land was full of the *indaaligande*. And he hated the pale eyes.

Among his people, the Chiricahua Apaches, he was called Yuyutsu. At first, the pale eyes had called him Eager to Fight—a good translation, for an indaaligande. After he had arrived at the hated school in the green state of Pennsylvania, a School Father had told him he could not be called Yuyutsu. He wasn't even allowed to speak his name ever again in the dreary buildings at the place they called the Carlisle Industrial School. They wouldn't even call him Eager to Fight. For four years, he had been forced to answer to the name John York.

That wasn't the worst of it, either. They had burned his buckskins, ripped the red calico band off his head, made him wash in foul-smelling water, and use brushes not fit to curry a horse, as one of the School Fathers had said, "to scrub the injun off your hide." And his hair, his long black hair that glistened in the sun and fell below his shoulders . . . had been cut off.

If he spoke the tongue of the Chiricahua, the School Fathers and School Mothers would crack his knuckles with a ruler. If he kept it up, they would beat him with the wooden paddles so he quit speaking it. They taught him English. Taught him how to read, how to add and subtract and multiply and divide. They taught him how to be a white man.

And now, they were sending him back to the Comanche-Kiowa-Apache reservation near Fort Sill in the Indian Territory. They were sending him back in a gray suit that itched, and wearing things they called Congress gaiters that pinched his toes and left blisters on his heels. They were sending him to his people as John York, indaaligande.

But Yuyutsu had had enough of being like the pale eyes. He would not go to the soldier-fort called Sill. He would go to his homeland. The land he remembered as a child, before the Long Knives had made Geronimo surrender and had shipped the Apaches off to rot in the stinking dungeons at the hot, wretched place called Florida. He would find his homeland. He would live—and this he knew all too well—and he would die in the Dragoon Mountains of the territory the pale eyes called Arizona.

Only . . . he was far, far from home.

He jumped off the train after it had pulled out from a city called Topeka and kicked off the Congress gaiters, replacing them with the moccasins made by his mother, which he had kept hidden from the prying eyes of the School Mothers and School Fathers at Carlisle all those years of being taught to follow the white man's road. The moccasins were all he had left that said he was a Chiricahua. His hair remained close-cropped, but he ripped apart the cotton shirt they had made him wear, using the blue sleeve as a headband.

He made his way to a pale eyes farm, where he stole some corn and ate the scraps the family had left for their dogs. He buried the suit there, but kept the blue vest. Finding a cowhide in the barn, he fashioned himself a breechcloth

All Yuyutsu had was a knife, which he had stolen from a passenger on the Atchison, Topeka, and Santa Fe who had drunk too much whiskey. A big knife, with a keen edge and long stag handle.

*Probably made by an Apache.* He should have slit the drunkard's throat with it.

Yuyutsu had seen seventeen summers. Tall and sinewy, the Apache girls had considered him handsome before the spotted sickness—another gift from the indaaligande—had left his face pocked and scarred. He did not know how long it had been since he had jumped off the train, but he figured the School Fathers and School Mothers already knew he was not going back to Fort Sill. They would chase him. Likely, the Long Knives were after him.

If there were any Long Knives left.

Once, the bluecoats had been as many as the grass that grew in the worthless flat land. Yet a few nights back, Yuyutsu had slept on the floor in one of the abandoned buildings at a soldier-fort called Harker. The Long Knives had not been in the place for ages. He had been lucky to find a building with a roof to keep him out of the falling rain. Pale eyes had been stealing from the old buildings that had once housed Long Knives.

He had listened to the rats chatter and the rain pelt the roof, and he could not recall seeing any Long Knives since he had reached the place called Kansas.

He remembered one of the School Fathers back at Carlisle telling him and his classmates, a mix of Apaches, Comanches, Lakota, and Pawnees, that "the frontier has been declared closed." Yuyutsu had not known what that meant, even after the School Father had explained that "all Indians are becoming more and more tame," and "in a few years you will be almost as white as us. Isn't that a good thing?"

There had not been an Indian uprising, he had been told at Carlisle, since Wounded Knee in 1890, when the recalcitrant warriors under Big Foot had been shot down, and the Sioux had given up, returned peacefully to the reservation.

A lie, a Lakota boy had told him. The Army had shot down women and children at Wounded Knee, and most of the Lakotas—even the men—had not even been armed.

Yuyutsu smiled as he thought, *Soon, the pale eyes will be saying that the last Indian war had been started not by a Lakota, but by a Chiricahua warrior who had lived up to his name Eager to Fight.*

But first, he needed a rifle.

### Pawnee Rock

It wasn't much of a landmark, Dehner McIntyre decided as he picketed his horse near what remained of the legendary citadel of sandstone. To hear the stories, Pawnee Rock had served as a lookout post for Indians. Not just Pawnees, but Arapahos, Cheyennes, and Kiowas had stood on the flat top and looked north, south, east, and west for wagon trains to attack and herds of buffalo to slaughter. Kit Carson had killed an Indian there, and emigrant after emigrant had carved his or her name in the sandstone.

Taking the Winchester from the scabbard, McIntyre walked to what was left of the landmark along the Santa Fe Trail on the western side of the Arkansas River. Up close, he could still see some names, even a date as far back as 1848, carved into the sandstone, but much of Pawnee Rock had been chopped off and hauled away by settlers who needed rocks for their chimneys.

A tree was growing from the top, and he made himself climb up the sandstone and get a good look at the country. He was a good ways northeast of

Dodge City—he didn't think he'd see dust from
Danny Waco—and Hays lay only maybe three days
from there.

When he pulled himself up to the top, he looked
in awe. He could see quite a ways from this perch,
and it wasn't as tall as it had been. He could see the
cottonwoods, leaves now golden, along the banks of
the Arkansas and the openness of the Kansas plains
in all directions. He couldn't make anything out,
but he knew that just down the trail stood the remains of Fort Larned, and up northeast, the Cheyenne Bottoms.

That was a bit out of the way, but he figured that
the wetlands formed by Blood and Deception
creeks would draw game—ducks and geese and
probably even a mule deer—something to eat other
than his hardtack and jerky, both of which were
running low—and rabbits, which he hadn't seen
much of since crossing the Rattlesnake.

He hadn't even had a chance to fire the big '86
Winchester since he had missed that white-tailed
doe just before he had reached the little settlement
of Greensburg before turning north.

He found an easier way off the rock on the other
side, and could already taste the venison he'd be
cooking at the Cheyenne Bottoms when he rounded
the last chunks of sandstone and saw an almost
buck-naked Mexican trying to slide up onto the back
of his horse.

"Hey!" McIntyre yelled, cursed, and saw the thin
pup of a horse thief leap onto the blue roan with

the gracefulness of a circus acrobat—which is when the gambler remembered the big rifle he held.

Quickly, he brought the stock to his shoulder, thumbed back the hammer, and aimed. He didn't remember pulling the trigger, but the roaring in his right ear told him he had done so. He stepped out of the smoke and cursed.

That fine blue roan lay on the ground, kicking and snorting savagely, blood already pooling underneath the mare's neck.

McIntyre cursed again. Then he saw the Mexican, only he knew it was no Mexican.

An Apache, wearing nothing but knee-high moccasins, a breechcloth the color of a brindle steer, and a thin blue headband, swept his right hand toward McIntyre's belly.

The gambler jumped back, only then seeing the flash of sinking sunlight against something metal. He heard the cloth of his frock coat rip.

The knife came back. McIntyre just managed to avoid seeing his guts spill to the ground. The Indian—a kid, probably not even out of his teens— came back, brought the long knife over his head, sliced it down savagely, grunting.

McIntyre brought the Winchester up, holding the stock and the barrel. The blade clanged against the barrel, just in front of the rear sight. He thought he saw sparks fly, but knew that had to be his imagination.

He jerked his left hand up, pitching the Indian to the ground and backed up. He worked the lever and fired from the hip. The gun roared, and the stock slammed into his shoulder, bruising the bone. Big-bore Winchesters—especially .50 calibers— weren't meant to be shot like that.

Hitting the ground hard, McIntire tried to roll over. Already, he had cocked the rifle.

The horse began screaming in pain.

The sun had disappeared behind Pawnee Rock.

His chest heaved. Heart pounded. It was October, yet he sweated as if he were back in Savannah in August. He swept the barrel around, but couldn't find that little Apache. *Apache? What in blazes is an Apache doing in Kansas?*

He jacked the lever again. Saw the shell fly out and land in the drying grass.

Dehner McIntyre cursed his luck. He had just wasted a shell, had forgotten he had already cocked the rifle—and as big as the .50-caliber cartridges were, the '86 didn't hold that many rounds in its tube. His head jerked left, right. The Indian was nowhere.

His horse had stopped its throes and lay motionless in a lake of blood.

Something sounded behind him. A stone, tumbling off Pawnee Rock. He spun around, saw the figure at the top, let the Winchester roar again.

Immediately, he realized his mistake. He had just put a .50-caliber chunk of lead into that tree that was growing atop the monument of a rock. Again, he turned back, trying to work the rifle's leather, but felt the breath knocked out of him.

He went backwards, landed with a thud. Tried to push the Winchester up, but it came down, crushing the breath out of him, bruising, if not cracking, his ribs. He could make out the Apache kid with the pockmarked face, eyes full of hate, hands locked on the rifle.

"This can't be . . . happening . . ." McIntyre managed to say. "For the love . . . of God . . . this is . . . 18 . . . 94."

The '86's forestock had slipped to his throat, and the Indian pressed down with all his weight. For such a puny boy, the kid had muscle. McIntyre tried to breathe, yet couldn't find air. His throat was being crushed, the world was turning black, and Dehner McIntyre realized his luck had finally run out.

He awoke to the light of the moon. "I'm . . . alive."

"Not for long, white man." Moonlight bathed the young Apache's face as he stood over the gambler.

"You speak English?" the indaaligande said.

Yuyutsu did not answer such a foolish question. He knelt before the pale eyes wearing the pants with stripes of many colors. The man's feet were bound and staked into the ground. His hands were likewise wrapped in rawhide. Spread-eagled. If the wolves did not come to him tonight, he would wish they had come by the afternoon.

"Do you feel the necklace I have given you?" Yuyutsu asked.

The white man swallowed. Fear shown in his eyes.

"The rawhide is wet. Very wet." Yuyutsu looked at the sky. No stars. Cloudy, cool. Maybe it would rain again. "It will stay wet on this night, I think. But come tomorrow, when the sun rises, it will not stay wet. And as it dries, it will become tighter . . . and tighter . . . and tighter. And you will find breathing harder . . . and harder . . . and harder."

He rose and held out the Winchester rifle. "I thank you for this present, indaaligande. Do not look so sad. When they teach more of our people at your Indian school in Pennsylvania, they will teach them of Yuyutsu, the last warrior of the Chirica-huas. Who killed many, many, many pale eyes with this fine rifle." Lowering the rifle, he grinned at the white man.

McIntyre knew that he would soon be dead.

"White man, what is your name?"

He had to ask the fool indaaligande again. The man managed to choke out an answer.

"Good, Dehner McIntyre," Yuyutsu said. "I am glad to know this, and maybe they will teach your grand-children's grandchildren your name. You will be famous. But always they will mention your name. I have given you honor. Because you, Dehner McIntyre, will be known by your people as the first man Yuyutsu killed on his great raid."

# CHAPTER THIRTEEN

Dark as those clouds had been off to the west, Jimmy Mann had expected to find himself drenched to the bone. But, typical for western Kansas, the storm had kicked up a lot of wind, only to release nary a drop of rain or stone of hail. Morning dawned clear and bright, the skies a pure blue, not one cloud, black or white, in the air.

Something else in the sky, however, caught his attention.

Seeing the buzzards circling a few miles off to the north, Jimmy spurred the roan colt into a trot, pulling the '73 Winchester from the scabbard as he rode, thumbing back the hammer as had been his practice since he first pinned on a badge.

In Dodge City, he had found nothing. No card-sharp named Dehner McIntyre. No .50-caliber Winchester repeater. No Danny Waco. No Gil Millican. No Tonkawa Tom. So he had gambled, deciding to light out toward Kansas City, a big city, certainly, with plenty of law, but a man like Danny Waco could find plenty of brothels, gambling dens, and hideouts on both sides of the Kansas-Missouri line. Jesse James and others had hidden out in the city or the surrounding farms, unmolested by peace officers. A long shot, Jimmy knew, but he had to do something, go somewhere. He had to keep looking.

The turkey buzzards kept circling, even as he neared the sandstone landmark along the Santa Fe Trail. That might have meant whatever the carrion had spotted wasn't quite dead. Then again, it could also mean that the wolves or coyotes hadn't finished with whatever lay near Pawnee Rock.

What caught his attention first were the colors. Dark red, gold, and stripes. He knew for certain then that what lay in the grass was no animal.

Jimmy swung down from the roan, keeping reins and Winchester in his hand, lowering himself to a knee, watching, and patiently waiting. His eyes scanned across the top of Pawnee Rock, down toward the scrub, the grass, the rocks. Not until he felt certain no ambush awaited, did he wrap the reins around a rock, and move toward the colors.

When he saw the man lying there, spread-eagled, arms and feet staked to the ground, a leather piece of string tightening around the throat, Jimmy let out a short breath, and again looked across the countryside. He thought the man was dead. He had to be dead. Then the eyes opened, and his swollen, cracked lips parted.

Instantly, Jimmy went to him, lowering the hammer on the rifle, before easing the Winchester to the ground. He drew the Barlow knife from his vest pocket. The blade opened, and he gently slid the metal between the man's sunburned neck and the rawhide. He cut the cord free, and the man sucked in a ragged breath.

"I'll be right back." Before he had even finished, Jimmy was up, Winchester back in his hands, heading for the roan.

"No . . ."

Even though the word came out as a ragged whisper, Jimmy caught the fear in the voice. He didn't stop, though. Didn't answer. He found the horse, grabbed the canteen, and ran back to the man.

He lifted the man's head gently, let a few drops of water trickle down the throat, and slowly lowered the head. In the clearings around the rock formation, Jimmy could see signs of a struggle, but no horses, nothing left of whoever had waylaid this stranger with outrageously striped pants. The pants were all he wore. Other clothes, including some worn boots, a gold ascot, and a crimson vest lay nearby. So did one sock. He could see other clothes that the wind had scattered during the night.

Jimmy also saw a few playing cards stuck in the grass and rocks. He took a guess. "Your name McIntyre? Dehner McIntyre?"

The man's eyes widened. His head barely nodded.

Without speaking, Jimmy moved to the gambler's bare arm. He cut it free.

Immediately, the gambler brought his hand over, massaging his throat. Once the man's bare feet and other wrist had been freed from the bindings, Jimmy removed his bandanna, soaked it with water, and handed it to McIntyre, who placed it on his throat.

The gambler stared at the canteen. "Please," he whispered. His tongue was so thick that he could barely wet his lips.

"Take the bandanna," Jimmy said. "Hold it over your mouth. Squeeze just a few drops." He stood, stared, but all he saw was the grass blowing in the wind. "I'm going to climb that rock. Take a looksee. You wait. Don't move too much. Build your strength back . . . slowly."

Atop the rock, he studied the land, but again, saw nothing out of the ordinary. Whoever had waylaid the gambler was long gone, and nobody was coming this way. After staying there five extra minutes—just to make sure—Jimmy went back down to the gambler, who had barely moved an inch except to move the wet bandanna to his overcooked forehead.

"Danny Waco do this to you?" Jimmy asked.

The man shook his head. His answer came in another hoarse whisper. "Apache."

That led Jimmy to think, *Sunstroke. His mind is gone.*

"What was his name again?"

The sunburned gambler sipped the coffee, which Jimmy had sweetened with the bottle of rye he had bought in Dodge City. Lifting the cup to his lips, setting the cup on the stone at his side, even swallowing the brew seemed to wear Dehner McIntyre out.

"Yo . . . Ye . . . You . . . something." His head shook slowly. "I'm not . . . I don't rightly remember."

"But he was Apache."

"That's what he said."

Jimmy Mann considered this. The only Apaches he had ever seen were illustrations in *Frank Leslie's Illustrated Newspaper* and *Harper's Weekly*.

McIntyre sipped more of the coffee. "It wasn't Danny Waco, Marshal. Because he would have killed me."

That, Jimmy realized, made sense. But an Apache Indian? That didn't. In fact, an Indian from any tribe didn't make much sense, not these days. Half-breed? Or a Mexican bandit? Either way, Jimmy decided, it wasn't his affair. It wasn't Danny Waco.

He turned, watching the sun make its way toward the horizon. The day was ending, and finding the gambler had cost Jimmy maybe twenty miles. Twenty miles farther away from catching up to Danny Waco.

The thought of Waco, of course, was what had steered McIntyre away from Dodge City. And only luck had brought Jimmy Mann to Pawnee Rock. He could have ridden straight north toward Hays City, or merely given up and returned to the Indian Territory and ridden back to Fort Smith, tail tucked between his legs.

Dehner McIntyre was in no condition to travel. Jimmy was still trying to figure out how to get him somewhere with only the roan to carry them both. Probably, Jimmy would just take the gambler back to the little community on the Pawnee River near old Fort Larned—which would cost him more time.

Fort Larned was southwest, toward Dodge City, and Danny Waco wasn't anywhere near Dodge.

The Winchester came up, and Jimmy stood, thumbing back the hammer, stepping toward the sound of hoofs. The gambler spilled the whiskey-seasoned coffee, tried to stand, but couldn't get his legs to work. He sank back into the grass, color draining from his face.

Jimmy spotted the riders coming hard down the trail, sending dust that the wind carried toward the east and south. Too far to make out the faces, and riding hard. But too many to be Danny Waco. And they certainly weren't a band of Chiricahua Apaches.

"Who . . . are . . . ?" The gambler couldn't finish.

"Rest easy," Jimmy said, and moved toward the roan, which was pawing the ground nervously, eying the newcomers.

*No point in hiding,* Jimmy decided. *No reason to, either.* Yet he kept the Winchester in his hands as he stood next to the horse.

A hand went up. The leader wore a gauntlet, was slowing down the dozen or so men behind him. Dark coats. Hats the color of wet sand.

Jimmy lowered the rifle, keeping the barrel aimed at the dirt—lest the riders get any wrong idea about his intentions—and called back to McIntyre. "It's all right. Army boys."

He pulled his vest over, so that the officer would be sure to see the badge.

* * *

The shavetail lieutenant, a kid maybe a couple years out of West Point, called himself Henderson. Said they were out of Fort Riley on the trail of a Chiricahua named John York, who had abandoned the ATS&F around Topeka.

McIntyre let out a mirthless laugh. "That's not the name he calls himself now."

"This Apache was educated at Captain Pratt's Indian school in Carlisle, Pennsylvania, and was being returned to the Comanche-Kiowa-Apache Indian Reservation near Fort Sill in Indian Territory," Henderson said.

Jimmy knew enough about that band of Apaches to know it spelled trouble. Henderson couldn't understand why an Indian might not want to go back there, but Jimmy kept his mouth shut. He also didn't say anything when McIntyre looked at him with an *I-told-you-it-was-an-Apache* expression.

The lieutenant's orders were to find the boy and bring him back to Fort Riley, where he had been shipped off to the agent at the reservation—or what was left of the reservation.

"It should not be a difficult assignment." Lieutenant Henderson did not see the bearded sergeant major behind him roll his eyes. "He is not armed."

"He is now," McIntyre said.

Jimmy Mann considered the gambler again. "How's that?"

"Took my Winchester," McIntyre said.

"You let him do that!" Lieutenant Henderson's swagger had dropped something considerable.

"Lieutenant," the gambler said, "I didn't have much of a say in the matter."

"What caliber?" Jimmy asked McIntyre.

"Caliber?" the lieutenant snapped. "What difference does the size of the cartridge matter? That Apache boy's got a repeating rifle and a chip on his shoulder."

Ignoring the pup officer, Jimmy waited.

"It's a .50," McIntyre said. "Won it off Danny Waco."

"A .50 caliber." The sergeant major sucked in a deep breath, then swore.

Jimmy echoed the non-commissioned officer's curse.

"Sergeant O'Donnell," Lieutenant Henderson snapped, "we must ride. I will not be responsible for another Wounded Knee." The green kid kept spitting out a bunch of other nonsense, while the patrol of cavalry troopers tightened their cinches, and prepared to ride.

"Did you see which way the Apache went?" Henderson asked.

McIntyre's head shook. "I was a little preoccupied at the time, Lieutenant. Getting ready to die." Still, the gambler jutted his jaw toward the west. "But my guess is he went that way."

"He's heading home, sir," Sergeant O'Donnell said.

"If he were heading home, Sergeant Major," the lieutenant said, "he would have stayed on the train."

"Home being Arizona Territory, sir," the noncom said stiffly.

"Whatever. We will pursue this miscreant if it takes us to the ends of the earth." He looked at McIntyre. "Do you wish to come along?"

The gambler grinned. "I think it's time for me to fold my hand, Lieutenant. Never been much of a prayin' man till yesterday and last night, so I think I'll leave the Apache hunting to you, and find a better place to deal cards."

Henderson turned to the deputy marshal. "And you?"

Jimmy looked at the lieutenant. He had a choice to make, but he knew the right one. The Winchester '86 wasn't important. He could find his nephew another Model 1886. What drove Jimmy was finding and killing Danny Waco. He wouldn't be chasing after an Apache.

"I'll take him"—Jimmy gestured toward the gambler—"down to Larned. Then I need to get after Danny Waco."

"Very well."

"But Lieutenant . . ."

Henderson turned, waiting with more than a modicum of impatience.

"That Winchester the Apache is carrying was stolen by the murderer Danny Waco. If you catch the Indian, would you send a telegraph to Deputy Marshal Jackson Sixpersons in Vinita, Cherokee Nation? We'd like that rifle back"—Jimmy thought up a lie—"for evidence."

"I'll send your deputy the Winchester and the Apache buck's scalp, Marshal."

Again, the sergeant major rolled his eyes. Henderson raised his gauntleted hand, motioned to the west, and spurred his horse. The other troopers followed at a trot, and the sergeant major tipped his hat, and shook his head.

"Good luck, Sergeant," Jimmy said.

O'Donnell spit out a mouthful of tobacco juice. "Thanks, Marshal. Reckon we'll need it." He spurred his bay to catch up with his commanding officer.

When the dust from the troopers' horses had drifted southeast, Jimmy Mann asked, "You think you can ride behind me? Just as far as Larned?"

"That's out of your way, isn't it?"

Jimmy was already tightening the cinch on his saddle. He shrugged. "Not that far. I can't leave you here." He looked over the horse's back. "Unless you want to ride with me."

"After Danny Waco?" Dehner McIntyre laughed without humor. "I reckon not, Marshal. No hard feelings?"

"'Course not." Jimmy moved around the roan and offered a hand to help the gambler to his feet. Actually, he preferred riding alone.

McIntyre grunted, his face masking in pain as Jimmy pulled him up and helped him to the colt.

Once Jimmy was in the saddle, he kicked his foot out of the stirrup, lowered his hand, and again assisted the gambler, pulling him up and onto the roan's back.

"Reckon those bluecoats will catch up with that buck?" McIntyre asked.

"Most likely. And some will live to regret it."

Jimmy kicked the colt into a walk.

McIntyre's arms wrapped tightly around Jimmy's stomach. "Where do you start looking for Waco?"

Jimmy could answer only with a shrug.

"Well, Marshal, I don't know if it'll help or not, but I did hear something at that poker table in Caldwell. It doesn't narrow down your search a whole lot, but one of Waco's minions said something about Nebraska."

# CHAPTER FOURTEEN

*Gove County*

The place along what the pale eyes called the Smoky Hill River reminded him of home. It was not the Dragoons of Arizona Territory, but the Monument Rocks jutted out of the Kansas plains. Not mountains, and certainly no trees, but the land offered some cover. It was where he would make his final stand. Where he could fight the bluecoats. He could make the Long Knives, and all of the indaali-gande, remember the name Yuyutsu.

Eager to Fight.

In less than a week, he had covered more than one hundred miles. Afoot. He had not gone south by southwest, thinking that would be the way the pale eyes would expect him to go. He had followed the Arkansas and Pawnee rivers, then turned north—not south—and made his way across the fields of winter wheat and prairie grass. He had killed an antelope along the North Fork of the Walnut with the rifle he had taken off the indaaligande with the ugly pants. Three times, he had considered killing other pale eyes between the Arkansas and the Smoky Hill. Miserable farmers who lived in homes made from the sod.

Yet what honor could be found in killing people like that? The women had been dirty as the men, and fat as the sows that waddled around the wretched homes. There would be no glory,

Ah, but killing bluecoats? *That* the pale eyes would remember. *That* would bring him honor and glory, for at least one of the men following him knew how to trail. That man was better than even some of the Apaches Yuyutsu had known before Geronimo had surrendered, and Yuyutsu and his people had been sent off to rot in the Florida prison.

The sun had begun to sink, turning the chalk buttes and arches from white to gold. Still, he could see the dust. Let the bluecoats come.

He worked the lever of the big Winchester '86 slowly, enjoying the sound of the mechanical clicks as the massive brass cartridge fed into the chamber. All around him was the flatness of Kansas. A man could seemingly stare from one end of the earth to the other—except at the place the indaaligande called Monument Rocks.

Formations of chalk—buttes and arches, nubs, crumbling ruins, and some that stretched as high as seventy feet—shot out of the prairie without rhyme and with little reason. Some close together, others far, far apart. The problem, of course, was that once the protection of the chalk fortress was behind him, Kansas would offer no protection from a bluecoat's long gun.

Yuyutsu, on the other hand, did not care. It was where he would die.

Summer and fall had beaten the grass into brown, and the skies were darkening into a deep blue. He had positioned himself against one of the taller monuments, one with a large opening, more a door than a window, long and angular, which gave him a view of the country to the southeast. He could see the slanting, flat-topped butte four hundred yards off. After that, there was little to be seen, except for some smaller chalk rocks to the west, another three or four hundred yards in the distance. Then nothing . . . except for the dust.

Placing the Winchester on his thighs, he pushed up the rear sight, then pressed his fingers gently on the metal, and raised the crossbar up to the numeral five. Five hundred yards. He checked the sun.

Yuyutsu waited.

Over the past few days, he had counted twelve riders and did not think any of the bluecoats would have quit chasing him. Bluecoats did not often quit, and these fools would soon regret that. Of the soldiers, he respected only one, but he did not know which one it was.

A few times, he had backtracked, then lay in the grass and waited for the bluecoats, blind to the ways of the Apache, to ride past. The first time, he figured he was done with worrying about the soldiers, but they had surprised him. They had picked up his trail.

At first, he had blamed himself for that, but when the soldiers found him again, he knew one of them had the eyes, the skills, of an Apache.

After that, it had become something of a game. He would lose the men trailing him, and they would find him again. Once it had taken the bluecoats a whole day to rediscover him. This last time, it had been less than three hours.

He was done playing with the bluecoats. Yuyutsu had not eaten in two days, and he was hungry. The soldiers would have food in their saddlebags. If not, he would eat one of their horses.

The dust grew closer, but Yuyutsu did not lift the heavy rifle. He did empty the box of shells, and spread out the brass cartridges beside him. He did not have that many rounds, but he figured he had enough.

A moment later, he heard the sound of hoofs loping across western Kansas. He worked up enough saliva in his mouth and swallowed, ran his tongue over his dried lips, and looked through the hole in the rock, carefully, not letting the soldiers see him. One, he figured, had a pair of binoculars. A few times, he had seen the sun reflect off the glass lenses, but he did not see that now.

It was time. Yuyutsu lifted the rifle, pressing the barrel against the chalk, feeling the crescent-shaped stock slip against his shoulder. He sucked in a deep breath, held it, slowly exhaled, and watched the soldiers ride past the butte.

The leader of the bluecoats raised his hand, and the soldiers stopped. Some let their horses drop their weary heads and graze on what little grass they could find. Others stretched in the saddles, kicking free of their stirrups, rubbing their backs. Most found their canteens and slaked their thirsts.

When the leader lowered his hand, he turned and began talking to another bluecoat, one with a bearded face and battered hat. They were too far away for Yuyutsu to hear what they said and their voices didn't carry.

His eyes swept across the men, wondering. He saw no one who forked his horse like an Indian, who looked like an Indian. So whomever the tracker was had to be a pale eye. A bluecoat. Yuyutsu had been almost certain that one of those men had to be an Indian.

He brought down the rifle, and lowered the sight to four hundred yards. The barrel went back up, rubbing against the chalk, but making no noise. He made himself relax, closed his left eye, and drew a bead on one of the bluecoats.

*No,* he told himself, *not him.*

He swung the barrel to one drinking water. *Let him drink.*

Another mopped his face with a yellow neckerchief.

*Too easy.*

He came back to the man the leader was talking to. He inhaled, exhaled, and looked at the bluecoat leader, trying to decide.

*I am like your pale eyes god,* he told himself. *I choose who lives. I choose who dies.*

Smiling, he found his target, and pulled the trigger.

"What is this place, Sergeant?" Lieutenant Troy Henderson asked.

"Chalk pyramids," Sergeant Sean O'Donnell answered, remembering at the last minute to include, "sir."

"Look like tombstones, don't they?" one of the troopers said with a laugh.

"Might be where you gets buried, Andy," came from another.

O'Donnell decided not to tell the soldiers to shut their traps. Instead, he told the lieutenant, "Monument Rocks, some folks called them. Heard some fellow at Riley once say they were something like eighty million years old."

"That's almost as old as you is, ain't it, Sarge?" Trooper Andy Preston said with a snigger.

Henderson turned in the saddle to stare down the trooper, but Sean O'Donnell didn't care what Andy Preston said. He was a good soldier, that Preston. Unlike Second Lieutenant Troy Henderson and most of the other boys who'd been assigned to this duty.

O'Donnell pushed up the brim of his hat, and looked across the plains. The sun would be down within the hour. After that, it would be too dark to follow the Apache runaway. If the green lieutenant would have obliged a sergeant major who'd been in this man's Army for twenty-nine years, O'Donnell would have simply said, "Good riddance, John York. Enjoy your walk to Arizona or New Mexico or Mexico or Canada or hell."

But the Army and Lieutenant Troy Henderson would never do anything like that. Anything that made sense.

The way Sean O'Donnell saw things, this pup of an Apache hadn't killed anyone—and he had had plenty of chances, seeing all those lone farms spread out across the plains. He hadn't even managed to kill the one person he had tried to kill, that lucky gambler they had found at Pawnee Rock less than a week ago. Let the boy go his own way. By Jehovah, the boy had grit, gumption, and guts. And some strong legs and tough feet to make it this far.

He wouldn't hurt anybody—not likely—unless Lieutenant Troy Henderson kept pushing. Then, there would be trouble.

And death. Plenty of death.

O'Donnell felt a shiver run up his spine. He hadn't felt anything like that since '65 when he had first seen the elephant. He'd been riding with the blue at Sailor's Creek in Virginia, just a few days and a few miles before General Lee had met General Grant to call things quits at Appomattox Court House. That would've been his luck, he remembered thinking, to get killed that close to the end of the war.

A similar thought pressed through his consciousness. He planned on retiring in three months.

"Sergeant Major!" Lieutenant Henderson barked.

Turning, O'Donnell listened to the lieutenant. At least, he tried to.

"You sure that Apache is heading this way?"

O'Donnell's head moved up and down. "He crossed the river, sir. He's been making his way this direction for some time." He pointed toward the rising pieces of chalk off in the distance.

In the fading light, Monument Rocks did look eerily like enlarged tombstones.

"No reason he'd stop now."

"No reason he'd continue, either, Sergeant." Lieutenant Henderson reached into his saddlebag and drew out a bottle of whiskey. He drank greedily and wiped his mouth with his sleeve.

Yes, sir. Sergeant Major Sean O'Donnell had to admit that a kid like Troy Henderson would find himself promoted to general the way he hit that bottle.

"You said he was bound for Arizona, Sergeant." Henderson corked the bottle, but instead of returning it to his saddlebag, slipped it inside his tunic. "Might I remind you—*again*—that we have been heading northwest for quite a while."

"That's right, sir."

O'Donnell thought for a moment, then added with a grin, "Maybe his compass is broke."

That got a roar of laughter and approval from the boys, and a reddening face and scowl from Troy Henderson.

"Let's ride!" the lieutenant barked.

Gripping the reins steady, O'Donnell kept his

horse from following the lieutenant's bay. "I'm not so sure I'd do that, sir."

Henderson reined in, turned around, glaring. "And why not?"

O'Donnell pointed by tilting his head and hat toward the chalk fortresses. "My guess, sir, is that that boy's lying in those rocks. Waiting."

"If he wanted to ambush us, Sergeant Major, he could have done that a day or more ago and saved us and our mounts saddle sores."

"Where, sir?"

"Where . . . what?"

O'Donnell didn't bother looking at the lieutenant anymore. He studied the rocks, hoping to see the sinking sunlight reflect off that barrel he knew had to be sighting down on the boys right about now. "Where would he ambush us, sir?" Again, he gestured toward the landmarks that jutted out of the plains. "Here he has cover. Plenty of it."

In what was going on thirty years, Sean O'Donnell had seen a lot of riding in the cavalry, most of it—practically all of it since the end of the Rebellion—in the west. Most of it on what folks back east called the Great American Desert.

"We are twelve men, Sergeant. He is a boy in his teens."

"He's an Apache, Lieutenant," O'Donnell reminded his commanding officer.

"Correct you are, Sergeant Major. He is an Apache. And we are soldiers. And as I told that tin-horn gambler and cowardly marshal, I will not be responsible for another Wounded Knee. The last

Indian uprising won't be cited in history books with historians pointing their yellow fingers at me."

O'Donnell kept looking, staring. He could feel fear, not just sweat, running down his spine. He wet his lips. He didn't agree with Lieutenant Henderson on many points. First, he didn't think that deputy marshal was a coward. Not by a long shot. And Wounded Knee wasn't on his mind. "I'm thinking more of the Fetterman massacre."

"How's that, Sergeant?"

O'Donnell almost grinned. "Little bit before your time, sir."

Over in Wyoming, shortly after the War of the Rebellion, an Army officer named Fetterman had disobeyed orders and led something like eighty men to death at the hands of the Sioux Indians.

"I don't see nothin'," Andy Preston said.

"I don't, either. That's what troubles me." O'Donnell made one final plea. "Sun'll be down directly, Lieutenant. We can camp here. Got this big rock for shelter. Protect our horses." He nodded toward the next growth of pyramids. "That's four hundred yards we'd have to cross."

"Sergeant Major," the lieutenant snapped, "I fear that you are becoming yellow—this close to your retirement. There is nothing out there to stop the United States Army except for a snot-nosed—"

# CHAPTER FIFTEEN

Sean O'Donnell ducked in the saddle, feeling and tasting the blood that had splattered all over his face. He tried to spit it out, but his mouth immediately went drier than a lime burner's hat. More out of instinct than anything else, he ducked in the saddle, reached for the Springfield .45-70 in the saddle boot, and heard the roar and echo of the rifle shot that had torn Lieutenant Troy Henderson practically in two.

Behind him came the screams, curses, and shouts of men. Horses reared. O'Donnell had trouble keeping his own mount under control, staying in the saddle.

Another shot roared. A horse screamed. Fell.

The rifle was in O'Donnell's hands, and he was thumbing back the hammer, trying to look, trying to find the smoke that would give away the Apache's location.

"Sergeant!" one of the men cried. Almost whimpering.

"Behind that butte!" O'Donnell roared.

A hundred yards away. Two of the soldiers were afoot, their horses loping toward the east, unlikely to stop until they ran themselves to death or reached the stables at Fort Riley. Another horse lay dead, its rider trying to kick himself free.

"Lie still!" O'Donnell told him. Through the dust, he saw another trooper catapult from his saddle, landing in the dirt, kicking up white sand and dust, with a sickening thud. Moments later, the report of the rifle reached O'Donnell's ears.

"Behind the butte!" O'Donnell yelled again. He had the Springfield against his shoulder, sweeping the barrel left to right, trying to train on something, an impossible task seeing how his skittish gelding kept stepping one way, then the other, nervous from the smell of blood and death.

Somewhere, the Winchester '86 stolen by the Apache boy once known as John York, spat again.

O'Donnell's horse was falling, but not from the bullet. That round had slammed into the head of the trooper—Martini was fresh off the boat and train from Sicily, could hardly speak a word of English—who had been pinned underneath the horse. He had managed to get free from the dead horse, stand, and get the back of his head blown off. Because he didn't listen to O'Donnell's orders to lie still.

No, because he didn't understand. Because Sean O'Donnell didn't speak Italian.

He triggered a shot just as the gelding stepped into a prairie dog hole. Then he was going over the horse's neck, hitting the ground, hearing the big dun climb to its feet, scurry off after the other riderless mounts.

He dug himself into the sand, would have dug his way clear to China if he could. A bullet slammed into the ground inches from his face, peppering his forehead and cheeks with grit.

The Springfield, hot to the touch, smoke snaking from the barrel, came up to him, and he worked the breech, had to pry the brass casing out of the chamber and slam in another cartridge.

"Sergeant!" It was Andy Preston.

O'Donnell rolled onto his back, watching the trooper who had served in his platoon for ten years spurring a black gelding straight for him. With a curse, Sergeant Major Sean O'Donnell raised his hand, trying to wave the trooper off, trying to get him to follow the rest of the boys back behind that butte.

The .50-caliber cannon ripped another round, but Preston kept riding, jerking hard on the reins, sliding the black to a stop. Preston lowered his hand, but O'Donnell was standing, turning, firing, and barking an order. "Get back behind that rock," he snapped. "I'm borrowing your horse."

"What the—"

He didn't have time to argue and grabbed Preston's proffered hand, jerking the unsuspecting soldier out of the saddle. An instant later, Sean O'Donnell held the reins to the black, and his left foot found the stirrup. As he swung into the saddle, he barked an order at Andy Preston. "Run like the devil. While that Apache buck reloads!"

He raked the black's sides with his spurs, and took off, leaning low in the saddle, almost over the gelding's neck. Moving north and east, he angled toward a series of buttes and arches.

O'Donnell made one mistake. He looked at the body of Second Lieutenant Troy Henderson, mouth open, never to finish the sentence, the curse, whatever it had been the green pup was trying to say, and eyes staring sightlessly at the sky darkening with the setting sun.

Deftly, Yuyutsu fingered the long brass cartridges into the loading gate of the smoking, hot-to-the-touch rifle. Most of the bluecoats, those not lying on the ground dead or dying, had made it behind the slanted butte. A few others were running or riding, kicking up dust.

He muttered a favorite curse among the indaaligande, and brought the big Winchester up, cocked it, jumping to the other side of the hole in the chalk monument. The barrel of the .50-caliber rifle followed the black-faced rider on the black horse.

He was the man. The honorable one. The pale eyes who had managed to follow the trail. Leading horse and rider with the barrel, Yuyutsu waited, squeezed the trigger, and felt the curved stock kick savagely against his shoulder, which throbbed from all the shooting and killing he had already done.

His eyes and nostrils rebelled from the smoke and the punishment the Winchester dished out. Blinking, he looked through the opening and saw that he had missed.

Maybe he should have shot one of the men running. Killed another bluecoat coward. But there would have been little honor in that.

He jacked another shell into the Winchester. Jerked the trigger, flinching even before he fired. He knew the gun would cause more pain on his throbbing shoulder.

Another miss. Horse and rider had reached the safety of the odd shaped chalk monument behind him. Yuyutsu swore a white man's curse again, turned, and tried to find an easier target.

A bullet spanged off the rock over his head. Not close. Probably even a scratch shot, but one of the bluecoats had seen his smoke. Knew where he was. He pulled himself inside, feeling his heart pound against his chest, blinking away the sweat.

He made himself stand, waited, and then jumped across the opening. Another rifle roared from the soldiers far away, but he did not even hear the bullet strike. Those soldiers were not great marksmen, and at four or five hundred yards away, posed no threat.

The one he must kill was over behind the rocks. When he reached the edge of the tall monument, he looked across the open flatness toward the other chalky series of rocks.

To the southeast, he saw the one that resembled the ruins of an adobe hut, like the corner of a building a pale eyes might have built in Arizona. Beyond that, rose a finger, dark underneath, white at the top. There was an opening, and then a large rock, longer, but not as high as either the adobe ruins or the finger. That one reminded him of one of the old prairie schooners that once traveled across the country, bringing more and more pale eyes into the lands once owned and ruled by Indians.

And behind that rock?

He didn't know. Maybe more buttes and smaller arches. Maybe nothing. Maybe the pyramids ended there, or another rock did not rise from the plains for a hundred or more yards. But Yuyutsu knew one thing. Somewhere behind those chalk formations waited the pale eyes soldier. He would have to kill him. Maybe steal his horse. Then he could either try to kill the other bluecoats or ride away to fight some other day.

To get there, he would have to cross fifty yards of flats. Not an easy shot for those troopers way off hiding, cowering, behind that slanting tower. But an easy kill for the bluecoat waiting for him.

Turning, Yuyutsu found the sun almost slipping behind the series of monuments off to the west. He would have to kill that bluecoat in a hurry, for he was still an Apache—no matter what the School Mothers and School Fathers had tried to beat into him at Carlisle in Pennsylvania—and Apaches did not like to fight at night.

He raised the barrel of the Winchester, thumb on the hammer, and cursed himself again. How many cartridges had he left in the sand by the window in the rock? How many shots had he fired since he had reloaded? *What a fool.*

Again, he wet his lips. The pale eyes behind those rocks was smart and patient. He knew that the first to move would often become the first to die. He was almost like an Apache. Yuyutsu knew he could no longer wait. Wait and the sun would set. He was not going to run away from a fight, anymore.

Besides, his feet hurt. He needed a horse. Food. And more rounds for the big rifle in his arms.

He leaped over the lower rocks, and ran, not even looking off toward the soldiers. A rifle roared, far off, but no bullet neared him. Another shot came, or maybe it was the first gun's echo. Either way, he kept running, kept studying the darkening rocks.

A third shot came, but missed, before Yuyutsu was safe behind the rock, slipping into the corner, looking through the opening, and carefully listening.

He waited until his breathing came back under control. Had to wipe his clammy hands on the chalky rocks. He slid along the side of the rock until he neared the opening. Waited. Listened. Looked.

At last, he jumped through the narrow entrance, landed in sand, spit out dirt, came to his knees.

Something sounded behind him, and he spun, falling back, bringing the rifle barrel up.

The shape came to him. He touched the trigger, then quickly released all pressure on it.

The horse stood still, sweaty and breathing hard. It pawed the earth with its forefeet. Otherwise, it did not move, and barely even considered Yuyutsu.

Shadows began lengthening, casting darkness all around him. He came to his knees, and considered the finger of rock just behind the dark horse. He even looked up, to the top of the finger, as if any pale eyes could have scaled that. Again, he wet his lips, and looked down the back of the wagon-shaped rock, but all he could make out were darkened shadows.

Suddenly, he felt cool. Night would be there directly. He moved toward the wagon-shaped rock, but quickly stopped and looked back at the horse. Instantly, he was heading straight for the worn-out animal. He slowed, speaking in quiet hushes as he approached the bluecoat's horse. He found its neck, rubbed one hand on the damp hide, and turned around, looking back toward the wagon-shaped rock.

His hand gripped the canvas strap of the canteen and jerked it up, pulled out the cork with his teeth, and brought the container to his lips.

The water was tepid, brackish, tasted of iron, and there wasn't much left, but he emptied it, dropped the canteen, and looked again at the rock butte.

He heard the footsteps.

Letting out a war cry, Yuyutsu scrambled toward the opening, sliding to a stop, bringing the Winchester to his shoulder. He saw a dark shape, but knew that shape had to be the soldier. The gun roared. He grunted. Jacked another round into the Winchester.

Somehow, the bluecoat had managed to dive behind the rock where Yuyutsu had perfected his ambush. Yet there was no cover there. The Winchester roared again.

The bluecoat kept running. Yuyutsu saw chalk and dirt and shrapnel of rocks fly from where the .50-caliber slug had slammed into the rock above the pale eyes' head. Again, the Winchester sang out, just as the bluecoat had reached the opening. He was diving, the pale eyes with the dark beard, and stretching out through the opening.

Yuyutsu's ears rang from the roar of the rifle, but he felt—he was almost certain—that he heard the man cry out before he disappeared through the door in the rock. He thought, though surely it was his imagination, he saw blood splatter against the crumbling white rock, now gold from the setting sun.

Yuyutsu fed another bullet into the rifle, and began hurrying to the rocks, to finish off that pale eyes tracker.

He had managed to make it only halfway, when a lead slug whistled past his ear. Another clipped the sand in front of him.

Whirling, he dropped to a knee and cursed his own stupidity, his deafness. So focused on catching and killing the one bluecoat, he had forgotten about the others. He had dismissed them, figuring they would be hiding behind that rock way off in the distance.

But they were all worthy opponents, solid warriors.

They had come, not on horses, but walking—marching bravely—crossing the flats, leaving themselves open to be gunned down by an Apache with a repeating rifle. And they had surprised him. He fired. Saw all of the soldiers either flatten into prone positions or drop to a knee. Guns roared, and Yuyutsu had no other choice but to stay where he was. To make his stand in the opening and be cut down like a dog and die.

Or run.

He made it back to the rocks, but not before a .45-70 slug slammed through his right leg, breaking the bone in his thigh, and making him scream like a newborn baby, wailing in pain, in misery.

# CHAPTER SIXTEEN

O'Donnell sat up, grunting, grimacing, gripping his right side. His left hand came away sticky with blood, and he whispered a curse. Unsnapping the flap on his holster, he pulled out the Remington revolver.

The silhouettes appeared, and he brought up the big .44, trying to keep his right hand steady. The left hand had returned to his side, making a feeble effort to stanch the flow of blood.

"Sarge . . ." one of the shades whispered.

Sergeant Major Sean O'Donnell mouthed a prayer of thanks as he lowered the revolver. "You get him, Andy?"

"Wounded him." Trooper Andy Preston sank beside O'Donnell. "I see he got you, too."

O'Donnell moved his hand and let Preston press a handkerchief over the wound. While he worked, O'Donnell leaned his head back against the chalk rock, his lungs still heaving, and pain burning his side.

"I'd say it's just a scratch, Sarge, but . . ."

O'Donnell knew what Preston meant. A .50-100-450 slug did not leave just scratches. It dug ditches. His side would sport one mean-looking scar, something he could brag about.

At least, the wound appeared far from fatal.

Another soldier knelt, ripping the sleeves off his calico shirt. He and Preston tore the garment and wrapped it tight around O'Donnell's waist.

While they were finishing, Trooper Roger Jones hurried over, sliding to a stop. "The Apache's back in them rocks. I know we got him. In the leg. He was hollerin' like a stuck pig for a minute, but he ain't sayin' nothin' no more."

"Bled out?" the soldier who had sacrificed his shirt asked hopefully.

"I doubt that," Preston muttered.

O'Donnell jerked his thumb back through the hole in the rock. "He doesn't have much lead to throw. There's a handful of shells on the other side. He left them in the dirt."

"How many will an '86 hold in the tube?" Preston asked the sarge.

"A .45-70 holds eight if it's a rifle or musket. I'd have to guess that a .50 would hold about the same. Maybe one fewer if it's a carbine."

"It's a rifle," Preston said. "So eight shots. Nine if he jacked one into the chamber."

"Likely less than that in that buck's repeater," Jones said. "He cut loose with a few shots."

"Still enough to kill a couple more of us, though," said the soldier without sleeves.

O'Donnell made himself stand. The sun had dropped well below the chalk pyramids off to the west, and it was growing darker with every passing second. He leaned back against the rock, wet his lips, and looked down at the .44 in his right hand.

"Let's finish this," Preston whispered.

"You bet," echoed Jones. "Win us some medals."

"Posthumously." Sergeant Major Sean O'Donnell tilted his head toward the sun. "Medals are one thing, if you're alive to get them. You boys itching to get killed?" He waited. "Chasing an Apache in the dark ain't my idea of having fun." Drawing a deep breath, he said, "Put some guards on both sides of those rocks. Tell them not to shoot Trooper Preston's horse by accident. Tell them don't fall asleep. We'll get Mr. John York come morning."

"Was that thunder?" Peggy Crabbe asked.

Her husband Matt was already tugging on the lines to the Michigan A Grade Combination Market and Pleasure Wagon. He called out, "Whoa" to the mules and looked across western Kansas toward the chalk monuments in the distance just beginning to show in the morning light.

"There it is again," Peggy said, shielding her eyes and fair skin, staring to the southeast. "But there's not a cloud in the sky."

He considered lying. Telling his new bride that certainly, it was thunder. She'd heard of heat lightning, no doubt. So what she'd heard was heat thunder. Common in western Kansas. A body gets used to things like heat . . . and the wind, which was just beginning to pick up.

He couldn't do it. "No, Miss Peggy, it ain't thunder."

The sound rumbled across the plains, despite the fact that the wind was blowing away from Monument Rocks.

She knew. "Gunfire?" The word came out like a gasp.

His head bobbed as he scanned the plains. He turned in the comfortable seat with the lazy back, reaching into the back, and pulling up his beaten-like-the-Dickens Spencer carbine.

"Hunters?" she asked.

He shook the lines, yelling at the mules to hurry, and slid the rifle onto the seat between his wife and himself. It struck him as one of his fool notions. But so had marrying the pretty little brunette who thought Terre Haute, Indiana, had been a wild, lawless town.

"Come on, you fool mules!" He found the whip and lashed out with it, just managing to catch a glimpse of his wife's horrified face.

Crabbe had twenty-three years on the twenty-two-year-old girl he had saved from a spinster's existence teaching school in La Crosse. He didn't know what that pretty young gal saw in him. Fresh out of Indiana, she could read, write, speak French, and make mighty fine biscuits.

And him? He had met a Frenchman once, had even hired out to serve as one of the monsieur's guides on a hunt the aristocrat had arranged with a couple generals, a consulate—whatever that was— from Washington City, and the commanding officer at Fort Wallace. That's as close to he'd come to speaking French. *Monsieur. Ouí.* And a couple cusswords that Frenchy, one evening after too much Champagne, had discretely told him . . . words he'd never mention to Peggy.

He could read sign, but not his letters, signed his name with two Xs and wasn't much for cooking anything that he hadn't killed. He'd never been to Indiana—hailed from Kentucky—although he had told Peggy that he had, back when he had been courting her.

He had worked on the Kansas Pacific, hunted buffalo, served as a beer-jerker in one or two hell-on-wheels, served as a deputy during the cattle seasons in Newton and Ellsworth, and scouted for the U.S. Army out of Fort Wallace. It was where he was taking Peggy, more or less.

The Army had closed up shop at Wallace about ten or twelve years ago, and since then he had spent his time working lousy jobs like gathering buffalo bones for fertilizer, even sweeping out the mercantile at Crider's place in La Crosse—which is how he met Peggy.

Actually, he was taking her to a hundred and sixty acres he had filed to homestead just spitting distance from Pond Creek. But first . . .

"Sounds like a gunfight!" he shouted. A regular shooting scrape. He hadn't been in anything like that since '89.

Swaying beside him, Peggy gripped the seat with both hands, her mouth open but her eyes screwed shut, trying to keep from tumbling out of the wagon.

He let the mules pull the wagon—which had set him back thirty-five dollars at La Crosse (and that did not include the mules or the harness or the ring Peggy made him buy for her)—off the track. The chalk monuments slowly grew off the prairie floor.

"Monument Rocks!" he called out, like he was offering a tour of western Kansas.

His wife didn't open her eyes to enjoy the view. 'Course, she couldn't see much anyhow. On account of all the dust the two mules kept kicking up.

Twenty minutes later, he could see the figures of men scurrying around the outcroppings. Smoke puffed from behind one of the rocks, and a moment later came the muffled report of a single-shot Springfield. Other men spread out. They seemed to have some ol' boy pinned up behind a series of chalk ridges.

A lawman he had worked with in Newton—before the peace officer had the misfortune of getting his head stoved in by an anvil—had once warned him to never go rushing into a fight. Not until he knew which side was the one he wanted to join up.

Crabbe pulled back on the lines, bringing the mules to a rough stop. Her set the brake, pulled the rifle off the seat, and leaped from the rig. "Stay here!" he shouted to his new bride.

She kept her eyes closed and her fingers tight against the seat.

*Maybe,* he thought as he hurried across the prairie, running in a crouch, *I should have at least kissed her cheek.*

Seven hundred yards from the pyramids, he stopped and knelt behind a clump of grass and scrub. He could make out the guidon flapping in that infernal wind and knew some cavalry boys had someone pinned down. He had never trained his sights on anyone wearing the blue.

*Deserter,* he figured.

All right. At least one thing had been settled. He knew which side he would pick in this scrape. He didn't care for deserters.

He started to snake through the grass, gripping the Spencer in his sweaty hands.

The leg no longer hurt. It did not bleed, either, but only because he had packed the ugly wound with the chalky sand. It had swollen up and was beginning to turn black.

Soon, Yuyutsu knew, he would die. From blood poisoning, thirst, or a bluecoat's bullet. He prayed for the latter, a fitting way for an Apache warrior to die.

It had not been much of a raid, after all. The bluecoats had outsmarted him more than once. For that, he blamed the School Fathers and the School Mothers at Carlisle, where they had taught him to follow the white man's road. Where they had made him forget what it was like to be a Chiricahua Apache warrior in battle.

Still, he had made some of them pay. Their women would cut off their hair in mourning for those who were no more. Their names would never be spoken again.

Well, if they had been Apaches—old Apaches, before the reservation days, before Geronimo had surrendered to the general called Miles—they would have done those things. The pale eyes would brag about how bravely their soldiers had died. They would erect marble monuments to their dead. They would tell lies in newspapers and books.

The only monument for Eager to Fight, the last great Chiricahua warrior, was the chunk of stone and sand he leaned against. He stared at the Winchester in his arms. Wondered if he had enough strength to lift the weapon or even to pull the trigger.

A rifle roared and the big slug bore into the butte far off to the right and ten or twenty feet over his head. Not even close. He wondered if the bluecoats planned on chopping down the chalk rock with bullets. Was that how they would flush him out of his hiding place?

"Stop wasting lead!" shouted the leader of the bluecoats—the man who had barked orders since Yuyutsu had killed their chief.

He wondered why they did not rush him. Just end the fight with one charge. He couldn't kill them all. Yuyutsu stared at the Winchester. He probably couldn't even kill one of them.

Last night, when the leg pained him so much, he

had thought about turning the big rifle on himself. But that was not a fitting way for a Chiricahua brave to die.

The sun baked him. Had the bluecoats been smart, they could have come at him from that direction. He probably wouldn't have seen them until it was too late.

But the bluecoats were stupid.

They could have charged him during the night, or immediately after they had busted his leg with a rifle shot, when the pain became too intense, when he could not have protected himself from a tiny ant. Or when he had drifted off to sleep, not to awaken until shortly before dawn.

The bluecoats would not wait much longer. The sun kept turning hotter, even though it was late in the year. The men and the horses Yuyutsu had killed would begin to bloat, to stink. The soldiers would want to end the standoff. Soon.

*He* wanted it to be over.

He dragged himself to the edge of the rock, leaving behind the soldier's black horse and a trail of blood the ants would follow. There was nowhere else for him to go.

"John York!" the leader of the soldiers called out.

Yuyutsu had tired of the man's voice.

"This is your last warning. Give it up, boy. There's no need for anyone else to die. Listen to me, John York. It's over. Let's end this peacefully."

*John York.* As if he would ever answer to that name. *I am Yuyutsu.*

A bullet kicked sand into his face, and he turned, surprised to find the strength back in his body, his wits keen. He blinked rapidly, cleared his vision, and brought up the big rifle. A soldier—a fool bluecoat—was running straight for him, firing a six-shooter. Smoke and flame belched from the revolver's long barrel, yet Yuyutsu felt no bullets tear into his body.

A running man could not shoot straight.

"Winfield!" a voice called out. "You fool!"

The big rifle boomed, jarring Yuyutsu's entire body and knocking him down. He landed with a grunt, felt the wound in his thigh open up again, and pushed himself up with the Winchester.

Just ten yards ahead of him, the foolish bluecoat named Winfield lay writhing on the ground, the sand darkening with his blood. He was crying, begging, coughing.

Yuyutsu sat up again, bringing up the rifle and levering a fresh cartridge. He aimed at the soldier, but did not pull the trigger.

Something in the corner of his eye caught his attention, and he turned and froze.

Another man stood only twenty yards from him, right knee on the ground, elbow braced on his left thigh, holding another type of rifle. "Drop the rifle, boy."

He was no bluecoat. He wore tan trousers and a muslin shirt. His cheek bulged with tobacco, and his hat wasn't even what they called hats out in this country. It was nothing more than a woolen cap of tweed, the kind Yuyutsu had seen in Pennsylvania. Not Kansas.

"Drop the gun." The indaaligande spoke with authority, but the big rifle trained on Yuyutsu's chest gave a man much power. "Drop it. Else I drop you."

# CHAPTER SEVENTEEN

It had been a good fight. They would remember
his name. His leg hurt . . . and he knew he wouldn't
be able to keep conscious much longer. Smiling,
Yuyutsu let the heavy Winchester '86 drop from his
fingers and land in the Kansas dust.

He told himself that he had no choice. After all,
the last bullet he had rested inside the bluecoat
named Winfield's guts.

"I got him, boys!" the white man yelled, but he
did not move, and took neither his aim nor his eyes
off Yuyutsu.

Yuyutsu turned, made himself smile again, though
even that action sent waves of pain throughout his
body.

The soldier, the last one he had shot, moved no
more. Other bluecoats, those still alive, hurried
around, stopping to check the man named Winfield, praying to their god, and muttering curses.
They gathered around Yuyutsu, the last great warrior of the Chiricahua Apaches. One bluecoat

picked up the Winchester, but mostly they stared, some at Yuyutsu, but the majority at the man with the rifle, the man with the funny cap, the man who had stopped Yuyutsu's great raid.

The leader of the bluecoats was the last to arrive, moving slowly. Yuyutsu enjoyed seeing the bloody bandage around the bluecoat's side. Had he not rushed his shot, had the gods not smiled upon this man with the stripes on his dusty coat, he would have been dead, too.

The soldier took the rifle from the other bluecoat, cocked it, shook his head, and gave Yuyutsu a spiteful look. He faced the man who had just stood and butted his rifle on the ground. "Who in blazes are you?"

Matt Crabbe slid the Irish eight-piece cap off his head, shoved it into his back pocket, and introduced himself as he nodded at the sergeant major. "Headin' for my homestead over near what used to be Fort Wallace. Heard the shots. Come to help."

"We thank you for that," the noncom said.

"Winfield's dead, Sarge," one of the troopers said.

*Most of the soldiers look mighty green,* Crabbe thought, *except the sergeant major and the soldier who's attending to the Apache buck's leg.* "You got any wounded? Other than yourself."

The bandage around the sergeant's waist was blackened with dried blood on his side.

"Four dead." The sergeant sighed. "No, five, counting Winfield. A couple are wounded, but nothing serious."

Five dead. Crabbe tried not to whistle as he looked at the Apache. *An Apache. In Kansas. In 1894.* His head shook. The Indian didn't look so fierce now, more like a little boy—probably had not even cleared his teens—in much pain.

"Bunch of our horses took off," the sergeant was saying, "and I'd like to get the lieutenant's body—and these other poor lads—to civilization for a proper burial. We lost a few horses, too, chasing this buck."

Crabbe nodded. "Nearest town's Russell Springs." He gestured toward the northwest. "County seat. Used to be the Eaton stop on the old Butterfield stage route. It's directly along the North Fork of the Smoky."

He looked over the troopers. They'd not likely be walking far. At least, not as far as Russell Springs—which is when he remembered Peggy. He slipped the cap out of his pocket, placed it on his head, and started walking, moving into a quickstep.

"Where you goin'?" one of the soldiers called out.

Matt didn't look back. "Be back directly. I gotta go fetch my wife."

"Wife?" the sergeant shouted.

She remembered her mother lying in that gray dress, the one she wore during the winter, arms folded across her chest, hair pinned back in that silver-streaked bun. Looking peaceful, beautiful. One never would have guessed how much pain she had endured before the consumption claimed her and sent her off to Glory. Father had let her lean over and kiss her mother good-bye. Then the preacher had nodded, they had closed the coffin, and taken Mother outside to be buried in the cemetery behind the First Congregational Church.

Until today, that had been the only dead person Peggy Browne Crabbe had ever seen.

She was a long, long way from the Wabash Valley.

She wouldn't get off the seat in the front of the market and pleasure wagon. Just sat nailed to that spot, wringing her hands, watching as the soldiers—and her husband—moved about the dead. Some of them had climbed into the back of the wagon, and she had heard her trunks scraping against the wood. It had made her skin crawl. She had watched them carry those trunks—with her clothes . . . her dowry . . . her books . . . everything she had to show for her twenty-two years—and place them behind one of those eerie white rocks that rose like tombstones in this bleak, foreign place.

She wanted to be back teaching children—even the wicked, wicked sons of Franklin and Maria Mitchell—in La Crosse. Wished she had never left Terre Haute.

Then they brought the dead, laying them beside the one she had seen. Some of the bodies seemed white as the chalk buttes and arches. Others black, bloated, hideous. Five men. No . . . five figures that once had been men. The soldiers did not even have the decency to cover the dead.

Yet it wasn't the bodies of the men that bothered her. It was the wind.

It just blew. Unrelentingly, it swept down from the north. The swallowtail flag one of the troopers had planted in the ground popped like firecrackers on the Fourth of July. The wind tugged at her dress, at her hair. She figured the bonnet she had bought in La Crosse was already all the way to Mexico. The wind peppered the back of her neck with grit and sand. And throughout the series of random out-croppings of rock—Monument Rocks, her husband had called them; another had said Pyramid Rocks—the wind moaned. Like the dead groaning. Like the earth ending.

Like her life ending.

She knew about wind. It blew in Terre Haute, and she vividly recalled trembling with her parents and three brothers when the tornadoes came through in those violent, stormy springs and summers. Yet the wind in Kansas was different. There wasn't a cloud in the sky, no threat of rain, just the wind, always blowing, always blowing.

"Miss Peggy . . ."

She saw her husband, that rough, uncouth man, looking up at her, his calloused hand on the edge of the seat. He still called her "Miss," even though they had been husband and wife for three days. *Miss Peggy*. She didn't know what she was supposed to call him, so she had decided not to say anything.

"We have to help these boys up to Russell Springs. A bit out of the way, but we have to help them. You see that, don't you, Miss Peggy?"

The wind blew.

She blinked. She did not even try to speak.

Her husband—what was his name?—turned, nodded to the sergeant with the bloody side. The sergeant said something, and the other soldiers re-acted. In horror, she watched—unable to voice any protest, not even able to lean over and vomit—as two men carried one of the dead soldiers around the wagon.

She felt the wagon dip and creak and heard the body of a dead Army officer—she had heard one of the soldiers say his name was Lieutenant Henderson—in the back of the wagon. Instead of hauling her life in trunks, they would be carrying corpses.

Instead of traveling in a market and pleasure wagon, she would be traveling in a hearse.

The wind moaned.

Two other soldiers picked up another dead man, one grabbing the man's boots, the other under-neath his shoulders. His long arms dragged across the dirt and remnants of grass.

She felt her heart twinge, and heard herself let out a little gasp when she saw the back of the man's head—or where the back of the man's head should have been.

Again, the wagon tilted. The corpse was laid down. She wondered if her husband would be able to scrape away all the blood. Once the bodies were gone.

The mules, she noticed, had no reaction to the dead men. Nobody even seemed sickened by the sight, by the fact that five men had been cut down.

The wind wailed.

She looked at the Indian. Two soldiers stood over him, guns pointed at his stomach, but the Indian boy looked as if he would soon be dead himself. She thought she might go over and help him, because the men who had doctored his badly wounded leg knew absolutely nothing about medicine. Maybe they didn't care.

He looked something like Rafe Mitchell, the most unruly of the Mitchell kids from La Crosse. Only darker. And skinnier.

*Yes,* she told herself, *I will go help that boy.* After all, she was a Christian. It was the Christian thing to do. Yes, she would help him.

Only she just couldn't get off the wagon. Couldn't let go of the seat.

If she did, she knew in all her heart that the wind would blow her away, and keep blowing her across Kansas, all the way to hell.

She watched as some soldiers carried another body to the back of her wagon. She closed her eyes. And felt the wind blow hard.

### Russell Springs

Take away the courthouse, and there wasn't much to Russell Springs.

The courthouse, a giant monstrosity of brick and stone, sat on the town square. The rest of the town seemed a hodgepodge of brick and stone, soddies, and cabins, even a handful of framed wooden buildings. Nothing looked permanent except the courthouse.

And the jail.

It stood behind the courthouse, tan stones, black bars, a giant red door, pitched roof, and a chimney off to the side. A white sign with black block letters spelling JAIL hung crooked over the door.

The county sheriff, a fat man named Barber, stood by the door, watching the troopers haul the dead bodies inside. On his head was a bowler, unusual for a sheriff.

Matt Crabbe stood beside the lawman and Sergeant O'Donnell, keeping his left hand clamped on his Irish cap to keep the wind from hauling it to the Netherlands. Every so often, he would shoot his wife a glance, making sure she hadn't moved.

Of course, she hadn't.

Hadn't moved . . . hadn't spoken . . . barely even breathed.

Well, he couldn't blame her. She was a schoolmarm from Indiana who had just seen what a .50-caliber repeating rifle could do to the human bodies.

When the dead soldiers were lying in one of the empty cells, two of the troopers came out to fetch the Indian and dragged him and his badly wounded leg into the jail.

"What'll happen to him?" Crabbe had to yell above the wind to be heard.

Sergeant O'Donnell shrugged.

Sheriff Barber sniffed and spit. "Hang, I reckon. Murdered five boys in blue."

Crabbe gestured toward the open door. "You don't fetch a doc to take that kid's leg off, you won't be hangin' 'im."

"Good." The sheriff grinned. Two of his front teeth had gold caps. "Save Logan County of the expense of a trial an' hangin'."

"Get a doctor." The words came from Sergeant O'Donnell with authority.

Barber sniffed again, sighed, and made his way to someone in the crowd that had gathered around the jail.

To Crabbe, it looked like half the town had come to see the show. Not that half the town of Russell Springs amounted to much. The sheriff said something to a black man in bib-and-brace overalls. He nodded and took off running, favoring his left leg. He disappeared around the courthouse, and Sheriff Barber returned.

"Sent the boy to see if Doc Kimball's in his office." The sheriff pointed at O'Donnell's side. "You wanna have 'im look at that wound of yourn?"

O'Donnell didn't answer him. He told his men to water their horses, grain them, and be prepared to ride out in two hours—those that had horses. The others would have to wait until the commanding officer at Fort Riley telegraphed other instructions.

*Lucky,* Matt Crabbe thought, *for the boys who would wait behind.* Unlike a lot of Kansas towns, Russell Springs still had a watering hole that served forty-rod and cheap beer. If Crabbe didn't have a new bride and a farm to plow, he would have joined them.

"Well," he said to no one in particular. "Reckon I should head for home."

No one said anything, and he returned to the wagon, put a new chaw of tobacco into his cheek, and climbed into the driver's box. He looked at his wife, tried to think of something to tell her, but couldn't. He reached for the brake, and found Sergeant O'Donnell standing at the side of the wagon.

"A marshal asked for this rifle, but he ain't here, and he didn't help us. You did." He held out that big rifle.

Crabbe reached for it, brought it to his lap. It was some gun, and even farmers needed something more than a shotgun out in western Kansas. The Spencer he had was showing its rust and shooting mighty loose lately.

"Only three rounds in the tube," O'Donnell said. "You might find a box in the mercantile here."

"Maybe." Crabbe hefted the rifle and turned to show it to his wife, but decided against that. He slipped it into the back of the wagon, leaned over, and shook the sergeant's hands. "Thanks."

"You earned it. Take it with the compliments of the United States Army."

# CHAPTER EIGHTEEN

*Wallace County*

Matt Crabbe pulled the lines, coaxed the mules to a stop, and set the brake on the wagon. "We're home, Miss Peggy," he told his new bride.

She merely blinked.

Well, *home* wasn't much to look at, Crabbe had to admit, but he had built the sod house shortly after filing his claim. Maybe that coyote that had bolted out of the door had frightened Miss Peggy. He would have to get that door fixed, so that the wind wouldn't blow it open, but, well, he had been gone for practically three weeks, getting married, carting Peggy all the way from La Crosse.

And that little fracas up at Monument Rocks had delayed them.

Actually, there had been two delays. First when he had joined the ruction and caught that Apache buck—which meant he'd had to haul the dead and wounded to Russell Springs. And second was their return to Monument Rocks to get all the luggage they'd left behind.

*Lucky,* he figured. Nobody had come along and made off with a right smart plunder. Yet his new wife hadn't seen things that way, on account that all she'd seen were the buzzards, coyotes, and wolves feasting on the dead Army horses.

She had just sat in the seat, hardly muttering a sound. Hadn't even offered to lift a hand to put those trunks and grips into the back of the market and pleasure wagon that had cost him a good month's wages. And some of those trunks weighed nigh a ton. That woman sure loved her books.

Crabbe dropped from the wagon, moved around the end, and came up on the other side, extending his arms, smiling his tobacco-flecked teeth, ready to help his wife down. Maybe he could even carry her over the threshold.

Or maybe not.

She just kept right on blinking, staring at him as if she didn't know him from Adam's housecat.

He lowered his arms. "Maybe . . . maybe I'll go check out our home. Make sure there's no varmints hidin' inside." After all, that coyote might have had some company.

He took the big Winchester with him. He hadn't bought any bullets in Russell Springs. He'd found the shells that tough, smart sergeant had told him about, the ones the Apache had left in the sand near a window in a chalk rock. Only six shells, but enough to make him feel a mite better. Besides, he had also gathered the empty brass casings, figuring he would buy some powder and lead at Sharon Springs next time he went to town and make his own ammunition.

Since the Army no longer manned Fort Wallace, folks would be apt to charge a small fortune for a box of Winchester shells in .50-100-450 caliber, and he had been making his own bullets, always reloading the empties, of his .50-.56 Spencer carbine for years.

Inside the soddy, he figured it might take awhile for Miss Peggy to adjust to her new home. Maybe once the odor of the dead skunk that coyote had killed and hauled back to a new den . . . well, once that stink had faded, Miss Peggy would feel a bit better, get back on her feet, and forget about those dead men she'd seen at Monument Rocks.

Best to leave the door open, air out their one-room home, he decided.

Crabbe walked back to the wagon. "Crick's just down the path yonder," he said, pointing. "This time of day, might be a deer or somethin' watering nearby." He patted the Winchester's stock. "I'll see iffen I can't scare us up something to eat. Antelope steaks sound good, Miss Peggy?"

Yeah, she was getting better. Her lips moved. She didn't say a thing, but she didn't blink, either.

*McCook, Nebraska*

Though a dozen years old, the town remained young, raw, and full of grit. It had been founded back in '82 once the Burlington & Quincy Railroad and the Lincoln Land Company reached an agreement to establish a railroad center. It made sense. McCook was roughly the halfway point between Omaha and Denver.

*Just like most railroad towns still sowing their oats*, Deputy U.S. Marshal Jimmy Mann thought. Riding down the main street, he kept studying every building, every face of every man who walked along one of the boardwalks. He held the Winchester, kept his thumb on the hammer.

A band practiced in one of the vacant lots. The leader, a man in a fine Panama hat and striped sack suit, kept stopping the assembly in mid-song, pointing out a mistake. Jimmy was no musician, couldn't carry a tune and could barely recognize a sour note, but he knew one thing—the band needed lots and lots of practice.

He rode a bit farther down the street, past the hotel, the bank, the land office, and a general store, until he came to the saloons, the gambling hall. Off beyond the privies and alleys, he could spy the cribs. That part of town he knew, even though he had never been in Nebraska, let alone McCook.

Immediately, he spotted a half-dozen horses hitched to the rail in front of the Platte River Saloon on the south side of the street and knew the cowboys drank there. Across the street stood the Lincoln Saloon. There were no horses, not even a hitching rail, and he knew that's where the railroaders got drunk. The massive, baldheaded man who came slamming through the batwing doors, spitting out blood and a few broken teeth onto the boardwalk kind of helped Jimmy make the determination. The man grabbed the wooden post out front to keep himself from falling into the mud.

Almost immediately, a man with red hair, a thick beard, and much smaller—though with arms as strong as two-by-fours—stepped through the still-swinging doors. He stopped on the boardwalk, spoke something in an Irish brogue, and waited for the bald man to turn around, wipe blood from his mouth, and bring up the fists. The redhead moved like a catamount.

Jimmy saw only the blur of the man's fists, the bald man's head snap back, and watched him stagger, grunt, curse, and fall into the mud.

The bald man did not move.

The redhead stepped to the edge of the board-walk, spit a glob of phlegm between the unconscious railroader's legs, and sucked on his skinned knuckles. Briefly, he looked up at Jimmy, dismissed him, and spun on his heels, pushing again through the batwing doors.

From inside came a cacophony of cheers.

The town founders had decided to name their new settlement after Union General Alexander McCook. He was one of the famed "Fighting Ohio McCooks." Apparently, the railroaders felt the need to live up to the reputation of the town's namesake.

Jimmy stared through the swinging doors and then turned to look across the street. Some tin-pin piano played inside the North Platte Saloon, sounding even worse than the band up the street. A few doors down, he spied another establishment.

## The Boiler Room

*A. J. Conrad*
LICENSED GAMBLER

It did not appear open, but it was still early in the day for gamblers.

He rode on a few doors past the gambling hall and swung out of the saddle. Looping the reins over the hitching rail, he walked inside the town marshal's office.

Marshal Cedric Hardesty was stunned by Jimmy's story. "Danny Waco?" The marshal whistled. "In Nebraska?"

Jimmy tested the coffee again. It tasted like gall, but it was hot and thick as tar. "He has been here before," he told the lawman, a pudgy fellow with spectacles, but his knuckles were crooked, his hands scarred, and his arms seemed as sturdy as railroad ties. "Killed that gambler in Omaha back in '88."

"Got acquitted," Hardesty reminded Jimmy.

"Yeah." The coffee went down slowly. *Acquitted.* That gambler had caught a .44-40 slug in his back, but he'd been wearing a revolver, had been accused of using a crooked faro box. That was enough for a jury of Union Pacific men to come in with a verdict of not guilty.

"Well." Hardesty tried his own coffee. He could drink the goo like water. "I wouldn't know Danny Waco if I saw him, but there haven't been any

strangers in town. Not that that would give me or
any of our businessmen reason to notice, that is."

"You'd notice Danny Waco," Jimmy said, "even if
you didn't recognize his face."

The lawman's head nodded in agreement. "You
sure he's in Nebraska?"

Jimmy wasn't sure of anything, but he said, "I
think so." Well, it was the only lead he had. The
trouble, of course, was that Nebraska was a mighty
big state.

"He'd be looking to gamble, to drink. Maybe
find a chippie. Somewhere the law wouldn't mind
an outlaw, as long as the outlaw didn't cause any
trouble."

Again, Hardesty nodded. "That's McCook. Least,
that's my philosophy when it comes to keeping the
peace."

Jimmy knew that to be the case in McCook.
Some lawmen would have broken up that fight at
the Lincoln Saloon.

"But Danny Waco is not here," Hardesty said.

Jimmy stared at the lawman, waiting.

"Because anywhere Danny Waco goes, he causes
trouble. And I like this job, this town."

That made sense. Jimmy nodded. Another trail
had gone cold. He could move from hell-on-wheels
to cow town to gambling den to those hog ranches
that sprang up in every parasite village near every
Army post. He could look forever, and never find
Danny Waco.

"If I were you," Hardesty said, "I'd ride up to

Ogallala. If Danny Waco's in Nebraska, that's where he'd wind up."

### Wallace County, Kansas

"When spring comes, the country really greens up," Crabbe told Peggy. *When the rains come, when we have a good winter. However, when there's a drought . . .* He figured it would be better not to mention those possibilities.

Peggy smiled.

Crabbe let out a breath. He knew she had forced that smile, had strained at the effort, but it was something, and it pleased him. "You get some wild-flowers, too." Suddenly, he was excited, seeing possibilities with his new bride. Maybe she was coming around, leaving the shock at what had happened at Monument Rocks behind her. "Not roses. Not tulips. Nothing like that, but . . . I dunno . . . it sometimes gets so colorful, reminds me of my ma's patchwork quilt."

Peggy's smile didn't seem quite so labored. "Why, husband, you are a regular poet."

He almost blushed, then wanted to take her in his arms, but the smile vanished, and she grabbed her sides, squeezing herself, suddenly shivering.

"Is it always . . . this . . . windy?"

*Windy? Child, you ain't seen wind till you've been here in March or April. And God help us when the thunderstorms hit in late spring and all through summer. Tornadoes . . . well . . .*

He turned to block the wind, watching a giant

tumbleweed roll across what was supposed to be
their front lawn. "Tumbleweeds." He spat. "Time
was when you never saw 'em things in the West.
Now a body can hardly go nowhere and not run
'cross . . ." Another spit. "Russian thistle. Wished
they'd strung up the rogue who planted 'em first
bushes."

He remembered her question, and turned to
face her again. "Might be a norther. Probably is one
blowin' in." He gestured at the open doorway.
"Might want to step inside. I'll get a fire goin'." He
looked back at the skies, darkening in the west.
"Could be a blue norther."

Tentatively, he put his arm over her shoulder,
feeling her flinch, and eased her around, guiding
her like a frightened child into the sod house.

He left her in the chair he had fashioned, which
he knew wasn't sturdy, handsome or relatively comfortable, but served its purpose. He quickly had a
fire going in the fireplace. She sat, staring at the
flames, listening to the wind howling.

"Be back in"—he shrugged, estimating—"maybe
an hour." He pointed at the trunk full of books.
"Pass the time some. Read one of your favorites."
Crabbe knelt on the dirt floor, opened the lid, and
pulled out the first book he found. He hoped it was
one by that Austen gal Miss Peggy so admired, but
he had no way of telling.

She took the book, gave him another weak smile,
and then set the book in her lap and rocked some
more.

A few moments later, Crabbe walked into the

wind, gripping the Winchester '86 in both hands. He didn't like the look of that sky, darkening in the northwest. Tried to remember what month it was, but he had never been good at such things. Out in western Kansas, months didn't really matter, anyway. He had sweated in November and had come close to freezing to death in June. The only thing constant, he knew, was the wind.

He pulled his hat down tightly and checked on the mules he had stuck in the corral. Both had turned their backs to the biting wind. His fingers already ached, even though he had pulled on gloves the minute he'd stepped out of the soddy. He heard the door to the potato cellar slamming. Another chore he would have to get around to at some point. But first . . .

He headed toward the creek, hoping he could find an antelope or something that would provide meat. But the way this norther was blowing in, he doubted if he would even find a frog to shoot at.

# CHAPTER NINETEEN

She hated it here. Despised the cold. Loathed this home of dirt. Detested that uncouth man she had married. Abhorred this frontier called Kansas. Reviled herself, her weakness, and her stupidity that had brought her into this marriage, and into this filthy place. She could not bear that everlasting wind.

Peggy Crabbe could get away from neither the wind nor the dirt. The wind blew always. Dirt came through the cracks in the door. Once, while she lay in bed, it sifted from the roof, and fell onto her. Not much, really, but it felt like an avalanche. She had awakened screaming, thinking the entire place was caving in on her, for she had read about the awful cave-ins at the mines in the West, and even in the East. Her husband, that fool Matt Crabbe, had come to her, tried to reason with her, and finally had slapped her—which had silenced her screams.

"Nothin' to worry 'bout," the cad she had married told her.

More dirt sifted from the roof, fell to the quilt her grandmother had made. She couldn't see the designs anymore, could only see the dirt.

"Might be a deer." Crabbe spoke with excitement, and he left her sitting upright in her bed— *her* bed—for her husband had been sleeping on his bedroll across the room. He grabbed that giant rifle he kept leaning by the front door.

*Front* door?

*Only* door. And it wasn't much of a door. No lock. Simply a latchstring he would pull in of nights.

He stepped through the door, which slammed shut behind him, then opened, then shut, then opened . . . the wind stirring up the dirt that had piled on the floor. The floor . . . of dirt. When the door flew back open, and held for a moment by a wild gust of wind, she saw the grayness swallow him.

The door slammed again, and she bolted out of the bed, grabbed the string, holding it, like she was a cowboy holding onto a rope. Pulling hard, she refused to let go, refused to let the wind blow open the door . . . again.

She breathed in dust and cold and the wretched odor of whatever he had cooked for their supper. The grayness had swallowed him. He had disappeared in the dirt and the tumbleweeds that blew across their home. If the wind had blown him away, out of her life, she would be free. Free to leave this awful place.

The door pulled open, and since she was pulling

on the latchstring, she fell backward as her husband stepped inside.

"What the Sam Hill is you doin'?" he called out, closing the door behind him and setting the bar in place. But the wind still rattled the door. It would rattle all night, and probably all the next day.

It would rattle for all of eternity.

"No deer." He sighed. "Think it was a coyot'. Nah. Too big for a coyot'. Wolf, most like." He leaned the rifle against the door, took a cautious step toward her, and then extended his hand. "You fall or somethin', Miss Peggy?"

She nodded.

"Hurt?"

Her head shook. She stared at his hand, rough, calloused, the first joint of his ring finger missing. She couldn't remember how he had lost it—shot off, cut off, or seared off with a lariat. She imagined it as a snake, the fingers fangs ready to strike her, release its venom into her veins. She suddenly thought that would not be so bad at all. She would have to wake up in a better place than this.

She took his hand, but sensed no sharp bite of fangs, only a rough grip that squeezed and pulled, and she felt herself lifted from the floor.

"Sure you ain't hurt?" her husband asked.

"I'm . . . fine." She began brushing the dirt off the skirt of her nightshirt. Dirt. Dirt. Dirt. Everywhere. She couldn't escape it.

Her husband moved to the uneven table, sat down, began pulling off his boots.

She kept at the skirt, watching the dirt and dust fall, beating the fabric . . . beating it and beating it. . . .

"Best stop that," her husband said.

She obeyed, looked at him. Even his face looked like a serpent. His eyes sparkling hypnotically like that rattlesnake that had bitten ten-year-old Marilyn Summers last spring during recess. Her thoughts drifted off to that time, what felt like a thousand years ago, in a place so far, far away.

It had snowed two days earlier. She remembered that. Could not believe that a snake would be out of hibernation, even though it had been warm for about a week before the cold front moved in. Had it been windy then? She couldn't remember. In fact, it amazed her that she could even remember La Crosse, let alone Marilyn Summers, who died.

Died.

Died.

*Peggy was grading papers when the other children came in screaming that Marilyn had gotten snakebit. At first, she thought those little pests were playing some prank, but all the girls were crying, and even the Dille boys' faces had turned pale as ghosts. She raced outside and found the girl crying and running around the swing, holding her arm that was already swelling.*

*"Where is the snake?" Peggy asked.*

*The kids pointed in different directions, but it did not matter. They never found the snake. It had struck, slithered*

*away, maybe even under the schoolhouse, and never
returned. Maybe it was the devil.*

*She got Marilyn to sit on the steps and wrapped her
scarf around the bite, two holes, two ugly holes, leaking
blood.*

*"His eyes . . ." Marilyn cried. "They just locked on me.
I . . . I . . . I couldn't . . . move."*

*Of course, she knew that the girl must have moved. She
had tripped and fallen while playing a child's game, and
the snake had coiled less than a foot from where she had
hit the ground. She had looked up, seen the snake, and the
rattler had struck.*

*Nobody thought Marilyn would die.*

*"My dog got bit three times," Mike Dille bragged, "and
he ain't dead."*

*"He didn't even cry," Mitch Dille sniggered.*

*Even Marilyn's father didn't think his daughter would
die. But she did.*


"That snake . . ." Peggy still heard that poor girl's
wail. "He was like the devil."

Suddenly, she was back from La Crosse, and
again inside this perdition that her husband called
a home. She watched him stoking the fire, bringing
it back to life, busying himself to heat up yesterday's
leftover coffee and corn pone. *Another great breakfast.* Coffee thick as tar, and no honey for the crumbling bread that tasted as if he had used more salt
than cornmeal.

*That snake . . . he was like the devil.*

Peggy stared straight ahead and knew that she

had made a horrible mistake. This home was under the earth. Well, practically. No other person lived anywhere close. Her husband's eyes were like diamonds, like the rattlesnake's. They had mesmerized her, tricked her. His hands . . . not hands. Cloven hoofs. So were his feet. She could really see . . . now that he had removed his boots. His socks were so filthy and full of holes . . . yes, she could see that his feet were likewise cloven hoofs. Why, she could see the tail, the horns, and the pointed ears. She looked at the rifle, but it was no rifle. It was a pitchfork.

Matt Crabbe was the devil. He was after her soul.

"You hungry?" he asked. "Sun'll be up in a half hour. Might as well start our day."

*Start our day.* Another day . . . that lasted an eternity. Another day of wind and dirt. Another day in hell. "I'm not hungry," she managed to say.

"Got to eat." He slid the coffee pot onto the grate over the hot coals in the fireplace.

A kitchen. Without an oven.

A home. Without a window.

A husband. Without a soul.

She moved to the table, sat down.

He did not put the bread into the Dutch oven, just pushed the awful stuff into a skillet and set it on the grate next to the pot. "I'll fix you somethin' then I gots to find us some game. That norther left a coat of ice an inch or two thick outside, but I warrant I should find some buck near 'bouts." He gestured at the pitchfork, which had transformed again into that hideous rifle.

Somehow, she managed to eat, and even wash down the horrible bread with black coffee. She wondered if Lucifer were trying to poison her.

He reached over with his hoof-hands and patted her hand that lay flat on the table by her plate. "I know it's tough. Takes some gettin' used to. But this is gonna be a good place for us. Got water. Good farmland, I'm thinkin'. Don't look like much right now, but it will. We won't always be livin' in this soddy. Don't you fret none 'bout that. Just got to clear the field first, plant some crops, get us some money. And I'm thinkin' that I might could set some traps along that creek. Sell us some skins in town. No, Miss Peggy, by the time our kids are maybe seven, eight years old, we'll have us a fine, fine place. Neighbors'll look on us with envy. Me especially." The diamonds in his eyes winked. "On account that I got the prettiest wife in western Kansas."

She stared at him, could not think of anything to say, and slid her hand from underneath his scratchy hoof, and picked up the coffee. She drank, smiling pleasantly at him, trying to think, trying to form a plan.

*How do you kill the devil?*

*How do you kill a snake?*

"Well." Lucifer drained his coffee and pulled on his boots. He pulled on his Mackinaw, tossed a bandolier of ammunition over his shoulder, grabbed his hat, setting it atop his head, and picked up the pitchfork-rifle. "I'll be back in a few hours."

He opened the door, letting the coming light

brighten their home enough so she could see the dust mites. She could feel the wind, but managed to follow her husband, the devil, outside. She clutched the neck of her nightshirt. It was cold, so cold, and the country was no longer the color of dead grass—beige, brown, ugly. It was white.

Her husband slipped a few times, then grabbed a stick from the woodpile to help him with his balance. He trotted off to the south, but stopped at the edge of the lean-to, and looked back. "You might want to chop up some wood. Stack it inside, in case we get another wet storm. Winter's comin'. Right soon, feels like. I'll be back, Miss Peggy. You just get settled in our home."

She nodded and he was gone. She looked at the woodpile, at the axe underneath the lean-to, its blade buried deep in the chunk of wood. *Wood.* There wasn't much, just some dry wood her husband, that devil, had scrounged up around the creek. Even that chunk he had brought from La Crosse. You could hardly find a tree in this country, so mostly what they burned in what passed for a fireplace was dung. Dried dung.

The devil was gone.

The idea struck her, and she hurried back inside, leaving the door open, pulling off her nightshirt, dressing quickly in warmer clothes. She picked up her stockings that she had worn yesterday, pulled them on, thought it would take forever to button up her shoes. The scarf went around her neck, and she raced outside, again leaving the door open.

Immediately, she slipped on the ice, falling, hitting the ground hard.

She felt like a total idiot. Pain raced up her arm, where her elbow had struck, and she figured the bruises were already forming on her thigh. She pushed herself up, shook her head, and saw her steamy breath. The sun was up, slowly rising, a white globe that seemed to slow, but not stop, the wind.

Tentatively, she rose and gingerly picked a path toward the lean-to. She did not care about the woodpile, about chopping up kindling. The bucket next to the fireplace in that awful home of dirt was full of dung. Antelope droppings. Mule waste. Even ancient discharges of buffalo, practically gone from Kansas for a decade. What fascinated her was the ax.

It took her five minutes to free it from that old chunk. "Bury the blade deep in the trunk," her husband, Lucifer, had told her earlier. "Keeps the blade free of rust, sharper, too." She didn't know if she believed that or not, but her husband, the devil, had certainly sunk that blade in deeply. As blisters formed on her fingers, she wondered if she would manage to free the ax.

A trick. Her husband, Satan himself, had fooled her. Tried to exhaust her so she would not be able to put up a fight when he came home this evening to take her soul.

At last, the blade pulled free, and she raised the ax. Heavy. She wanted to rub her finger over its edge, to test its sharpness, but she feared the ax. It looked like a snake's fang. Impossible. But . . .

It did not matter. She had the ax. She knew what she must do.

How do you kill the devil? The same way, she had decided, as you kill a rattlesnake.

You chop off its head.

# CHAPTER TWENTY

*Ogallala, Nebraska*

Danny Waco remembered those good old days—wild and raucous, with cheap booze, cheaper women, and stupid cowboys who expected to be cheated in the gambling dens and promptly were by shady card sharps and crooked roulette rigs. Ogallala sure hadn't changed much with the times, and to him, Tonkawa Tom and Gil Millican, that was a good thing. Oh, the town had grown some, and progress had reached parts of it, but River Street remained a fine place for debauchery. Ogallala seemed just as lawless as it had been back when it was nothing more than a hell-on-wheels along the Union Pacific line. The Pony Express had come through first, then the railroad, but Ogallala's claim to fame came as a cattle town, one that some say rivaled Dodge City. It had catered to cattlemen ever since the burg had been plotted, official-like, back in '75. Plotted, yeah, but nobody had ever gotten around to incorporating it.

The Great Western Trail came through there, bringing cattlemen, cowboys, and longhorn beef to stock the ranges in Wyoming, Montana, the Dakotas, and even a few in the rolling hills of western Nebraska's boot heel. Stupid Texas waddies came in and got drunk, and often got killed. Boot Hill, for the longest while the only cemetery in town, had more than a hundred graves. When you realized that the town's population seldom topped more than one-twenty-five, that was saying a lot.

It brought in the likes of Luke Short, a gunman mighty handy with cards, and Sam Bass, an outlaw who'd met his maker down in Texas in the late '70s. And on a clear autumn day of blue skies, a modest wind, and temperatures in the fifties, it brought in Danny Waco.

For three days, Waco had enjoyed all the comforts of Nebraska. He had settled into a high-stakes poker game for some more comfort. What he didn't realize was how fate would soon make Ogallala uncomfortable.

Though the Texas cattle trade wasn't as prominent as it had been before that Texas fever outbreak back in '84—which led to Nebraska banning Texas cattle and ending the trail-herd business— Ogallala hadn't finished sowing her oats.

The stores stood along Railroad Avenue, south of the UP rails. River Street, where the cowboys had raised Cain back in the '70s and '80s, ran south of the rails just above the South Platte River.

The town jail, the lone stone structure along Railroad Avenue's false-fronted frame buildings, sat empty, and the lawdog minded his own affairs. He didn't care what happened in the saloons, gambling dens, and brothels, as long as no one disturbed the business section or made fools out of themselves by the railroad depot where people might see them and get the wrong idea about Ogallala, Nebraska. Nor could anyone cause a ruction and disturb anyone eating at the Ogallala House, because S.S. Gast, the owner, didn't want anyone spoiling his supper or unnerving his chef.

Danny Waco had no plans of disturbing any peace, unless the dealer at the poker table inside the Cowboys Rest riled him. Gil Millican stood with his boot on the brass foot rail at the bar, working on his sixth beer of the day. Some hurdy-gurdy gal stood beside him. A handful of other men lined the bar, and two more card games were being played.

Waco studied his hand. Two jacks, two queens, and the ten of hearts. He checked.

The man in the derby who kept sucking his teeth checked as well.

The skinflint beside him tossed in his cards and swore. "It ain't even good enough to check with." He reached for his flask. Man was even too cheap to buy whiskey.

The lady gambler bet fifty. The dealer, a gent with a crooked nose and brown bowler, matched the bet, and it was back to Danny Waco . . . who saw their fifty and raised a hundred.

"Checking and raising," said the dealer, "can get a man killed."

"So can a crooked nose, bowler hat, and big mouth," Waco said.

The gambler's face turned ashen. The lady gambler laughed softly, but was already reaching for her chips.

She was all right. Waco decided that he would hate taking all her money.

The teeth sucker folded, saying, as every fool seemed to say, "Too rich for me."

The skinflint, who had already folded, pushed his chair back. and stood. "I'm callin' it quits, friends."

Waco watched him weave through the batwing doors.

The lady gambler saw Waco's hundred and raised again. The dealer folded.

Waco wondered about her. Red hair. Green eyes. Not pretty, but not like that soiled dove who was still pestering Gil Millican. Without looking at his cards, Waco called the lady's bet.

The dealer asked, "How many?"

Waco took one. A five of clubs. No help. But two pair, especially jacks and queens, still proved to be a powerful hand.

The lady said, "I'm good."

"I expect you are," Waco said, grinning and watching her reaction.

She had none.

*Straight? Flush? Nah.* Waco figured her to be bluffing. A good bluff, too. He looked at the stack of

cash, coin, chips, and the skinflint's pocket watch.
He had made up his mind to call and raise her two
hundred, let her sweat that one out, when Tonkawa
Tom pushed through the batwing doors and made
a beeline for Waco's poker table.

Jimmy Mann crossed the bridge over the South
Platte River, barely pausing to look at the saloons,
gambling dens, and brothels that still lined River
Street. Late in the year, and late in the life of the
once wild and woolly cow town, there weren't as
many saloons, gambling dens, and brothels, and
certainly not as many horses tethered to the hitching rails out front as in the past. He followed
Spruce Street over the rails, past the depot, and to
Railroad Avenue, where he found the jail and the
marshal's office.

Inside, he found a deputy who sent him to the
Platte House.

The lawman, a short, squat man named Munroe
was eating an early supper. Jimmy introduced himself. The lawman motioned at the empty chair
across from his ham and biscuits, and Jimmy slid
out the chair and sat down, resting the battered old
Winchester on the tabletop.

Munroe stared at the carbine, pulled out the
napkin he had stuck in the neck of his shirt, and
dabbed the gravy off his mustache. The napkin
dropped onto the table. He pushed back his chair
and sized up Jimmy Mann. "What brings a deputy

United States marshal to this part of the world?" He reached for his coffee cup.

Jimmy was aware that everyone in the dining room had stopped eating. He couldn't hear a knife scraping a plate or anyone slurping coffee. Outside, through the big window, he saw people walking down the boardwalk, a freight wagon rumbling down Railroad Avenue. Inside, they stared. That Winchester had gotten their attention.

"Danny Waco," Jimmy answered in a bare whisper.

Munroe left the coffee cup on the table. His hand disappeared. "You sure?"

Jimmy's head shook. "It's a guess." He knew not to waste time asking the town marshal if he had seen him. Munroe's reaction had already told him the answer. His paling face also told Jimmy there was no need in asking for assistance in arresting Waco, if Waco were indeed hanging his hat in Ogallala.

"So . . . knowing what you know about Danny Waco . . . where would I look?" Jimmy figured the lawman would have read all those articles in the *National Police Gazette*, whatever the Ogallala newspaper called itself, and the wanted posters . . . maybe even the two Beadle & Adams dime novels that glorified the outlaw the way they made heroes out of Jesse James, Sam Bass and Billy the Kid.

Munroe found enough strength to grab his coffee cup and drank some. Probably would have preferred whiskey. Inhaled deeply, blew it out, and motioned with a tilt of his head. "River Street."

"Any place in particular?"

"This town used to bring in floaters from all over, but they'd go back to Omaha or Cheyenne, Deadwood or Denver City once the cow business ended. Come back in late spring, early summer. Wouldn't be but one saloon open in December."

Jimmy waited impatiently. He didn't care one whit about a lecture on *The History of Ogallala, Nebraska*. He repeated the question.

Munroe shrugged. "Would Waco want to get drunk or get . . . ?" He looked over his shoulder, and let the sentence die.

"Whiskey," Jimmy answered. "Poker. And a woman."

"The Cowboys Rest," Munroe answered.

"It still around?" Jimmy had heard of it, mostly from older lawmen talking about the wild old days ten to twenty years back.

"More or less," Munroe said. "Ol' Tuck sold out after the herds stopped coming in, but the place hasn't changed much. Quieter, maybe, but there's still loose women, roulette wheels, poker tables, and plenty of John Barleycorn. Local cowboys come in, mostly. Most of them don't even carry revolvers."

Danny Waco would. Jimmy knew that. He thanked the lawman, grabbed his Winchester, and stood.

"Marshal?"

Jimmy waited.

After clearing his throat, Munroe said, "Our jail was built back in '75. Stone building. Folks called it 'the most substantial jail west of Omaha.' It wasn't, of course. And it sure isn't strong enough to hold a man like Danny Waco."

Jimmy nodded. "It won't have to," he said, his voice cold, emotionless. "Boot Hill will hold Danny Waco. I aim to kill him."

Waco always sat facing the door. That's one reason he had lived so long. He held up on raising the lady gambler and let Tonkawa Tom make his way to the poker table. The barkeep and a few others frowned at the sight of an Indian, even a half-breed, in the Cowboys Rest, but none had enough guts to say or do anything about it.

The Tonk knelt at the table on Waco's left and whispered, "Lawman just met with town law. Wears badge like Parker's deputies."

Waco grinned at the patient lady gambler. "And his horse?"

"Been on the trail long time."

"Now what would a deputy from Arkansas and the Indian Territory be doin' this far north?"

"Didn't ask. But he carried a carbine. On his lap. Not in scabbard. Him ready. Him lookin' for somebody. Me guess . . . you be who he after."

Shaking his head, Waco sighed. "A body can't get no rest no more, seems like." Well, he could wait. Nothing like a good gun fracas to get one's blood a-boiling.

On the other hand, there was a time and a place to fight, and Ogallala, Nebraska, wasn't it. The way

Danny Waco figured things, it would take the lawdog from Indian Territory an hour or two to round up enough brave, law-abiding citizens to cross the railroad tracks and walk down Railroad Street to chase out or kill that undesired element. Best thing to do, then, would be to light out right away, move north and follow the North Platte and the old Oregon Trail northwest, then turn north toward the Black Hills.

Maybe a body could find a good card game and no persnickety lawdogs in a place like Deadwood up in Dakota Territory. No, it was *South Dakota* these days. A regular state. More progress. That was the problem with the West—not enough frontier left anymore for an owlhoot to get any rest.

"Where are our horses?" Waco asked.

"Outside."

"Fetch Millican from that hussy. Tell him we're leavin'."

With a nod, The Tonk rose, and crossed the room toward the bar.

Waco smiled at the lady gambler. He hated doing it, but he moved his hand from his winnings, and laid his cards on the table. "I always hate foldin' a winnin' hand, little lady, but I am a gentleman and decided to let you bluff me." He started to rake his winnings into his hat.

The woman—he wished he could remember her name—shook her head at Waco's high two pair and laid her own cards on the table as she swept the pot in front of her. She didn't have to show her cards.

Waco knew that. She was classy, this dame, and he would have enjoyed getting to know her better. A lot better than that strumpet who had been trying to woo Gil Millican into spending an extra dollar or two on her.

"It wasn't a bluff, Mister Waco."

He stopped and stared. Not only did she know his name, she knew how to play good poker. It was a good thing Tonkawa Tom had come in with that news. Else Waco would have lost a whole lot more money.

The lady had a full house. Aces over eights. Not the Dead Man's Hand—that was two pair, which would have also beaten Waco's cards—but a sure-fire winner.

"Maybe I'll see you down the road." He went to the bar to cash out any chips he had. And to have a shot of rye for the long trail north. "And have some better luck."

"Maybe."

When he had his money stuffed inside his jacket pocket and the thickening money belt he wore under his shirt, Waco stepped onto the boardwalk. Millican and The Tonk were already in the saddle.

"We runnin'?" Millican seemed a bit testy since Waco had interrupted that budding romance.

"Nope," Waco lied. "Playin' the odds is all. Three days is long enough in one town. I hear Deadwood callin' our names, boys."

That made both of them smile.

Waco loosened the reins, but said before he started to climb into the saddle, "Let's get us a little grubstake out of that little ol' bank up in Chadron."

Their smiles widened.

And quickly faded when a voice called out, "Hold it, Waco. Move and you're dead!"

# CHAPTER TWENTY-ONE

Jimmy Mann understood, and immediately regretted, his mistake. He ducked as all three outlaws palmed their six-shooters and cut loose.

Give a man like Danny Waco a chance, and you might get killed. Jimmy knew better. He should have just drawn a bead on Waco's back and pulled the Winchester's trigger. Then maybe the other two vermin might have given up. If not, by the time the shock had worn off from seeing their leader shot dead, Jimmy could have dropped both Millican and the Indian from their saddles.

As soon as he'd shouted the warning, Jimmy moved, ducking and dropping behind the abandoned frame building that once had likely been a saloon.

Two bullets tore into the dust of the street behind him. A third shot blew out a chunk of rotting wood. A couple other rounds hit the boardwalk. Jimmy's Winchester roared.

The deafening sound of gunfire caused Waco's

big horse to back away, jerking the reins from the outlaw's grip.

The Tonk wheeled his horse around, and bolted down the street, toward the river.

*Smart man.* Jimmy would give Tonkawa Tom that much credit. His loyalty was to himself. It wasn't his job to save his pard's life.

Millican's horse began rearing in the street, but Gil Millican was game enough not to drop his revolver and start pulling leather to keep from being bucked off. He even managed to loosen a bullet, but it went high, not close to Jimmy's position.

Moving the barrel, Jimmy tried to find Waco in his sights, but that horse kept getting in his way. The Tonk was gone. Shouts came from all directions. One idiot even came through the doors of his shop across the street, saw the smoke, the panicking horses, and then stupidly ran to his windows, trying to close the shutters to protect the glass.

Jimmy aimed, fired, and saw splinters fly from the column that held up the awning to the Cowboys Rest. Waco ducked. His horse skedaddled, taking off down the street, not toward the river, but toward town proper. Cursing, he fired twice from the hip as he ran, making a beeline for the nearest side street.

Jimmy braced the carbine against the wall below where a bullet had torn out a good-sized piece of plank, but before he squeezed the trigger, Millican managed another shot. That one proved a whole lot closer than his others.

In retaliation, Jimmy jerked the trigger, but

missed. He turned away, pulling the Winchester with him and jacking another cartridge into the chamber. He quickly turned back and put a bullet through the crown of Millican's hat. The gunman had regained some control of his mount, spurred the horse hard, and took off. Not even stopping, barely slowing, he helped Danny Waco swing up behind him. They disappeared around the side of a brothel. Jimmy could see the upstairs curtains moving, and could make out the distorted figures of painted ladies staring at the ruction on the streets below.

He imagined what they were saying. *"Haven't seen nothin' like this since eighty-four or eighty-five."* *"Ain't nobody dead yet. So we ain't lost no customers."*

He cocked the Winchester and turned to his own horse, which he had tethered to a rain barrel. It was nervous, eyes wild. Sure wasn't Old Buck, but it could run. Jimmy grabbed the reins, leaped into the saddle, and sent the horse into a lope. Rounding the corner, he put the reins in his mouth and charged after Danny Waco and Gil Millican.

It surprised him that none of the outlaws went south, toward the South Platte and the bridge over the river. They had turned north, even The Tonk. Jimmy didn't think they were setting him up for any ambush, but going north meant they would either have to cross the North Platte or ride alongside it. Not that the river ever held much water. Or was deep. But crossing any stream or river would slow them down, and riding midstream offered no protection, no place to hide.

He saw the dust, dug the spurs in deeper, felt the horse find even more speed. Generally, a man did not shoot from a moving horse expecting to hit anything, but Jimmy let another .44-40 slug fly. As he left Ogallala proper, he saw Millican and Waco galloping past the hill northwest of town.

He pulled the trigger, and the horse carrying the two outlaws went down hard.

Millican flew over the horse's neck as it fell, and Waco dropped to the side and rolled over. He came up firing from the supine position. Two shots. Both wide.

*How many rounds had Waco fired?* Jimmy shook his head. It didn't matter. He grabbed the reins from his teeth, pulled hard, slowing down his mount and leaping from the saddle even before the horse had stopped. Somehow, he landed on his feet, jacked the lever, fired as he ran, and then dived into the ditch.

Waco was running up the hill. Too fast. Jimmy realized the man was running up some sort of steps.

Millican had rolled over and was on his knees. His hat was gone, and he spat something that looked like blood. Jimmy fired. So did the outlaw as he dived behind the dead horse. His hand reached for the scabbard.

Jimmy started to fire, but a bullet dug into the sod next to him. Waco had found a spot up the hill to shoot from. Jimmy flattened himself in the ditch, moving forward a few rods. He knew getting caught underneath another man's gun—even a six-shooter—was not favorable. He came up just in time to see Millican running up those steps, carrying a repeating rifle.

Something squeaked. Shut. Squeaked. Shut. Squeaked. Shut.

He wanted to fire, but Millican shot with his revolver as he scrambled up those steps. A moment passed, and he was gone. Up the hill. With a carbine or rifle.

Jimmy moved as fast as he could through the ditch, keeping his eyes open, watching as he scooted through the tall grass lining the hillside. It was dead, yet waving in the wind. Soon he detected the steps, and looking up toward the top of the hill saw a picket fence and gate that the wind kept blowing open.

He felt a chill race up his spine and remembered his mama's old superstition she'd always say whenever he shivered for no reason. *"Someone just stepped on your grave, Jimmy."*

He tried to spit—not enough saliva in his mouth—and moved up the hill, near the steps but not on them. The wood and stone might give him some cover. Keeping the rifle trained up the hill, he moved slowly, carefully. He covered the last few feet in a lunge, and leaned against the fence, the gate next to him opening and closing, banging, fraying his nerves.

Peering through the broken fence, he saw plenty more dead grass, some cactus, and a few shrubs. Mostly he saw the markers, wooden crosses and wooden slabs, faded with time. There were no fresh mounds. Not yet. By tomorrow, he realized, it might change.

Again, he thought *Someone just stepped on your grave, Jimmy.*

He moved through the gate, rifle ready, and sank into the grass, flattening himself, bringing the stock against his shoulder, his finger on the trigger. He chanced a look up at the nearest tombstone. The words were faded, but he could make them out.

### RATTLESNAKE ED

KILLED BY
LANK KEYES

1884

He was in Boot Hill. Maybe for all of eternity.

"Give me that Winchester!" Danny Waco jerked the rifle from Gil Millican's hand before he had even finished issuing his order. He looked at the gate to the cemetery, and shoved his own revolver into the holster. He pointed with his head, but never took his eyes off the fence. "Get on the other side of this boneyard. We'll cut that Johnny Law down when he comes over the fence."

"How about the gate?" Millican asked.

"He ain't that dumb. He figures we'd expect him to come right through that gate. Do that, and we'd fill him with lead." Waco laughed and brought his arm up to wipe his nose, leaking blood from the horse wreck. "Move!" he snapped, and heard foot-steps as Millican rushed, hunched over, through the old, pretty much abandoned cemetery.

The wind kept banging that gate. Annoying, it was, but Waco had learned to block out such noises. He looked off in the direction of town, figuring the law would come up somewhere on that side. But where?

The wind blew the gate open again, and he saw the flash, the cloth, the sudden movement, and he turned, coming up, leveling the rifle, but that marshal from Judge Parker's court had dived and landed beside an old tombstone.

Waco cursed and flattened against the grass.

This lawman would be someone to play poker against. Made the predictable seem unpredictable. Might have seen Waco, so he crawled through the grass, over one or two graves, and came to one of someone with a bit of class or at least some money. That body's kinfolk or friends had erected a little fence around his grave. Of course, weeds had over-taken it, and the whitewash had been blasted away by wind, snow, and rain.

Waco glanced off to his left. Gil Millican had found a spot along the last row of dead men.

*Where in blazes had The Tonk gone? Gutless wonder.* Waco cursed and spit. No better than those fool, loudmouth kids they'd gotten to go along on that Katy job. He should have remembered what his pa had told him all those long years ago. Don't trust no Indian. And trust a half-breed even less.

Gently, Waco eased himself up, resting the rifle between the pickets of the fence around the grave. He noticed for the first time the size of the grave. Too small to be a full-grown man. Must have been some kid. He aimed in the general direction of where he believed that law to be hiding. Then the heat of a bullet practically seared him as it roared past his face, blowing off the pointed end of the old one-by-two-inch picket.

Cursing, screaming, Waco fell backward, the rifle spinning up and over, landing in the grass.

He recovered quickly, rolled over, grabbed the rifle, and scurried along the graves through the tall grass, over one grave with the cross lying on its side—no name, and the date too weathered to make out anymore—to a marker that was nothing more than a slab of wood. No name, no date, nothing likely ever had been written on it, probably because the poor fool was unknown and unclaimed.

Waco rose and yelled, "Go get him, Gil!" He pumped three quick shots across the boneyard and ducked, laughing to himself as he heard Millican cutting loose with something that might have been a Johnny Reb yell, firing his revolver as he ran.

A rifle roared, and Waco came to his knees, firing, cocking, cocking, firing, then moving over three or four graves, aiming at the smoke from that law's long gun.

Millican had emptied his Smith & Wesson, and he found another tombstone to hide behind while he reloaded. Waco aimed, waiting for the lawdog to show his head, if he wasn't already barking at the devil, dead from one of Waco's bullets. Suddenly, a figure appeared on the far edge of the grave. Too far away to be the law—unless he was a ghost. Waco turned his barrel and almost pulled the trigger before he understood exactly who it was standing there.

The Winchester's barrel felt scalding hot as Jimmy quickly fed shells from his gun belt into the carbine's loading gate. He felt around the belt. Ten more cartridges. Plus the six he had in his Colt, still holstered. *Stop wasting lead,* he told himself. *You know better than that.*

The way he figured it, Waco was off on the town side of Boot Hill, and Millican about even with the gate, maybe twenty yards in front of him. He rolled onto his belly, took a deep breath, and moved up a few feet.

"You loaded?" Waco's voice calling out to Millican.

"Yeah? You?"

"To the brim. Charge that gent, Gil. We'll get him this time. The town laws will be here shortly."

Jimmy came up, saw Millican running. Almost immediately, he caught something out of the corner of his eye and turned just as Tonkawa Tom pulled the trigger on a single-shot rifle.

Waco laughed as the lawman went flying backward, his carbine's stock going the other way, and the rest of the Winchester flying over Millican's head.

That half-breed had come through. But Waco figured any praise would have to wait. "Come on, boys!" he yelled. "Leave the law for the buzzards, and let's get out of here."

They were all running. Couldn't wait around to check to see if that lawman was dead or merely dazed. Ogallala's finest would be coming to help that marshal. Waco hurdled the fence, then tripped, tumbling down the hill, but never letting go of his rifle. He came up and saw Tonkawa Tom already on the road.

*Now there is a good man,* Waco figured. Good ol' Tonk had even fetched the lawdog's horse. Waco also saw something else. Men. Most of them on horses, not riding hard, but coming toward Boot Hill. The town law. And some were armed for bear.

He looked up and found Millican running through the gate and down the steps.

"Posse come." The Tonk was already in his saddle.

"I know."

"Didn't know your horse dead."

Millican reached them, slid to a stop, turned, and aimed his Smith & Wesson at the gate . . . waiting for that marshal, who might or might not be dead.

"Must ride double," The Tonk said. "Till find another horse."

Waco knew that would just slow them down. With a posse on their tail.

Millican had the reins to the lawman's horse.

"Let's go," Tonkawa Tom urged.

Waco hated to do it, but, well, he didn't want his neck stretched. Hated it. But not that much. He raised the rifle and blew Tonkawa Tom out of the saddle.

# CHAPTER TWENTY-TWO

*Wallace County, Kansas*

The days never changed. Dreary. Cold, Always growing more frigid. The nights stretched on for an eternity. Breakfast was always some gruel or nothing more than black coffee. Because fresh game proved scarce, salt pork usually wound up on the plate for supper.

The wind always blew.

Peggy Crabbe had grown to accept this as the wind blew out October and November roared into the treeless plains of western Kansas. Each morning she awoke to find the cot on the floor where her husband spent each night empty and Matt Crabbe gone. She made her breakfast, swept the dirt and dust out of the sod house, and went about her day—feeding the mules, breaking up the ice out of the trough so they could drink, preparing supper. She had forgotten all about ever eating a noon dinner or having tea . . . the thought of having tea made her laugh.

She never expected her husband, Old Beelzebub, to return, but late each afternoon, she heard the mules snorting, and knew the Devil had made it back to Hades. He always returned with the pitchfork, which he made her believe was a rifle, and he hypnotized her into thinking that his hands and feet were those of humans, that his ears were not pointy, and that his eyes were not soulless.

Peggy knew better, though.

Sometimes her husband, the Devil, brought home scrawny jackrabbits for supper. Other times, he would leave the pitchfork-rifle in the soddy, and take a shotgun with him, returning with a pheasant or some other birds—Peggy did not want to know what they had been—and she would fry those up in a skillet and serve with a thick gravy she had learned how to make that was stout enough to fill their stomachs more than the thin, greasy meat of the fowls. She had even grown accustomed to spitting out the birdshot that wound up in her teeth.

Other times, her husband, Lucifer in disguise, returned home with nothing.

On those evenings, even he sat at the table, head hung down, and sang out in despair. "God as my witness, Miss Peggy, I didn't know things would be this rough. I thought—still think, mind you—that this is a good place for a homestead, but . . . but . . . but . . . well, I jus' don't know where all the game's got to. We got water. And it ain't like this place coulda been hunted out afore we settled here. It's jus' . . . well . . . it's peculiar. I even tried fishin' in the crick, but"—he let out a long, weary sigh—"nary a bite. At least we got us salt pork."

*Not tonight,* she thought as she ladled a thick mess of gruel and gravy into his bowl.

"I just can't figure this out. Bad run of luck." His head shook again. "It's like—"

"We are cursed," she finished for him.

He laid his spoon on the table and studied her, long, thoughtfully. "I—" He never could find the words. "Don't reckon I'd say that."

*Of course not,* she knew. Because he was cursed. Cursed to rule in Hades. Tossed out of Heaven. Because he was Satan. Maybe she would find her courage, and God would give her the strength, and she could chop off the head of this serpent.

But, it wouldn't be that night. She knew it when she pulled up the covers and heard the Devil snoring on his cot by the door. She was too tired. It proved hard to keep up one's strength with the slop they had been eating for two weeks. If Matt Crabbe were not Lucifer, he would have given up, taken her back to La Crosse. By Jehovah, she would have settled to be back at Monument Rocks, looking at the bloated bodies of horses and soldiers.

She tried to say a prayer, but could not remember any. Another trick of her husband, she knew. Corrupting her mind. Blinding her. Stealing her memories.

The wind howled. She could see the dust already

forming under the bottom of the door. She could hear something banging outside, while her husband, the Devil, snored, oblivious to everything going on outside.

The quilts and blankets could not warm her, no more than the fire. Old Beelzebub had banked it before he had lain down on the floor and quickly fallen to sleep.

Briefly, she looked at the books she had left on the bed. The Bible. Charles Dickens. But she did not feel like reading. Not that night. She was too tired and needed her strength. Tomorrow, she knew, would be the day she would kill the Devil.

### Ogallala, Nebraska

Marshal Theodore Munroe and his posse of stalwart, brave, God-fearing citizens stopped to stare at the body of the dead half-breed.

Shirley Sweet shook her head in disgust and tossed her Remington Rolling Block rifle to the haberdasher named Belton. Lifting her skirt, she hurried up the steps, went through the gate, and found the young, bearded deputy U.S. marshal on his knees behind a wooden grave marker he had knocked over. The tombstone was broken. The man who wore the six-pointed star wasn't in much better condition.

He kept shaking his hands, trying to make the feeling return, sending streams of blood onto the dead grass, weeds, and sunken grave.

Turning, Shirley took a few steps back toward

the gate, staring down the steps. Marshal Munroe and others were pointing down the road at the fading dust left by Danny Waco and his one surviving partner. None of the posse seemed interested in the cemetery, although a few had walked around the dead man to look at the dead horse.

*The day had been going pretty good,* Shirley thought. She had bested that murdering outlaw in a poker game, had a good stake already, and Colonel Tom C. Curtis had not even arrived in Ogallala with the rest of his Wild West Show.

*Wild West Show?* No, Curtis's was not anything like Buffalo Bill Cody's or Pawnee Bill's. It was more like a dog-and-pony show, but Shirley Sweet was Curtis's star attraction, a sharpshooting wonder. Munroe and a couple men had come into the saloon—conveniently a few minutes after Waco had left and gunfire had erupted on the streets of Ogallala. The marshal had asked for a posse, anyone in the saloon who could help them. The only volunteer in The Cowboys Rest had been Shirley Sweet.

Munroe and the others did not like that one bit, but when Shirley had produced the handsome Remington Hepburn, no one had the guts to stop her.

A single shot, the Rolling Block was a No. 3 Sporting Model, firing .38-55 Winchester from a 30-inch barrel. She rarely missed, even figured she could give Annie Oakley a run for her money. Of course, hitching her career to a confidence man like Colonel Tom C. Curtis, she knew there was a fat chance of that ever happening.

Belton stared at it stupidly, like he had never held a gun before. Probably hadn't, but gave him credit. Haberdasher or not, he had joined the posse. No one in the saloon had.

"Hey!" she shouted, and everyone looked up. "That lawman's up here. Hurt, but he'll live. I could use a hand."

Men in the posse looked at each other, but no one moved. Shirley Sweet gave up and returned to the lawman.

"Where's my rifle?" he asked when she knelt beside him.

She had spotted part of it—the stock—on the main path when she had entered Boot Hill.

"I need my rifle," he repeated.

"Not anymore." She ripped a piece off her skirt, and grabbed the man's left hand. The cuts on that palm seemed deeper than the cuts on his right. He did not resist, and she wrapped the cloth over his hand, securing it tightly.

"Huh?"

She let his left hand drop, and reached for his right, noticing how he touched the center of his chest—right on the breastbone. She saw the hole in his shirt. "You're lucky," she told him as she began to wrap his right hand.

He blinked. "How's that?"

"Way I figure it, one of those gunmen shot you. Only the bullet—had to be from a rifle, a powerful one." She kept on talking as she worked on his right hand. "Bullet hit your rifle, which you must have been holding right next to your chest. Probably hit the stock, right above the lever. Blew your rifle apart." Her head tilted. "I saw the stock laying over yonder. Reckon you'll find the rest of your gun"—her head tilted the other way—"over there somewhere."

She tied off the ripped piece of skirt. "Bullet popped you in the chest. Dead center. Lucky. But it was spent by that time. Might have just been a fragment of the bullet. By all rights, you should be dead. I reckon that rifle you were shooting saved your life."

He blinked. Reasoning and sanity seemed to be returning. He looked at his hands. Blood already seeped through both of her bindings.

"You're like a cat, I reckon," Shirley Sweet told him.

Somehow, he managed to laugh. "Nine lives?"

She smiled at him. "Something like that."

"Well." He sighed. "Reckon I just used up Number Nine."

"Then don't get caught under Danny Waco's gun sights again."

His head lifted, and he stared at her hard. "What's your name?"

Shirley smiled. "I thought you Westerners frowned upon such things as asking a body his or her name."

"My name's Jimmy Mann," he told her. "Sorry for being forward. Deputy marshal out of Fort Smith."

"You're a long way from home."

"I got my reasons."

Yeah. She knew his reason. Danny Waco. Probably personal, not legal.

"I'm Shirley Sweet. Originally from Zanesville, Ohio."

"You're a long way from home, too."

She shook her head, laughing without humor. "I haven't had a home since I was fourteen years old. How's that you put it out here, 'I live where I hang my hat'?"

He looked up at her. "You're not wearing a hat."

"'Cause I hung it here. In the hotel. For now."

For the past eight years, since Colonel Tom C. Curtis had found her shooting squirrels for the Zanesville Café, she had lived in hotels, but only when Curtis was flush. Mostly, they slept in the wagon yards or under the wagons when they couldn't afford what a wagon yard charged.

The Colonel Tom C. Curtis Wild West Extravaganza Featuring Shirley Sweet, the Sharpshooting Wonder of the World included four wagons; one bear with only three teeth left; an Italian who passed himself off as a great Sioux warrior; a Texas roper who, Shirley had to admit, was pretty handy with a lariat, as long as he laid off the hooch; a twelve-year-old runaway who could blow a trumpet; Colonel Tom C. Curtis, whose only dealings with the military came when he slicked soldiers in his shell games; and Shirley Sweet, twenty-two-year-old dead shoot . . . and not a bad poker player.

The Colonel had sent her ahead, instructing her to get the lay of the land at Ogallala and maybe win some money at the card tables, while the rest of the

Extravaganza waited for him to finish his thirty days in jail in North Platte, Nebraska.

Served Curtis right. Shirley had warned him against running his con games or trying to set up the show in North Platte. That was Buffalo Bill Cody's stamping grounds, and Cody was friend to everyone—excepting, naturally, a money-grubbing fraud like Tom C. Curtis who cheated, swindled, disavowed every Code of the West, and competed with Buffalo Bill for a buck.

"You know a lot about guns," Deputy U.S. Marshal Jimmy Mann was telling her, "for a . . ."

She waited. He didn't finish. A good thing, she figured, though she was really used to such comments.

"Sorry," he said.

That surprised her. She smiled, and pointed at the Colt in his holster. "I take it you're handy with guns, too."

He looked at the revolver. "Not so much with short guns."

She laughed. "Me, neither. Never even fired a six-shooter. Just rifles and shotguns."

He looked at his bandaged hands, back at the holstered Colt, then at her. "I got to go after him." He started to rise, only to fall against her shoulder.

She caught him as she heard the gate to the cemetery opening. At least one of the posse members had found his courage.

She eased Jimmy back up, waited for him to regain his balance and the dizziness to pass, and then released her hold. "Honey, you ain't going nowhere—especially not after a man like Danny Waco. You can't even hold a gun. Not it them hands. And you won't be holding one for a spell."

Frowning, Jimmy Mann looked at his hands.

Marshal Munroe squatted beside them, his knees popping, and his lungs working hard from all the exertion of walking up those stairs to the cemetery. He had come into Boot Hill alone, leaving the six other men from town to gawk at the dead man, the dead horse, and watch Danny Waco and his pard get farther and farther away. Shirley figured they were already out of Munroe's jurisdiction. The newspaper would probably write that Munroe had run Danny Waco out of Ogallala.

"You got one of them, Mann," Munroe said.

The deputy marshal stared, not comprehending. "What are you talking about?"

# CHAPTER TWENTY-THREE

*You got one of them.*

The marshal's words ran through Jimmy Mann's head again. *Got one?* Jimmy had not killed The Tonk. The half-breed had been shot dead by his pard, his boss—the man whose life he had saved.

Jimmy nodded. That had to be how things had played out—which meant Danny Waco had only Gil Millican riding with him.

For now.

As Shirley Sweet stepped into the hotel room with a platter of food and coffee, Jimmy stared at his heavily bandaged hands.

*For now.*

### Wallace County, Kansas

On that November morning, Peggy Crabbe woke to find the pitchfork leaning against the dirt wall. Satan himself had left it there before daybreak.

He'd walked out of the soddy wearing his winter coat and carrying the shotgun.

Cold and tired, she sat up in her bed, watching the dirt tumble down the quilt and fall to the floor. The door pattered with the howling wind, and, despite the fire burning—the Devil, always adept at building fires, must have stoked it before he left— she saw her breath. The temperature must have dropped forty degrees since yesterday, and it had been cold yesterday.

Funny, she never thought hell would be so cold.

When she found enough resolve to face another lifeless day, she pushed off the dirty quilt, swung her feet to the cold dirt floor, and looked again at the pitchfork. It had turned again into the rifle, that big Winchester that fired those big cartridges.

For one moment, as she made herself stand, made herself walk to the fireplace where the coffeepot rested on a hearthstone, Peggy Crabbe had a lucid moment. She even felt sane. And she thought, *Could I take that rifle, put the barrel under my chin, and somehow pull the trigger?*

It sounded so easy, but she knew she would never have the courage to do such a thing. Not yet anyway. Not until she killed Satan.

*With*—the thought made her stop as she bent down to pick up the coffeepot. *Kill the Devil with his own pitchfork.*

When she straightened, she looked at the rifle, which again had become a pitchfork. The tines beckoned her like a finger, coaxing. She could even hear the angel's voice, telling her how easy it is to kill Lucifer, to save the world, to save all of those souls—even her own—simply by killing this evil, evil monster. It would be so easy. So simple. And then, as the extreme sacrifice, once the Devil was dead, once she had shot him and cut off his head, she could sacrifice herself. Put the rifle barrel under her chin, lean back, reach down, and push down on the trigger.

And walk the Streets of Gold.

It felt heavy. Weighed much more than she had expected. She lifted the Winchester '86, surprised at how cold the barrel felt. Even in the freezing soddy, the rifle was cold. Being the pitchfork of the Devil, Peggy had expected it to be hot to the touch. Even the walnut stock and forestock chilled her.

She moved back to the bed, sat on it, resting the Winchester on her lap. Her fingers slipped inside the lever, and she tried slowly to move the lever, yet found she lacked the strength. She pulled her hand out of the lever, gripped it with her fingers, and jerked the lever away from her. Even that was difficult, but she heard the clicks, heard the demons screaming, and felt something pop against her.

The big .50-caliber cartridge lay between her legs, and she picked it up—the brass also felt frigid—studied it, then let it fall onto the dirt at her feet.

Pushing the lever down felt much, much easier. When the lever lay back in its normal position, all the screaming stopped. She looked at the gun, brown and black and gold. And silver. The firing pin, or whatever it was, waiting for the cocked hammer to strike.

It had no smell, this rifle, this pitchfork. This tool of Satan. She let go of it, and looked at it, marveling at it. Outside, the wind howled. Inside, the fire crackled. She examined the fireplace, feeling the shroud of coldness blanket her until she shivered. She knew. She should go to the fireplace, stoke it, toss on some of the logs the Devil had left to keep her warm. Yet that was just a trick of his. To make her leave the pitchfork, his tool, on the bed. Then he could return, and take the rifle. Use it to kill her. To take her soul.

She would not give him the chance, and in an hour or so, the fire died.

Crabbe had warned her. Told her she must never let the fire go out. Said something about a hard winter coming, a big freeze—early, but deadly—and one did not want to let the sod house get cold. That, he had told her, was how folks died. Died . . . froze to death . . . in their own homes, even though a soddy could be downright comfortable in the hardest of winters, and cool in the hottest of summers.

She did not believe him, of course. She had not been comfortable since she had left La Crosse.

Peggy remained on the bed. She forgot about the fire, forgot about the freezing temperature. She looked at the pitchfork in her lap, watched it change again into a Winchester. When she touched it again, it no longer felt cold.

The hammer remained cocked. She saw the

scars on the wood, the big dent in the walnut just underneath the rear sight, the smudges and finger-prints on the iron, steel, whatever they made guns out of.

Her right hand fell onto the stock, moved for-ward, and her fingers slid inside the guard, her thumb found the hammer. Her left hand found the forestock, and she tried to lift the rifle.

The Devil was strong. Fighting her. Making it hard to raise the Winchester, but she had the Lord on her side, and the strength of the Apostles, of John the Baptist, of the saints, and even the sinners who wanted to escape from purgatory, from perdi-tion, from all the levels of hell. The rifle came up, shaking, but up.

Pressing her left elbow against her chest, she managed to keep the Winchester balanced, level—more or less—and she slipped the stock against her right shoulder.

Outside, the wind blew.

The demons howled.

Dirt fell onto her hair from the roof, onto the unmade bed she sat on. The door rattled. She could not hear the mules but knew they must be moaning, kicking impatiently, waiting for her to break the ice in the trough so they could drink, waiting for her to feed them.

*Feed them?* When the mules ate better than she did?

The candles her husband, Lucifer, had lighted before he had left that morning, had blown out, or gone out, and the soddy turned dark. She could see only the light of day shining through the cracks in the door, the cracks in the ceiling, the holes in the wall.

For all of eternity, Peggy waited. She refused to obey the demons screaming at her to put the rifle against her head, to end her own life. She refused to go to sleep, to answer nature's call, even to throw the quilt over her shoulders.

She sat on the bed, kept the rifle pointed at the creaking, moving door, and waited. Her fingers grew numb, the rifle seemed to add weight, but all of that merely made her focus her resolve. She knew what she had to do, and knew that great would be her reward in heaven.

Sometime later—how much later she could not fathom—she heard Lucifer's return. He cursed over the wind. Stamped his boots. Yelled at her. Asked if she were all right. She saw the door moving, a movement that could not be caused by the wind, and Peggy Crabbe pulled the trigger.

The report deafened her, like all the souls trapped in the hereafter screaming, and she had not prepared herself for the Winchester's kick. That crescent-shaped stock seemed to break her shoulder in two, and as she fell backward, her hand slipped from the lever, and the barrel came up, slamming hard against her face. The sight ripped into the bridge of her nose, and she felt the cartilage give way—then she was somersaulting over the bed.

Something slammed against what passed as a bedpost. The rifle. Or was it a pitchfork again?

Peggy didn't know, but she no longer held the Winchester. She landed on the sod floor and felt more dust fall into her eyes. Her nose was busted. A knot formed on her forehead. Her shoulder throbbed. Her fingers on her right hand ached. Her wrist felt as though someone had tried to rip off her hand.

Peggy tasted blood.

She smelled the brimstone of Hades.

And outside, she heard the Devil's curses.

She had not killed him after all. Lucifer would surely kill her.


A patch of ice saved Matt Crabbe from getting his head blown off. Trying to force open the door to the sod house, he slipped—just as a bullet blew a hole through the wooden door and warmed his right ear—and landed hard on the frozen ground.

His ears rang. He rolled over, cursing, coming up, and pressing his back against the sod wall. Both legs and his left elbow ached. He grabbed the shotgun and pulled it close.

From inside their home, the big Winchester '86 roared again, and another chunk of wood flew a good rod from the soddy before disappearing in the snow.

He knew it was his rifle—well, the rifle the soldier boys had given him. He cursed himself for leaving it behind. He should not have brought the shotgun, but, by jacks, he hadn't thought some scoundrel would go into his home.

Then . . . the thought struck him. What had that ruffian done with Miss Peggy?

"Who are you?" he yelled. "What've you done with my wife?"

No answer.

He feared for his bride, maybe trapped inside with some scalawag. Maybe . . . maybe . . . He shuddered at the thought.

"I got a shotgun, a rifle, and two Colt's revolvers!" he lied. "And if you don't haul your sorry carcass out of my home, I'm gonna kill you deader than a doorknob."

He came up, moving toward the door, thumbing back both barrels on the shotgun. Silently, he cursed his luck. He had loaded the shotgun with birdshot. Strong enough to bring down quail, maybe a duck or two—if he had found them.

Crabbe thought of something else. When he had left that morning before daylight, it was cold. It had not warmed any. The clouds had continued to dump snow and ice for three or four hours, and the temperature continued to plummet. He had acted like some greenhorn settler, not considering a winter storm. Had not prepared for this, though his Mackinaw and gloves kept frostbite at bay. For now. But not for much longer.

If he did not get inside that cabin, he was dead. "You best come out of there!" he yelled.

A few moments later, the wind died down and the ringing left his ears just long enough for him to hear "Go away."

That was no scoundrel. No thief or vagabond.

"Please . . . go . . . away."

He mouthed her name. *Peggy*. It was his wife who had fired two shots through the door. He yelled, "Miss Peggy . . . it's me . . . your . . . husband!" He breathed hard, seeing his icy breath.

"No," she called out. "You're the devil!"

For weeks, Crabbe had tried to convince himself that Peggy was fine. Newlywed jitters and all. Nothing to worry about. She'd been through a lot, after what had happened at Monument Rocks. But she would bounce right back. She had to. Those faraway looks in her eyes, the vacant stares, and the crazy-woman talk was nothing. She was a schoolteacher, by grab, and . . . and . . . and . . .

He cursed himself for a fool.

"Miss Peggy," he called out. "It's me, Matt." He set the shotgun down, stock in the small snowdrift next to the soddy, barrel leaning against the frozen wall. He inched his way to the door, took in a deep breath, and pushed it open. "It's me. See."

He saw all right. He saw the Winchester aimed, saw his wife holding the big rifle, and he swore he even saw the muzzle flash. She was bleeding. Her nose busted. He saw that, too, and felt the bullet rip between his right arm and his side. The kick of the big gun knocked her backward. He saw all that while he cursed and jumped to the side, slipping again in the snow. His head hit hard, but luckily the snow pile was softer.

*She's tryin' to kill me.*

He came up, shaking out the cobwebs, refusing to believe the thought that flashed through his mind. Pulled himself up to his knees, moving with the wind, feeling the snow on his back and neck.

Inside, he saw his wife, saw her on her knees. Fear masked his face. His throat contracted.

She had the Winchester butted on the sod floor, had the barrel under her chin, and she was reaching for the trigger.

Matt Crabbe came up. He wanted to yell, but didn't have the voice or the courage. He moved through the doorway and leaped over the end of his wife's bed. His outstretched right hand grabbed the Winchester's burning hot barrel just as the rifle boomed again, and he landed on the floor, hand burning, and pain shooting through his shoulder. He couldn't hear anything but the ringing in his ears that felt as if it would never cease. He smelled the gun smoke, the urine, and the foul odor of this ugly, horrible home he had built for his wife.

He cursed himself for stupidity. He had brought her, the woman he loved, to this hellhole. He had driven her mad.

And maybe, he thought, as he lifted himself up, he had damned himself for all of eternity.

Maybe, he had driven sweet Miss Peggy into taking her own life.

# Chapter Twenty-four

*Ogallala, Nebraska*

Bundled up against the cold, Shirley Sweet stood at the Union Pacific depot when the westbound pulled into town. As was his style, Colonel Tom C. Curtis stepped off the train, bowing as he removed his oversized Stetson—and the wig almost came off with it—with those extravagantly beaded gloves.

Shirley was already smiling, but she was thinking, *How did I ever manage to hitch my future to this scalawag and fraud?*

Marshal Theodore Munroe was also at the depot, and he intercepted the good colonel before Shirley Sweet had a chance to move. "You can put that hat back on, Mr. Curtis, because you won't have time to hang it in Ogallala."

"Why, my good man—" Curtis began in his booming voice.

"You're not 'good-manning' me, Curtis. You're

not kissing any babies. You're not running out of any hotel leaving a bill it would take me four months to pay off. And you sure aren't setting up your stupid show in my town." Munroe reached into his pocket. "I even bought you a ticket. West. Get back on board, Curtis." He shoved the ticket into the colonel's big hat still in the faker's hand and stepped back. He opened his black coat, revealing the big Schofield in its holster.

*Of course,* Shirley thought, *the good marshal didn't act this brave when Danny Waco was in town.*

The engine hissed, squeaked, and belched smoke while porters helped arriving passengers with their grips and trunks. Loved ones greeted each other. Others bid friends and family farewell.

When the commotion diminished, and carriages and farm wagons took passengers to hotels, homes, or saloons, Colonel Tom C. Curtis finally found his voice. It went from thunderous orator to demurred jailbird. "Is it all right, Marshal . . . if I have a few words with my associate yonder?"

Munroe chanced a look at Shirley. His face registered surprise.

"You know this fool, Miss Sweet?" the lawman asked.

"Unfortunately," she said.

Munroe shook his head. "Train leaves in fifteen minutes, Curtis. If you're not on it, twenty minutes from now you'll wish you were." The lawman walked away, but did manage to tip his hat as he passed her.

"How was the jail in North Platte?" Shirley asked Curtis as he dragged his feet, defeated, in her direction.

He pasted on that fake smile of his underneath a walrus mustache. The mustache was real. The goatee was glued on. "I have struck worse. And I have spent time in better. How things been here?"

She shrugged. He would ask her for money. Yeah, she knew Tom C. Curtis better than the quirks of her firearms.

But the faux colonel studied the ticket. "This'll get me to Julesburg, Colorado." He sounded disappointed.

"Did you expect the marshal to splurge and send you to San Francisco?"

Sticking the ticket in his coat pocket, and putting the hat back atop his wigged head, he shook his head in disgust. "You do enjoy your jokes at my expense, don't you?"

"At my expense," she corrected. "When's the last time you paid me one quarter of that thousand-a-month you promised me eight years ago?"

"Well . . ." He turned, looking past the depot at the gray sky and the rolling plains that stretched along the South Platte River. "Julesburg."

"Want to set up there?" Shirley asked.

"Nah. We were there three years back. Remember?"

Of course she remembered. It was mighty hard to forget that tar and those feathers. A couple patches on her thighs still bore scars.

"Besides," the colonel said, "I've got us booked up around Fort Meade. Thought we might winter there."

"Where's Meade?" Shirley asked.

"South Dakota."

"Winter . . . in South Dakota?"

"Deadwood ain't far from there." He faced her again. "How's your poker and faro?"

She had to laugh, shaking her head. "Where are the boys?"

"On their way with the wagons. Had to sell one of them. To pay the fine."

"Had to sell a wagon? Or one of the boys?"

"Don't be smart. They should be here in a few days. Providing that the weather holds." Curtis stamped his feet, then looked at her with those boyish, pleading, Mama-loving eyes. "You want to buy a ticket? Come with me to Julesburg?"

Her head shook. "I think I'd better stay here. So the boys will know where to go. We'll meet you at Meade."

"Town's called Sturgis. Used to be known as Scooptown, because folks scooped up their pay from the fort. This winter, we'll scoop up a ton of money." He said it as if he truly believed it, causing Shirley to shake her head in wonder. "Reckon I'll see you there."

"Safe travels," she told him. "Don't get tarred and feathered . . . again."

Curtis shook his head. "I bet that blowhard of a

lawman sent me there a-purpose. Knowed what they done to me back in '91."

She kept quiet. *Me?* They had tarred and feathered the whole troupe.

He started back toward the train, even made it a good rod, before he stopped, turned, and came back to her. "You wouldn't happen to have . . . say . . . twenty dollars or so I could borrow, would you, Shirley?"

### Wallace County, Kansas

She came to her knees, smelling the pungent odor of sulfur, thinking she was in hell, and raced through the open door. Once she stepped outside for the first time that day, the bitter cold snapped her thinking, and she slipped on that icy spot, falling to her knees, landing in the snow.

"Miss Peggy!" a voice called, and she recognized it as that of her husband.

She pushed herself up, staring at the whiteness, the purity of heaven, and the tears began to fall, burning her cheeks. "My God. My God . . . my God . . . my God . . ."

Peggy shook her head, heard the snow crunching and the heaving of a man's lungs, and smelled that sour odor of Matt Crabbe. He sank beside her in the snow.

She looked up at the heavens, feeling the snow stinging her face, and then felt her husband grab her, pull her to her feet. "I must have lost my mind," she said, bawling on his shoulder.

Odd. She no longer minded his smell, or the cold, or that dark hole in the earth that they had called their home.

"It's all right, Miss Peggy." He spoke in a quiet whisper. His hands, rough, callused, but certainly not cloven hoofs, felt gentle. She cried even harder.

She had tried to murder her husband.

She had tried to kill herself.

Somehow, she had even thought that this gentle, kind man was Satan, that he had tried to lead her to the eternal pit.

It wasn't his fault that their homestead had failed. What had she done to help? Sit in bed? Read Jane Austen or Honoré de Balzac? Mope around the place? Pity herself?

Yet her husband was telling her, "It's my fault, Miss Peggy. I knowed how you was feelin'. Knowed you didn't like it here. When I couldn't find no game, nothin' fit to eat, I shoulda packed us all up and left this awful place."

Peggy made herself move off her husband's shoulder. She didn't feel cold, though it had to be pushing single digits out there. A mule snorted, and she laughed. He was probably cursing her. She hadn't fed them, and they had not had any water. Wiping her nose, she looked into her husband's eyes. They were so gentle. Full of love.

For her.

"You probably want to have our marriage annulled," she told him. "I wouldn't blame you. Being married to a lunatic."

"You don't say that, Miss Peggy . . ." he told

her, speaking forcefully. "Don't say that at all, Miss Peggy."

Her smile grew, and she put her hands on his broad shoulders. "Not Miss. Please . . . call me Peggy."

She kissed Matt Crabbe. She knew she had made the right choice in picking her husband. They would leave this place, this pit of despair, and they would try to start over. If that proved possible, if her mind recovered, if her husband did not abandon her as he should. But he wouldn't. Matt Crabbe would start over, too. Most likely, he would leave that awful rifle behind.

She had almost killed him with that Winchester. Had almost killed herself. Let it rot. Let it be buried in the soddy that had, for a while at least . . . along with that wind that didn't seem to be blowing so bitterly hard anymore . . . driven her insane.

### Ogallala, Nebraska
### Winter 1894

The doc, a portly man with a patch over his left eye and a wicked-looking scar that ran crookedly from the bottom of that brown leather oval all the way to his chin, managed to pluck the stitches from both of Jimmy Mann's hands. Didn't even hurt too much.

By December, Jimmy was sick of Ogallala, sick of Nebraska, sick of the cold, sick of just about everything—except Shirley Sweet.

Doc Gurney was one thing, but Shirley made a

mighty fine nurse. She had sent the rest of her Wild West show northwest to Fort Meade, giving the boys and a decrepit old bear instructions to tell Colonel Curtis that she'd be there when she felt like it. And she had nursed Jimmy back to health.

A few days after the solstice, the skies cleared and morning dawned cold but passable. She took him to the outskirts of town and set empty whiskey bottles on posts. "Reckon you can shoot?"

Jimmy looked at the scars on his hands, flexed his fingers. The left hand remained numb, without any feeling. Doc Gurney had said he'd likely never have much feeling in that hand, but he wasn't crippled. Jimmy didn't mind the severed nerves. In fact, he kind of liked that lack of feeling. It matched the rest of his mood. "Let's see."

She went to one of her long trunks in the back of the livery wagon they'd rented and opened it. Out came a Winchester in practically mint condition. "Here."

When Jimmy took the rifle she offered, he smelled the oil, the grease. Doubted if the weapon had ever been fired more than a handful of times. He studied the rifle, instantly feeling the pain, the sadness, and wished the rest of his body could be like his left hand, without any feeling.

"It's an '86," he told Shirley.

"Uh-huh," she said as she brought out her Rolling Block. "Short rifle. Twenty-four-inch barrel. Shoots .45-70 gov'ment." She opened the grip she had also brought, tossing him a box of shells.

He caught the cartridge box in his right hand,

rested them on the gate of the wagon, and looked again at the rifle.

The stock was walnut with a satin finish, deep grains, gorgeous, a work of art—like Shirley Sweet. The grip was straight, the crescent butt plate steel. He knew the front sight, its brass bead made by Marble Arms, and he pushed up the rear sight.

"Lot of gun," he said, his words ringing hollow. He saw his brother, lying dead in an express car in the Cherokee Nation. He saw his nephew at home in Texas, waiting for the present Jimmy had promised him.

He dammed those feelings, opened the box, and withdrew a long cartridge, which he fed through the loading gate. In an easy motion, he jacked the round into the chamber, brought the weapon up, bracing the butt against his shoulder. Sighting on the farthest bottle, he pulled the trigger.

"Jiminy!" Shirley blinked away her surprise. "You don't waste no time now, do you?"

Smelling the pungent odor of gun smoke, he cocked the rifle, lowered the hammer, sat on the wagon, and began feeding eight shells into the Winchester. When that was done, he levered the carbine, lowered the hammer again, and put in a ninth shell.

"This is just target shootin', honey," Shirley said.

He didn't listen. Nine shots later, he reloaded the Winchester and walked to those posts, taking with him a sack of whiskey and beer bottles. He moved with a purpose, brushing off the busted glass, replacing the targets—Jimmy had not missed one—and returning to the wagon.

The horse snorted, uneasy, unnerved by the gunfire, but the brake was set, and Jimmy had placed rocks in front of the wheels as added insurance to keep the rented livery Percheron from running back to town.

"Do I get to shoot?" Shirley asked.

He shrugged. "Go ahead." He sat again on the wagon, staring at his hands.

"They hurt any?" she asked him.

Jimmy shook his head. His shoulder didn't hurt, either, and it had been a long time since he had fired a rifle.

"I got three Winchesters, this Rolling Block, a Savage, two shotguns, and a Creedmoor," Shirley told him. "But I shoot targets."

She aimed, fired, and busted the top off one bottle. Reloaded. Shot again, hitting the glass again, but not dead center. Just nicking off another chunk of glass. Three shots later, there wasn't enough to shoot at.

"That's what folks pay to see," she told him, walking to the wagon. Sitting next to him, she brought out some cleaning supplies and began working on the target rifle. "Small caliber, I can do them kinds of things."

"Usually, I don't shoot at bottles."

"Yeah." She slammed an oily batch down the barrel with a ramrod. "Your targets shoot back. That's how come you got laid up these past few weeks with them ripped up hands of yours."

"You've been a good friend," he told her, adding, "Shirley."

"Got a soft spot for untamed souls and fools."

"Which am I?"

She smiled and fished a fresh cartridge from her vest pocket. "I ain't rightly sure."

"Danny Waco killed my brother." He hadn't told her that, merely that he was a lawman chasing a train robber. Jimmy wasn't even sure he had meant to tell her, but the words had shot from his mouth, and he couldn't take them back. "Murdered him." He looked at his hands. "Blew his head off . . . for no good reason."

He stood up, shattering three more bottles into specks of blue and green glass. Now, his shoulder did hurt, and he sat back down.

"Feel better?" she asked.

"No," he replied.

"Didn't think so." She sighed. "You're goin' after him, I take it."

His head nodded.

"Any idea where to look?"

He shrugged. "Deadwood. Miles City." He let out a heavy sigh. "This is all new country to me."

"Yeah. It's winter. Might be a long one. I don't reckon you'd like to ride up to Fort Meade—that's in South Dakota—with me?"

"Oh." He was reloading the .45-70 again. "I'd like to, Shirley, but . . . I'd best go it alone."

"Figured. Don't make no never-mind to me." She had sent the boys on up to Sturgis after they had arrived. She knew Colonel Tom C. Curtis would be mad at her for not going along with them, but she had hoped . . . well . . . that's what a sharpshooting girl from Zanesville, Ohio, gets for hoping.

"There's a pack train headin' that way in a week," Shirley said. "I'll hitch up with 'em." She opened her valise and pulled out a purse. "But you'll need money."

"I've got some. Don't you—"

"Hush." She handed over a wad of bills. "You take this. I won it off Danny Waco. I don't want it. I got plenty."

"You won it?"

She grinned. "I cheated."

He almost laughed, but he took the money and slipped it inside his coat.

"You'll take the Winchester, too."

"That I can't do."

"Yeah, you can. All that cannon does is sit in that crate. Only time I ever take it out is to clean it. Take it. And welcome. I shoot bottles, Jimmy Mann, and targets, and smokes out of mayors' mouths. I ain't no big woman. That's too much rifle for me. In my line of work."

He looked at the rifle, then at her, and leaned over and kissed her. She kissed him back. Again, Jimmy Mann wished that all of him could be dead like his left hand. He pulled away, sighed. "We best get back to town."

He'd be gone by daylight. He knew that. Back after Danny Waco. Likely, he would never see this girl again. Yep. He knew that. So did Shirley Sweet. Jimmy could tell by the tears in her eyes.

*Wallace County, Kansas*

The way McNally figured things, that soddy out in the middle of nowhere saved their lives.

Why, they had merely stumbled upon it, just about when McNally and Tyron figured they were done for. Blizzard in full force, them lost, nowhere near Nebraska as far as they could tell, and lo and behold, the sod house appeared.

They kicked open the door. Wasn't much of a door. Had two big old holes in it. They led their horses inside, along with the pack mule.

"It's a blessin'," Tyron said. "Blessin' from the Lord."

In answer, the mule began peeing on the dirt floor.

"Ain't nobody home," McNally said.

"Not in no long while." Tyron sat on what passed for a bed. A bed that had been ripped apart by thick claws of skunks, coyotes, wolves and maybe a badger or weasel over the past week or two or month or year. Hard to tell with the snow coming down sideways, and the soddy dark as McNally's soul.

"Get a fire started, Tyron," McNally said.

"Start it yerself," Tyron chimed back.

"You wanna freeze t' death?"

"I ain't cold."

"Start that fire, Tyron, else I'll—" McNally saw it first, laying on the floor by the fire. He ran forward, bent over, and heard his pard say, "That's mine!"

But McNally snatched up that rifle and said, "Ya want it. Come a-take it from me." He worked the lever, surprised to see a fresh cartridge ram into the chamber.

"It's a Winchester!" Tyron cried out.

"An' it's got bullets!" At least, McNally knew, it had one.

"Golly."

"Get that fire started, Tyron!"

"Don't ya point no gun at me."

McNally brought the rifle up, laughing. Even Tyron managed to cackle some.

"Wolves is a-gonna regret that I found this here Winchester," McNally said.

"All of Nebrasky is." Tyron busied himself trying to gather enough kindling and wood to put in the fireplace. "We'll make a passel with pelts come spring."

"Once we get to Nebrasky."

Tyron laughed. "Can't wait till this blizzard ends."

"When ya gets that fire a-goin', let's celebrate. Gots some liquor in my saddle bag."

"Ya been hoggin', McNally."

"Savin' it for a special occasion!"

He studied the rifle, reading the numbers. "It's a big one." He couldn't read his letters, couldn't tell A from Z, but he did know his numbers and could even cipher things like 2 plus 2 and 5 minus 1.

"Says here fifty, one hundred, four fifty."

Tyron looked up. "What's that mean?"

"Fifty caliber, I reckon."

"In a repeatin' rifle?" Tyron clucked his tongue.

"That's what it say."

Tyron laughed. So did McNally. "'Em wolves up in Nebrasky is really gonna regret us happenin' 'pon this here homestead."

Tyron's head bobbed. "It's a blessin' from the Lord."

# CHAPTER TWENTY-FIVE

*Hay Springs, Nebraska*
*Winter 1895*

Even to a couple of weasels like McNally and Tyron, there wasn't much to Hay Springs, just a collection of shanties, tents, and soddies on both sides of a trail that seemingly led to nowhere. The only way to tell what each place sold came from reading the sloppily scribbled or badly carved signs stuck in front of the businesses, but neither man had ever learned how to read.

Of course, there were other ways of telling.

Like the banjo music, laughter, and cusses coming out of a big tent structure on the north side of the muddy street, and all the horses tethered out front, peeing and crapping in the frozen mud and snow.

The town had sprung up some years back when folks were grading railroad track to Chadron. The depot was about the only thing permanent to Hay Springs, if anyone would call an old boxcar converted into a business, *permanent*. But the town had plenty of springs nearby, and those springs and the railroad had been bringing in farmers to grow hay—hence, the town's name—and ranchers, and cowboys, and on that bitterly cold January morning, a couple wolfers up from Texas named McNally and Tyron.

They tethered their horses and mule, stamped their feet in the hard-frozen ground to get their blood flowing again, and walked through the flap into the warmth of Hay Springs's biggest tent saloon.

"Caint I carry the big Winchester, McNally?" Tyron asked.

"No."

"Well, ya been a-hoggin' it since we was in Kansas."

"It be mine."

"Ain't so."

"Well I gots it."

"Well I just mights take it from ya."

McNally laughed and pointed the barrel at an empty table. There they sat, enjoying the warmth of the pot-belly stove, listening to the banjo player claw out that song about Jesse James, and picking lice out of their hair until a barmaid came wandering by, stopping a few feet from them because of their smell.

"What'll you have?" she asked.

"How much do a whiskey cost?" Tyron asked.

"Twenty cents a shot."

He frowned.

"Two beers then. They's only a nickel, right?"

"Right." She quickly left.

When she returned, sliding two mugs of warm porter in front of the wolfers, McNally said, "We's lookin' fer someone."

She stepped back, waiting. Each man drank about half his beer. McNally wiped his beard with his filthy coat sleeve, and said, "Name Clements."

She waited and did not answer.

"Big rancher in these parts."

Still, she said nothing.

"Ya gots a hearin' problem, lady?" Tyron asked. "We's a-waitin'."

"I'm waiting," she said, "for ten cents for those two beers."

Cursing, McNally unbuttoned his coat, reached inside his vest pocket, and withdrew a pouch, and counted out ten pennies, which he stacked on the side of the table.

The waitress stared at the pouch. "What is that thing?"

"Bull-wolf scrotum," Tyron answered. "We's wolfers." He said it proudly.

"Clements," she said, her face showing disgust, "runs the Circle C-7 down by Box Butte southwest of here. He ain't here."

"Didn't expect luck t' favor us," Tyron said.

"But his foreman is," she said.

"Well, ain't that somethin'. Ya mind sendin' 'em

over here. Tell him we's the wolfers Clements sent fer. Wants t' discuss the particulars an' such."

She left.

"An' have 'im brings a bottle if he's a-mind," McNally called out. "Talkin' business works up a body's thirst."

She did not answer.

"Hey, lady!" Tyron shouted.

She stopped and turned.

Tyron pointed at the ten pennies. "Ya forget yer money for our beers."

"I'll get it later." She made a beeline for the bar, which was nothing more than a two-by-twelve plank stretched across two whiskey kegs.

Laughing, McNally picked up his pennies, dropped them into the smelly pouch. "Works ever' time, don't it, Tyron?"

"Shor does." He sipped his beer and then dropped his hand on the table.

"Don't touch my rifle, Tyron," McNally warned him.

The Circle C-7 foreman brought his own beer, but no bottle, introduced himself as Ferdig, and pulled up a chair. "Mr. Clements didn't say nothing to me about hiring a couple wolfers."

"Ya got wolves, don't you?" McNally finished his beer. "I knowed that even jus' from the string a carcasses we seed ridin' up here."

Mr. Clements had not exactly sent for the two wolfers, but a cowhand who had quit the Circle C-7 and lighted down Tascosa way for the winter, had mentioned the wolf problem on the ranges of western Nebraska.

When Ferdig did not answer, McNally laughed. "Word come all the way down t' Tascosa 'bout yer troubles with wolves. 'Em wolves can be a pest. 'Specially when a winter's bad as this'n."

"Might be," Tyron chimed in, "that when yer steers start birthin' baby cows, ya won't have no little cows to round up. They'll all be breakfast fer a pack of vicious wolves."

"Steers don't birth baby cows," Ferdig told them.

"Well, ya gets our meanin'." McNally flagged the waitress over. "Three more beers, lady. Ain't that right, Mr. Ferdig?"

He didn't like it, but the foreman nodded at the waitress, and finished his own beer.

"What's your price?" Ferdig asked.

"Well," McNally said, "I hear the bounty is—"

"No bounties. Tails or pelts. Two years back, we found some wolfers we hired were showing a part to one of the magistrates for payment, then going to the next county and showing another part of the same wolf to collect from that magistrate. Mr. Clements pays per pelt or tail."

"I swan," Tyron sang out, "some wolfers ain't got no pride, an' give us honest tradesmen a poor name."

"What's your price?" Ferdig repeated.

McNally chuckled. "We ain't greedy. Goin' rate's five dollars a pelt an' ten cents a tail. Don't want no advance. We'll take our pay when we brings in our haul first a spring."

Ferdig leaned forward. "The going rate is two dollars a pelt and half a cent per tail."

Leaning back in his chair, McNally shook his head, then turned to look at his partner. "Ya hear that, Tyron?"

"I heard. Reckon the markets a-glut since we left Texas."

"Reckon so."

Ferdig leaned back and let the waitress deliver the three beers. "On my tab, Charlotte."

"Thanks, Mr. Ferdig," Tyron said as he practically lunged for the beer.

The waitress left. Ferdig did not drink.

"You use wolfhounds?" Ferdig asked.

"Nah." McNally sipped his beer. "Dogs cost money. Eat too much. Rough work, too, ridin' hard, tryin' t' keep up with a pack a wolfhounds." He laughed and gestured toward his partner. "'Sides, Tyron here, he don't eat as much as dogs, though he does have just as many fleas."

"Shut up, McNally. Ya's one t' talk."

"Ya best hold yer tongue, Tyron." He patted the Winchester's stock.

Ferdig waited until the two men had sipped more beer, letting the tension pass.

"Mr. Clements don't like strychnine," the foreman told them. "I don't neither. You can trap the wolves, but come spring, you take your traps with you. And if you use poison, Mr. Clements and me and our boys will ride you down and make you two eat it."

"Trappin's fine," McNally said. "Tyron an' me, we don't cotton to strychnine, neither. Hate the stuff. Ain't no sport in p'isonin' no deer or cow carcass. Tyron an' me, we's professionals. An' I got this." He patted the Winchester's stock.

Ferdig merely glanced at the rifle, then pushed himself up from his chair. "I'll see you come spring." He strode back to the bar, leaving McNally and Tyron to finish their beer and wait for that bar gal with the poor attitude to return. She never did.

They set up camp a few miles southeast of town near the two lakes—imaginatively named East Lake and West Lake—that some land developers had connected with a four- to six-feet-deep ditch.

Camp was a Sibley tent they had stolen when Tyron had deserted from some infantry outfit stationed in Missouri. They picketed their animals near the ditch, breaking the ice so the horses and mule could drink. They laid out their traps, figuring they would find likely spots to distribute them the next morning, cooked a supper of salt pork and beans, and then retired to the tent to finish the bottle of whiskey they had splurged on down in Alliance.

"Dead deer on tuther side of that ditch," McNally said. "Ya see it?"

Tyron shook his head and blew on his fingers.

The little stove he had stolen from a mercantile in St. Francis had yet to heat up the tent. "Expect it froze t' death."

"Afore ya go t' sleep t'night, ya stick some strychnine in 'im."

Tyron lowered his fingers. "Didn't ya hear what that ramrod tol' us 'bout p'isonin' such things?"

"Yeah. But we gots all that strychnine we taken from that outfit on the Pecos River."

Tyron shook his head.

"Two dollars a pelt and half a penny a tail," McNally reminded him.

Tyron grinned. "It's a blessin' from the Lord."

The way Tyron and McNally decided things over half the bottle of forty-rod liquor that would blind most men, they'd only use a little bit of the strychnine. Unless there came a real hard blizzard or cold front. If they came across a dead carcass, they would just naturally poison it. Make things easy.

They planned to set traps along the ditch and on the two ponds where they found any wolf tracks or droppings in the snow.

"We gonna do things like we done down in Texas?" Tyron asked.

"Certain-shore," McNally said. "We come 'cross a she-wolf with some pups, we jus' kill the pups. Let that she-wolf find herself a mate this spring or summer, an' give us some more business."

"Providin' we stick around here," Tyron said—

which meant providing the good citizens and up-standing ranchers around Hay Springs didn't run them out of the state.

Down in Texas, they had laid down a line of strychnine more than a hundred miles north to south, but it was a right smart warmer down in Texas than it was around East Lake and West Lake. And those Texians weren't so high and mighty when it came to things like strychnine as that Ferdig and Mr. Clements seemed to be.

So McNally and Tyron used the poison modestly. They did shoot one steer, even saw it branded the Circle C-7, and packed it with strychnine, but not until after they had carved up some beef and removed the hide that revealed the Hereford's brand. A rich rancher like Mr. Clements could spare one bony steer.

When the cold front broke, lifting the temperature to thirty degrees, and the sun reappeared, Tyron and McNally left camp. They had managed to poison twelve wolves, but the carcasses were too frozen to skin, so they piled the bodies behind the tent, and covered them with snow.

A week or so later, they rode to West Lake and followed wolf tracks in the snow, hoping the tracks would lead to a den. There, they could kill any pups, and let the mama live to bring them more business.

No such luck, though. They found the wolf, a he-wolf, by one of the springs. Upwind of the cur,

McNally slid from the saddle and tugged out the big Winchester. He aimed over the saddle—his horse was seasoned to gunfire, and he wasn't walking anywhere in that snow. He pulled the trigger.

The wolf fell dead.

Tyron pulled his fingers from his ears, shaking his head. "That sounds louder than the cannon they used t' fire at that fort in Missouri." He whistled, then saw McNally on his knees, rubbing his shoulder. "Ya hurt?"

McNally's ears were ringing, and his shoulder throbbed from the Winchester's savage kick. He cursed the rifle, which lay in the snow in front of him, and looked up at Tyron. "Gun like t' 've tore my arm off at the shoulder."

"Ya gots to hold it tight agen yer shoulder, pard. Won't kick so hard iffen you does that."

"Ya ain't tellin' Rafe McNally how t' shoot no rifle, you two-bit peckerwood."

"Well, ya's the one a-writhin' on the ground."

"Ain't writhin'. Gun jes kicks like a mule."

"Maybe ya should lets me shoot it. I knows how to handle a rifle."

"I'll give you tuther end of this 'ere gun." He grimaced, had to bite back the pain, wondering if that .50-caliber cannon had broken his collarbone, but managed to pick the Winchester out of the snow. Still, he had to use the rifle, butting it against the ground, to push himself back to his feet.

Still on his horse, Tyron cackled.

"Shuts yer trap!" McNally told him.

"Ya's a sight," Tyron said, still laughing. "Ain't

seen ya hurtin' so since that barkeep in Abilene broke ya nose with 'is bung starter."

"I whupped him, though. Sure as I'll whup ya."

"Yeah. Sure ya did. That's how come I had to drag yer carcass out of that bucket o' blood to the livery stable in town."

"Shuts yer trap." McNally brought the Winchester up, even though bracing that hard crescent-shaped butt against his shoulder pained him something fierce, and jacked a round into the chamber. "Ya gets to that wolf I jus' kilt—or I'll be stuffin' yer carcass with p'ison for 'em wolves t' feed on."

"Ya oughten not to talk t' me like that, McNally." Tyron practically pouted. "We's pards. Been pards for quite a spell now."

"I'm gettin' a mind to dissolve this 'ere partnership."

Tyron swung down from the saddle, his boots crunching the snow. "That there rifle's changed ya, McNally."

"Jus' fetch that wolf. Ain't as cold as it's been. Might be able to skin 'im."

Drawing the curve-bladed knife from his sheath, Tyron smiled a broken-teeth grin. "Might not be jus' a wolf I skin this day."

McNally laughed, keeping the rifle trained on his partner. "Skinnin' knife ag'in' this 'ere Winchester. Who ya reckon'd win that fight?"

# CHAPTER TWENTY-SIX

*Deadwood, South Dakota*

He had a Winchester '86 in .45-70 caliber, a Colt revolver that fired .44-40s, $128.32 left, and a job.

Not much of a job, especially for a deputy U.S. marshal, but working in the mines got him three squares to eat, a bunk to sleep in, and the room he rented at the hotel was warm. Winter had been cold, hard, and miserable.

Jimmy Mann had found the trail of Danny Waco in Chadron, Nebraska. Seems that sometime in November, four men had robbed the bank there of $1,320 in script.

"Four men?" Jimmy had asked the county sheriff. "Not two?"

"I think the cashier knows how to count," the sheriff had said, and Jimmy had to laugh at that one.

"Two wore masks. Grain sacks over their head. Figured them to be local boys. The other two didn't care who saw them. Slim fellow with crazy eyes, and a tall hombre with a Smith & Wesson."

"That would be Danny Waco and Gil Millican."

The lawman had shrugged. "Possible. They didn't introduce themselves. We lit out after them, but they crossed into the Pine Ridge Reservation, and that was as far as my badge carries me." He had leaned over to spit tobacco juice into a spittoon. "Maybe the Sioux scalped them."

No such luck. Jimmy had crossed the White River and moved into South Dakota, into the Black Hills, warming himself and his bones in Hot Springs, then up to Hill City. He had seriously considered riding to Sturgis to see if he might run into Shirley Sweet, but he thought that he was too close to catching up with Danny Waco. Knowing Waco, Jimmy figured the outlaw would have gone to Deadwood.

If he had, he wasn't there anymore. No one remembered seeing him, but people in Deadwood had short memories. Waco might have been here, probably had, but Deadwood wasn't as wild as it had been back in the '70s when Jack McCall had sent Wild Bill Hickok to his Maker or even the '80s. Men and women in mining towns had never been overtly friendly to lawmen, especially deputy marshals practically a thousand miles out of their jurisdiction.

Besides, nobody wanted to get on Danny Waco's bad side, if in case he did show up in Deadwood.

So where would Waco be? Belle Fourche? Even

farther north into one of the ranching towns in North Dakota? Or Canada? Montana, maybe? Miles City or points east? And were those two local boys he had pulled in to rob the Chadron bank still with him? Those were all questions Jimmy had asked himself.

He had considered heading out for the cattle town of Belle Fourche, but then the first blizzard hit. Deadwood, nestled in the Black Hills, was pretty much protected from the rough winters that could turn the Northern Plains of the Dakotas, Nebraska, and Montana into a white, freezing hell. Maybe Danny Waco would get caught in a snowstorm in Montana and freeze to death.

Jimmy hoped not. He wanted to be the one that ended Waco's life.

So Jimmy decided to wait out the winter in Deadwood. Earn some money. He had hated accepting that handout from Shirley. But not the rifle. He loved the Winchester '86, once he managed to push those lousy memories out of his mind, and it shot true. His nephew would love handling the weapon. Yet taking money from a woman galled him. But he needed cash.

So he earned it. Twelve hours a day in a pit. He didn't drink. Didn't gamble. Hardly ate. The work was grueling, but Jimmy liked it. He added muscle. Stamina. Even resolve. And his wounded hands got tougher, stronger. Yeah, he would be ready for Danny Waco come spring.

Few of the miners talked to him, and he never

sought out conversation. He retired to his room with newspapers, scanning the print for any mention of the outlaw or any murder, bank robbery, train robbery, anything.

Nothing showed up . . . but it was winter. Likely Waco had been forced to hole up somewhere, too.

Spring would come. Jimmy Mann knew that. Spring would come, and he'd pick up Waco's trail. That had always been easy.

He just followed the dead men.

### Hay Springs, Nebraska

They ate wolf steaks, fried up in wolf grease. Wolf stew, seasoned with wolf grease. McNally always called it "an acquired taste," but it didn't cost much. Of course, they knew to eat only the wolves they had caught in traps, or those McNally shot with the .50-caliber Winchester, not the ones they managed to get with strychnine.

They were careful about the poison. Didn't want anyone with that big ranch to learn they were using the stuff, and when they found a dead coyote or dog or anything by one of the carcasses they'd stuffed with strychnine, they always carted it back to camp and burned it in the fire. The ground remained frozen too hard to bury anything, and, well, neither McNally nor Tyron really cared much for digging.

"I gots an idea-er, McNally," Tyron said one bitterly frigid night in February.

"Yeah?" McNally alternated between cleaning the

Winchester and sipping the jug of whiskey they'd traded a wolf tail for from some passing colored boy that had just mustered out of the Army.

"Well, we cut offen that wolf tail for that jug ya's a-hoggin' . . ."

McNally cursed and tossed the jug to his pard.

After downing a couple swallows, Tyron smacked his lips—though the hooch was awful—and wiped his mouth with the sleeve of his coat "Well, I was thinkin' that maybe we could cut offen the tails of a few more. Tell that segundo at that big ol' ranch that that wolf, well, she musta jus' gnawed it off or somethin' like that. He gots the skin an' all, an' I'd 'spect he'd think, that iffen that wasn't the case, iffen we was a-lyin' t' him, well, all we'd get was a half a penny. Ain't no skin offen his nose."

Again, McNally cursed. He set his rifle on the folding desk they'd erected in the tent.

"Fer a half-penny?" He shook his head. "Toss me that jug."

Before he obeyed, Tyron took another long pull on the forty-rod.

As McNally drank, Tyron said, "No, it ain't fer jus' half a penny. See, what we does is we takes that tail down south." He shivered. "An' sooner the better iffen ya was to asks me. Didn't think it'd get this blasted cold up here. But say we take that wolf tail down to Ogallala or Dodge City or someplace likes that. Where they still gots magistrates payin' bounties on wolves. We show 'em that tail, and they ain't that particular. So we get whatever they's payin' bounties."

The jug came to rest on the table near the rifle. McNally wiped the snot from his nose, mustache, and beard. "An' what happens if they don't pay us no bounty?"

With a shrug, Tyron said, "Then they'd pay us the half-a-cent fer the tail. Don't ya reckon?"

McNally replied with a grunt and reached for the jug once more.

"Half a cent more'n we'd make if we taken the whole skin to that Ferdig gent at the Circle-somethin' outfit we's a-workin' fer."

"Half a cent," McNally said in disgust.

"Adds up," Tyron told him.

"You think that Ferdig's a fool? How many wolves do ya think 'd gnaw off their own tails?"

"It ain't like we'd tear offen all 'em tails. Just a few. Got us, what, thirty-forty wolves already. And ten-twelve coyot's we'll pass offen as wolves. Plus 'em three big dogs ya p'isoned."

"I ain't p'isoned 'em dogs. Ya done it!"

"'Cause ya tol' me t' do it."

"Didn't say p'ison no dog."

"Well, I didn't tell that dog to eat that bad meat. None of 'em dogs."

"Well, they's deader 'n dirt, sure-nuff."

"Yeah, an' 'twas yer idea-er to pass 'em off as wolves."

"Bes' hope the owners don't come a-lookin' fer 'em."

"Mangy as 'em curs was, they was strays is all."

"Well . . ." McNally had another drink.

"'Spect we'll have us a hunnert or more by spring. Ya taken two-dozen tails. That's . . . what?"

It took some studying. Might buy them two draught beers . . . if all they got down south was half a penny. But if they sold those tails for a full bounty, well, that would add up a mite. Of course, McNally would never let Tyron know that idea he'd come up with wasn't such a bad one after all. Might work.

"Can ya pass that jug ag'in, McNally?"

With another curse, McNally sent the jug sailing. He knew he had thrown it too hard, and too high, and when it sailed through Tyron's fingers, and fell on the hard ground, spilling out at least a tumbler's full of rotgut, McNally leaped from his chair.

The fight was on.

"Ya fool!" McNally yelled. "Ya wasted good whiskey." He kicked his pard in the ribs, grabbed his hair, and slammed his head down onto the hard earth. "Idiot."

He rolled Tyron over, slapped his face, then punched him hard. Once. Twice. Three times.

Tyron groaned.

"Ya ain't good fer nothin'." McNally grabbed the beaten fool by the neck and bottom of his coat. He heaved Tyron through the entrance to the tent, hearing him crash into the snowdrift, moan, and sob. He found the hat that had been knocked off his pard's head and threw it out into the cold, too.

"Ya ain't good fer nothin'. That's how God cusses me. Gives me a fool for a pard. All ya knows how to do is p'ison dogs."

When he stormed back to the desk, picking up

the jug, and taking a sip, he knew he had over-reacted, knew he should apologize. He told himself that it wasn't Tyron's fault that he was a moron, an incompetent fool. He blamed that outburst on his lousy luck. Should apologize. He knew that. He also knew he couldn't do it. Even an hour later, after Tyron had recovered enough to step back inside the tent, sniffling, his face covered with frozen blood, McNally couldn't do it.

They didn't speak that night, but McNally did toss him the jug. To him, that was as good as an apology. Of course, there wasn't but two or three swallows left, and most of that was McNally's back-wash.

For two more days, they didn't speak. But then they came across five poisoned wolves, killed three others they had found in their traps, and McNally even shot one dead at three hundred yards.

He said that was cause for celebrating, and Tyron agreed to cook a supper of wolf steaks while McNally took a coyote pelt they figured they could pass off as a wolf's to the guy who operated a hog ranch three miles south of town. He returned with a bottle of awful, but cheap, liquor.

So they ate wolf steak fried up in wolf grease, bitter as gall, tasting like dead rats and rotting ravens, and washed it down with liquor that tasted even worse. They laughed anyway, thinking about all that money those pelts and tails would bring, how they would have enough cash to get them back to Texas and maybe even do some real drinking.

They felt good . . . until McNally gripped his

belly, slipped out of his chair onto the cold ground, and groaned.

"I am . . . sick . . . as a . . . dog." His face paled. He had to use his right hand and arm to keep himself sitting up. "Bad . . . likker."

Tyron started to come to him, started to say something, then laughed, and grabbed the bottle of forty-rod. He drank, wiped his mouth, and shook his head. "Ain't nothin' wrong with this stuff. I reckons I fed ya a steak from one of 'em wolves that got holt of yer strychnine." Another pull from the bottle. "Accidental, o' course." He slapped his thigh and howled in delight.

"Ya p'isoned me." McNally shook his head. He couldn't believe a simpleton like Tyron could have gotten the better of him. He thought about how those wolves had suffered before they died. Thought about how long it would take the poison to kill him.

"I reckons I'll be a-shootin' that big ol' rifle of yourn. Wonder how much yer pelt'll bring me come spring." Tyron kept laughing and drinking until McNally pushed himself up and reached for the Winchester '86 that was leaning against the table.

Seeing that, plus the rage in McNally's eyes, Tyron dropped the bottle and stepped forward. "Wait a minute, pard, I's just a-teasin' ya . . ." He realized then that he was too late.

The table overturned, and McNally was levering the rifle, bracing it against his roiling stomach. Tyron screamed, and reached for his skinning knife. Gripped it, charged.

The rifle roared at point-blank range, spinning Tyron around. He landed on his knees, right beside McNally, who had to brace the gun against the hard ground, trying to work the lever again.

Tyron stared at the bloody mess that was his shirt and had been his stomach. "Ya kilt me. I was jus' fun—" Rage filled his eyes, and he realized he still held that curved Green River skinning knife . . . and McNally was vomiting . . . and the Winchester was falling to the ground.

McNally looked up. "Ya son of a—" He never finished the curse.

Tyron had just enough strength, just enough hatred, just enough life in him to bring up his arm, and slash his partner's throat with the knife.

McNally fell first. Then Tyron dropped on top of his partner.

The Winchester rifle lay beside them.

Outside, somewhere in the extreme cold, wolves, coyotes, and perhaps a few feral dogs howled.

# CHAPTER TWENTY-SEVEN

They had come down into Nebraska on their way to Hay Springs for—what else?—winter hay. Sergeant Jay Chase, 6th U.S. Cavalry, didn't care much for the assignment, wet-nursing eighteen new recruits. Most of those green peas either drove or sat in the backs of big wagons. Three, though, rode half-broke, poor excuses for horses that should have been shipped to a glue factory, not an Army post in South Dakota. But orders were orders, and there he was—cold, butt hurting, thighs chapped—riding herd on those nitwits the idiotic lieutenant had saddled him with. They included some kid from the New York slums who knew nothing about horses, three fools fresh off the boat from Italy or Spain or Portugal or some such place, and two drunks who spent more time in the guardhouse than in the field. The rest were even worse.

Then they saw the wolves.

Snarling they were, inside and outside some ramshackle tent that the wind had half blown over.

Something inside that tent sure held those big curs' attention. A couple horses and a mule, all looking like something even the stock buyers for the 6th Cavalry would have passed over no matter how much of a kickback the mustangers offered to pay, were tethered in a miserable structure behind the tent.

Yet, for the moment, those wolves did not pay any attention to that poor excuse for livestock. They focused on whatever lay inside the tent.

Carcasses, some skinned, others still frozen solid, were stacked all around what remained of the tent.

That trooper from the Fifth Ward got bucked off by the gelding. Scared senseless by the wolves, it bolted down the road toward the flea-bitten town of Hay Springs. Another trooper's mount started side-stepping, but at least that idiot had the sense to slide off the saddle into the snow and get a good hold on the reins.

"Halt!" Sergeant Chase yelled. He looked around at the wagons, filled with hay from the farms east of town. The drivers had set the brakes, and sat still, staring at the wolves, color draining from their faces. One dark-skinned foreigner in the back of the third wagon vomited on the hay.

The sergeant's horse became skittish, but it wasn't some half-dead mount. It was a solid, smart dun—Captain Thurston's horse—Chase had bribed the saddler back at Fort Meade to give him.

"Easy, boy," Chase told the horse. He reached for the Springfield sheathed in the scabbard. It was awkward pulling that heavy single-shot .45-70 carbine, his heavy woolen coat flopping in the wind, his gauntlets stiff from the freezing cold. He had considered ordering one of the recruits to do this job, but after looking at those green pups, he decided they would likely either shoot a horse or mule, or Sergeant Jay Chase.

The wolves had not run off, had not been scared by the arrival of these noisy, lumbering wagons and horses. Of course, it had been a bitter winter, and they had found something in that tent—or what was left of a tent—that made them defiant.

Chase's carbine would stop that.

He aimed at the closest wolf, squeezed the trigger, and heard the roar as the Springfield's stock slammed against his shoulder. The dun horse, trained by Captain Thurston, barely flinched. The wolf slammed into a snow bank, spraying the canvas of the tent crimson.

The wolves lost their nerve and beat a hasty retreat into the frigid landscape.

Chase shifted the Springfield into his left hand and fumbled with the leather cover that protected his Army revolver. When he had the snap released, he drew the .45 and popped three rounds into the air. Just to make sure the wolves did not return.

It caused two more horses to buck off their troopers, and the lead wagon to run about twenty-five yards before the driver managed to stop the frightened mules.

Chase barked a few choice curse words at the Greek driver, yelling at him for not having the brains to set the brake earlier. Then he cursed the fools who pulled themselves out of the snow, brushing off ice and shame. He shook his head, holstered the Colt, sheathed the Springfield, and brought the dun to the nearest wagon, tethering him to the rear wheel.

"You." He told the driver. Chase couldn't remember the man's name. "You and you." He pointed to two other troopers. "Follow me."

Snow crunched underneath their boots as they trudged through the snow. Soon, the smell hit them, and they stopped to bring up their kerchiefs or woolen scarves to cover noses and mouths. Chase spit and stepped over the wolf he had killed. Drawing his Colt again, he used the barrel to push open the flap in the tent.

He was the first inside. Only the driver followed him The other two recruits stood outside, shivering.

He cursed and spit into his yellow kerchief. He pulled it down and spit again, the saliva freezing in the air. He shook his head. Behind him, the driver muttered some prayer in his native tongue and began bawling like a newborn.

"Out," Chase managed to tell him. "Get out."

The trooper did not need any further orders. He staggered through the canvas, ripping part of it as he tumbled beside the two waiting soldiers.

Chase had read fanciful stories about wolves attacking men, but as far as he knew, all those stories were hogwash. Outside, he could hear other soldiers moving cautiously from their wagons, listening as the driver muttered what he could in English, trying to tell them that those beastly wolves had attacked and ripped apart two human beings.

"No." Chase told himself. He eased forward, dropped to his knees, and used the barrel of the Colt to move one of the corpse's arms. Tried to, anyway. It wouldn't move. Either frozen from the cold or stiff in rigor mortis.

The man's arm had fallen over his face, and the wolves had made a mess of things, but he could see the bloody hole in the man's belly—at least, where the wolves hadn't gotten to it yet—and the powder burns on the man's coat. He had been shot at point blank range. Chase also saw the Green River skinning knife still gripped in the man's right hand and the frozen blood on the blade.

Chase looked at the second dead man.

The wolves had moved the bodies around some and had gone for the fleshy parts, but if Chase read things right, these two men—skinners of some sort—had killed themselves. The camp was squalid. So were what remained of the dead men.

*Maybe the Army isn't such a bad place to be.*

He could see the busted and broken jugs, flasks, and bottles. These two fools must have been drunk. Gotten into some quarrel. One pulled a gun. One pulled a knife. A few moments later, both were shouting at the devil.

Well, he had seen things like that happen with his own troopers in all his years in the Army.

He asked himself, "What were they fighting over?"

Then he saw the rifle.

* * *

"Wolfers," Ferdig told Chase. "Mr. Clements hired them for the Circle C-7. They've been a pest of late."

"Wolves?" Chase asked. "Or the wolfers."

Ferdig smiled and sweetened the sergeant's coffee with a little rye from his flask. "Honestly, I don't even remember their names. Mac-something. The other, I don't know. Figure they killed themselves?"

Chase nodded. They were sitting in the coffee-house, half-tent, half-soddy, but warm and cozy. The coffee tasted better than anything the chowhounds poured at Fort Meade. Of course, maybe that rye whiskey had something to do with it.

"Don't surprise me." Ferdig had ridden in from someplace called Box Butte.

Chase had sent a rider to the ranch after some girl at a bucket of blood had said she seemed to recall two sorry-looking cusses asking about bringing in wolf pelts for the bounty or reward or whatever they called it. It was a month or two back, but she remembered them asking about Mr. Clements, who owned the Circle C-7.

"Too cold to bury them, I reckon," Ferdig said.

Chase wasn't sure if that was a question or a statement or just some idle thought. He sipped more of the coffee. "You wouldn't know if they have any kin, would you?"

Ferdig laughed so hard he had to draw a rag out of his coat pocket to wipe his nose. "Wolfers? I don't rightly expect their own mothers would have claimed them." He tasted his whiskey straight from the flask. "Guess we'll just send them off like Vikings. Burn 'em. And the wolf pelts they got. How many did you say?"

"I didn't," Chase told him.

"Well, we'll take care of them, I guess. After all, they were working for the Circle C-7, and Mr. Clements takes care of his men. Or wolfers. Whatever the case may be. You've done your job, your duty, Sergeant. Might as well ride on back to your fort with your hay."

"Might as well." Chase decided that he did not care much for Mr. Ferdig. He had a strong hunch that, yes, Ferdig and his cowboys would burn the remains of those two dead wolfers, but he might take the pelts for himself and collect the bounty or whatever was being done in Nebraska. But that was none of his affair. Besides, he had just learned what he needed to know.

Those two dead men didn't have any kin.

Sergeant Jay Chase thanked the Circle C-7 foreman and finished his coffee. "Guess I need to get that hay back to Fort Meade before all our mounts starve to death."

The horses were usually half-starved anyway. But this, he did not say.

"All right, Sergeant." Ferdig stood. "You say wolves were eating the bodies?"

Chase nodded.

"Sounds sort of like justice, don't it?"

"I don't know a thing about justice. I'm a career Army man."

They shook, and Chase left the coffeehouse, hating to be back outside, and then swung into the saddle and eased the dun down the road to where he had left his command. They had found their horses, and most had recovered from the shock of the wolves and the wolves' meal.

Chase knew they could have stayed in Hay Springs for a night, but he wanted to be shun of this country. He had the boys ready to ride fifteen minutes later, and they eased their way north and west toward Chadron. They would move along the White River, crossing it at Crawford and heading to Fort Robinson.

Eat some Army chow for a change and sleep in warm bunks. Let their horses and mules rest a day or two, before moving into South Dakota, crossing the Pine Ridge Reservation and moving through the Black Hills and on to Fort Meade.

Chase's first thought, his first plan, was Fort Robinson.

They made only five or six miles that day, camping along the side of the trail. The next day, after five more miles, he let them halt for a while.

Sergeant Jay Chase tied the captain's dun horse to the last hay wagon's rear wheel and walked through the snow to the lead wagon. "Martin," he told the driver as if *Martin* was that bloke's real name. "I'll take that Winchester now."

The trooper dumbly reached under the seat and fetched the powerful weapon.

"Don't hand me a gun barrel first, you bloody idiot!" Chase snapped. "That Winchester might blow me in half." He jerked the weapon out of the green trooper's hands, almost pulling the poor kid down from the wagon and into the snow.

"What you gonna do with that repeater?" the recruit from New York City's Fifth Ward asked.

"Shoot it," Chase answered. "What else." He jacked the lever. Needed oil. A good cleaning. No, a thorough cleaning. He doubted if those wolfers had ever rammed a greased patch down the barrel. He should clean it, but he wanted to try it first.

"Fifty caliber." He shook his head, grinning. "Never seen the likes of a rifle like this." He whistled. "Fifty caliber."

"I thought they was only found in buffalo guns. Or mountain men's guns."

Chase ignored the trooper, then turned and barked an order. "Every brake on every wagon had best be set, and every trooper on a horse better have his feet on the ground and the reins wrapped firmly around two hands." He wasn't about to lose any more time chasing after runaway stock. "You can walk the hundred and thirty miles to Fort Meade."

"Do they let sergeants carry repeaters?" another kid asked.

"It'll be my personal rifle"—Chase glared at those kids—"which I'll use on any fool that asks me another fool question."

The rifle came up, and he smiled. That crescent stock fitted his shoulder like a glove. He drew a bead on the top center of a fence post, and sighed, remembering all those times when a soldier could have crossed this country without seeing a fence post or a cow or anything but Sioux and Pawnee.

He drew a deep breath, held it, let it out, and squeezed the trigger.

His shoulder throbbed, but he wouldn't let any of the greenhorns see how much that rifle's kick had hurt. He grinned and pointed at the post. The .50-caliber slug had blown the top of the fence-post off.

A few of the troopers cheered. Some whistled. Most just kept their fingers in their ears.

"That's some good shooting, Sergeant," the New Yorker said.

Chase stared at the Winchester. Yeah, it was some good shooting, seeing how he had not even sighted in the weapon or cleaned the filthy rifle. He imagined what he could do once he had the '86 Model spotless, oiled, and ready.

"What do with that you?" asked another trooper in broken English.

"Win money," Sergeant Jay Chase said. "Win lots of money." He wondered how many of the soldiers at Fort Robinson thought highly of their own marksmanship . . . and how much of their pay they had left and were willing to bet.

# CHAPTER TWENTY-EIGHT

*Crawford, Nebraska*

*The town has growed some,* Danny Waco thought as he sat at a table in one of saloons, *since my last visit in 1886.*

Back then, there hadn't been anything but a bunch of tents. Tent saloons. Tent cathouses. A tent hotel. Even Calamity Jane had pitched a tent and filled it with ten dance-hall girls and plenty of soldiers and railroaders who wanted to see them girls—ugly as sin, the way Waco remembered, just like Calamity Jane—do the can-can. That had been back when some railroad, the Fremont, Elkhorn, and something or other Valley, had been laying rails into Wyoming.

They had named the little hell-on-wheels after some dumb Army officer who had gotten himself killed down in Mexico. Made sense, Waco figured, since the bluebelly had once been stationed at Fort Robinson.

Most of the tents were gone, replaced by frame and picket buildings, even a brick structure or two. Another railroad had reached the village by '87. Crawford had a newspaper, the *Crawford Clipper*, stores, warehouses, and solid hotels. Of course, the soldiers stationed at Fort Robinson still demanded gambling dens, brothels, and saloons, which is why Waco had decided to come down this way after spending most of the winter in Belle Fourche and Rapid City. He hadn't even gone to Deadwood, figuring that's where the law would expect him to light out for after robbing that sorry old bank in Chadron.

Chadron wasn't far at all from Crawford, but Waco figured the law had forgotten all about him and the money they had taken. Besides, nobody would look for him that close to where he had pulled that job.

The losers he had conscripted into pulling the Chadron job were long gone. Waco and Millican had left them in Hot Springs. For all Waco knew and cared, the boys had been captured and lynched. He had picked up a big, tall, mean-looking Sioux Indian. The cuss stood six-foot-six in his moccasins He wore his long black hair filled with silver streaks in braids, and had the meanest face Waco had ever seen. Man didn't say two words a month, and Waco liked it that way. The Indian didn't even remind him of Tonkawa Tom.

The big Sioux—Waco and Millican merely called

him "Indian," for they did not know his name—
carried a Winchester, too.

Not an '86, of course. Waco shook his head,
thinking about that rifle, wondering what had ever
become of that .50-caliber cannon, or that weasel of
a gambler who had cheated him out of that repeater down in Caldwell all those months ago. No,
Indian carried a Model 1866, the first repeater produced by Winchester. It chambered the old .44
Henry rimfires, but it was sure better than those old
Henry rifles. Nelson King had improved the design
of the old Henry, tweaked those quirks, put a loading gate on the side. It shined, too, because of the
brass gunmetal receiver. That's why most folks
called the Winchester '66 the "Yellow Boy."

A month back, Waco had gotten a better look at
that rifle. He saw the name Winchester's original
owner had carved into the stock. He couldn't read
the name because Indian had nailed a bunch of
studs into the stock. Waco never could understand
why Indians always did that. They had to decorate
things all the time. Make them pretty. Indians were
like stupid petticoats in that regard. Waco couldn't
see the name, but he could see something underneath all those studs—7TH CAV.—which made him
believe Indian had killed some bluebelly officer
with Custer back in '76 on the Little Big Horn.

Waco saw the Yellow Boy first, then the big
Indian as he pushed his way through the batwing
doors. A few people stopped their drinking and
their idle chatter to stare at the tall Sioux, and the
barkeep frowned hard, then turned to busy himself

cleaning glasses with a dirty towel. No one said anything to Indian.

Waco had to smile at that. They were probably so scared of the big cuss, they would have served him a whiskey had he asked for a drink, and even told him it was on the house.

Indian stopped at the table where Waco sat emptying a bottle of rye with Gil Millican. "Soldiers come."

Waco snorted. "Soldiers are always coming. There's a fort here, ain't there?"

"These come other way. From Chadron."

That made Waco frown. It was probably nothing. He had robbed that bank in Chadron, but that was a civilian affair. The Army wouldn't be involved. Those bluecoats were probably heading over to Fort Robinson on some military matter.

On the other hand, he had been thinking about trying for Cheyenne. Get out of these rawhide dumps like Crawford and Belle Fourche and Ogallala and see a real bona fide city. The morning had dawned clear, sunny, and warm. He figured the temperatures might even get above freezing. "Well," he said at last. "I reckon it's a nice day for a ride."

"Where we goin', Danny?" Millican asked.

Waco finished his rye. "Cheyenne. That's what I'm thinking."

"Ain't never been there," Millican said.

"Sure you have," Waco reminded him. "That's where you killed Burl Scott back in '89."

"I thought that was in Laramie."

"No. Cheyenne."

"Well, then, you reckon it'd be safe for me there, Danny?"

"Nobody remembers Burl Scott. He was a two-bit saddle tramp. And nobody remembers you, Gil. They remember Danny Waco. They fear me, too. We'll be safe. Let's ride."

Indian grunted, turned, and headed for the door. The menfolk in the saloon began to drink again, and talk, and stop staring. Waco tossed some coins on the table, pushed back his chair, and grabbed his rifle and six-shooter, which he had laid on the table—just to be safe.

When the Colt was back in its holster, he buttoned his coat, pulled on his gloves, and made for the horses, all tethered in the muddy street.

The soldiers were coming by. The big wagons were filled with straw or hay or something like that. No, those boys weren't coming to arrest him.

Waco snorted and grinned at Gil Millican. "That's what's become of the Army, Gil. Bluebellies are now protecting convoys of straw."

Millican laughed and moved for his horse.

Waco slid in beside him on his own stolen mount, grabbed the reins, and backed his horse in the street after the last wagon had passed. "Let's ride. Cheyenne's waiting."

He kicked his horse into a trot and passed the first wagon full of feed for Army mounts. Or maybe the U.S. Army was feeding its troops straw these days. He laughed at his joke, and pulled his hat low, kept his head down as he passed the other wagons and lead riders. Just to be safe. He didn't want to take any chances and be recognized.

It's why Danny Waco rode right past Jay Chance, and did not notice the Winchester '86 the sergeant was carrying.

### Fort Robinson

"Why don't you make it twenty dollars, Captain?" Sergeant Chase told the officer. "These .50-100-450 shells don't come cheap."

"Do you have twenty dollars, Sergeant?" the captain said with a smirk.

Chase handed the Winchester to the trooper from New York, named Eustis. "Hold this, Useless." Looking at the captain, he said, "Let me check my poke, sir," and pulled out his pouch from the deep pockets on his trousers. Methodically, he opened the pouch, and fished out a few coins. Nodding, he returned the gold pieces into the pouch, which disappeared inside the mule-ear pockets.

"Yes, sir," he told the captain. "Appears that I have fifty-five dollars. In coin, too. Not script. Never did trust that paper money."

The captain, a tall, wiry cuss, whipcord thin and ramrod straight, streaks of gray just appearing on his Burnside whiskers, took the bait. Practically swallowed the hook. "Well, Sergeant, should we make our bet fifty-five dollars then?"

Chase smiled. "Do you have fifty-five dollars, Captain?"

The captain glared. Did not even bother to

answer, and snapped his fingers. A black corporal, likely the captain's striker—or slave, maybe, Chase thought—hurried forward with a leather case.

Other soldiers gathered around, and even a few of Chase's recruits whistled skeptically at their sergeant's chances when they saw the rifle that came out of the case.

"That's a High Wall, Sarge," Trooper Eustis Whatever-his-last-name-was whispered to Chase. "I saw a sharpshooter win a contest with a gun just like that at Creedmoor back in '89."

Creedmoor would be what once had been Creed Farm on New York's Long Island. It had opened back in 1873, and the National Rifle Association had been holding target matches on a yearly basis ever since.

"They let you in to Creedmoor?" Chase asked.

"Yes, sir."

"Don't *sir* me, boy." He nodded, though, at the New Yorker and looked at the rifle the captain held. Before he stepped forward, he told the recruit, "You might not be so worthless after all, Useless."

The High Wall, Model 1885 single-shot Winchester was what many marksmen considered John Moses Browning's best-designed rifle. The one the captain was showing off to his troopers and junior officers looked mighty fine. It had that strong, case-colored falling-block action—an element that had led many people to consider the model the best single-shot, long-range rifle ever made. Better than the Sharps. Better than the Remington—which was saying a lot.

The captain's weapon had the full octagonal barrel, just a couple inches from being a full three feet long, and was gloss-blued with gold engraving. The stock was walnut, satin finished with a pistol grip, and the forestock cut checkered. It even had one of those fancy recoil pads, not the steel, shoulder-crushing crescent butt plates most High Walls sported, but the same kind of butt plate Mr. Browning had put on the 1886 Model Winchester that Trooper Eustis still held.

The captain's High Wall had a long brass sight that ran almost the full length of the barrel to just past the trigger, hammer, and fancy lever. The whole shebang likely was fifty inches in length.

"Naturally, Sergeant," the captain said as he removed his eyeglasses, handing them to the corporal for cleaning. "I shall remove the telescopic sight. For sporting purposes, of course."

Chase spit out tobacco juice. "No need to bother with that, Captain. You'd just have to sight it in again when you put it back on. My eyes are fine. I don't need telescopes."

The orderly was returning the officer's glasses.

"Or bifocals." Chase enjoyed seeing the captain's face flush.

"Suit yourself," the captain said. Testy. Mighty testy—and that, Jay Chase figured, was a good thing.

"What does she shoot?"

"A .45-90," the officer replied.

"How much she weigh?"

"Thirteen pounds."

"What's the length of pull?"

The captain considered the sergeant with something more than curiosity or contempt before he answered. "Roughly thirteen and one-half inches, Sergeant. You know something about guns, I take it. More than the average noncom in this man's Army."

Pushing back his winter hat, Chase grinned. "Well, I reckon we'll find that out in a few minutes, won't we, Captain?" He decided that he liked Fort Robinson. It didn't have all the trees that he found at Fort Meade, and it certainly felt colder, but it was a good post. With good people.

It had been founded in the early to mid 1870s after the government had established the Red Cloud Agency. This part of the state wasn't flat, but pretty. Not Black Hills pretty, but filled with rolling hills, now covered with snow and ice. Chase knew it would green up come spring.

Crazy Horse, that big Sioux leader, had been killed there, bayoneted by another Indian. Another year later, a bunch of Dull Knife's Northern Cheyenne bucks had busted out of the guardhouse, or wherever they were being held, killing a bunch of soldiers. And many, many Indians died, too.

The fort was manned primarily by a bunch of blacks. The 9th Cavalry of those so-called "buffalo soldiers" had called Fort Robinson headquarters since 1895. Lots of soldiers and officers, Chase didn't care much for those black boys in blue, but he knew the 9th was a fine outfit. He would gladly have traded some of his greenhorns for these soldiers—but that would not have gone over well with the commanding officer at Fort Meade.

In fact, Chase figured some of the buffalo soldiers could give him a run for his money in a target-shooting match, but he wasn't shooting against that tough-looking soldier or that corporal who acted as if he had yet to hear that President Lincoln had freed the slaves a few decades back.

They reached the clearing. Two black troopers carried paper targets and hammers. Two others had posts. Apparently, they were used to the captain and his target shooting. And they were a long way from Creedmoor, New York.

Other officers, white men—for most of the 9th was commanded by white officers, although Chase had heard of a black lieutenant in the regiment named Young, a West Point graduate. He'd been stationed out there for a year or so before being shipped off to Utah for a while. He was teaching military sciences at some college in Ohio that educated Negroes.

"Shall we say two hundred yards, Sergeant? To start." Captain Wilbur Lincoln grinned. He had a crowd of black soldiers he commanded, white officers, even a major and the post surgeon, for his cheering section. The captain adjusted his spectacles.

Earlier that day, Chase had cleaned the rifle, had sighted it in, test-fired half a box of cartridges, and had bought several more boxes in Crawford. He took his rifle from Trooper Eustis and felt the wind. Little of it, just a slight breeze blowing north to south. The sky was clear. He doubted if it was any warmer than thirty-five or thirty-eight degrees.

The Winchester felt right in his hands. The captain kept grinning, figuring he had already won that fifty-five dollars.

"Oh, I don't know, Captain Lincoln," Chase said casually. "How about if we make it five hundred, sir?"

# CHAPTER TWENTY-NINE

"Fifty-two . . . fifty-three . . ." Captain Wilbur Lincoln, eyes red, face pale, countenance embarrassed, had to dig for change. Quarters and dimes and finally, pennies. "Fifty-four . . . fifty-five." He sighed.

Sergeant Jay Chase beamed and slid the much heavier pouch back into the deep pockets of his trousers. "Thank you, Captain Lincoln."

The captain turned to a young lieutenant, probably fresh out of West Point, with fuzz for a mustache and pimples on his cheeks. "Don't worry, Mr. Rush, I will pay you back come payday."

"Whenever you can afford to, Captain Lincoln." The green pup of an Army officer grinned at the sergeant. "I bet on the winner."

Chase had to laugh as he took the Model 1886 Winchester from Trooper Eustis.

"You bet on him?" Captain Lincoln found that hard to believe.

"Yes, sir," the kid beamed. "You're darn-tooting I did. I saw Sergeant Chase at Creedmoor seven years ago. My father took me to see the contest."

Chase reconsidered the snot-nosed lieutenant. As if he could remember that kid from that far back.

It also made Captain Wilbur Lincoln reconsider the noncom who had just bested him, first at five hundred yards, then at a thousand. With a repeating rifle that looked as if it had been marched over by the entire command at Fort Robinson. "You? You shot at . . . Creedmoor?"

Turning toward the officer, Chase spit tobacco juice onto the ground. "Oh, I did not do that well," he said sheepishly. "Why five, no six, yes, six fellows outshot me that time. Come on, Useless." He strode back toward the enlisted men's barracks, where the post adjutant had graciously agreed to house the boys from the 6th Cavalry for the night before they continued their journey north to South Dakota. Trooper Eustis followed close behind him.

A black sergeant handed Chase the paper targets. "That was some groupin', Sergeant."

"Thanks, Sergeant. I appreciate that." Chase would study the targets later.

Four others cheered him as he ambled past. Others, of course, those idiots who had so unwisely bet on Captain Wilbur Lincoln and his fancy little target rifle, sent him looks of bitter derision. He greeted them with pleasant smiles, anyway. Just to make them feel worse.

Speaking of feeling worse, Chase felt the urge to rub his shoulder or at the least send Trooper Eustis to the post sutler to buy some liniment. It felt as if it were black and blue. Actually, he sometimes wondered if he had chipped his collarbone. That Winchester kicked like an elephant.

But it had won him fifty-five dollars from a snobbish officer who had been spotted a fancy brass telescope and a long-range rifle. At five hundred yards. And then a thousand. And that took a bit of the bite out of the pain Sergeant Jay Chase was feeling.

"What you thinking, Sergeant?" Trooper Eustis asked.

"I'm thinking what a bunch of suckers there are stationed at Fort Meade these days."

### Meade County, South Dakota

George Washington's birthday proved sunny, calm, and even warm as Sergeant Jay Chase rode to the designated sharpshooting contest cheered by those green kids he still was trying to whip into shape and cheered by some of the leading gamblers in Sturgis.

It had been decided to hold the contest around a little lake or pond or whatever you wanted to call it—still frozen over, although the ice didn't look that firm—that lay north of Fort Meade, almost on a line that ran from Sturgis to Bear Butte off to the northeast. If he looked behind him, Chase knew he could make out Sly Hill and Oyster Mountain, maybe even Granite Peak and Crook Mountain in the Black Hills. Instead, he focused on his competition.

He rode under a banner proclaiming THE MEADE COUNTY SHARPSHOOTING SPECTACLE OF THE WORLD.

*So,* Chase wondered, *will the winner be world champion or county champion, and will this truly be a spectacle?*

He saw an Indian with a big, battered flintlock rifle. A buckskinned vagabond with a beard to his belly. Cowboys with Winchesters and Marlins, one with a Spencer, another two with Henrys. Six or seven trappers or buffalo hunters or wolfers with Sharps rifles, one of which even had a telescopic scope. That reminded him of Captain Wilbur Lincoln. He wondered if the uppity captain had ever paid back that snot-nosed lieutenant.

The barber from Sturgis had shown up, too, trading in his razor and strop for a Ballard No. 5 Pacific single-shot rifle and several boxes of .40-63 cartridges. The barber, Chase knew, had been one of those snake-in-the-grass sharpshooters under Hiram Berdan's command during the Rebellion—back when his eyes and muscles had been thirty years younger. Even a couple of enlisted men and two officers from Fort Meade were in the competition.

He saw an 1866 Springfield that had been modified into a .50-70 sporting rifle. Chase didn't remember the shooter's name, but he knew that gun. He had beaten it in the Fourth of July contest three years back.

Turning his head right and left, he saw a Chaffee-Reese bolt action . . . a Howard .44 single-shot carbine . . . a .43-caliber Keene, the first bolt-action rifle Remington had produced . . . two Colt Lightnings, both probably in .32 caliber . . . even a few rifles Chase couldn't identify.

He shook his head, amazed at just how many people came out thinking that they could outshoot him. Well, it wasn't every day that somebody put up a purse of $1,500, winner take all.

No second place this go-round.

He rode past the field they would be shooting across, starting at fifty yards. Colonel Tom C. Curtis had sure done his best, lining the shooting grounds with barbed wire that had been decorated with bunting. Buggies and wagons were parked all along the lakeshore, and corrals had been thrown up, with hay for the horses and mules to eat scattered across the ramshackle affairs.

Chase smelled stew and bread. One tent appeared to be more popular than the rest, and he guessed Colonel Tom C. Curtis had hired a few beer-jerkers from the Sturgis saloons. Folks must have come from Deadwood . . . from Rapid City . . . maybe as far away as Pierre or even Montana or Wyoming.

As he reined in his horse, Sergeant Jay Chase saw the woman.

It never ceased to amaze her just how many men couldn't shoot worth a hoot. Colonel Tom C. Curtis's harebrained shooting championship started with paper targets at fifty yards, which was nothing more than a pot shot for Shirley Sweet.

The day proved perfect for shooting. No wind. Not even cold, and the paper targets had been painted red to make them easier to spot. But plenty of men swore bitterly, blaming their rifles and not their own incompetence, when their shots missed the bull's eyes, missed the circles, missed the entire bright red paper square.

Shirley, of course, did not miss.

She had brought along her No. 3 Remington Rolling Block Sporting Model.

Colonel Curtis pleaded with her not to shoot so straight in the early rounds. Build up her odds. Make the bets higher. Nobody would bet on a woman to win, not in South Dakota. Not anywhere in the West. Probably not anywhere in the world.

"I'm here to win," Shirley said. "And nothing's guaranteed."

"Just make it interesting, sweetie," Curtis begged.

She rammed a cleaning cloth down the Remington's 30-inch barrel. "Do you have $1,500 to pay the winner?"

"I will. Once all the bets have been collected, sweetie." That was the colonel's scam. The bets would pay for the bartenders he had hired and the whiskey and kegs of beer he had bought.

Knowing Curtis the way she did, he also would be collecting a percentage of the take from the soiled doves in their cribs and from the church collection plate.

Everyone bowed for the parson's invocation and prayer and the passing of the plate, and then Shirley finished cleaning her rifle and waited for her turn in the firing line for the second round— iron discs, probably removed from plows at the Sturgis stores that catered to farmers, at a hundred yards.

A steel target at one hundred yards was more to her liking. No spyglasses needed for the judges to announce where the bullets had hit. You just fired, and waited to hear the *ping*. Or not.

She beat the gentleman with the bolt-action Keene, and he bowed graciously and kissed her hand. She liked him . . . and his Remington .43.

But that cowboy with the dirty Henry that she beat in the next round, iron discs at two hundred and fifty yards? She didn't care much for that louse. He cursed his luck, cursed Colonel Curtis, cursed his pards who heckled him so mercilessly, and cursed her as a man decked out in women's garb. Then he stormed away to the tent saloons.

Five hundred yards made things more interesting— shooting cracker boxes, also painted red with white bull's eyes. Shirley used her tang sight for the round.

And then there were three.

Shirley Sweet. Libertino Adorante, a silver-headed barber from Sturgis who had a Ballard No. 5 Pacific .40-63. And a wiry sergeant from Fort Meade, who called himself Jay Chase. To her surprise, he was shooting a beat-up Winchester repeating rifle in .50 caliber that reminded her of Deputy U.S. Marshal Jimmy Mann.

Actually, she had hoped he might have been there. She even looked around for any sign of Danny Waco, but if he was at the competition, he was in the saloons or brothels. Probably not at the church tent, unless he was robbing it.

"Children, ladies, and gentlemen!" Colonel Tom C. Curtis spoke through a red, white, and blue megaphone. "Our three finalists will be shooting at a target that has been posted on the far side of Lake George Washington."

Shirley figured that was not the name of the frozen pond out on the flats.

"Its distance from here is one thousand yards—almost a full mile."

*More like six-tenths,* Shirley thought as the crowd oohed and ahhed.

"The target is a church bell—"

"That, Colonel, is sacrilegious!" the preacher bellowed.

Curtis lowered the megaphone and found the parson. "It's from an abandoned Catholic church, sir."

The preacher was Protestant, and he nodded his acceptance and withdrew his protest.

"As I was saying . . ." Colonel Tom C. Curtis returned to his megaphone. "The bell has been painted red, white, and blue in honor of our glorious nation's first president, on this, his . . . his . . . his . . . one hundredth birthday!"

Applause. Shirley didn't know exactly when George Washington was born, but she had to guess he would have been a bit older than a century mark, but she decided to stop listening to Colonel Curtis and focus on that target. If she could see it.

"How will we know if we hit it?" the barber asked.

"Why, my good man," Colonel Curtis answered, "church bells ring, don't they?"

Laughter erupted. Even Sergeant Jay Chase chuckled. Shirley, who was trying her best not to listen to that blowhard and cheat she worked for, had to smile.

"Shooters will fire from the prone position. Shooting sticks are allowed at this stage in this round." The colonel waited as the Sicilian barber from Sturgis and Shirley went to their tables and grabbed their shooting sticks. The barber carried a fancy tripod. Shirley's was just a couple old fire-hardened limbs tied together with rawhide, which she had been using since her childhood in Ohio.

Sergeant Jay Chase just rubbed the front sight of his Winchester '86.

Of course, the colonel waited five more minutes to allow more bets to be placed before he returned to his megaphone.

"After a random drawing of lots, our finalists will fire in this order. Liber . . . tin . . . o Adorante . . ." Curtis butchered the barber's name. "Sergeant Chase of the finest cavalry in the world. And Shirley Sweet, second only to Annie Oakley among our nation's shooters of the fairer sex."

Shirley had never met Annie Oakley, but figured she could give Buffalo Bill's sharpshooter a run for her money. She shook her head at the colonel's attempted compliment and whispered, "I've never shot one of the fairer sex. Not even a man, though I'm tempted right now."

"So am I," she heard Sergeant Jay Chase say.

She turned, saw the soldier, and smiled. He grinned back.

Three minutes later, the crowd hushed as the barber stretched out on the ground and sighted down the Ballard. They waited. The rifle boomed.

A moment later, the bell beyond the pond chimed.

Locals cheered, but fell silent as Jay Chase stepped to the line.

"Sergeant," Tom Curtis said as the soldier stretched out on his belly. "Would not you prefer to use shooting sticks?"

"He may use mine," the barber offered.

"Thank you, no." Chase levered the Winchester, waited, and fired.

The crowd exploded in delight at the *ping* of the bell.

Shirley Sweet allowed the Sturgis mayor to help her to the ground and braced the Remington's stock against her shoulder. She drew a breath, let it out, found the bell in her sights, and squeezed the trigger. She didn't hear the sound, but the crowd did. Everyone cheered, except those who had bet against her. They cursed.

"What's next?" the mayor asked. "Do we move the bell?"

"Let's put 'er atop Bear Butte!" someone joked.

When the laughter died, Colonel Tom C. Curtis said, "I think it would be easier to have our shooters back up fifty yards than move that bell." His head shook. "It weighs a ton."

So they moved back and fired again.

Shirley went first. She knew she had hit it, and immediately moved back to her table to clean the Remington while the other two men shot. People slapped her on the back. A few ladies even deemed to compliment her. Most of them, however, looked at her as if she were some freak of nature.

The sergeant fired.

When she heard the chime, she stopped cleaning her rifle. She thought for sure that Jay Chase would miss. He was shooting a repeating rifle, for goodness sake.

It was the barber who missed. He bowed graciously, but Shirley saw the tears in his eyes as he accepted condolences and disappeared.

"I guess," Colonel Curtis said, "we should back up another fifty yards."

"Good," a cowboy joked. "We'll be closer to the whiskey."

"That's a mighty fine rifle you got, lady," Sergeant Jay Chase said as he cleaned his Winchester.

"I'm impressed with yours as well, Sergeant," Shirley told him. "I just got rid of a Model 1886 Winchester myself."

"What for?"

She shrugged. "Honestly, I didn't think that rifle would work in long-distance shooting. I must have been mistaken. It wasn't a .50-caliber, of course."

"Of course." Withdrawing the ramrod, Sergeant Chase winked at her. "Maybe you'd like to make things a might more interesting. I can give you a chance to win it."

"Are you wagering your rifle, Sergeant?"

He nodded. "I've been admiring your Remington, lady."

She extended her hand. "Well, Sergeant, I think we have a bet."


"In this final— Well, I don't know. Maybe it shall be our final round or perhaps our two shooters will be shooting from Montana, perhaps even Idaho, before long. At any rate, this round our two finalists will be shooting from standing positions."

Shirley tried not to listen to Curtis's rambling. She tried to focus on the bell. After so many rounds, the Remington Rolling Block felt heavier than a mountain howitzer. She also felt the wind picking up just a little, blowing northwest to southeast. Her throat was parched, her lips cracked, and her heart pounded.

She didn't know why. She hadn't felt a case of nerves shooting at targets in three or four years.

"Sergeant Chase, you have the honor of firing first," Curtis explained.

Shirley drew a deep breath, let it out, and butted the Remington on the ground, turning to watch the soldier lift his Winchester to his shoulder.

Sweating, Chase worked the lever, but lowered the hammer and the Winchester. He took a deep breath.

*So,* Shirley thought, *he's nervous, too. Well, who*

*wouldn't be with fifteen hundred dollars and a rifle on the line? Not to mention, bragging rights in Meade County, South Dakota.*

After wiping his hands on his blue Army-issue trousers, Chase brought the '86 back up. He slipped the crescent-shaped butt plate against his shoulder, thumbed back the hammer, and took a deliberate aim. The rifle spoke.

People held their breath and waited. There was no chime. The crowd gasped, groaned, moaned, whistled then everyone was looking at Shirley, even Jay Chase, who stood shaking his head, amazed that he had missed.

Eleven hundred yards. Could she even see that red, white, and blue bell?

She set the sights for that distance and brought up the heavy rifle. It began to weave. She cursed her boss, the scalawag Tom Curtis. He had to eliminate shooting sticks in *this* round? He thought she could outshoot a career Army soldier who had probably fought against Indians? She wondered if the good citizens of Sturgis and the Black Hills would tar and feather her along with Colonel Tom C. Curtis when they realized he couldn't pay off the winner or the bets.

She sighted, wet her lips, and waited until her arms held the Rolling Block just slightly steady.

Finally, Shirley inhaled deeply, exhaled slowly, and squeezed the trigger. The gun roared. Her shoulder ached. Lowering the rifle, she waited and listened.

# CHAPTER THIRTY

For an eternity, there was no sound. And then . . .
*Ping.*

Shirley almost threw up. The crowd roared, and Colonel Tom C. Curtis mopped his brow with a polka-dotted bandana.

Somebody clapped her back. Another tousled her hair. She stepped away from the congratulators and made herself take a deep breath, staring across the plains, across the pond or lake or whatever it was, and shook her head in disbelief.

"Miss Sweet?"

Slowly, she turned to see Sergeant Jay Chase standing beside her, holding out that Winchester rifle. "I believe that this belongs to you, ma'am. Nice shooting."

She glanced at her own rifle, before shaking her head. "Sergeant Chase, it was a silly bet. I couldn't—"

"No, ma'am." The soldier cut her off. "A bet is a bet. I am a lot of things, Miss Sweet, but one thing

I'm not is a welsher. Take it." He grinned, lowering his voice into a conspiratorial whisper. "Besides, I bet on you."

That news made her straighten her posture. "Sergeant, are you saying . . ."

Again, he stopped her and thrust the gun toward her. "No, ma'am. I tried my best. My bet won't match that fifteen hundred bucks you're about to get . . ."

*Fat chance,* she thought, of me ever seeing a dime of that purse.

"But it'll tide me over for a few months."

She took the rifle.

"Besides, on a sergeant's pay, just keeping this .50-caliber cannon in cartridges will leave me busted."

She knew he was lying. A man like Sergeant Jay Chase would never bet against himself, but she thanked him and watched him bow graciously in defeat and then walk away, leaving her alone with her victory. Well, not alone. People still clapped her back with their massive hands. One shoved a bottle of bourbon at her, but took it back and drank greedily before staggering away.

After a while—she wasn't sure how long—she found herself standing alone on the plains of South Dakota, feeling the wind begin to pick up, still hearing the cheers and curses, songs and celebrations. But the ruckus was coming from the tent saloons.

She held a Remington Rolling Block in her left hand, butted against the ground, and a Winchester

1886 in .50-100-450 in her right, the still-warm barrel aimed at the earth.

### Deadwood, South Dakota
### Spring 1895

"Well, Mann, I hate to see ye go," the boss said in his Irish brogue as he slid the envelope across the table. "Ye makes a bloody fine miner."

"Another month," Jimmy Mann said, "and I'd be a bloody fine mole."

The boss laughed, then tapped the envelope. "Took out, of course, what ye owed the bloody company."

Jimmy stared hard through the barred windows that separated the boss and the payroll from the line of employees.

"Don't fret, Mann. Ye ain't like most of 'ese blokes. Keeps to yeself, ye does. Don't drink, don't fight, just read bloody newspaper after bloody newspaper. An' the only time I ever seen ye at the sheriff's office was when ye was readin' dodgers an' the like." His hand lifted, and Jimmy dragged the envelope, opened it, and seemed satisfied at the cash.

Behind him, another miner grumbled, cursed, and told him to hurry along.

Ignoring the rudeness and impatience, Jimmy nodded at the boss. "Thanks for everything."

It wasn't something a mine boss heard often in a place like Deadwood. He actually appeared taken aback. "Well, Mann, as long as I'm here, ye'll have a job waitin' for ye."

Jimmy nodded again and left the payroll line for the last time. He had bought a horse—a blue roan with some thoroughbred in her—a new saddle, and plenty of cartridges for his Colt and his Winchester .45-70. He had money, new clothes, some grub, and a full stomach, having splurged on breakfast at the café closest to his hotel. He had seen everything he needed to see in Deadwood, including—on a whim—Wild Bill Hickok's grave. All he wanted to see was Danny Waco, in the sights of his Winchester '86 short rifle.

The question was, where was Danny Waco?

Jimmy had almost gone blind reading every issue of every newspaper that arrived by stagecoach in Deadwood and every issue that the local newspapers had exchanges with. No newspaper had mentioned his name. Nothing. Maybe Waco had gotten caught in a blizzard. Or killed by some road agent. But Jimmy did not believe that.

He ruled out riding east. Pierre, Sioux Falls, and even Yankton just didn't seem to be towns that would have appealed to Waco. And if the outlaw had had enough of winter, the way Jimmy had, he didn't think Waco would ride up into North Dakota or Canada, either.

*So . . . Montana?* Miles City or Billings or even farther west into the mountains and gold camps there? *Wyoming?* Sheridan or Buffalo or maybe start heading south and find Cheyenne or Laramie? He wouldn't want to risk Nebraska, especially not after that fracas in Ogallala and the robbery in Chadron.

Jimmy stood inside the sheriff's office, staring at

the map. He was about to choose Cheyenne when he happened to look up. Belle Fourche was closer and a cattle town. He might as well hit it on the way out of South Dakota.

### Cheyenne, Wyoming

About two or three years back, maybe four, some hired gunmen had left Cheyenne by train to take care of cattle business in Johnson County. The plan was to run off some rustlers. Well, kill off plenty of rustlers and be well paid by the big Wyoming ranchers. Of course, things didn't turn out that way. Oh, the armed force managed to kill a few rustlers— Danny Waco didn't rightly remember just how many—but the way Slick Amos told him, the Wyoming cattlemen were a bunch of idiots, nobody could or would command, and before long the gunmen were under siege themselves. They tried to fort up at some ranch near Buffalo, and likely would have all been killed by some testy citizen-rustlers had not the U.S. Army arrived. The so-called invaders had surrendered to a bunch of bluecoats from Fort McKinney. The gunmen, many of them from Texas, were supposed to have been tried, but since Wyoming cattlemen still called the shots in Cheyenne, most of those old boys, including Slick Amos, just wandered back to Texas.

That little fiasco still weighed on the minds of the people and the law in Cheyenne.

It was why Danny Waco sat at a corner table in

the Paradise Saloon rereading the little letter he had been delivered that morning.

"I'm cold, Danny," Gil Millican said as he poured himself a morning bracer. "I don't rightly think I'll ever warm up."

"Where's Indian?" Waco asked.

"In the wagon yard, I reckon." Millican downed his rye. "How long we gonna hol' up here, Danny?"

Waco laughed and slid the paper across the table. "Find out yourself, Gil."

"I don't know what this means, Danny." He picked up the letter, read it, shook his head, and turned to Danny. "What's it mean?"

"It's what I hear folks are callin' a white affidavit. Basically, it's an informal request that we take our business and pleasure out of the state of Wyomin'."

Millican lowered the letter. "They's runnin' us out of Cheyenne."

Waco snatched the letter, wadded it up, and tossed it onto another table. "In a friendly sort of way."

"We gonna let 'em do that, Danny?"

His head shook. "Nah. We're gonna leave on our own volition." He had heard some gambler say that earlier. *Volition.* Didn't know exactly what it meant, but it sure sounded like something an educated man would say. Besides, the marshal who had asked that gambler to take his marked cards elsewhere had laughed and hadn't arrested the sharper, merely escorted him to the depot.

Danny Waco had found Cheyenne to be dull.

Not much excitement to be found in the town, not even in most of Wyoming, at least the parts he had seen. Gil Millican was right. It was spring, and the streets were covered with a dusting of snow. They had had to spend a right smart of money on winter coats, and Danny's luck at cards had turned a bit in February.

"Find Indian. Get our horses and gear." Waco fished a banknote from his vest pocket and tossed it at Millican. "Pay our bill. Because we're honest citizens. Then bring the horses here. We'll head south. Where it's warmer."

"Mexico?" Millican asked hopefully.

"Hell," Danny Waco answered.

### Belle Fourche, South Dakota

The owner of Wertheim's Mercantile shrugged, glancing at his wife as she laid out the new scarves on the counter down at the end of the store. Finally, he reached up and touched the barrel of the Winchester 1886 .50-100-450 that Shirley Sweet had brought inside.

"Well, Missus Sweet," he began, "I just don't know."

"It's Miss Sweet, Mr. Wertheim. This is the rifle that finished second at that shooting contest near Sturgis."

"Yes, ma'am, I know. I mean. I heard you. But it's pretty beat up."

"But it shoots pretty."

Sweating, he removed his spectacles and again

looked at his wife then back to Shirley. "You see, ma'am, most folks here buy shotguns. Deer rifles. Those new Winchesters in .30-30 calibers. The '94 models. They are popular. And we sell a lot of Marlins. But this here is—"

"A .50-100-450. Not many of them around."

"No, ma'am."

"You could hang it above your stag horn yonder." She tilted her nose up at that ugly, pitiful excuse for a trophy of deer antlers that hung above the work-boxes, writing desks, crayons, pens and slate pencils, and the calendar from 1891. She guessed that the Wertheims liked the painting on the calendar. Considered it art.

After a heavy sigh, Mr. Wertheim walked to the cash register, reached underneath the counter, and pulled out a catalog.

Montgomery Ward or Sears & Roebuck, Shirley could not tell.

He thumbed through some pages, pursed his lips, closed the book, and returned the catalog to its place below the cash register. Once he was back in front of Shirley, and after another cautious glance at his wife, he said, "New ones go for nineteen or twenty dollars. I can give you ten."

Her head shook. "New ones did not finish second in that shooting contest."

"Yes, ma'am, but . . . maybe if you were to sell your winning rifle."

"That's not on the table."

"Well, you see—"

"Thirty dollars." Grinning, she leaned forward just enough to squeeze her breasts with her arms and give him an eyeful.

He backed up and wet his lips "Thirty dollars?"

"Yes."

"Is . . . the rifle . . ." He had gotten up some courage. "What else are you"—he took another quick glance at his wife—"selling?"

She straightened. "Perhaps, I should discuss this matter with Missus Wertheim?"

The woman in question had already left for the storeroom. And Mr. Wertheim was heading to the cash register, hitting some lever or button that popped open the cash drawer, and he was soon back with thirty bucks in greenbacks, counting them out for her, and taking the rifle, which he put behind the counter.

Shirley couldn't believe her luck. She would have settled for ten. Expected no more than that, but her luck had returned.

It had certainly soured after winning that shooting match near Bear Butte. Oh, she had traveled with Colonel Tom C. Curtis and his winning attitude after the match, and they had landed in Belle Fourche, a cattle town on the Belle Fourche River near the Montana border.

Belle Fourche was a good town for a man like Colonel Tom C. Curtis. It had grown from a stagecoach station on a line that ran from Medora to Deadwood into a thriving cattle town. Cattle had been shipped out on the railroad for four or five years, bringing in herds from North Dakota, Montana, Wyoming, and South Dakota. Town leaders kept saying that the Middle Creek Stockyards would likely ship some 2,500 cattle cars full of beef this year, which would make the town the largest cattle-shipping yard in the world.

Perfect place for con jobs, shooting contests, and that dog-and-pony wild west show.

Shirley had awaked one morning to find that the trains had pulled out the previous night with not just cattle, but with Colonel Tom C. Curtis and some hussy he had found at the Livestock Saloon. He had left her and the rest of his "Extravaganza" with one extravagant bill.

The Colonel Tom C. Curtis's Wild West Extravaganza Featuring Shirley Sweet, the Sharpshooting Wonder of the World was no more. The three wagons had been confiscated for auction. The old bear with only three teeth left had been shot, skinned, and his tough meat sold to a restaurant. The Italian who tried to be a great Sioux warrior hadn't even made it to Belle Fourche, having drunk himself to death in Sturgis. The Texas roper had quickly found a job at some ranch, and was working probably before Colonel Tom C. Curtis and his hussy had stepped off that train. The twelve-year-old runaway with that loud, ugly-sounding trumpet had probably caught a freight.

Shirley Sweet, twenty-three-year-old crackerjack shot, was alone.

She had sold her medals, her signed copy of

Buffalo Bill Cody's autobiography, and much of her pride. About all she had left was that valise with a few extra clothes, and the case that carried her Remington Rolling Block. Her other guns were gone and she had just sold the Winchester '86.

Mr. Wertheim was staring at the closed door to the storeroom, waiting for his wife to return.

Shirley decided to test her luck. "Mr. Wertheim," she cooed.

He turned, and she tilted her nose at the counter.

When Wertheim looked down, he saw her hands resting on a deck of playing cards, right next to those neat stacks that amounted to thirty dollars in script.

"What would you say about . . . double or nothing?" Shirley asked.

Ten minutes later, she walked out of Wertheim's Mercantile with ninety dollars in script and coin, and bought a ticket on the next Freemont, Elkhorn, and Missouri Valley train heading east. Her luck had held.

She'd get off at a stop down the road and make her way somewhere . . . Texas, maybe. Texicans considered themselves good shots and loved to gamble. Likely she could keep her luck going down south.

That train was just about to pull out of Belle Fourche, so she settled into a seat, leaned back, and fell asleep.

She did not see a lean, leathery former deputy U.S. marshal named Jimmy Mann ride toward the saloons along the stockyards on a blue roan mare, holding a Winchester '86 at the ready. Nor did she see a slim, wiry, nervous cuss named Noble Saxon leave the stockyards with a wad of cash and make a beeline for Wertheim's Mercantile.

# Chapter Thirty-one

Lady Luck had favored Noble Saxon for some time, and he felt pretty good. He had made a sizable profit this fine spring day, selling thirty-two beeves for thirty-one dollars and twenty-seven cents a head. He figured out his expenses—ten dollars (including a bonus) for the two hired hands who had helped him herd the cattle from around Sundance, Wyoming, to Belle Fourche, a few bucks for grub and whiskey and three-and-a-half days in the saddle, and twenty-five dollars for some fresh duds and a Winchester Model 1886 rifle in .50-100-450 caliber.

The latter was the sweetest part of his run of luck. He happened to walk into the mercantile when Mr. and Mrs. Wertheim were having a rollicking row. Saxon smiled at the memory as he walked across the street to the Cattle Baron's Saloon. Mrs. Wertheim was about to rip her husband's head off, and made him sell that rifle or toss it out the door. Either that rifle went or she was going straight to the preacher, the newspaper, and the offices of Bodeen & Masters, Attorneys at Law. It had something to do with the previous owner of the rifle. Saxon wasn't sure of the particulars and didn't care, because he had walked out of that mercantile with a hard-kicking rifle for fourteen dollars and fifty cents. A used saddle in this part of the country cost more than that.

He pushed through the doors to the saloon, and got directions to a washroom, where he went to change into his new store-bought duds and wash the grit off his face and hands. He had thought about taking a bath, but, well, he had to ride all the way back to the Thunder Basin, so it did not make sense to spend money on a bath.

After a steak and fried taters, some whiskey and a woman, he'd likely leave Belle Fourche with maybe better than $900.

Sweet.

Yes, sir, Lady Luck sure loved him.

And the best part about it. Those two hired men would be leaving Belle Fourche in the morning to hire on at some ranch in southwestern Nebraska. He wouldn't run into them ever again. Nor the Thunder Basin stock detectives. Or those ranchers whose beeves he had gathered, then doctored their brands with a running iron. Besides, he had a legitimate bill of sale, and his brand was duly registered in the state of Wyoming in Cheyenne. He was, after all, a legitimate rancher.

Even though the Thunder Basin Confederation

of Stock Raisers often questioned the size of his herd.

Freshly scrubbed, more or less, wearing new underwear and a scratchy woolen shirt and duck trousers, he went back to the saloon proper, set his rifle atop the table, and leaned back in the chair, adjusting his new hat. It was an awesome hat, something that Wertheim gent called a "Chief Moses," with four silver stars on the four-and-a-half-inch crown and eight more on the four-and-a-half-inch brim. The color of nutria. Cost him seven dollars. But, to Noble Saxon, it told him and everybody else that he was a man of means, a man of property, and a cattle baron who knew what he liked and liked what he knew.

Noble Saxon knew he was a lucky man.

He called out to the bartender, "Bring me the best Scotch you got." He called it out like he was somebody, because Noble Saxon was somebody. He grinned as the cattlemen standing at the bar with their cigars and whiskeys turned to admire him, and watched them stare as he pulled out the greenbacks from that thick envelope. He was a man of means. Richer than God, he figured. Rancher. Empire builder. Cattle rustler.

### Eastern Wyoming

He killed a mule deer, and ate his fill, cutting out a few steaks, but leaving most of the meat for coyotes and ravens. Noble Saxon could do that. He was a wealthy cattleman, and coyotes and ravens needed to eat, too. He might as well make things a little easier for them.

That Winchester rifle shot true, just like the gent up in Belle Fourche had told him. Saxon rubbed his shoulder after shoving the rifle into the scabbard. 'Course, that mercantile owner had not told him just how hard a .50-caliber Winchester kicked. Punched like a mule. Might even leave a bruise.

He followed the Belle Fourche River, running high now from the spring thaw, keeping along the eastern side, not pushing the bay gelding, merely enjoying the ride back to the grasslands of Thunder Basin. Eventually, of course, he had to leave the river, and ride south. Returning to those 160 acres he had proved up, more or less, after homesteading.

Homesteading had proved to be more work than a man of means and ideas like Saxon felt like he should be doing. Rustling came much easier, although he did run a few head of his own. He wasn't exactly sure just how many cattle he really had.

The hills rolled along under a blue sky filled with plenty of white clouds. The grass was greening up; even some wildflowers had begun to bloom, attracting bees and flies. He patted the envelope in his vest, smiling at all that money he had, and wondered if maybe he should find a saloon, have himself a whiskey, let the members of the Thunder Basin Confederation of Stock Raisers see just what a man of property he was. The problem, of course, was that a cowhand or wealthy cattleman would find a lot of grass, a lot of hills, and plenty of cattle in the

Thunder Basin, but not too many saloons. The nearest watering hole was a day and a half's ride from Saxon's dugout and corral.

On the other hand, there was that bottle of Scotch he had bought at the Cattle Baron's Saloon in Belle Fourche.

In fact, he was just about to rein in the bay and unbuckle the saddlebag, cut the dust, when he saw the turkey buzzards circling off to the right. He stopped to think about what that could be, then laughed, and said out loud, "Might be one of my cows."

It wasn't.

It was Kelly Farson, deader than a doornail.

Noble Saxon took a drink of that whiskey. He wiped his lips, dismounted the bay, and walked closer, rifle in his right hand, bottle of Scotch in his left. Farson's horse stood up on a hillside, grazing contentedly, still saddled. Farson, however, was stretched out, like he was sleeping, his arms folded across his chest, his feet crossed at the ankles. At least, he had been, before a couple vultures had come along. Saxon had scared them off with a rifle shot, which left his shoulder throbbing again.

A man could have thought that Kelly Farson had dismounted his horse, lay down on the grass, and died. Excepting, of course, those two bloody holes in his belly, holes that had not been caused by vultures, but bullets. Another purple hole had been drilled right in his forehead. Shot so close, his head had been burned by powder.

The corpse had something between the fingers on his right hand, and Saxon made himself go over, and pluck the paste card from the dead man's stiff fingers.

Ace of spades.

Like Saxon, Kelly Farson was a rustler, a small rancher who supplemented his herd with beef belonging to the Thunder Basin Confederation of Stock Raisers. Only Kelly Farson shunned whiskey and cards.

After taking another long pull from the bottle, Saxon returned to his horse, gathering the reins, and swinging into the saddle. He put the bay into a good lope and left Kelly Farson and his horse alone. Saxon had thought about taking Farson's horse. After all, it wouldn't do the dead man any good, but he sure didn't want to give any stock detective reason to pin Farson's death on his own hide. That's probably why they had left the horse there, hoping they could lure some unsuspecting small rancher into taking a horse and getting himself lynched.

Late that afternoon, Saxon happened upon another small rancher, Ryan Banding. Young fellow—honest as far as Saxon knew—with a good-looking wife. Banding waved his hat and reined in, and Saxon rode up, took another sip of Scotch, and offered the last few drops to Ryan Banding.

Banding didn't drink, either—which relieved Saxon, who finished off the Scotch and tossed the empty bottle into the grass.

"Jay Hyatt's dead," Banding said.

Jay Hyatt. Another rustler.

Saxon almost said, *So is Kelly Farson,* but merely asked, "How?"

Banding shook his head. "Don't know who done it, but he was found three days back. Shot twice in the back, and once in the head. With a rifle." He shook his head again and spit out the bad taste. "I found him. By a fire. With a running iron."

*Caught red-handed.* Saxon nodded, and let out a mirthless chuckle. Or maybe the stock detectives had brought along that running iron, just to make it look like Hyatt had been caught rustling. Of course, Jay Hyatt never had Noble Saxon's luck. No doubt, he had been rustling when he had paid the piper.

"Stock detectives, I reckon." Saxon wished he had bought another bottle of Scotch in Belle Fourche.

"Not the ones we've been dealing with," Banding said. "This one stuck an ace of spades in Jay's hand. I gave it to the sheriff."

Like that gutless wonder, a pawn for the big ranchers in the basin, would do anything about it.

The big ranchers had brought in a hired killer.

Saxon slid from the saddle, fell to his knees, and threw up all that good Scotch. Coughed, gagged, tried to throw up again, only he didn't have anything left in his belly.

"You all right?" Banding asked after a while.

"Yeah." Saxon's knees didn't want to cooperate, but he managed to stand, even got back into the saddle. He was sweating. Smelled bad. Maybe he should have taken a bath in Belle Fourche. "That all the news you got, kid?"

"Well . . ." Banding shrugged. "I reckon. Figured you might ought to know. Mr. Lyman and Mr. Rivers. They don't care much for you, you know."

"I know." Lyman and Rivers were the leaders of the Thunder Basin Confederation of Stock Raisers.

"Be careful, Noble."

He laughed. "Don't need to be careful, kid," he said, as he nudged the bay into a walk. "I'm lucky."

For the longest time, Noble Saxon studied his dugout and corral before riding down the hill to his place. He had decided that maybe he should be a mite careful, but the place looked deserted, and he saw no signs of anybody paying him a visit. He rode down at last, unsaddled the bay, turned the horse loose into the corral, and walked to the dugout he had cut inside the hill.

He pushed the door open, and stepped inside, holding the Winchester in his right hand, and taking off his "Chief Moses" hat with his left.

"I wondered," a Scottish voice called out from inside the dark dugout, "if ye'd ever make it home, Noble Saxon."

The rifle fell to the ground, and Saxon backed into the wall.

"Aye, that's a good laddie, letting that rifle fall."

He almost vomited again. He could felt the sweat pouring from every pore as if someone had hit the lever on a beer tap.

"Leave the door open, laddie, for so long 'ave I been waiting for ye, I feel like a blind man. No light and all, and, besides, the sky looks lovely this time of day, don' ya think? Pick up the rifle, though, if ye don't mind, Noble Saxon, me lad. I'd like t' 'ave a look at 'er."

He obeyed, hoping he could get a look at the stranger, but the man moved back into the shadows. Saxon laid the '86 on the table, then backed up, against the doorjamb, wondering if he could dive out of the dugout and get away.

Right. Where could he run? No trees. He would never get to the corral before the gunman, this stock detective—no, this murderer for the Thunder Basin Confederation of Stock Raisers—gunned him down and stuck an ace of spades in his dead grip.

"Aye. A fine rifle ye have here, Noble Saxon. What caliber? A .45-70?"

"Fifty," Saxon muttered, amazed that he could even speak. "Fifty-something."

"Impressive." The man shifted in the chair, but Saxon could only see the gloved hands that rested on his Winchester. "Me? Been using a new Marlin, I 'ave. Shoots a .38 WCF. Not a bad rifle, but methinks how I could use one with a wee more punch. Do ye know what they say of the '86 Winchester?"

Saxon saw the rifle disappear, then saw that cavernous barrel sticking out of the shadows, pointed at his chest. He heard the lever being cocked.

"They say"—the Scottish brogue chuckled—"that it kills on one end. And cripples on the other."

That reminded Saxon of just how much his right shoulder hurt from shooting that big rifle.

It was the last thing Noble Saxon ever thought.

Later, after sticking an ace of spades in the dead man's right hand, the killer walked out with Saxon's rifle. His right boot crushed the dead rustler's expensive "Chief Moses" hat on the dirt floor.

# CHAPTER THIRTY-TWO

***Denver, Colorado***

"Jimmy, do you know who's drinking in the Brown Palace right now?" Deputy U.S. Marshal Will Drake let out an exasperated sigh and jerked open the top drawer to his desk, hoping he could find the writing notebook.

"Unless you tell me it's Danny Waco, I don't rightly care who's drinking anywhere in this city, Will." Jimmy Mann's voice came out filled with intensity and anxiety.

"It ain't Waco." Drake found the writing tablet and slammed the drawer shut.

"I know Waco left Cheyenne and got to Fort Collins, then sold his horses and took a stagecoach here." Jimmy sighed. It seemed the closest he had been to the outlaw since Ogallala, Nebraska, last winter.

"He didn't stay long, if he even got off the stage." Drake was up, leaving the notebook on the desktop, hurrying to the window. He pulled back the curtain and watched people passing by the office on foot, in carriages, on horseback. Denver bustled. It always bustled.

"Ian Nisbet," he said to the window.

"Who?" Jimmy turned in his chair, waiting.

"The Ace of Spades." Drake muttered an oath and let the curtain block out the light. "Hired killer for various outfits up north. Montana, Wyoming, the Dakotas. Killed a bunch of rustlers. You know the type."

Jimmy did. Well, he had heard of men of such ilk, but in Arkansas and Indian Territory, he didn't run into many cattle barons who killed small ranchers and rustlers. He ran into murderers who would kill for a nickel or half a bottle of rotgut. He ran into whiskey runners and drunks, train robbers and bank robbers. He ran into every type of cutthroat that had worn out their welcomes in Texas and Kansas. Stock detectives, though? No, those were to be found in Texas and mostly on the ranges of the Northern Plains.

"Ace of Spades?" Jimmy asked.

Drake nodded. He returned to his desk and opened another drawer. He pulled out a flask and two dirty glasses. "Most recently, he hired on with a conglomeration of ranchers in eastern Wyoming. He killed six men. Rustlers. A few of them caught red-handed. One or two, maybe they were honest small-timers, but we'll never know."

The flask was opened and whiskey poured into the dirty glasses. Drake didn't wait. He lifted his glass in a toast and killed the shot, then refilled the glass. That one, he sipped.

Jimmy lifted his glass and took a small taste. He didn't know what kind of whiskey it was, other than dark, and that it practically blistered his lips and tongue. "How do you know he killed them?"

"He left a calling card," Drake answered. "He stuck an ace of spades on each victim."

"So you're looking for someone with a lot of playing cards?"

Drake swore at Jimmy's attempt at a joke.

"I'm looking for a butcher who blew away a woman who stepped out of her shack to go to the well or privy."

That caused Jimmy Mann to kill his whiskey. "A woman?"

"Carol Banding," Drake said. "Nineteen years old. Married to a cowhand who had filed a claim in the Thunder Basin. The way everyone in Wyoming suspects it happened was that Nisbet was waiting for her husband, figured he was in the house. The kid wasn't. Had gone out to work his herd. Came home, found his wife dead. And here's where this Nisbet had gall. He stuck an ace of spades in her hand, too." He polished off that statement with a vile curse.

Jimmy had to echo that curse.

"And he's here."

Drake nodded.

"You need help?"

Drake sighed and shook his head. "That's not the way we do things in Denver, Jimmy. This isn't the Creek Nation. And we don't have a Hanging Judge. We have"—he laughed, the whiskey having gone to his head—"law and order . . . justice. We'll let Nisbet, the Ace of Spades, hang himself."

"All right." Jimmy sighed. He stood up, extended his hand. "Been a long time since we rode together, Will."

Drake shook Jimmy's hard grip. "Lot of water under the bridge since I left Parker's court."

"You've done well for yourself. Read your book. Almost rode down to Dallas two years back to hear your lecture."

"Be glad you didn't. And I know you didn't read my book. I didn't either. Didn't write it. Didn't read it. Just let some ink-spiller put my name on it."

Jimmy Mann had his left hand on the doorknob when Will Drake called out his name. Slowly, Jimmy turned, keeping his hand on the doorknob, but his right on the Winchester '86.

"Tascosa," Drake said.

"How's that?"

Drake started to pour another couple fingers of whiskey into his glass, but thought better of it, and screwed on the top, then dropped the flask into the drawer. "If you're looking for Danny Waco, I'd make a beeline to Tascosa."

Jimmy's lips pursed. His eyes then hardened. "It's a long way to Texas, Will."

"It is. Word is, though, that German Stevens is planning on robbing the bank there when the ranchers get ready to pay off their crews. End of May, I'd say."

"German Stevens?"

Drake's head nodded again. "And I got a tele-graph from the county sheriff in Trinidad. Seems that Danny Waco was through there a week ago. So was German Stevens. They were seen chatting in some bucket of blood. Waco left. Stevens stayed an-other day or two. But they shook hands before they parted company."

"You trust that lawman in Trinidad?"

After a shrug, Drake said, "No reason not to."

"Why'd he send you that message?"

Will Drake had to laugh. "I don't know. I imag-ine he thought I might like to put it in my next book."

A few minutes after Deputy U.S. Marshal Jimmy Mann left Will Drake's office, the reporter from the *Denver Post* showed up. Drake tossed him the note-book and left the office without a word, letting the reporter close the door and hurry to keep up.

They made their way to the Brown Palace.

By any city's standards, The Brown Palace was an amazing structure. Built of onyx—the most used in any one building—it had opened for business less than three years earlier. Newspapers had proudly proclaimed it as the greatest hotel between St. Louis and San Francisco.

They charged a pretty penny to get into one of the rooms, but they allowed anyone who had enough greenbacks stay there. Ian Nisbet had plenty of cash. By the time Will Drake and reporter Paul English had arrived at the hotel's bar, he had also consumed a lot of the bar's best bourbon.

Drake gave English his orders and then pushed back his coattail and moved to the bar. He joined the drunken killer and extended his right hand. "Mr. Nisbet, I presume."

The man whirled. His eyes had trouble focusing, but he must have made out the badge on Drake's lapel "Aye, and who might ye be?"

"Will Drake."

Nisbet's head cocked. "The author?"

Drake bowed.

Nisbet slid his bottle toward Drake. "Gunman, lawman, man of letters." He laughed a drunken laugh. "Ye plan to put me in that book ye must be working on?"

"Well, sir, we are two of the best of our business."

"How's that?"

"Come now, sir, let us not play games. You are the Ace of Spades."

Nisbet laughed. "Aye, and if I remember the note in *The Wyoming Review,* 'Will Drake will never be a Hickok or Hawthorne.'"

Drake laughed, too, although he had written a scathing letter to that imbecile who had written that vindictive article in that rag of a newspaper in Laramie.

"It's noisy, here, sir," Drake said. "And crowded. I propose we retire to a place where we can speak in confidence. You have a room here, sir?"

They made it to the fifth floor, and Drake had to use the key to open the door to Nisbet's room. The gunman was seriously in his cups.

The bed was unmade. Whiskey bottles littered

the floor and dresser. The chamber pot had not been emptied.

Drake was surprised, though he guessed that Nisbet had run off any maid. Only one thing appeared to be clean in the room, and that was an 1886 Model Winchester lying atop a chest of drawers. "Is that the rifle, sir?"

"What rifle?" Nisbet staggered toward the chamber pot and began unbuttoning his britches.

Drake had picked up the Winchester. It was a .50-100-450. He ran his fingers along the barrel and then the stock before he picked up an enormous cartridge as Nisbet's urine splashed into the pot and onto the rug. He spoke up, raising his voice, making sure Mr. English would be able to hear in the room next door.

"Is this your rifle? The one you used to kill all those notorious rustlers in Wyoming."

Nisbet cursed and turned. Not even trying to button his pants, he moved toward the chest of drawers. He slapped the cartridge out of Drake's hands and opened a drawer, found a bottle, tossed it onto the floor because it was empty, then pulled out another. No more than three swallows remained in that bottle. Nisbet did not offer any to Will Drake.

He crashed on the bed, scattering bottles and poker cards across the comforter, and leaned against the headboard. He drank greedily. "I used a Marlin. Till I met the leader of those swine who stole good men's beef."

"Banding?" Drake asked.

Ian Nisbet cursed. "Banding. No." He laughed and hurled the empty bottle across the room. It shattered against the wall.

Drake had to wonder, *Did that scribe next door put that in his notebook?*

"I don't recollect the name. Good rifle, though. Won a shooting match in . . . I don't remember where. Girl shot it." The word *girl* caused the drunk to close his eyes. They stayed closed.

Drake tried to remember some of the names. "Hyatt?"

No response.

"Folsom?" No, Drake shook his head, cursed his stupidity. That was not the name, but he couldn't think of that dead rustler's handle. Another name came to him, and he asked, "Noble Saxon?"

The drunkard's eyes opened. He laughed. "Aye. Noble Saxon. Shot 'im at point blank range, I did. Blew 'is sorry hide out of the hole he lived in. Aye. Aye, yes, that was 'is name. Noble Saxon." Nesbit waved a finger. "A good rifle. Shoots true."

"You proved that when you shot Carol Banding."

Nothing.

"What was the distance? Five hundred yards? Seven?"

Nothing. At least, not for a minute or two. But just when Drake was about to give up, consider this a fool's game, Nisbet sniggered. "Nine hundred. Had to raise the sight. Adjust for the wind. Ye wouldn't think a man of my ability would mistake a pretty woman child for a two-bit rustler at any distance shorter than five hundred yards, would ye?"

"No." Drake's words were barely audible. He cleared his throat. "No." He wet his lips. "So you shot her?"

Nisbet held out his hand and closed it into a fist. "The hole that bullet left when it came out was bigger 'n this, it was. True. True, I say."

"But you still stuck an ace of spades in her hand."

He laughed, though his eyes were closed again. "Marry a rustler, die like a rustler. Makes no never mind to me, Will Drake."

A tapping came from the wall. Drake looked at it, knowing what it meant.

"Rats." Ian Nisbet had opened his eyes. "Rats in The Brown Palace."

*Yes,* Drake thought with disgust. *Rats.* "Yes, rats in The Brown Palace." He felt like one, too.

The door in the next room opened. Footsteps sounded down the hall. Will Drake felt as disgusted with himself as Ian Nisbet felt. That feeling of loathing. Years back, when he had left Judge Parker's court, folks said that Will Drake was the greatest lawman in the West. Now look at him. Getting a confession from a drunken killer, a man who had been something himself, a feared man, until he had accidentally killed a woman.

He looked at the rifle in his hand. Nesbit, the "Ace of Spades," had killed her with it.

The reporter from the *Post* was going to the newspaper office to print his story in what the publisher would undoubtedly print as an extra. There would be a trial, a conviction, and a hanging in

Cheyenne. After all the other newspaper stories. The extradition. All that legal bartering and politicking.

People would laugh at Will Drake. The greatest lawman in the West had to resort to John Barleycorn to get an arrest. What would happen when the press found out that he had sent a former colleague, a veteran lawman himself, to Tascosa on a fool's errand? Oh, sure, Danny Waco and German Stevens had met in Trinidad. And maybe Waco would join Stevens for that bank job in Tascosa, but what the lawman had also put in that telegraph was that Danny Waco was going to Elizabethtown, that old mining camp in the mountains of New Mexico Territory first.

After all, the money wouldn't be filling that bank in Tascosa until later this spring.

"Do you have a gun, Mr. Nisbet?" Drake asked.

The killer's eyes opened. "Aye."

"Let me have it, sir."

He reached inside his coat, and withdrew a Harrington & Richardson's self-cocking .32. He held it in his right hand. "I didn't kill 'er with this, Will Drake."

"I know."

Nisbet tilted his head at the Winchester. "I didn't mean to kill 'er with that."

"I know that, too."

"Once," Nisbet said, "ye an' me, the both of us, we were decent men."

"Once." Drake brought the Winchester up to his shoulder.

"Kills on one end," Nisbet said with a laugh. "Cripples on the other."

"Huh?"

The drunk laughed. "Ye'll learn."

His eyes closed a moment before Will Drake pulled the trigger.

# CHAPTER THIRTY-THREE

*Elizabethtown, New Mexico Territory*

The way Will Drake figured things, he had done Ian Nisbet a favor, killing him in the room at The Brown Palace, saving him the shame of being hanged in Wyoming. Maybe, Drake thought, he had done himself a favor, too.

Certainly, he had gotten his name back in the newspapers. Will Drake, legendary lawman, had killed the "Ace of Spades" in Denver. Self-defense. The mad-dog murderer of an innocent woman in eastern Wyoming had pulled a gun, tried to gun down the legendary lawman and author, but Drake had shot him first. Even used the killer's rifle.

"Poetic justice," was how that scribe had put it in the *Denver Post*.

Eastern newspapers had picked up those reports, and Will Drake was again on top. But he needed to go a bit higher, and he knew how to do that.

Bring in Danny Waco, the West's most notorious outlaw.

Drake knew where he would most likely find him.

Elizabethtown. E-Town for short. Or, as some of the more colorful writers put it, "Hell Town."

Lying in the shadow of Baldy Mountain, E-Town had seen its ups and downs since it was founded after the discovery of gold back in 1866. In fact, it became New Mexico Territory's first incorporated town. For a while, E-Town was gloriously wild and wicked, the Colfax County seat, boasting a population of 7,000—during spring and summer. You didn't want to be there in winter, not in those mountains, so folks would pack up, move south, then come back after the thaw.

That was until the gold played out, the county seat moved to Cimarron, and everyone left. But not for long. One thing about some mining towns—they lived, died, and were reborn. E-Town had been reborn a couple times, never regaining that glory from the late 1860s and early 1870s, but it just would not stay dead.

Miners had started dredging, although, to Will Drake, such an idea sounded ludicrous. How could you dredge in a place with so little water? But, somehow, they had managed to make it work, loading the ore into huge wagons and hauling the cargo up and over Raton Pass to Trinidad, Colorado.

Riding down the main street, Drake heard a fiddler playing in some stone saloon. Most of the buildings were rotting cabins and crumbling ruins, leftovers from early E-Town. The walls of the livery looked as if they wouldn't stop the wind, but he heard the whistle of wind from one of the mines or maybe one of the dredges. He wasn't sure.

He glanced up at the hill, saw the iron fence around the cemetery, and found the saloon with the fiddler. Several idlers were hanging around on the boardwalk, and the hitching rails were full of horses.

He figured he would find Danny Waco there.

As he rode into the town, Drake wondered if perhaps he should have leveled with Jimmy Mann. After all, they had been friends once, had ridden across the Indian Nations together, probably had saved each other's lives a few times. Jimmy was a good shot, a good man to have around. Besides, he had a legitimate reason to go after Danny Waco.

All Drake wanted was the glory, the prestige, a few more book deals, and another lecture circuit to take him around the country. New York. Chicago. Boston. San Francisco. Seattle. Charleston. Richmond. Kansas City. Omaha. Salt Lake City.

He could go to the local law, but decided against it. Maybe in the old days, E-Town had a tough lawman, but the sheriff or marshal or constable or whatever they called him was probably some portly old man who minded his business and didn't even pack a gun.

In front of the two story saloon, which had no name painted outside, Drake reined up and smiled at one of the loafers. "Full up, I see." His tone was friendly as he pointed at the rails. In answer, one of the horses lifted its tail and began to urinate.

"Yeah," the loafer said.

The loafer, Drake knew, was an Indian, a big, stout hombre with hair in braids, taller than any Navajo or Apache that Drake had seen around that part of the country. It reminded him of something else that lawman up in Trinidad had mentioned. Danny Waco had arrived in the Colorado town with two men, one of them believed to be Gil Millican, his longtime accomplice. And the other? A Sioux Indian.

"Well . . ." Drake nodded at the building next door. "Reckon I should get a little food in my belly before I start drinking, eh?" He eased his horse down the muddy street, and dismounted in front of a log cabin that had no name, either, but was obviously a café.

He removed his linen duster, took the Winchester 1886—the rifle he had used to kill Ian Nisbet—from the scabbard and stepped onto the boardwalk, trying to get most of the mud off his boots. He did not look back toward the saloon or the Indian and moved inside, walking straight toward an empty table. He slid the rifle atop the table and sucked in a deep breath.

"What'll it be?"

He pushed his hat brim up, wet his lips, and smiled at the young waitress, a plump girl, red hair, and freckled face. Drake had expected to find some Mexican waitressing in a town like E-Town. "The back door."

"Huh?"

"Where's your back door?"

She blinked. Finally motioned. "Through the kitchen."

"Is there a back entrance to the saloon next door?"

"Huh?"

He wished the waitress had been a Mexican. Or anyone with a brain in her head.

He repeated the question.

"Yeah . . ." She said after a long pause. "I think so."

He pulled a coin from his jacket pocket. "Good." He rose, taking the rifle with him, and moving past the redhead toward the door that led to the kitchen.

*That is,* Danny Waco thought, *the worst fiddler I have ever heard.* He checked his watch, wondering just how much longer he would have to sit in the poor excuse for a saloon in the poor excuse for a town.

At last, the door to the storeroom opened, and the man with the bowler hat came inside, Winchester at the ready.

Sight of that big rifle caused Waco to leap from his chair and bellow, "That's my gun!"

The lawman whirled toward him and tried to bring the '86 up to his shoulder, but he was too late. Fool never had a chance.

Indian had been standing with his back to the wall, behind the fiddle player, waiting for the John Law to come sneaking into the saloon. It made Waco think that he had been smart, killing Tonkawa

Tom like he had done, replacing him with the Sioux.

The big Indian stepped forward and slipped that pig-sticker of his between the lawdog's back ribs. The man gasped, but that was all, because Indian had stuck him good. The rifle fell to the floor. Indian grabbed the dead man's shoulders and dragged him back into the storeroom, probably outside, leaving just a trail of blood.

The music had stopped—for that, Waco was grateful—and the patrons and barkeep stared as he moved to the floor where the law had just expired. He snatched the rifle from the floor, lowered the hammer, and screamed in delight. "It's mine, I tell you!" he shouted to no one in particular.

"Sure it is." Gil Millican had been standing at the far end of the bar, holding that big Smith & Wesson revolver in case he needed to kill the law.

"No!" Waco stepped to the bar. People gave him a clear path, and the bartender quickly filled him a shot glass of rye. "It's the one from the train."

Millican holstered the revolver and walked down the creaking floor. At that moment, most of the drinkers decided to take their business elsewhere. Indian stepped back inside, wiping the blood off his hands.

That lawman had been a fool. Figured he could ride into a town like E-Town and get the drop on Danny Waco. As if he or Indian or Gil Millican or half the outlaws hiding out in such a town, wouldn't recognize a man like Will Drake, legendary lawman and author. Will Drake, deader than dirt because he was a fool.

Waco held out the rifle for Millican to study.

"The train?" Millican said.

"In the Nations, fool. The one in the express car. Look!" He pointed at the barrel, the marking of the caliber

$$50\text{-}100$$
$$450$$

"You sure?"

"Of course, I'm sure. It's the rifle that sharper cheated me out of. In Caldwell."

Millican looked at the Indian. "But it wasn't *that cheat* that Indian just knifed. Wasn't him at all. That was—"

"I don't rightly care who that was. Will Drake, a cardsharper from Caldwell or German Stevens. He's dead. And he brung me my rifle. My rifle!" Waco rubbed the stock and barrel and laughed before turning back to the bar to pick up the shot glass and down the whiskey. "Mighty nice of the law, don't you think so, boys?"

Millican scratched his chin. Indian just stood there, waiting.

"What's it been?" Waco asked. "Six months. No, closer to eight." His head shook. "But now it's back with me." He shook his head again. *Luck. Fate.* Whatever you wanted to call it. He had that rifle, the 1886 Winchester in .50 caliber. He had a job waiting for him in Tascosa. That bank would go down a lot easier with this rifle. Then he could just kill German Stevens and not have to worry about splitting the take with that cutthroat.

Waco laughed again. *Fate.* That's what it had to be.

After shaking his head, he motioned toward the door. "Might be time to leave this burg, boys." He knew that knifing that law would rile the good, God-fearing citizens of E-Town and maybe even the territorial law.

It was, after all, a long, hard ride to Tascosa, Texas, and German Stevens was waiting.

# CHAPTER THIRTY-FOUR

*Tascosa, Texas*
*Late Spring 1895*

The town blended in with the sand, and the dust, and the canyons, mesas, and perhaps even the river—if anyone would call the Canadian River a river at that time of year. Maybe a creek, although it looked no bigger than those irrigation ditches the Mexican sheepherders had dug back when the settlement was called Plaza Atascosa.

It was a town of adobe huts and jacales. You wouldn't find a frame home or a log structure larger than a lean-to or outhouse. In fact, you would hardly even find a tree in that part of the world, even along the shallow sand bog they called a river. About the only things that country grew, other than scrub and grass, were tombstones, and most of those were rocks or crosses manufactured from broken spokes of wagon wheels or planks pulled from wagon beds with names carved with pocket knives into the faded wood. The graveyard, however, seemed to be a veritable garden.

Although Tascosa dated back to the last years of the Comanche troubles, it had boomed in the 1880s, serving as shipping quarters for the big ranches of the area—the XIT, the LIT, the LS, the Frying Pan, and the LX. During those years, Charlie Siringo, Billy the Kid, Dave Rudabaugh, and Pat Garrett had done their share of drinking and gambling in the saloons. More cowboys passed through there on the Tascosa-Dodge City trail, herding beef to the railroad in Kansas. Tascosa had become the county seat in 1880, and the stone courthouse still stood, although it had been converted into the bank.

Oh, Tascosa remained the Oldham County seat, but the courthouse had moved into a smaller building. That was merely another sign of the times. You would hardly be able to count forty or fifty people, although Boot Hill quadrupled the population. By Jacks, they probably let the dead vote, which was the only way that Tascosa hadn't lost its designation as county seat.

The beginning of the end came back in 1887, when the Fort Worth and Denver City Railway laid tracks on the other side of the riverbank. Most businesses and entrepreneurs had moved to the rails, but the ranchers were a stubborn lot. They liked Tascosa, and wouldn't let it lose its designation as county seat. They liked the country, and the whiskey, and the rawness of life and liberty. They liked a town where a man could wear his pistols on his person and not have to worry about getting arrested or his skull bashed in by some gun hand with a badge. They liked those old days, when a man could shoot another man in a quarrel and not have to worry about a hangman's rope or a wasted day or two in that hot courthouse listening to some pettifogging lawyer.

They liked the money the cattle and cowboys brought in to Tascosa.

Danny Waco and German Stevens liked that, too.

"*Ja.*" The German gunman grinned and refilled his stein with more thick black beer. "Dat is plan. Ja." He nodded and sipped his beer, leaving thick sudsy foam on his handlebar mustache. "Ya do vell, ve be rich."

"Yeah." Waco walked to the window, pulled back the curtain, and stared out the dirty glass at the dirty street and the dirty saloon. "So let me get this right. While Gil, me, and my Indian are in the bank, you and those two ol' boys"—he tilted his hat slightly at the two gunmen German Stevens had brought along—"will be waitin' in that grog shop." He cleared his throat. "Ahem. . . . makin' sure nothing goes wrong."

"Ja." The Hun's head nodded.

He was a big man with a big head and big mustache. Despite the heat of the Texas Panhandle, he was dressed in a black broadcloth suit that didn't fit well at all. In fact, it looked as if his buttons would pop off at any moment. His blond hair was close-cropped, probably shorn so no one would really notice how bald the fat man was getting. The eyes were cold blue, but for such a big man with a fat belly, his feet and hands were downright tiny.

German Stevens carried two Remington .44s, nickel plated with pearl handles, stuck in a red sash. He must have thought he was Wild Bill Hickok or some gunman like that, instead of a fat, beer-swilling idiot who had stepped off the boat and found a pretty good job as a hired thug in the Five Points region of New York killing men and maybe two women. When the law started coming after him in New York, German Stevens had moved west, killing men and maybe two other women in Kansas, Missouri, the Indian Territory, and Texas.

He had decided to branch out. Rob a bank. With help from Danny Waco.

"Sounds simple." Waco stepped away from the window and found a bottle of some sweet-tasting syrup that Stevens considered whiskey. Tasted like peppermint candy. A petticoat's drink.

Stevens kept nodding as he swallowed down the rest of his beer. "Ja," he said happily. "Ja. Very easy. Ve vill be rich."

The two gunmen tagging along with Stevens were young men, slim, out-of-work cowhands by the cut of their clothes and the condition of the six-shooters in their holsters. They had likely been fired by one of the ranching outfits along the Canadian River, had a grudge, or like German Stevens, just didn't cotton to work.

"And if something goes wrong?" Danny Waco asked.

German Stevens belched. "*Nein.* Vat could go wrong?"

"Reckon it's about that time," Oldham County Sheriff Clete Stride said on that Saturday as he compared the time on his Illinois pocket watch with what the Regulator clock on the wall showed.

Jimmy Mann answered by jacking a shell into the chamber of his Winchester .45-70, lowered the hammer, and fingered out another cartridge from the box, sliding the long brass shell into the loading gate on the rifle.

"The way it'll work"—Stride snapped shut the case on his watch, and let it fall into his vest pocket—"is this way . . ." He went at it again, the same way he had told Jimmy for two weeks. The payroll would come by stagecoach from the railroad, with riders from various outfits serving as guards. The moneyboxes would be unloaded into the bank, which once had been the county courthouse. It was the sole permanent structure in the dying town, made of stone more than a foot thick. The boxes would be loaded into the vault, and closed up until payday on Monday. "I hope you're wrong, Mann," Stride finished.

"So do I, Sheriff." Jimmy Mann knew that was a lie. He had come this far. He needed to end it. Today.

He saw his reflection in the mirror and practically

did not recognize who he had become over the fall, winter, and spring. He was leaner, harder, his hair grayer, but he was not an old man. His face was bearded and the whites of his eyes red. His left hand still had no feeling.

*Much like the rest of me,* he thought.

Jimmy had been in Tascosa for weeks, waiting. His brother and his brother's family, including young James Mann were maybe a day's ride from there. If he had any feeling left in him, he would have ridden to see his brother, to see James, to rejoin the living. Instead, he had remained in Tascosa, waiting for Danny Waco.

He had become a dead man, living on hate, living for revenge.

However, he had pinned on that deputy marshal's badge and could see how tarnished it was. He told himself that he should not wear it, that he did not deserve to wear it. Everything he had sworn when he had first became a lawman he had trampled in the dust along the trails through Indian Territory, Kansas, Nebraska, the Dakotas, Wyoming, Colorado, New Mexico Territory and Texas.

No, his search for Danny Waco needed to end today.

It had to end today.

"I've got two men atop the roof of the bank," Stride said. "Five more waiting inside the bank. Three at the livery, up in the loft, two at the undertaker's on the south side of town. Got two men with spyglasses atop Boot Hill. And that busts my budget for two years, Mann, paying these boys."

"You'll get it back, Stride." Jimmy made himself stand. He pulled on his hat. "Rewards for Danny Waco and German Stevens will make you richer beyond your years even after you pay off those . . ." He had almost said *clowns.* Instead, he said nothing.

Jimmy touched the knob, looked down the street, and opened the door. "I'll wait in the saloon. Keep you covered in case anything happens."

"All right," Clete Stride said to the door as it slammed shut.


Fluid piano keys rang out an off-key version of "The Yellow Rose of Texas" from the Canadian River Saloon as Jimmy Mann pushed through the batwing doors. He kept the big rifle in the crook of his arm and did not step inside the saloon until he was certain Danny Waco and German Stevens were not around.

He could see only the back of the piano player's head. A woman who didn't look like she fit in the place. The saloon seemed quiet, with only a few cowboys drinking beers, their boots propped up on the brass rail that ran underneath the bar.

The owner of the establishment had spent a small fortune in freight charges to have that bar and back bar hauled to Tascosa during the glory days. Likely, he would move it to some other town as soon as Tascosa was dead and buried.

Jimmy moved to the end of the bar and signaled the barkeep, a thin Mexican with a well-groomed mustache, for a beer. The Winchester went atop the bar. The piano music stopped.

As Jimmy lifted the glass of lukewarm beer, a voice said behind him, "Nice cannon you got there, mister."

Caught off guard, Jimmy stared into the face of Shirley Sweet.

She laughed, but Jimmy had no laughter left inside him. He wiped the suds off his stubble and swallowed the beer. "You playing piano? Here?"

"A girl's gotta eat."

"What happened to your rifles?"

Her head shook. "That, Jimmy Mann, is a long sad story. Should be told over a drink."

He turned, started to call out for another beer for the lady, although what he really wanted to do was send her out of Tascosa and out of the Canadian River country. He didn't get a chance.

The batwing doors pounded, and in walked someone Jimmy Mann did not want to see.

"What are you doing here, Millard?" Jimmy called out to his brother, who had rushed inside and embraced him in a bear hug.

"I could ask you the same question," Millard said, swearing. "Haven't heard from you since after Borden got killed. Thought you were dead yourself, feeding buzzards somewhere. You quit your job. You don't write. You—"

"I asked you—"

"I work for the Fort Worth and Denver," Millard shot out. "Remember?"

Jimmy finished his beer and lowered his voice. "How's the boy?"

Millard slumped at the bar, saw the barkeep, asked for a beer, and noticed Shirley Sweet. He started to introduce himself, but seeing the rifle on the bar stopped him.

"James is fine. Good boy. But we've all been worried sick about you. Is that . . . ?"

Jimmy's head shook. "No. But I'm gonna get that rifle. I'm gonna see that James gets it."

A silence filled the saloon, and Shirley took the moment to clear her throat.

"Millard," Jimmy said. "This is Shirley Sweet. Shirley, my big brother, Millard."

Neither the sharpshooter nor Millard looked away from Jimmy. Their eyes burned into Jimmy, and Millard was about to speak again when the saloon doors opened.

"Millard," Jimmy whispered, "do me a favor and escort Miss Sweet out of here. Off the streets. Into a building with solid walls. But not the bank. Or the livery. Or the undertaker's." He grabbed the '86 Winchester and moved down the bar, watching two lean, young cowhands wander to a table in front of the piano.

Jimmy paid them no mind. He focused on the stout man in a tight-fitting black suit, who had removed his black Stetson, and was wiping the sweat off his face while ordering a beer from the barkeep.

"German Stevens." Jimmy thumbed back the hammer on the Winchester, although he kept the barrel pointed at the floor and one eye on the back bar's mirror, studying the two cowhands who had entered the saloon with the German murderer.

"Ja." The big man smiled, and pointed at Jimmy's badge. "And ya are a peace officer. Ja." His fat head nodded. "Ya vant me?" Stevens slipped his thumbs inside the sash near the twin revolvers. His fingers dribbled against his pants.

Jimmy answered by shaking his head. "Not at all. But you know where the man I want is."

German Stevens laughed. "Indeed? Ack. Who is dis man?" He stepped away from the bar, widening his stance.

"Danny Waco," Jimmy said.

The two gunmen by the piano were staring, hands hovering above their holstered Colts. Jimmy chanced another look in the mirror and frowned. Neither Shirley nor Millard had moved.

"Tsk-tsk." Stevens shook his head. "I do not know *vere* dis man is."

"No?"

Stevens's big head shook again. He tilted his fat chin at Jimmy's rifle. "A Vinchester, no? Da 1886 model? Big gun. Go boom loud, no?"

"A Winchester '86, yes," Jimmy said. "Danny Waco has one like it."

"I vud not know." The killer's left hand was coming out of the sash, ostensibly reaching for the beer the barman had served, but Jimmy Mann was not that green.

He brought the Winchester up savagely, the barrel catching Stevens hard in the groin. Jimmy screamed, "Where is he? Where's Waco?"

Stevens, however, could not answer, nor could he even speak. The killer's pale face turned even whiter, and he groaned as he sank to his knees, one Remington falling to the floor.

Jimmy did not consider the German again. Even after he had shouted at the man-killer, he had started to whirl toward the two gunmen, bringing the Winchester up. Behind the bar glass shattered, though Jimmy never heard the pistol fire.

He saw the cowhand holding the gun, saw the fool thumbing back the hammer on his Colt. The kid had rushed his shot. The other one was struggling with his revolver, which had caught in the holster.

Jimmy saw it, then he saw nothing but white smoke.

He had fired the Winchester from the hip. He ducked, stepped away and up, and levered the rifle.

Someone screamed. The piano clanged. The punk he had shot had been slammed against it, moving it all the way to the adobe wall, and spraying the ivory keys with crimson as he slipped to the floor in a pool of blood.

Jimmy fired again, taking time to bring the crescent-shaped butt plate against his shoulder and aim. He knew his bullet had been true, and dove to the floor, rolling over, working the hammer, aiming at German Stevens.

The big gunman had managed to draw his other revolver with his right hand. His left hand clutched the edge of the bar—the only thing holding him up. The man's face was pale. He had vomited from the wicked blow to his privates.

He had the Remington up, but was having trouble cocking the hammer.

Jimmy did not wait. At practically point-blank range, he pulled the trigger, and smoke blinded him. He couldn't see the big gunman's face, but saw the knees buckle, the back slam against the bar. Then he saw German Stevens, sitting against the bar, his legs stretched out, his head tilted at the side, a giant, bloody hole in his breastbone. The black cloth material smoldered from the gunshot soon erupting in flames.

Every button on the dead man's vest had popped off.

His ears ringing, Jimmy stood, grabbed the German's beer, and poured the brew on the dead man's burning chest. The fire went out, and Jimmy turned to find Millard, standing in front of Shirley, protecting her—ever the dutiful, good brother. Quickly, Jimmy glanced at the other two men, both dead by the piano.

Outside, something else sounded as if a war had begun on the streets of Tascosa.

Jimmy Mann rushed outside to join the fight.

# CHAPTER THIRTY-FIVE

Never trust a fat Hun who drinks too much beer and sissy-tasting sweet liquor.

That's what Danny Waco should have remembered.

He had followed German Stevens's orders. Let the hired guns deliver the money to the bank, let them ride out with the stagecoach. Then he, Gil Millican, and Indian had walked into the bank to make a little withdrawal.

They walked straight into an ambush.

Those miserable John Laws gave them no chance. As soon as they were through the door, Waco—who had yet even to draw his piece—heard someone shout, "It's Danny Waco!"

And they started the ball.

Indian caught the first three bullets, started to fall back, his Winchester Yellow Boy clattering on the floor. Waco took advantage, catching the dead man and using the massive body as a shield as he backed out the door. Waco's revolver leaped in his hand, and he was blasting away, although the thick smoke made it downright impossible to see anything.

He could hear, though, and he heard more bullets pumping into Indian's body, but by that time, that big Sioux was beyond caring or feeling. The dead man must have weighed more than a mustang, and at six-foot-six, using the dead Indian as a shield, while firing a six-shooter, proved to be one mighty tough thing to do.

A bullet even sheared off one of Indian's silver and black braids.

Waco cursed, kept moving, kept backing up, kept shooting, even though the hammer kept striking empty chambers.

As soon as he was out the door, Waco let Indian's body fall and headed for his horse, the one he had tethered to the rail in front of the big stone building. He jerked the Winchester from the scabbard, thumbed back the hammer, and aimed, sending a .50-caliber bullet through the window.

Gil Millican, miraculously, had made it out, too, though blood poured down his head from what once had been his left ear. His hat was gone, and as he turned, he staggered. The smoking Wm. Moore & Grey twelve-gauge, that beautiful shotgun Waco had used to kill that idiot lawman over in Denison, slipped from Millican's grasp into the dust. Millican clawed for his revolver.

Waco whirled. More men had opened fire from the rooftops, from the livery, and he could hear a war commencing inside the saloon.

"Stevens!" he yelled. Immediately, Waco shut up. Like that drunken fat German could hear anything above the deafening roar of rifles and pistols from all over Tascosa.

"Danny," Millican groaned. He turned again, caught a bullet in his back, and fired into the bank's door. He kept staggering, weaving, and heading right for the undertaker's. A hearse was parked out front. One of those Rockfalls beauties, made in Sterling, Illinois, with shiny black wood, thick drapes, pretty tassels, and golden lamps.

Fitting, Waco thought, as he swung up on the horse, put the reins in his teeth, and spurred the fast gelding into a lope. He blasted away with the Winchester as he rode, seeing more bullets slam Millican against the hearse and other bullets splinter that well-polished black wood and shatter the glass.

He didn't see his partner drop to the dust. He didn't see anything but the road and a lean, leathery man with a bearded face and badge crash through the saloon's batwing doors, take aim with a huge Winchester, and send a shot that tore off Waco's hat and carved a furrow across the top of his head.

He saw something else. A boy . . . no, a teenager . . . Running right down Tascosa's boardwalk, stepping right into the sights of the .50-caliber Winchester.

Jimmy saw the boy and thought it was his nephew. He even screamed out James's name and lowered his Winchester '86. Moving, becoming human again, he stepped in front of the kid, pushing him aside and feeling a massive lead slug tear through his stomach.

Down he went, but almost immediately, Jimmy was up, on his knees, driven by hatred and the need to kill Danny Waco. He brought up the Winchester, firing as Waco galloped out of town. Jimmy pushed himself to his feet, staggered against the column, and saw the boy.

It wasn't James. Younger, this kid was, with red hair and freckles. Jimmy heard the boy's mama calling out the name, but he couldn't hear clearly. A young woman was running, tears in her eyes, hands lifting the hem of her skirt, chasing after her son. The boy was all right, though, and Danny Waco was getting away.

Jimmy clutched his bleeding belly, managed to swing into the saddle, and spurred the gelding, catching a glimpse of Shirley Sweet and Brother Millard as they ran through the saloon's doors.

Deputy U.S. Marshal Jimmy Mann focused on the dust left by Danny Waco's horse.

Blood flowed down the back of Danny Waco's sweaty neck. His spurs gouged the horse's sides as he fired at one side of the street, then the other, and then knew enough to hold his fire. A Winchester '86 had a limited capacity. It wasn't one of those .44-caliber 1873 models, the kind some old boys used to say, "You could load on Sunday and shoot all week."

The horse cleared town, and nothing but the

Staked Plains of the Texas Panhandle stretched ahead of him. If he could only make it past Boot Hill . . .

He didn't.

The rifleman came up from atop that boneyard, and the rifle shot tore into the chest of Waco's horse. Down went the horse, and Waco flew over the mount, landing with a thud, busting his left ankle. For a moment, he thought the horse would roll over on him, crush him, and kill him, but he came up in an instant and found the '86.

A bullet kicked up sand in front of him. He blinked, aimed, drew a bead on the gunman and killed him. More bullets sliced through the air. The townsmen, those cowardly John Laws, were racing after him. He cracked a shot at them and then saw the second assassin standing beside a crooked tombstone. The man's shot creased Waco's side, but didn't spoil his aim. The Winchester kicked mightily, and the man went flying.

Waco pushed himself to his feet, snapped another quick shot at the charging posse, and knew the only place he could run was up that hill.

Except he could not run, not with a busted ankle, but he could walk pretty fast. He had to. If he didn't he was dead.

Well, he was dead anyway, but he could at least take a few more Texicans to the burning pit with him.

*Just like that time back in Ogallala, Nebraska*, he thought. That posse had him dead to rights, too, but Danny Waco had showed them he was mighty tough to kill.

*But . . .* he suddenly remembered . . . *on that day, the Tonk saved me from a bullet or a noose, and I shot the Tonk dead.*

The cemetery wasn't on much of a hill. Not in that part of the country. Certainly not as tough a climb as that hill in Ogallala. It was sandy and rocky, and he kept slipping, despite using the Winchester as a crutch. He staggered, felt two more bullets whine off rocks in front of him.

More luck. Those Texas bushwhackers were shooting uphill, and that was a lot harder to do even for experienced marksmen.

He reached the top. No gate, no fence, surrounding the boneyard. He came to a chunk of wood, already rotting—like the sorry cuss six feet under—and fell on his face. He rolled over, worked the rifle's lever, and saw the man riding hard, flame and smoke belching from his Winchester.

Some lawman called out for the fool to stop, but that hard-riding hombre refused to listen. The horse carried him up the hill. His rifle barked, and Danny Waco felt the bullet slam into his back.

As horse and rider rode past, Waco rolled over onto his back, made a snap shot. The horse squealed as it reared and fell to its side, crashing onto three crooked crosses. The rider went off to the right. Smart man, diving in the opposite direction from where the horse was falling.

Waco came up to his knees, had to strain, using

practically every ounce of strength he had left to get that rifle up and cocked. The rider came up, and Waco's Winchester roared. He saw the rifle the man was holding fly apart, and the man slam into the dirt.

Laughing, Waco spit up blood. Then another shot caught him in his left arm, and he fell down.

"Waco!" a voice yelled. "This is Sheriff Clete Stride. Come on down with your hands up."

Waco laughed. His left arm was busted. He couldn't raise it if he tried. Ignoring the lousy law, he took his Winchester, pulled a couple cartridges from his vest pocket and fed them through the gate. He wasn't sure how many shots he had left—if he had any. But he had at least two bullets.

Determined, he crawled to the man he had shot.

Below, that fool lawman kept calling up at him to surrender.

Another voice yelled out, "Jimmy! Jimmy Mann! Are you all right?"

That stopped Waco. He spit out another bloody froth and made himself crawl faster.

*Jimmy Mann.* He tried to place the name, but it was hard, shot to pieces like he was, knowing it was the end of the line for Danny Waco.

*Jimmy Mann?*

Waco remembered him. *That deputy for Judge Parker's court.* The lawman who had arrested him some years back. He stopped again, looked at the '86 Winchester, and remembered something else. *Yeah, that's right. This big rifle.* The one he had taken off that train in the Cherokee Nation. He remembered the express agent and laughed. He had killed that ol' boy, that brother of lawman Jimmy Mann.

He wondered how far the deputy U.S. marshal had been tracking him.

They would die together atop Boot Hill in Tascosa, Texas.

The man's leg came up, bending at the knee. The lawdog groaned, turned his head, and clutched his belly.

Danny Waco laughed. He had got that John Law good. Busted his rifle, and the bullet still plugged him. The John Law lay there, bleeding like a stuck pig. Waco remembered something else. He had shot this lawman on the streets, out in front of the saloon. Had almost killed that fool boy, but the lawman had pushed the kid aside, taken that heavy .50-caliber slug.

And he would take another one. In the head. At point-blank range.

When he finally reached the lawman, Waco had to leave his own Winchester on the ground. He grabbed the arm of a cross and tried to use it to pull himself up. The cross collapsed, and Waco flattened against the rocks and dust. He coughed, cursed, and made himself stand, first to his knees, then using the rifle to pull himself up.

Jimmy Mann tried to push himself up, but couldn't. His eyes burned with hate.

Danny Waco laughed.

Weaving on his legs, Waco brought the big rifle to his shoulder. Blood seeped from multiple wounds.

He had to blink some from his eyes and finally wiped his face.

"I'll . . ." It hurt to talk. "I'll make you . . . one promise." Waco spit out more phlegm. "Same I gave . . . your . . . brother." He almost fell, but somehow kept his feet. "Promise . . . you . . . Jimmy Mann . . . promise you this. Your . . . funeral will . . . have . . . a . . . closed coffin . . ."

He aimed and screamed in agony as he dropped hard to the ground. Cursing, he reached for his leg.

"Jimmy!" a voice called out.

Waco ignored what was left of his right knee and whirled, forgetting the lawman. "A . . . petticoat." He laughed. "A woman"—he cursed—"shot me." He could see her holding some odd-looking rifle, nothing like anything he had ever seen.

A man came up alongside her, holding a shotgun. They stopped, crouched, waiting. He figured they couldn't see him, not lying on the ground like he was, protected by some scrubs and what remained of tombstones.

"I'll fix . . . your . . . flint," Waco whispered. "Both of . . . you. The lady . . . with the rifle . . . first."

Jimmy knew who it was. His brother, his always-solid reliable brother, Millard. And Shirley Sweet. Coming for him. Coming to save him. Coming right into the gun sights of Danny Waco's big Winchester. The rifle that had killed his other brother, Borden.

Yet he wasn't sure he could even move. His stomach felt as if someone had filled it with coal oil, then dropped a match. He managed to turn his

head and could see the mangled remains of the
Winchester Shirley had given him. The stock wasn't
there anymore, just some splintered wood and
twisted metal, torn apart by the lead of a .50-caliber
bullet, parts of which rested in his gut.

He thought about his pistol, but when his hand
touched the holster, he felt only leather. The Colt
must have flown out when his horse had been shot
from under him.

"Jimmy!" Shirley Sweet's voice.

The answer chilled him.

"Over . . . here." Waco sniggered, spit out blood,
and laughed again.

The man was crazy, but he could still finish
Shirley and Millard before he died.

That made Jimmy move. He wasn't sure he had
it in him, wasn't sure of anything, but if he could
save Millard and Shirley, maybe that would make
everything right with God, make him justified . . .
or something like that.

He had saved that boy's life out in front of the
saloon. If he could just save two more lives. Not his
own. That, he understood, was beyond hope.

Rolling to his side, a sudden searing pain almost
paralyzed him. He was close, close enough to stretch
out his right arm. His hand gripped the barrel of
the remains of the Winchester, still warm to his
touch, almost burning his fingers.

Another thought panicked him. *Do I have any
shots left in this rifle?*

He rolled back over, braced the ruined end of
the rifle against his side, and thumbed back the

hammer. He also prayed. Prayed for the strength to pull the trigger, prayed for the weapon to fire.

Danny Waco spun around, coughed, pressed the Winchester Model 1886 in .50-100-450 caliber against his chest. He laughed and started to bring the big Winchester—the rifle that was supposed to go to Jimmy Mann's nephew—around.

Still moving cautiously, tentatively, were Millard and Shirley. Jimmy could just make them out. He had to do this. Finish it. Before he was dead, too.

"That . . . thing . . . will . . . never fire." His eyes full of laughter, Waco turned away from dying Deputy U.S. Marshal Jimmy Mann and drew a bead on Shirley Sweet. "It'll never . . . fire," he whispered again.

But it did.

# CHAPTER THIRTY-SIX

Shirley Sweet lifted Jimmy Mann's head into her lap. She refused to look at what was left of Danny Waco after that .45-70 slug had struck him in the back of his head. On his knees, Millard unbuttoned Jimmy's vest, and tore away the shirt, then stopped, color draining from his face. Swallowing down the bile and blinking away the tears, he wadded strips of cloth into some sort of ball and pressed the makeshift bandage against that ugly wound. Or wounds. The bullet that had destroyed the rifle that once had belonged to her must have splintered into fragments, and most of those pieces had gone into Jimmy's gut. But it was the bigger hole, the bullet he had taken when he had saved that young boy's life back in front of the saloon, that would likely kill Deputy U.S. Marshal Jimmy Mann.

Changing her mind, Shirley looked at the dead outlaw—or at least what was left of him—and the rifle by his body. She looked at the rifle near

Jimmy Mann's right hand, or what was left of the rifle. It had been hers. She'd given it to the lawman, and he had used it—somehow—to save her life and his brother's life. How it had even managed to fire befuddled the sharpshooter in her.

It seemed impossible, but Jimmy had gotten that mangled rifle to shoot. To kill Danny Waco.

Shirley blinked away tears.

"Mann!" That was the voice of the sheriff.

"Up here!" Millard yelled. "Waco's dead. I need a doctor. Now!"

Jimmy laughed and spit out blood. "You need . . . an . . . undertaker."

"Hush," Shirley heard herself say. "You're gonna be fine, sweetie. We'll get you to the doctor's office. We'll . . ."

Again, Jimmy laughed. "You're not . . . getting me . . . off this . . . hill." He moved a finger on his right hand, pointing . . . or trying to point. "The . . . rifle."

"It's ruined," she told him.

Jimmy's head shook. "No. Not . . . that one." He coughed before he could finish, squeezed his eyes shut against the pain, and pointed toward the one by Danny Waco's body.

Millard fetched it and placed it in his brother's hand.

It was the 1886 Model Winchester Jimmy had been chasing for months. He had caught the killer of his brother Borden in the wind-blown cemetery of a dying Texas town. He had retrieved the stolen rifle, the one he wanted to give to his nephew.

*But,* Shirley had to think, *at what price?*

With a weak smile, Jimmy managed to open his eyes. "You'll give . . . this to . . . James . . . you hear?"

"I hear you," Millard said.

That gave Shirley some comfort. Jimmy was happy. Satisfied. He had finished his job. Done what he needed to do.

By that time, the sheriff and others had gathered around. Some pointed at the dead outlaw, others at the dead horse. A few began removing the bodies of the two deputies shot dead by Danny Waco.

One man whispered, "By golly, I can't believe one of us killed Danny Waco."

"Shut up," Shirley snapped. They hadn't killed Danny Waco. This brave, determined lawman had killed Waco.

Jimmy lay there with his eyes closed. He wet his lips. Shirley could hear death's rattle in the lawman's voice when he spoke. "Might give . . . him my . . . badge, too. Maybe . . . Millard, you . . . ." Another coughing spell silenced him.

Again, he opened his eyes and grinned. Blood trickled from one corner of his mouth. He managed to swallow, and said, "Gonna be . . . one . . . cold . . . winter." He shivered. "Already . . . freezing."

Sweat dripped from Millard's face and mingled with the tears on his cheek. May in the Panhandle could be hotter than a furnace, and it was even hotter up on Boot Hill.

"You rest, Jimmy." Millard had become resigned to the fact that his younger brother was dying.

Shirley tried to steel herself for what would soon, what must, happen.

"You deserve a long rest, Brother." Millard smiled weakly. "You've traveled far."

"Yeah." Jimmy smiled, and Shirley thought he would die then, but his eyes filled with some sudden purpose, something he needed to say. He almost lifted his head off her lap.

"He'll be a better man than me, Millard." Jimmy said it without pause, maybe without pain, but he began slipping. "Me and . . . you . . . both." He coughed again. "Badge and . . . this rifle. You hear?"

Millard nodded. "I hear."

Shirley could tell that he seemed confused. The rifle, yes. She knew that Jimmy wanted his nephew to have it, that it was a gift for him before Waco had stolen it and stolen another Mann brother's life. But the badge? *That,* Millard did not understand.

Shirley, however, did. She had never met the young James Mann, son of Millard, nephew of Jimmy, but she could picture him. She imagined him looking just like Jimmy in better days. She could see him, the young nephew of a lawman, wearing that brave but flawed lawman's badge. Removing its tarnish. Standing proud.

Jimmy swore softly and chuckled again. "That was . . . some . . . journey."

And Jimmy Mann closed his eyes one last time.

# EPILOGUE

*Fort Smith, Arkansas*
*Spring 1899*

Katie Crockett pulled the empty mug from its place in front of Deputy U.S. Marshal James Mann. "You want another beer?"

They had finished two pitchers of the brew. Mostly, Katie had done the drinking. James had been too busy talking.

He shook his head. His hands lay flat on the table, not far from that big rifle, that big rifle that everyone joked about.

Katie finally understood. James had opened up to her, just a little. No, a lot. It had taken a lot of courage. And it had taken a lot out of the young lawman.

Silence filled the Texas Corner Saloon briefly, although no one but Katie had heard James's story. She knew why. Another deputy marshal, fat, lousy, cowardly Riley Monaco had lowered his voice to a whisper, and the hangers-on were eagerly waiting to hear his stupid joke.

"You are a better man than your uncle, James," she whispered. "Better lawman, too."

The people erupted with laughter at Riley Monaco's punch line.

Katie ignored them and stared across the table at the deputy.

He chuckled without mirth. "There are many who'll argue that point."

"Not with me. Thanks for telling me that." He looked up, and she smiled. "Don't fret. I won't run off to the newspaper and give them an exclusive. That's between you and me."

He said nothing.

"You don't go by *Jimmy*. I've never heard anyone call you anything but James."

His head shook. "My name's James. Jimmy . . . That was . . . that was his name."

She could understand. He didn't want to be his uncle. He had to be himself. He was his own man, and, from what she had heard about that wild young lawman, the man who had paid for that Winchester '86 with his life, it was a good thing.

"How often do you think about him?"

James shrugged. He was still young, practically a boy, but his face was hard, and his eyes even harder. How long had he been riding for Judge Parker's court? Three years? No, it was getting closer to four.

A lot of lawmen, a lot of experienced marshals,

never lived that long. Life was cheap in the Indian Nations.

"On bad days," James answered. "I think about Uncle Jimmy. Like today. But never when I'm on a job. Jackson Sixpersons told me years ago that that would get me killed."

"He's a good man, too," Katie said, smiling. "Jackson." She saw life in the young lawman's face.

"Yes." Warmth filled his smile. "Jackson is. The best."

"The best."

Katie's smile widened, and it pleased her very much when James returned the grin.

The chatter died again. Men stared at the doors to the saloon.

Katie and James turned to find a tall Cherokee standing in the doorway, a big Winchester shotgun, a Model '87 lever-action twelve-gauge, in his hands.

The Cherokee's long hair was completely gray, and he wore spectacles and a mangled black Stetson. He also wore the six-pointed star of a deputy marshal pinned on a Cherokee ribbon shirt.

"Speak of the devil." Katie wasn't sure how old he was, but figured he had seen sixty years many years ago.

The Cherokee lawman's face was impossible to read, at least, impossible for her to read. But James read it. They were partners. Had been for some time.

Deputy U.S. Marshal James Mann was already sliding out of his chair, standing and reaching for the rifle, that big Winchester rifle in .50-100-450 caliber, which he had lain atop the table when he had first entered the saloon.

Deputy U.S. Marshal Jackson Sixpersons nodded grimly. He didn't need to say anything, not after years together.

Already, James Mann was moving toward the doors.

The Cherokee turned, leaving the entrance to the saloon and moving down the boardwalk to where his horse was tethered.

Now, Mann was moving through the batwing doors.

She knew where they were going. Off to the courthouse to get warrants, then cross the ferry into Indian Territory, and go chasing after some other outlaws. Murderers, maybe. Robbers. Whiskey runners. The worst lot of men, if you could call those hardcases *men*.

A team of two men going after who knows how many outlaws.

No, Katie figured, there were three of them. James Mann. Jackson Sixpersons. And the spirit of Jimmy Mann.

"Hey, Mann," Deputy Marshal Riley Monaco called out from his perch on the bar. "That big gun of yourn will sure come in handy . . . iffen you run into a herd of wildebeests."

His crowd of fans hooted and laughed and punched one another as they watched James Mann's back.

James did not reply. The batwing doors of the saloon banged back and forth, and he was gone.

"Riley," Katie said as she slid her chair back and pushed herself up. "Shut up."

That prompted more laughter from the bar flies, who now began to tease Monaco.

Katie didn't care. She went to the entrance, stopped the swinging doors with her hands, and pushed herself partway through, leaning out for a better view of two lawmen, watching, staring, and wondering.

Jackson Sixpersons and James Mann had mounted their horses. They let a freight wagon pass, and then they kicked their mounts into slow, deliberate walks down Garrison Avenue. Down the muddy street they rode, ramrod straight, determined, a tall, gray-haired Cherokee and one young deputy marshal.

Jackson Sixpersons rode a paint horse and carried a Winchester Model 1887 lever-action shotgun and a badge.

Riding a brown mustang named Old Buck—Jimmy Mann's old horse—Deputy U.S. Marshal James Mann carried a Winchester Model 1886 in .50-100-450 caliber across the pommel of his saddle. He, too, wore a badge.

He also carried the name of Mann.